Harlach, dazedly, slipped into a chair, unconsciously pressing his chest.

His shirt, thus revealed, was black as well, obviously expensive. "I'm so terribly sorry," he said. "Entirely letting the side down. But I...something *jumped out at* me, I don't know where it came from, and I think it must have...thrown something at me? Something sharp?"

Varney hissed. "Are you hurt? Did it scratch you?"

Harlach lifted a shaking hand to his shoulder, pushed aside the collar of his (soaking-wet) Armani shirt, and his fingers came away red. He looked from them to Varney and Greta, eyes huge in his white face.

Praise for Vivian Shaw

Strange Practice

"*Strange Practice* is written with elegance, wit, and compassion. The prose is gorgeous, the wit is mordant, and the ideas are provocative. Also, there are ghouls."

—Laura Amy Schlitz

"An exceptional and delightful debut, in the tradition of *Good Omens* and *A Night in the Lonesome October*."

—Elizabeth Bear

"Shaw balances an agile mystery with a pitch-perfect, droll narrative and cast of lovable misfit characters. These are not your mother's Dracula or demons....*Strange Practice* is a super(natural) read."

—*Shelf Awareness*

Dreadful Company

"A playfully witty confection...framing London's supernatural residents as delightfully normative while still capably evoking the frisson of the uncanny."

—*Publishers Weekly* (starred review)

"Shaw's elegant writing makes this series a standout in the genre."

—*Booklist*

STRANGE
NEW WORLD

BY VIVIAN SHAW

THE DR. GRETA HELSING NOVELS
Strange Practice
Dreadful Company
Grave Importance
Bitter Waters (novella)
Strange New World

STRANGE
NEW WORLD

A
DR. GRETA
HELSING

NOVEL

VIVIAN SHAW

orbitbooks.net

Copyright © 2025 by Vivian Shaw
Excerpt from *Bitter Waters* copyright © 2024 by Vivian Shaw
Excerpt from *The Scholar and the Last Faerie Door* copyright © 2024 by H. G. Parry

Cover design by Will Staehle and Lisa Marie Pompilio
Cover illustration by Will Staehle
Cover copyright © 2025 by Hachette Book Group, Inc.
Author photograph by Emilia Blaser

Orbit
Hachette Book Group
1290 Avenue of the Americas
New York, NY 10104
orbitbooks.net

First Edition: May 2025
Simultaneously published in Great Britain by Orbit

Orbit is an imprint of Hachette Book Group.
The Orbit name and logo are registered trademarks of Little, Brown Book Group Limited.

The publisher is not responsible for websites (or their content) that are not owned by the publisher.

The Hachette Speakers Bureau provides a wide range of authors for speaking events. To find out more, go to hachettespeakersbureau.com or email HachetteSpeakers@hbgusa.com.

Orbit books may be purchased in bulk for business, educational, or promotional use. For information, please contact your local bookseller or the Hachette Book Group Special Markets Department at special.markets@hbgusa.com.

Library of Congress Cataloging-in-Publication Data
Names: Shaw, Vivian, author.
Title: Strange new world / Vivian Shaw.
Description: First edition. | New York, NY : Orbit, 2025. | Series: Dr. Greta Helsing novel
Identifiers: LCCN 2024044927 | ISBN 9780316537971 (trade paperback) |
    ISBN 9780316538077 (ebook)
Subjects: LCGFT: Fantasy fiction. | Paranormal fiction. | Novels.
Classification: LCC PS3619.H39467 S77 2025 | DDC 813/.6—dc23/eng/20241001
LC record available at https://lccn.loc.gov/2024044927

ISBNs: 9780316537971 (trade paperback), 9780316538077 (ebook)

Printed in the United States of America

LSC-C

Printing 1, 2025

For Laura, who first told me not to stop; for Jane, who was there from the beginning and without whom this world would be a hell of a lot less rich; for Linden, my heart and home, my first reader and best cheerleader; for Stephen, best and most angelic of agents; for all the editors I've worked with throughout this series; for my friends, who provided encouragement and guidance and single-malt where profoundly needed; and, not least, for anyone who ever sought and found family in unexpected places.

For thou wilt mark here many a speck, impelled
By viewless blows, to change its little course,
And beaten backwards to return again,
Hither and thither in all directions round.
Lo, all their shifting movement is of old,
From the primeval atoms...

—Titus Lucretius Carus,
De rerum natura (*On the Nature of Things*)

We love you more than you know.

—AWOLNATION, *Kill Your Heroes*

PROLOGUE

Victoria Embankment, London

November, in the ancient city: the sky fading through ultramarine in the east, here and there sparrows beginning to sing in the trees along the Embankment. People bundled up in coats, hunched against the chill, hurrying on the day's earliest errands; a hundred thousand stories trundling on independent of each other, layers of history like a vast temporal cake standing against the fading night. By Blackfriars Bridge a figure in a neat camel-hair topcoat leaned on the parapet of the Embankment, looking down into the water, paying no attention to the few people passing by.

Haliel *liked* London. It was somewhat of a failing in an angel; surface-operative duty was supposed to be something one did because one had to do it, with the understanding that being in Heaven was enormously preferable, rather like being a diplomatic attaché assigned to Soviet-era Moscow. But Haliel liked the city, liked its huge weight on reality that came with being ancient and built on its own past, liked the way the old and new rested against one another without fighting terribly hard. (He didn't like the proliferation of horrible new mirrored skyscrapers, but practically no one else seemed to, either, except the people who kept putting them up everywhere.)

He wasn't thinking of anything in particular, just enjoying the way the water was still ink-black against the brightness of the reflected lights, just beginning to be tinted with the dawnlight running up the eastern sky: the awareness of how *old* the river was, how slow and patient it must be, on its way to the unknowably distant ocean. If such a thing had thoughts, Haliel mused, they would be *slow* thoughts.

It was still cold out, this early; too cold for the coat he had on. In a minute he'd go and have breakfast in one of the cafés that catered to the early crowd, and spend the morning in his tiny flat poring over last night's essograph traces, as he was a conscientious surface operative and enjoyed his work. In a minute—

The pain came out of nowhere, a sharp horrible sting in his back. He staggered, clutching at the parapet, staring wildly around: no one was there. Had something *bitten* him? He reached clumsily over his shoulder and felt an object stuck in his back, just above where his left wing-root would be in his ordinary form—some kind of arrow? Dart? What was going *on*?

When his fingers brushed the thing, it moved slightly and sent the pain into reeling, swooping heights. Haliel felt his grasp on the edge of the stone lose its strength, dizziness washing over him, pale color fading from the world—his knees threatening to give out—with a supreme effort, he forced his mind clear enough to translocate.

The damp London pavement vanished, replaced with bright white pearlescent stone, and the dimness of a November dawn flared into the sourceless white light of Heaven's main courtyard, looking up at the sapphire battlements still not quite completed after months of repair work. The pain in Haliel's back flared briefly; he gritted his teeth and gave the thing lodged in his coat a sharp tug, which hurt badly enough to send spots dancing across his vision—but it came away in his hand, and as soon as it was out, the pain in his back settled down to a more bearable kind of throb.

He stared at the thing. It was made of metal, about the size of a bullet but much narrower, with a flared base and a sharpened tip, now faintly stained with his golden blood. Haliel sniffed at it and blinked: it smelled like—herbs, rosemary and rue, and a little like salt. Very obviously something made for the sole purpose of sticking into somebody, but he couldn't imagine why anyone should want to puncture *him* with little herb-scented metal darts; he didn't have a single enemy on Earth that he was aware of. He and Hell's London surface operative, the demon Harlach, even had coffee together sometimes in one of the little shops near the cathedral (well, Harlach had coffee with lots of crunchy sugar; Haliel preferred delicate herbal tea with honey) and talked to each other about things they might both find of interest. Nobody in London paid any attention to Haliel except to take his money; he couldn't think who could possibly have mistaken him for someone they had reasons to damage.

He reached over his shoulder and rubbed at his back; it hurt a little, dully, but nothing like so badly as it had with the dart still in place. Slipping the thing into his pocket, Haliel hurried toward the main entrance of the Heavenly citadel. This wasn't the sort of thing he was supposed to deal with; this was very much a matter for someone higher up in the ranks than him.

Inside, the pearl terrazzo floors glowed softly as they always did, the glory of the jewel-set windows—they looked like stained glass, but the panes were cut and polished slices of gems—throwing warm colors over Haliel as he hurried through the corridors. As soon as he'd passed through the main entrance, the camel-hair coat and casual clothes he'd been wearing turned themselves into a white robe, his wings flickering into visibility; by the time he knocked on a particular office door he appeared no different from any of the other angels going about their proper business. He knew Gabriel preferred it when people looked like what they actually were.

"Come," said the beautiful voice from inside, and Haliel let himself into the office. "Ah, Haliel. What brings you here?"

All angels looked roughly the same, other than variable skin and hair color: inhumanly beautiful, neither entirely male nor female, curly hair and vast white wings, narrow ring of halo, blank golden eyes, but Gabriel was ever so slightly taller than most. His wingspan was broader, and his halo was noticeably wider, than Haliel's; the smaller angel had to squash a brief urge to cower, his feathers fluffing instinctively. "Um," he said. "Sorry to intrude, sir, but something a bit strange—happened to me. On Earth. Sir."

"What sort of something?" Gabriel asked, his lovely mouth turning down in a faint moue of distaste. Haliel knew Gabriel didn't *like* the idea of angels being on Earth; it wasn't where they belonged, and he tolerated the necessity of the surface-operative system with what on a lesser archangel might have been considered bad grace even as he received their reports. Haliel had never been quite sure whose idea it had been to station operatives from Heaven on the Prime Material plane to keep an eye on things, the way the demons did, but Gabriel—despite being in charge—had never seemed to consider it worthwhile.

Haliel took the little dart out of his pocket and set it carefully in the middle of Gabriel's white desk blotter, innocent of ink. The desk had a golden inkwell on it, containing a quill pen, and a single very neat stack of paperwork; other than that it was simply one very large cultured pearl. Against the snowy whiteness the dart looked even uglier, alien and out of place.

"I was—just standing there looking at the river," he said, looking down at it instead of at Gabriel, "and something *shot* me with this. In the back. It hurt quite badly for a minute or two. I can't think why anyone should be going around shooting at *anybody* with little dart things, let alone me. I didn't see who'd done it, either; when I turned around there was nobody there."

Gabriel picked the ugly thing up, narrowing his eyes at it, and went through the same basic forensic examination as Haliel had, sniffing at the point. He recoiled slightly, the downturn of his mouth sharpening.

"I see," he said. "Well. You did right to come to me and report the incident, Haliel. I will consider the matter. You are to visit the infirmary and have Raphael look at the wound, and then return to your assigned duty once he passes you fit."

"Oh, I don't think that's necessary, it doesn't hurt that badly now," Haliel said, and then caught himself before Gabriel's expression could change. "I mean. Yes, sir, right away. Thank you, sir."

"That will be all," said Gabriel, setting down the dart, and Haliel retreated from his presence, glad when the white door closed behind him with a faintly musical click. He'd go to see Raphael and get some honey-nectar salve or something to put on the tiny wound and then get back to *work*, those esso traces wouldn't review themselves—and he could stop at that little sushi place on the way to his flat, that sounded like a wonderful idea—and by the time he got home all of this would be nothing more than a weird, brief aberration.

Haliel smiled the sort of smile that would have left a human briefly dazzled, and straightened up, mantling his wings more neatly—and got on with it.

CHAPTER I

Alessio's Italian Restaurant, the Bowery, New York City

Nobody could remember exactly when this place had first opened; it had stood on the corner of Bowery and East 3rd for as long as people's memories generally lasted in this particular neighborhood, although it had been apparently shuttered for a good twenty years. This past spring it had opened up again, under new (or possibly old-but-new-again) management, and was doing good business on a street where practically every block featured at least one red-sauce joint. Perhaps lighter on the garlic than others, but generally unremarkable.

It was midnight; the place was closed, but a dim light was visible behind the blinds in the front windows. A very curious person might have sidled up to the window to see if they could peek through the gap and get a look inside; an even more curious person might have gone around the back to listen at the door of the kitchen, but neither of them would have stayed curious for long. The little black bulbs of security

7

cameras studded both the front and back of the building like architectural pimples, keeping a close eye on passersby.

That incautious person might have heard a few muffled curses from inside, followed by a nasty bubbling scream. The scream was choked off into more cursing.

"—shitting mother of fuck, Jesus, get your hands off me," whoever it was spat. "I told you I didn't see nothing—ah, *fucking Christ* that hurts—"

"So you said," another voice cut in: this one held both authority and the hint of a lisp. "Mario, put some of that rotgut *inside* him instead of in the hole; it might have a more salutary effect. One more time, Radu. Slowly."

The three men were in the restaurant's kitchen, lit only by the green glow of the EXIT sign over the door and the sodium-vapor streetlights outside; apparently what they were doing didn't require a lot of illumination. The unfortunate Radu, stripped to the waist, was sitting on a café chair turned around backward, his face buried in his folded arms on the chair's back. Mario, as directed, splashed some of the cheap vodka he'd been pouring over a wound in Radu's back into a glass instead. Slow dark blood trickled from the wound, which looked ugly even by the limited light available: its edges were puffy, swollen as if whatever had made it had been coated in something corrosive.

Radu took the glass, knocking back the shot in one gulp, and coughed explosively; when he could speak again he sounded a little more steady. "Like I said. Didn't smell anything weird, just ordinary humans, I didn't think anything of it, minding my own business when suddenly this fucking thing hits me in the back like a fucking icepick, and by the time I can turn around there's nobody there, not even the goddamn bums, everybody's split the scene. Fucking dart *hurts* like I got shot, plus I have to puke my guts out, and when I'm done doing that, all I can do is get my ass back here for some fucking back-alley surgery—fuck, Mario, gimme another drink, I feel like *shit*—"

Mario obliged, and poured another splash of vodka from the plastic handle over a linen napkin, dabbing it at the hole in Radu's back. "I got it all out," he said. "Thing had some kinda shit on it, must be what's makin' him sick, but I got the pieces outta him, Mr. Contini. Saved 'em in case you want someone to look at it or somethin'."

"Thank you, Mario," said the third voice, presumably Mr. Contini. "Your presence of mind is admirable. Radu, you said you smelled humans in the area before the attack. Were they wearing perfume or cologne, or in need of a shower? Any details would help."

"Just humes," said Radu, swallowing his second drink. "Maybe coulda used a shower, but not real funky. No perfume or nothing. Smelled like—floor polish, that pink liquid-soap shit they put in public bathrooms. Bad food."

"Bad food," repeated Contini.

"Soup-kitchen food. Shit you make in those big old vats, cheap noodles and sloppy joes, that kinda stuff."

"Not the scent of people living their best lives," said Contini. "Mm. Did you get any whiffs of anything else once the thing hit you?"

Vivian Shaw

"Couldn't smell a fucking thing, I was too busy hurling," said Radu, sounding as if he might repeat the process in the near future.

"Here's the thing I dug outta him, Mr. Contini," said Mario, offering a folded-up napkin wrapped around something. "Smells kinda like herbs and metal to me, but I ain't so great with smells since last time my nose got busted."

"I see," said Contini's voice, and its owner moved out of the deeper shadow to take the handful of crumpled linen: tall and very thin, with high shoulders and long fingers made longer by clawlike nails, the green EXIT light sliding over slicked-back black hair. The eyes were invisible in deep-sunken sockets, except for two sparks of reddish light. "Well. I suppose you'd better stay here tonight; try not to be sick on the floor if you can help it. Mario, go ahead and lock up once you've put a bandage on that, and then call around to warn people there's someone playing stupid games in the city. I'll be in my office. Don't bother me without a very good reason indeed."

"You got it, sir," said Mario, glancing at his colleague, and grabbed for the trash can just in time.

Erebus General Hospital, Dis

Behind his desk, Dr. Johann Faust's floor-to-ceiling office windows looked out over the central plaza of Dis with the shimmering opalescent flames of Lake Avernus in the background. The view was largely wasted on him; as medical director of the Erebus Health System he was either too busy in

10

the hospital itself to spend much time in his office, or on video calls with the windows opaqued behind him. Today, however, he had the glass set to transparent and had rolled his chair a little to the side so as not to block the view.

On his desk's big central monitor, an angel—winged, androgynously beautiful, identifiable from a demon only by the halo and the blank golden eyes—sighed. On closer examination, it looked rather more tired and worn than one might have expected from the host of Heaven; there were shadows underneath those golden eyes, and the beautiful features sagged a little. Behind it was a wall of pearl white, with no windows whatsoever.

"You get used to the view," Faust said. He looked rather like the woodcuts: stocky, not so much fat as solid, bearded, wearing a dark velvet robe trimmed with fur rather than a doctor's white coat; he wasn't seeing patients this afternoon. "The burning lake is a bit much to ignore at first, but you do stop noticing after a while."

"I wouldn't want to," said the angel, sounding wistful. "Something that beautiful should never be taken for granted—but I would find it a distraction, I admit."

Unlike some of the angels Faust had encountered, this one lacked the constant expression that suggested something in its vicinity smelled regrettable; there was a certain rueful, self-aware set to its otherwise anonymous features. It was also the only one of the archangels with whom Faust had any desire or patience to engage in conversation, because it was the closest thing Heaven had to a physician. He didn't envy that position one tiny little bit: the badly-hidden exhaustion on the angel's face spoke of an endless round of frustrations. "You ought to knock off for a bit," he said, characteristically blunt. "Go to the celestial equivalent of the Spa and soak in holy water or whatever it is you do, get some actual *rest*, Raphael. You're looking a bit seedy, and that's a professional medical opinion."

"We haven't got a spa," said Raphael, not without a tinge of regret. "We shouldn't *need* any such thing, you understand. That sort of sybaritic pleasure-seeking is supposed to be for your sort. We're above physical infirmity."

"It says so in the handbook, then?" said Faust. "'How to Angel: Be Constantly Exhausted but Not Complain'?" Actually, that did ring fairly true, he thought.

"I'm not exhausted," said Raphael automatically, and then put a hand to his face. "All right, perhaps I'm a little tired, but it's only because there's much more work than usual. Since the—the reset, and the signing of the Accords, and the—*collaborative initiative*. All the exchange work-gangs here and down in Hell. It must be a great deal more work for you as well, surely?"

"That it is not," said Faust, "for the clear and simple reason that I've got delegation going on, unlike you lot. I don't have to do all the work myself. The hardest thing we've had to deal with since the Accords has been managing the allergic reactions—some of it's just sniffles, but I've had several people need emergency care—and the high-energy mirabilics labs are working on that as we speak. We're getting some interesting results from Lake Avernus water run through the scanner, based on what I had to use for plasma for your angels during emergency surgery." He tilted his head. "Come to think of it, what *are* you doing up there about allergies with the exchange work-gangs?"

"Masks," Raphael said, sounding as dolorous as he'd ever heard an angel. "And lots and lots of nectar for the angels, but we haven't got a thing other than masks to help it in demons, the poor things. We, uh, tried the nectar, despite my strong recommendation against the idea, and it—really didn't go well at all, I'm afraid."

Faust snapped his fingers. "Two months ago. Right? We got a group of demons in the ER down here with acute GI distress, looked like they'd ingested something mildly corrosive, didn't want to talk about it."

"I am *so* dreadfully sorry about that," said Raphael unhappily. "I did submit an official report to the Council beforehand to point out that giving demons any food or drink from Heaven was probably not going to do them any good at all, but that was interpreted to be a, a xenophobic and defeatist attitude, and Gabriel came and counseled me about it. And how we all need to pull together to fulfill the Accords and there's no room for negativity."

"Fuck's sake," said Faust over the angel's wince. "It wasn't really that much of a problem, gastric lavage with lake water and some empirical treatment sorted them out nice and quick, but do your lot really refuse to listen to the voice of reason *that* much?"

Raphael looked so miserable that Faust had to hold up a hand. "Never mind. Not my business, my circus, or my monkeys. Point being, soon as I get anything useful out of the labs that works on our end to knock down the allergic reaction—and *won't* set it off on your end—I'll send it up to you at once. By the pallet-load if necessary."

"I don't know," said Raphael, "I don't think Gabriel would like that, but maybe he could be convinced?"

Right after the...events...of the recent post-apocalypse reset, which Faust didn't want to think about in much detail, there had been reason to believe that the angels responsible for bureaucratic management in Heaven had perhaps had their horizons broadened, but it sounded to him like they had settled directly back into their old ways. The official inferno-celestial Accords that had been signed by Gabriel and Samael after the fighting was over, witnessed by the massed hosts of both Heaven and Hell, included a clause decreeing that both sides should actively collaborate in joint projects to accelerate the rebuilding process in Heaven. Faust had said a great number of bad words in German when he'd read that particular subsection. He'd known perfectly well why it was in there, after the blank horror of the war itself and the clear and present need for Heaven and Hell to work together to prevent any such thing happening again, but that didn't make it not intrinsically stupid: philosophy and good intentions were all very well, but they didn't trump physiological reality. Angels and demons in the full manifestation of their power were unavoidably *allergic to one another*, and nothing was going to make angels in Hell and demons in Heaven *not* suffer the physical repercussions even if it sounded good on paper.

He'd said so to Samael, in the Devil's white-on-white office, leaning with his hands flat on the white-wood desk: *If I haven't made it sufficiently clear, my lord, the clinical reality here is that this is not going to fucking work out just because it's narratively convenient and people want it to, I can't fix the basic nature of the goddamn universe to fulfill political goals,* and just for a moment felt a flicker of mindless atavistic fear as Samael's eyes had gone from brilliant butterfly blue to blank scarlet, lid to lid. It was the worst argument they had ever had—Samael had never *refused* to listen to him before when he'd pointed out reasons why something wasn't going to work—and even thinking about it now made Faust's stomach feel unsettled.

Thank you for your clinical input, Doctor Faust, the Devil had said, enunciating. *You may go,* and for the first time since he'd shaken hands with Mephistopheles all those centuries ago, Faust had been *afraid* of his employer.

(He had known, of course, that Samael *knew* as well as he did that this was impossible, no matter what they tried to get around the physical reality of it. He'd just hoped Samael could unmire himself from politics enough to point that out to everybody else.)

He was not afraid now; he was frustrated. And Raphael, poor bastard, had to deal with the frustration of an entire divine bureaucracy trying to make him do the impossible without any of the resources Faust had to draw upon. Nothing could *prevent* the reaction. It was built into the nature of the universe itself. You could hope to ameliorate the *symptoms* of that reaction, but you could not prevent it from occurring. As long as demons were helping with the debris-removal and construction gangs in Heaven, or angel volunteers were helping organize library stacks in Hell, this would be a problem.

As long as . . .

"You know what," he said, slowly. "I've just had a brilliant idea. Again."

"Oh?" said the angel, blinking.

"So we know that demons in *Heaven* and angels in *Hell* are viciously allergic, yes? Well, what about if they *don't* swap places? What if they work together on the Prime Material instead, neutral ground? It'd be interesting to see if the reaction is still as intractable when the individuals are no longer affected by their physical location magnifying its intensity. We know from the surface operatives that at least limited and periodical contact—when they have coffee together or occasionally meet to talk—doesn't seem to trigger it, but what if we increased the direct, prolonged exposure to one another in a relatively neutral environment?"

"You mean—send an angel and a demon to Earth specifically to work closely together?" said Raphael, blinking again before a smile like sunrise broke through the visible fatigue. Faust was briefly stunned by the beauty, glancing hurriedly away. "They could . . . *further the missions* set out in the Accords," the angel said, as if realizing this out loud. "Couldn't they?"

"They absolutely could," said Faust, still seeing afterimages. "And provide both of us with valuable data in the process."

"They'd have to *work closely together*," said Raphael. He now appeared faintly lit from within. "To...collaborate. Setting aside differences. And achieve some sort of common good in the mortal world. As an example of, of infernocelestial bipartisanship."

"That, too," said Faust, reflecting that as a human he himself had had a much easier time learning how to be a medical administrator than an archangel must have, even one like Raphael who'd occasionally had a thought cross their mind. "Get 'em to build a house together or something. Be all constructive. We'd need a pretty young and enthusiastic demon for the role, of course. I'm sure we can find someone." Fastitocalon was always complaining about his interns; maybe one of them could be pressed into service.

He couldn't quite read Raphael's expression, but he could have sworn for a moment that something quite like glee flickered across his lovely features and was gone. "And *we'd* have to find a young and driven angel," Raphael said. "Who really is *passionate* about things. Who could bring *energy* to the project. Wouldn't we."

"Just so," said Faust. "Look, why don't you have your people start looking for potential candi—"

"I've got one," said Raphael, very fast. "I've got the perfect candidate."

And you want to get him the hell out of Heaven posthaste, Faust thought, not without sympathy, wondering what exactly this candidate had done to get up the angel's nose; Raphael was a very great deal more patient than Faust himself had ever managed to be, even when he'd been alive, but apparently even archangels had limits. "Excellent," he said out loud. "I'll ask around, see if we can find someone suitable on our end to volunteer. They ought to have some sort of specific project to work on while they're paired up, I'll have to think about it— probably building houses isn't quite the ticket, but I'll come up with something."

"Do," said Raphael. "I think it will be of *extreme* use to everyone involved. Our candidate is . . . to some extent trained to work in healthcare, but he is very inexperienced and would need professional oversight." There was a delicate weight on *professional* that said a number of things at once; Faust wondered again what the mysterious angel had done, and decided he didn't want to know.

"I'm not up on my roster of surface operatives," he said, "that's all Monitoring and Evaluation, but presumably someone up there would be capable of taking on a couple of inexperienced beings and provide *professional oversight*—"

He snapped his fingers again, the idea coming to him all at once. "No. Even better. We needn't necessarily place them with a Hell surface op at all; I'm acquainted with a human physician on Earth, a personal friend of the archdemon Fastitocalon, who might possibly be able to help figure out something vaguely useful to do with them. She was of some use down here in the worst of the fighting and I'd trust her to keep basic order between an angel and a demon for a bit."

"Your arches have human friends?" said Raphael, blinking. "Is that strictly ethical?"

"We're Hell," said Faust, with a less-than-pleasant grin. "We approach ethical from a somewhat unorthodox direction." He felt ever so slightly guilty about dropping Greta Helsing in the soup, but she'd think of something. Of that he had no doubt. She was good friends with Fastitocalon, wasn't she? Being involved in infernocelestial politics shouldn't really pose much of a challenge for someone who knew as much as she undoubtedly did about the subject, and she'd done a pretty decent job of emergency surgery with zero experience to back it up; he thought she'd do at least as well keeping an angel and a demon in order when the world *wasn't* ending all around them.

"Let me make some calls," he said. "I'll be in touch."

Harley Street, London

The difficulty with cosmetic reperfusion for Class A revenants, colloquially known as zombies, was not the actual physical drainage and replacement of the old embalming fluid; that was easy, if mildly unpleasant. The real challenge was getting your *tints* right.

They'd come a long way since the "suntan" and "natural" dye formulations of the sixties. Back then, zombies had had to make do with varying shades of orangey-pink if they didn't want to go with formaldehyde grey; these days you could mix up a custom blend of hues to add to the embalming fluid, and it was somewhat rewarding for the physician as well as the patient to watch the color change as the dyed fluid perfused the tissues.

Greta Helsing was very good at it. Greta Helsing had a

state-of-the-art Porti-Boy embalming machine that could pump a full dose of fresh embalming fluid through a patient's body in about half an hour, start to finish, and she was extremely skilled at mixing her dyes to get the right color balance in the finished tissue. She hated doing it, because the formaldehyde—even in her well-ventilated procedure room—gave her a foul headache. At least this morning's patient had left well satisfied with the results of his procedure, brand-new trocar buttons glued in and sealing the incisions through which the fluid was pumped and drained, and she didn't have to do anything *else* complicated for a little while.

Her phone rang for the fourth time in half an hour while she was still rootling around in her current enormous handbag for the ibuprofen, and it took her a moment to winch her professional smile back into place before picking up. "Greta Helsing," she said, and gave in, briefly making a horrible face that no one but her office wall could see.

"Greta? Arne Hildebrandt. Have you got a moment?"

Hildebrandt was in charge of one of the major labs in Göttingen doing research on supernatural medicine, a sort of grey area between the ordinary world and the one her patients inhabited, kept safe by a blanket of obfuscation that to the casual eye merely indicated normal-type biological research. He'd been instrumental in publishing one of her early papers on mummy medicine; she considered him a valuable colleague.

"Hello, Arne," she said. "What's on your mind?"

"Well, it's a little hard to explain. It's our records," said Dr. Hildebrandt. His German accent was noticeable but not distracting. "We've been going through last year's lab records prior to moving everything to a new building, and there's this…*discrepancy* no one can seem to explain."

Greta's talking-on-the-phone smile did not so much falter as diminish, like a radio with the volume slowly turned down. "What sort of discrepancy?" she asked.

"It's very subtle," said Hildebrandt. "But it seems that halfway through one day's transcription, every single record changes as if one author left off and another suddenly took over. I could ignore it if it was just one or two documents, but it's *every single record*. All the papers. Every computer file. Parameters ever so slightly altered. No one knows why."

Greta shut her eyes, the headache clanging louder than ever. She'd been afraid of this; she'd hoped like hell that it wouldn't happen, but on some level she'd always known it was just a matter of time.

Almost every human on the planet lacked *conscious* recollection of the moment last year when the entire world had undergone an elemental change: an apocalypse averted, a universe's parameters reset. Only creatures made largely out of magic and memory itself, like mummies and certain other monsters, or people who hadn't been *on* Earth while the crucial bit happened, like Greta, had any clear recollection of that particular moment in time.

"It's like some sort of—I don't know, pressure-wave went through and moved every single recording instrument, every measurement, every *thing*, ever so slightly, all at once." Hildebrandt sighed. "I want to think of this as just an aberration—a seismic tremor, or something, but I can't make it work with the evidence we've got."

Of course you can't, she thought, pressing her fingers to the rim of her eyesockets. *You're sometimes deeply annoyingly smarter than the majority of humans, and you are a scientist, so you are very clearly not going to let this go, and I have no idea what the hell I'm cleared to tell you.* She didn't even know what the official Hell position *was* with regards to information the humans were allowed to share; Faust had only given her limited information about the science of magic because she'd asked him, but she was pretty sure that was supposed to go no further without official permission.

"…Greta?" said Hildebrandt. "You still there?"

She opened her eyes to find herself staring at the dog-eared pile of textbooks on her office credenza, and turned her attention back to the phone. The books had titles such as *Principles of Mirabilics*, fifteenth edition, and *Applied Mirabilics: An Introduction.* "I'm here," she said. "And—maybe I might have some idea about what's behind the discontinuity, but I can't be sure until I talk to some colleagues of mine." *Or ask them what I'm allowed to say.*

"Well," said Hildebrandt, sounding a little puzzled. "Thanks, I think?"

"Let me get back to you, Arne. I won't be long."

Monitoring and Evaluation Director's Office, Dis

Fastitocalon put out the morning's third cigarette and stared at the man sitting across his desk, fur-trimmed robe and floppy hat not much changed from the day he'd arrived in Hell several centuries ago. Over the years Fastitocalon had spent a great deal of time glowering at Faust, one way or another, while the doctor lectured him or told him to do painful things or—occasionally—reassured him, but this might be the first time he'd ever been on *this* side of a desk from Samael's personal physician and the medical director of Erebus General. He'd only had this particular desk for a few months, but it was still a tiny flicker of pleasure to recognize each *first time* he experienced something as an actual archdemon instead of a third-rate excommunicated ex-accountant with chronic bronchitis and melancholia. Going from onetime employee to running the entire Monitoring and Evaluation department, in charge of the surface-operative business of keeping an eye on the Prime Material plane, was still a little difficult to fit inside his head; he wasn't entirely sure he *wanted* to lose that repeated sense of wonder.

Faust looked right back at him and did not react at all when Fastitocalon very deliberately reached for his cigarette case, extracted another Dunhill, and lit it with a fingertip. "Run this by me again, slowly," he said, blowing out a thin quill of blue smoke.

"I," said Faust, with large pauses, like a British tourist trying to get a foreigner to understand English, "want your friend, the human doctor, to drive an angel—and a demon—and presumably a selection of ancillary people—around America— in a bus." He eyed the burning cigarette-tip. "The angel's some sort of terribly keen orderly or intern or something who's apparently driving Raphael nuts, and I'm sure we can find an equally annoying demon counterpart to send up there with it; possibly you can recommend someone who would benefit from the experience. The point of this entire endeavor is to fulfill the very particularly idiotic bit in the Accords that goes on about infernocelestial collaboration and bipartisanship. By doing field research."

"Yes," said Fastitocalon, "that was more or less what I thought you said. Field research on supernatural creatures and their various ailments?"

"*Précisément*, Director. I am told this will be handled by External Affairs through a major European university's coffers, under the guise of an ordinary research trip. All Helsing needs to do is stop the angel and the demon biting bits off each other or pushing each other in front of large vehicles, record how they are physically affected by being in the other's presence—mostly this whole business is *actually* research to find out what the hell happens when you get them interacting on the Prime Material rather than Heaven or Hell so nobody goes into anaphylaxis—and do a bit of doctoring on the way."

" 'Record how they are physically affected,' " said Fastitocalon.

"Record with *scientific detail*," said Faust, nodding seriously. "She need not draw diagrams, you understand. But in-depth discussion of how they interact is to be desired. One can cling to a faint hope that actual data might prompt the powers that be to *revisit* that section of the Accords."

Fastitocalon lost the battle and burst out laughing, passing a hand over his face. "I am so enormously glad I am going to ask her this over the phone, Faust. Not face-to-face."

"*I* am so glad," said Faust, getting up in comfortable triumph, "that it is *you* asking her, and not me."

London

It was already getting on for full dark when Greta locked up the clinic at five-thirty, carrying several heavy files with her, and went to meet her ride home. This time of year there was no desire to linger and watch the golden light of evening slant its way across the river or warm the ancient stones of the city: she was cold, she was hungry, she had a filthy headache, and she wanted to go *home*, damn it all. The conversation with Hildebrandt had done nothing but engender a general sense of dread regarding what the hell she was allowed to say and to whom.

Ordinarily she'd have been able to stay at Edmund Ruthven's Embankment mansion. She'd spent a lot of time there recently, one way or another, and she'd finally escaped the lease on her horrible little Crouch End flat by dint of throwing Ruthven's money at the landlords and never looking back, but Ruthven and his partner Grisaille were in Romania. With Count Dracula and his latest ward, ten-year-old vampire Lucy Ashton, whom Ruthven and Grisaille had housed and sheltered for a few somewhat-complicated days this spring.

Lucy was an orphan who had been turned by a thoroughly unscrupulous American vampire, who had subsequently been tracked down and killed by Dracula's people, and was now living her best unlife in the luxury of the Voivode's castle learning how to turn into bats and wolves and mist and not having to put up with the vagaries of the English foster system. Ruthven had had conniptions over the entire process of trying to find somewhere for her to live before the Draculas had offered their home, but he seemed to have regained his general suave self-possession and jumped at the chance to go and visit with the family.

Greta rather envied every single one of them.

The demon giving her a ride to Varney's country house was supposed to meet her at the end of Harley Street in the Cavendish Square park, a little circular oasis of trees and grass in the middle of an expensive chunk of city, and normally he was waiting for her to get there—she *did* try to be on time or at least text him if she was running late—but there was no sign of him anywhere on any of the benches they usually used for rendezvous. It wasn't entirely unheard-of for Harlach to be late; generally he was about as good as she was in terms of texting ahead to let her know he'd been held up, but her phone was blank and clear.

Greta sat down crossly on a bench with her files in her lap and waited. It came on to rain.

Ten minutes late, she thought, checking her watch. *Another five and I'll text him.*

Another five and I'll text Varney *so he doesn't start to get concerned.* It was very much not like her to be late home to Dark Heart House without letting him know; it wasn't as if she had to deal with traffic. She wanted to be *home* so she could talk to Varney about the bloody, bloody discontinuity problem and what the hell she was going to tell Arne Hildebrandt.

The rain intensified.

Another two—

"Greta?" It was Harlach, hurrying out of the darkness, hugging his coat tightly around him, soaked and shivering, his face very white in the dim streetlamp illumination. "Lady Varney—I'm so sorry I'm late, are you ready—"

Fuck, she thought. He didn't look anything even close to okay, and it had been months since she'd got him to stop calling her *Lady Varney*. She didn't know him too terribly well; in her experience Harlach was pale at the best of times, his dark curly hair and heavy eyebrows and lashes giving him a (hopefully) unintentional Byronic air, but right now he looked *grey* in the flat streetlight, his hair wet and black. Grey in a way she hadn't seen for several months, since her last encounter with the demon Fastitocalon. "Yes, of course," she said, getting up, the files tucked under her arm. "What happened? Are you all right?"

Harlach just reached for her hand, and his fingers when they curled around hers were warmer than they should be, given the night's chill. "Hang on," he said, and the world went blank and brilliant white.

She had never liked translocation but she had to admit that reducing a multi-hour commute to a matter of seconds was definitely worth the brief disorientation. Cavendish Square vanished around them, and in the space of a few heartbeats that brilliant whiteness was fading to disclose the familiar terrace of Sir Francis Varney's country seat: Ratford Abbey, generally and romantically called Dark Heart House for the sake of the copper beeches surrounding the old mansion. It wasn't currently raining in Wiltshire, for which she was vaguely grateful.

Harlach stood beside her, still breathing hard; now he was wheezing faintly, his hand very warm in hers. Greta made a decision, pushing aside the worry over Hildebrandt's question for now. "Come inside," she said. "You don't look at all well. You can have a drink and tell me what the hell is going on, if it happens to be something I'm in any way cleared to hear, and I'll look you over properly."

"...if you insist," he said, pushing the wet hair out of his eyes, capitulating much too quickly. He was still wheezing, very pale, brownish crescents under his eyes, and he let her draw him toward the warmth and safety of the house. She'd never seen him like this in the half a year he'd been taking her to and from her London clinic; he'd always been the kind of suave, urbane, slightly overdressed type of chic you associated with surface-operative demons. This version lacked his usual polish.

"Come on," she said, and opened the French doors leading into the blue drawing-room, into warmth and light and safety.

Sir Francis Varney was reading the newspaper in one of the large squashy armchairs pulled up to the fireplace. His ward Emily's stacks of veterinary textbooks and notes and Coke cans were not in evidence: Emily had gone off for a week with some friends to climb mountains in Wales, of all things, and the house felt much larger and emptier without her. When Greta and Harlach came in, Varney first smiled and then put down the newspaper, looking concerned, and got up.

"Good God," he said, staring at Harlach. "You're drenched— was it raining or *snowing* or couldn't it make up its mind? —Here. Have a drink."

"I'm quite all right," Harlach said, not sounding it, but he took the glass Varney pressed into his hand. "Just. Something of a shock."

Varney flicked a glance to his wife, who was putting down the stacks of records she'd brought on the credenza, and both of them shared a single thought: *What in London could possibly shock a surface-operative demon*, and then *Do we want to know?*

Harlach swallowed half the brandy in his glass and coughed violently, setting it down on a little rosewood table, and when Greta offered to take his coat he shrugged out of it with a noticeable wince. "I'm sure it's nothing," he said, still wheezing slightly.

"It's obviously *something*," she told him, going to hang the coat up to dry. "Sit down and get your breath back, and *then* tell us what's going on." She couldn't help thinking again how much different the Harlach she sort of knew was to this white shaking creature, and pushed away a thoroughly annoying spike of impatience. He'd tell them if he wanted to tell them, and it wasn't necessarily any of her business except inasmuch as she wasn't a hundred percent sure he could *manage* the return journey to London in his current condition.

Harlach, dazedly, slipped into a chair, unconsciously pressing his chest. His shirt, thus revealed, was black as well, obviously expensive. "I'm so terribly sorry," he said. "Entirely letting the side down. But I...something *jumped out at* me, I don't know where it came from, and I think it must have... thrown something at me? Something sharp?"

Varney hissed. "Are you hurt? Did it scratch you?"

Harlach lifted a shaking hand to his shoulder, pushed aside the collar of his (soaking-wet) Armani shirt, and his fingers came away red. He looked from them to Varney and Greta, eyes huge in his white face.

Fuck, thought Greta, meeting Varney's eyes over the demon's head, and slipped into her calm talking-to-patients voice. "Fetch my bag, would you, Francis, the big one, by the mud-room door. It's going to be all right, Harlach. Just try to relax—finish that brandy—and I'll have a look and sort you out."

Neither she nor Varney could shake the mental image of a quite different drawing-room with a different creature laid out on a couch, suffering from a poisoned wound. Harlach didn't look anything like as awful as Varney had on that night years ago, but he clearly wasn't well, and she wanted a closer look at his bleeding shoulder. While Varney fetched her bag, she went to wash her hands before pulling on a pair of nitrile exam gloves.

Harlach was still very white, but beginning to be flushed

high on each cheekbone, breathing audibly, and she couldn't help thinking of that previous poisoning incident even as she had him ease the fabric down over his shoulder to expose the wound—and then let out her breath in a sigh of relief. It wasn't even close to the cross-shaped stab wound that had brought Varney half-collapsing to Edmund Ruthven's house. It was, in fact, just a scratch, but a bad one that was puffing up angrily and much too red and hot: something in the wound was irritating him.

"Right," she said. "This isn't very nice but I ought to be able to sort you out quite quickly, Harlach, and then you can tell us everything you remember."

"There isn't much," said the demon, his eyes closing. "Just . . . I was on my way to come pick you up and something in an alley just jumped out and . . . *threw* something at me, or shot it—I wasn't paying attention, I was on my phone—and it got me in the shoulder. I couldn't see who'd thrown it, whoever it was had gone, and by the time I got to Cavendish Square to meet you I was unavoidably late."

"Never mind late," said Greta, taking a thermometer out of the bag Varney had brought. "Under the tongue, please. And you're sure it didn't scratch you anywhere else?"

He shook his head, and obeyed: 100°F, not fantastic, but not terribly dangerous for a demon. Greta got out sterile saline, disinfectant, antibiotic salve. He didn't seem to be having *worse* difficulty with his breathing, at least, although she didn't like the sound of it. "Varney, could you fetch me a towel? Thanks."

She looked closer at the puffy, swollen scratch: yes, something still in there, tiny fragments. That swelling, plus the shortness of breath, told her she needed to get whatever it was out of there. Hadn't the fucking Holy Sword people been *sorted out*, as Samael had put it? Were there now copycat idiots of some kind running about cutting holes in demons for the sake of eternal salvation, or was this just—terrible luck? Wasn't the whole bloody reset supposed to have done away with disturbances like this?

One thing the past several years had taught Greta was that one made one's own luck, by and large. Varney returned with a clean towel and a couple of her pairs of forceps still drying from the isopropyl he'd soaked them in rather than boiling them for several minutes, and she had to smile, remembering the moment when Edmund Ruthven the vampire had brought her instruments neatly arranged on a tray. She'd said *Since when are you a scrub nurse*, and he'd told her he had driven ambulances in the Blitz and that there was more in heaven and earth, Horatio.

He'd been right about that. Greta took the forceps and bent over Harlach's shoulder while Varney held the light for her. Yes: a couple of tiny fragments of something deep in the scratch, the flesh almost too swollen to see them. "This will hurt," she told Harlach. "It'll be over soon, but it will hurt."

"Understood," he said between his teeth, and she bent closer and reached into the shallow wound to pluck out the residue, whatever it was. Varney, to his eternal credit, had brought her a clean saucer along with the forceps, and she straightened up and dropped a couple of tiny shreds of metal onto the porcelain.

Harlach had held still with visible effort throughout the nasty little operation; now she could irrigate the wound to clear any residue, and cover it with antibiotic salve, close it with a couple of Steri-Strips, and sit back on her heels. "There," she said. "I've stopped, and you ought to feel much better soon, Harlach."

"Thank you," he said, eyes still shut. His breathing wasn't what she'd call *great* but there was quite a lot less of the wheezing effort he'd demonstrated earlier, and he wasn't pressing his chest. It really did look like that might have been some sort of allergic reaction to whatever she'd taken out of his wound. "I do . . . very much appreciate it, Doctor."

"You're staying here tonight," she said, "we've got loads of spare rooms; don't worry about a thing."

Harlach nodded after a moment. "Can you lean on us long enough to get you upstairs?" she said.

"I can walk," he said, and pushed himself upright, went grey-green, and nearly collapsed into Greta's arms. He was shaking. "—Ugh. I'm sorry. Apparently I *can't* walk terribly well at present—I really am so sorry about this—"

"Harlach," she said. "Hush. Let me. Okay? This is my job. Let me. Go upstairs with Varney and I'll bring you something hot to drink and you can lie down and heal. One thing: did you happen to get any idea of the shape and size of the weapon that hurt you?"

He shook his head and then looked miserably dizzy, passing

a hand over his face. "No. Didn't see it at all, just the pain, the blade must have been…hidden somehow, or just too quick—"

"Never mind," she said. "Go on up to bed. I'll be up to see you in a bit. Varney?"

Varney nodded and slipped his arm around Harlach's shoulders with iron strength held in very careful control, taking most of the demon's weight as they slowly trundled out of the room.

Greta sat back, looking at the detritus of first-aid paraphernalia, and covered her face with her hands. Hadn't Samael said that the fucking remnant-thing was *gone*, that the Gladius Sancti were over and done and not going to harm them or anybody else ever again? What was lying in wait for random demons on the course of their normal pursuits and why, other than your standard anti-demon zealot? Those at least were generally too insane to pose any reasonable threat. What the hell was going on, and what did it mean in terms of *what she could tell Hildebrandt?*

Her phone rang, and after a moment she stripped off her gloves and fished it out of her pocket, staring at the caller ID. Fastitocalon never just *called* her on the phone. He simply spoke inside her head, courtesy of the mental link they'd shared for most of her life. Why he was suddenly *calling* her was—

Was maybe as explicable as her amiable surface-op demon acquaintance who took her to work every day being randomly attacked by something that harmed supernaturals.

Fuck.

"Fass?" she said, lifting the phone to her ear. "Tell me *you* know what the hell I'm supposed to do?"

"Funny you should say that. As a matter of fact," he said, "I absolutely do."

CHAPTER 2

Dark Heart House, Wiltshire

W hat's that supposed to mean?" Greta demanded. "Fass, is the Gladius Sancti thing *back* somehow?"

"What?" he said, sounding distracted. "No. Not as far as I know. I need to ask you to do me, and Hell in general, an enormously huge favor."

"Me?" she said. "What on earth can I do for Hell?"

"You can supervise a couple of perishing neophytes in the process of determining whether or not angels and demons are hideously allergic to each other *on Earth* rather than in either of their bases of operations," said Fastitocalon. Since he'd shaken his chronic cough, his voice had smoothed out into a pleasant, faintly golden-toned tenor, but he still *sort* of sounded like the Fass she'd known all her life: cut-glass BBC accent, wry and sardonic. "And in the process of doing so, you can conduct field research on supernatural physiology and pathology. In America."

Greta took the phone away from her ear and stared at it for

a moment, as if this would clarify anything, before replacing it. "You are making no sense whatsoever," she said.

"I'll try again. The powers that be are having some difficulty with the infernocelestial Accords as signed on account of how angels and demons do not do so well when pressed into close proximity with one another in either Heaven or Hell, and therefore this whole collaborative work-together-for-greater-good bit isn't actually a thing anyone can really hope to carry out with any grace, no matter how flowery the language may be."

"*I* could have told them that," she said. She could clearly remember the medical demons' allergic reaction to the angel patients undergoing triage in the Dis hospital, in the middle of the chaos, and Faust's expression as he told them to get the hell out of it and mainline antihistamine until they could breathe again.

"Yes, well," said Fastitocalon, "so could Faust, and he tried, but apparently it wasn't a thing that could politically *be told* to anyone, even Sam, so here we are and we've got to make the best of it because nobody wants to destabilize the current political climate any further, myself very much included. What they want you to do is trundle about America for six weeks or so in a scientifically appointed vehicle of some description with an angel and a demon—the angel's some sort of celestial orderly and the demon's one of my own misbegotten interns, for which I apologize in advance—and observe how they work together while educating the pair of them in basic clinical procedure. If they swell up and stop breathing as soon as they get within five feet of one another, you can shoot them full of adrenaline *and* you will have obtained a valuable data point for the research teams of both Above and Below, who will undoubtedly both feel better knowing that the problem is being examined properly. Who knows, there might be enough actual data to prompt the powers that be to revisit the wording of that particular section, although I hold out little hope."

"Who's going to pay for all this?" she asked, ignoring the bit about wording. When Heaven and Hell had both signed something, it sounded vanishingly unlikely that they'd consider changing it, even if it was patently absurd. The pretext for this trip seemed somewhat flimsy to her, as well; they knew angels and demons could *coexist* on Earth, as evidenced by the fact that several surface operatives from the two sides were at least vaguely friendly with one another. She was inclined to blame *the current political climate* rather than any direct scientific research objective.

"Göttingen University, I'm told. It's being handled through Hell's External Affairs office, and the Göttingen people have been subconsciously instructed to think of this as their idea in the first place."

"Göttingen," she repeated, slumping back against the edge of the sofa, pinching the bridge of her nose, eyes shut. "*Fuck.* Fass, I had a call from Arne Hildebrandt at Göttingen this afternoon. It's what I'd been afraid of this whole time: he's noticed the discontinuity in records that came with the reset. He doesn't *remember* the reset, like he's supposed to not remember it, like *everybody's* supposed not to, but he's noticed the slight change and he isn't going to let it go. It's probably going to just be a matter of time before he twigs a lot of useful information and starts asking less-than-useful questions— he's a supernatural-medicine researcher, but as far as I know he is currently blissfully ignorant of Heaven and Hell and the cutting edge of mirabilics. He asked me if I had any idea what might have caused the discontinuity, and I told him I'd talk to some people and get back to him. Do *you* know what I'm allowed to say and not to say?"

"Hildebrandt," said Fastitocalon heavily. "Yes. That would be the name I've been given. It is in fact his department that's been leaned on to decide they want this field-research expedition to occur."

"What the hell am I supposed to tell him? 'Yes, I know; no, I can't say anything about it, so please pretend you didn't notice anything at all'?"

"Actually," he said after a moment, "this might add weight to the theory that they came up with this idea for the trip themselves." He sounded thoughtful, and she could hear a faint tapping noise on the other end of the phone. Fastitocalon's fingernails were ever so slightly longer than men usually wore them, quite pointed and very clear, and he tended to tap them on things while he was trying to work out some particularly knotty problem. For a moment she missed him so badly it almost hurt.

"I would suggest," he continued, "that you inform Dr. Hildebrandt—when he calls to officially request your participation, and not before—that yes, you will be undertaking this research trip for Göttingen, for reasons *among which* is the need to determine if anybody *else* has noticed any similar discontinuities in their own records. And if so, to potentially discover what the reason or reasons behind said anomalies could be."

"So something more like 'I don't know,'" she said, wry, "'but I intend to find out'?"

"Along those lines, yes. I recommend something a bit more science-y sounding, but of course that is entirely up to you."

"I've been neatly maneuvered, haven't I," she said, feeling both weary and affectionate. "Damn you, Fass."

"Already done, my dear doctor, already done. Look, I know this is a lot to take on, but—"

"But someone's got to do it," she finished for him, "and I am the logical answer. Fine. One question, though."

"Ask away," he said.

"Who the hell is going to *drive* the bloody bus to and fro across America and up and down in it, because I can tell you right now it is very definitely not going to be me?"

Fastitocalon laughed: a familiar sound, without the painful, raspy edge on it she'd grown to know so well. "I will see what can be done. For now, do accept my apologies for this whole business; I do *know* it's a lot—"

"Yes, you said," Greta told him. "I don't relish the thought of telling Varney about this, by the way. Sincerely doubt he'll react with untrammeled delight. Have some coals of fire."

"...thoroughly well-deserved," said Fastitocalon, sounding wry. "If he cuts up rough, I expect I could have a word with him?"

"I shall remember you said that," she said. "Right. I'd better start working out what the hell one *wears* for multiply-mendacious supernatural field-research trips across the States, hadn't I? Good-bye, Fass. You owe me."

"Hell owes you," he said, the levity gone from his voice. "Thank you, Greta."

"It most certainly does," she said, and hung up the phone. It wasn't until several minutes later that she realized she hadn't told Fastitocalon about Harlach and the business of the mysterious not-Gladius-Sancti attack; the relief of telling him about the discontinuity problem had driven it out of her mind.

Some physician I am, she thought sourly, dropping the phone onto the coffee table and heading for the house's grand staircase.

By the time she got upstairs Greta had more or less fabricated her planned response to Hildebrandt in her mind: yes, she'd do it; yes, she thought it was a jolly good idea; yes, she thought it might actually shed some light on the discontinuity he'd called about earlier, and she'd be sure to record all discrepancies they came across in clinical records during the fieldwork trip. Everything would be quite all right. She'd wait to hear from Göttingen on next steps.

She'd wait to hear from Hell's External Affairs department on the *other* next steps. Greta had never had to supervise anyone as an official teacher or minder, and she hoped like hell she'd be able to handle an angel and a demon who might or might not be able to work together. Her vague impression of what to expect was basically a couple of undergrads, completely ignorant of the modern world—perhaps the demon less so than the angel, which might be easier to deal with, not that she'd have much of a choice. At least she might get a chance to talk to Faust about their individual medical requirements, and possibly to get a better idea of the clinical picture with regard to angel-demon reactions and what if anything could be done about them.

God, this was going to be potentially interesting and also *so insanely tiring* and Varney was not going to be happy about any of it at all.

Fass, you owe me, she thought again.

"How is he?" she asked quietly from the door of the green bedroom. Varney got up just as quietly from the chair by the bed and came over to meet her.

"He seems to be sleeping now," he said. "Too warm still, but I didn't fetch the thermometer to see how bad. The scratch is definitely healing, albeit slowly; whatever it was clearly doesn't seem to be anywhere as damaging as the…the previous substance we encountered." Unconsciously his hand rose to touch the spot just under his left collarbone where the Gladius Sancti weapon had wounded him years ago. "He just seems ill and exhausted."

"Thank you," she said, meaning it. "Go get yourself something heartening to drink, love. I'm going to sit with him for a while. I need to talk to you about something later, but I want a look at him first."

"As you wish," he said. "Should I bring you up a sandwich or some vile instant noodles or something to keep body and soul together?"

"Thanks, but I don't think I'm tremendously hungry," she said. "You are the best of men, Francis Varney."

"I try," he said with a hint of a smile, lovely and odd on that melancholy face, and left her alone with Harlach.

The demon didn't seem to be in terribly bad shape, but Greta still didn't like how she could hear his breathing, or how the pink irritation was still visible around the healing scratch—or the way he was sweating a little, dampening the hair at his temples; he was still definitely too hot.

Harlach was mostly out of it, but could be roused to open his mouth for the thermometer, and she really did not like what it told her at all: 103.7, edging into significant even for a demon, especially since he'd been at 100 when they arrived. That was...maybe forty-five minutes ago, and he was spiking.

She thought again of the way he'd been wheezing earlier, before she got the stuff out of his wound; that really had seemed like it might be an allergic reaction to whatever it was. And Fastitocalon had said the research trip was a front to investigate allergic reactions in angels and demons on the Prime Material plane. Was someone *already* doing hands-on experiments in that particular field of inquiry?

What would happen if that got worse? Would he respond to the emergency adrenaline shot she'd use on a human, and what the hell could she do if he did *not*?

Greta gave up and shut her eyes and reached for a faint but

present mindtouch, rather than trundling downstairs to fetch her phone; she preferred talking to him this way anyhow, both for convenience and privacy. *Fass. Fastitocalon. I need you.*

Silence for several minutes, then his voice in her head, sounding more familiar than he had on the phone line. *Greta, what is it, I'm a bit busy.*

You've been a bit busy for what, a year now—never mind, I need you. It's Harlach, I forgot to tell you earlier. Something's hurt him, he's not well. You said the Gladius Sancti thing was gone, but I think something else seems to be trying to take its place—

Shit, he said delicately, and she could tell she had his full attention. *What happened? Tell me exactly.*

He was late picking me up tonight from work, and when he did appear he was in obvious distress—he got us back to Dark Heart but then more or less collapsed, and said he'd been attacked by something with a... I don't know, tiny crossbow, dart gun, something with a blade—he didn't get a good look—and tiny bits of it broke off in his wound. He was dizzy and short of breath and wheezing and the scratch itself was red and puffy, so I got the bits out quick as I could with tweezers—shades of Francis with the Gladius Sancti weapon, years ago—and he seemed a bit better, but he's not healing as fast as a demon should and he's spiking a fever and, Fass, I can't help thinking this might have to do with the allergy problem you were talking about, and I think I need someone to take him Below before it turns into something I can't fix. I want him seen by someone who knows what the hell they're doing and has the equipment and staff to manage serious medical emergencies.

Damn, said Fastitocalon, sounding sharp. *Right. I'll have someone come up to fetch him. Stay put. Do you have the fragments from the wound?*

Of course I do, I put the bits into a ziplock bag like somebody who has seen a forensic-medicine drama once in their lives. Have Faust make somebody run it through whatever your equivalent is of a GC/MS.

All right, all right. I'm sorry. I'll have someone up there in a minute.

The mental link did not exactly cut off but shrank all at once, like a radio station with the volume turned down. She was at least grateful that Harlach would be taken under Dr. Faust's care and not be *her* worry anymore—and wanted to pick a bone or two further with Fastitocalon, once this was taken care of.

When the promised demon arrived to fetch Harlach, she was unsurprised to see it was Irazek, the ex–surface op they'd met in Paris, earnest and carroty-orange-haired as ever, and was slightly grateful for the familiarity: it was comforting. "Hi," he said. "Oh dear, he doesn't look good at all, does he… will you be coming with him, Doctor?"

"Definitely not," she said, handing over the bag with the tiny bloodstained bits. The last time she'd been in Hell's central medical facility, she'd had her hands inside the chest of a dead angel trying to get its heart to agree to beat again, and she wasn't terribly keen to revisit the memory, no matter how good the view of the lake might be. "Don't lose those. Best just to get him back to Hell right away, get him to the hospital, have someone test that to find out what's in it. Give Dr. Faust my best, and could he possibly have someone update me on Harlach's condition when it's convenient? He's...a friend." Sure, not a very *close* one, but you didn't take and hold someone's hand twice a day for months at a time and not develop some sort of fondness.

"I'll ask," said Irazek, taking the bag, his other hand around Harlach's wrist. "I'm sure it can be managed...thank you... here, just—" He vanished, as did the demon on the bed, in a tiny little thunderclap.

Greta stayed put, eyes shut, until her eardrums decided to equalize from the pressure differential of two beings popping out of existence, and then opened her eyes and looked at the now-empty bed and decided on the whole she didn't need to make it. In fact she didn't need to do anything for a few moments—but didn't startle when Sir Francis Varney came up quietly behind her and rested cool hands on her shoulders.

"Will he be all right?"

"I don't know," she said, twisting to look up at him. "But he's a damn sight better off in Erebus General than in our green bedroom. Christ, Varney, nothing about this makes any sense."

"Are they likely to want you again tonight?"

"Sincerely doubt it. Faust has staff, and imaging, and technology, and everything I haven't got in my lovely country manor that is *not in any way* designed to handle medical emergencies. There's nothing I can do that they can't do much more efficiently."

"So they wouldn't mind terribly if I did this," said Varney, and lifted her into his arms as if she weighed no more than a rolled-up duvet, and carried her briskly down the hall to their own room. Greta—taken by surprise—squeaked, and then clung to his neck with both hands, and pressed her face against his chest, and did not want to let go when he set her down on the edge of their own bed. Being carried by Varney was one of the great and unexpected joys of marriage: simply lying in the strength of his arms and thinking of nothing was a pleasure she seldom allowed herself, but God was it nice.

"Thank you, darling," she said. "I'll deal with this in the morning—there's something else I need to talk to you about, it's complicated—"

"It is always complicated," said Sir Francis Varney, settling beside her against the pillows, and pulled the covers over them both. Wordlessly Greta wriggled into his arms, resting against his shoulder, and he curled his arm around her, a warm weight against his side. "Everything is always complicated."

"That is *deeply* philosophical," said Greta with a sigh. "Look, there's no good way to say this, but: I've been asked to do a field-research trip in America, and I owe Hell any number of favors at this point; I couldn't really find a way to say no with any grace. I'm so sorry about this, Varney."

"Field research?" he said. "For Hell?"

"Technically for Göttingen University, but yes, basically for Hell." She sighed. "There's something else as well. My friend Dr. Hildebrandt at Göttingen has realized *something* happened even though he can't remember the reset, and I don't know what the hell I'm supposed to tell him—I don't think *Fass* knows, either—but this trip business is different. It's something to do with the way angels and demons can't seem to be near each other without setting off a sort of allergic reaction, and they want to know if that holds true on Earth as well as in the empyrean, and so they're sending me and an angel and a demon to trundle about America with the pretext of gathering data on supernatural populations. I think they said it was going to take six weeks? Maybe two months, tops. I refuse to spend much more time than that away from work. I really am sorry, love, I know it's a long time to be separated—"

"Could I come, too?"

"What?" She sat up to be able to look at him properly. "You *want* to come with?"

"I very much would like to," he said. "If it wouldn't be getting in the way of your work." He looked entirely earnest.

"I thought you'd hate the idea," she said. "*America.* Months of not being here. Doing favors for other researchers."

"I should like to see America," he said, with no detectable hint of irony. "I think it would be extremely educational, and I could perhaps help with some of your data-gathering, or at least stay out of your way."

"And help me deal with the angel and the demon?"

"And that. I can instruct them in the ways of the world, or something." He smiled, that singularly sweet smile only she and a very few other people ever got to see. "Teach them how to pretend to be human when anyone's looking."

Greta was still having trouble parsing this. "I seriously thought you'd hate the whole concept," she said. "But— Christ, it'd be lovely to have you with me, and not just for moral support; you could very much be of use in wrangling clueless creatures. It'd be so much easier not to have to manage on my own."

"Then that's settled," said Varney. "When Göttingen or Hell or whoever rings up in the morning to request your services, ask if their protocol would allow for one more participant. I think if you're doing them this much of a favor, they'll find it hard to say no."

" 'Specially since *you* stopped the apocalypse and saved the world for them and everything," she said with a smile, and lay back against his shoulder. "Useful bargaining chip, that."

"It seemed like a good idea at the time," said Varney, and she couldn't help laughing, despite the lingering worry over Harlach and whatever was apparently abroad in London with sharp pointy things *this* time around, and what she was going to tell Arne Hildebrandt about the apocalypse Varney had prevented, and exactly how she was supposed to get to work tomorrow with her usual ride emphatically nonavailable. She'd think of something.

One way or another, she always did.

New York City

There's an art to street preaching in the mortal city: you have to know the laws, be able to cite shit, there's a couple of websites set up for that very purpose so all you have to do is whip out your list of legal precedents and hope you don't get the cops who've had a rough day. There's the art of preaching itself, how to gather attention and keep it, draw a crowd, while you tell the story, spread the word, bring the gospel. There's the art of not listening to the hecklers. After a while you can tune 'em out, because you are here for a reason, and that reason is very simple.

Afterward you mostly always meet up in someone's basement or back room to talk about it, to share the stories of your witnessing, how many people you think you reached that day. And if you're lucky, very, very lucky, *he'll* be there. Gideon. Brother Gideon. He never once told anyone to call him Brother, but it wasn't like he needed to. Some things you don't need to get told.

He talks to you like he knows you, like he knows everything inside your head and loves you anyway, even if you've got some stuff way down deep you don't actually want anyone to look at too close. When Brother Gideon's there you all feel blessed, pure and simple, and it's like you get filled up again with all the energy you need to go back out tomorrow and share the word of Christ. Because like he says if you reach just one soul, that whole day will have been worth it.

You don't always remember exactly what he says, after he's gone. And sometimes you lose time while he's talking. But you feel it in your heart all the same, that blessing.

Sometimes people ask you why you do this, and you say: because it needs to be done.

Heaven

The Archangel Gabriel did not pride himself upon his open-door policy, because pride was a sin and his door was closed except when in active use; if people had business with him, they made appointments, or took their chances knocking on said door.

Prior to the reset—and the Accords—there had been fewer instances of Gabriel's *not* answering such knocks, but over the past few weeks several of his colleagues and subordinates had found themselves standing in the corridor wondering if it would be politic to try knocking a *second* time, in case he had not heard, or if doing so would be exactly the opposite of helpful. Gabriel did not appreciate it when he was interrupted in the middle of something important, and technically anything he did was classified as *important* because it was him doing it.

Only occasionally had anyone bothered looking under the door to see if there was light in the office, because that wasn't the sort of thing angels went in for thinking about; but in fact there had been a clear white glow visible, the color an angel gave off when praying very intensely indeed. The more savvy of the angels had stopped thinking at that point and merely gone about their business, returning in a few hours to see if he could be disturbed; the less intellectual had wondered vaguely what he could be praying about, and if there was something going wrong with Heaven again. No explanation was forthcoming, and there did not appear to be any new disaster on the horizon, so the matter remained a vague source of confusion rather than active concern.

Haliel had chosen his moment wisely when he'd come to deliver the little dart-weapon to Gabriel after his attack; the archangel had merely bid him *come*. He had no way of knowing that after his visit, no one in Heaven had seen Gabriel for nearly half a day, and would not have known what to make of this intelligence had he been informed; he rarely came up to Heaven to meet with his immediate supervisor.

Now, another angel was standing in the corridor, hand still raised, wondering if they should try knocking a second time, and if it might be worth going to see one of the *other* arches to ask if Gabriel was quite all right... and almost immediately dismissing the thought.

It was so very much not their business, after all, and asking for information they did not already possess was simply *not the done thing*.

Göttingen University, Germany, Professor Hildebrandt's Office

Arne Hildebrandt replaced the phone in its cradle, looking satisfied. A good morning's work so far: Dr. Helsing had agreed to undertake the research expedition as he had hoped she would, with an eye to tracing down any other strange disturbances or inconsistencies in data and records in the various places she would be visiting. Yes, all right, her husband could come along if he was absolutely sure to stay out of the way of any significant experiments or tests Dr. Helsing was called

upon to perform; yes, the two students who would be joining her, with the odd names, had all their visas and passports
and so on in order; he could go ahead and make the official
request from the bursar and contact the correct people to set
the plans in motion.

(Just for a moment, a flicker of uncertainty touched Dr.
Hildebrandt's mind: those two postdoc students, J. O'Lack
and Adam Riel, how long had they been in his department?
They'd transferred in, that was right, but he couldn't quite
seem to recall them being noticeably *present* at any given time
in the recent past...no, he was sure it was simply slipping his
mind the way little things did when one had to keep an entire
department's research running under a fairly shallow disguise.)

All in all, it was shaping up to be a fine day. In some ways
Dr. Hildebrandt wished he were coming along on this particular expedition: there were bound to be some absolutely
fascinating populations of supernatural creatures to investigate, and he'd always wanted to see more of America than the
research university campuses he'd visited in his professional
capacity. Ah well, another time.

(When exactly had he come up with the idea for this trip,
anyway? He'd...been planning it for months, hadn't he? It
was just the knotty problem of who could take on the lead
research position and mentor the postdocs, and the business
of getting the university to agree to advance the funding, that
had taken so long.)

Dr. Hildebrandt put his fingers to his temples: he'd been
having these strange transient headaches just recently, he kept

meaning to go to one of his colleagues and get a professional opinion, but there never seemed to be time, and in any case the pain never lasted very long. Perhaps it was anxiety-related or something. Or he simply needed new spectacles.

The fact that these flashes of slight pain were directly correlated with the flickers of uncertainty he sometimes experienced—was he forgetting something important?— had yet to dawn on him, and he pushed the matter away as unimportant and reached for his keyboard. Time to send out a number of official emails and set this expedition in motion: there were layers and layers of logistics that needed to be triggered, all of which had balanced on this single phone call to the English doctor.

Dr. Hildebrandt pressed his temples again, unconsciously, and then got on with it.

CHAPTER 3

Erebus General Hospital, Dis

Y*ou* look like you haven't had any sleep," said Dr. Faust,
looking up from his clipboard. He was leaning on the
counter of the main nurses' station on the inpatient floor and
did not appear tremendously pleased to be bothered with this
particular visit. "What do you want?"

"Good morning to you, too, Doctor," said Fastitocalon, giving him a reptilian look. He was in rolled-up shirtsleeves and
yesterday's tie and looked slightly greyer than usual. "Your
sunny disposition is as always such a treat to encounter. No,
I haven't had any damn sleep, and yes, I do want something:
I need to know what was in that muck that came out of Harlach's shoulder. No one at the lab will tell me without your
say-so. How is he, anyway?"

"He'll do," said Dr. Faust. "Although Helsing was quite
right to get him down here when she did; we had a bit of a
time of it getting his fever to come down and stay down, even
with lake water and some minor applied thermodynamics,

and I don't enjoy thinking of what we'd have done without those. I think he's mostly over the worst of it, but I want to keep an eye on him for a while longer." He straightened up with a sigh. "Come on, I can tell you're not going to leave my poor lab staff alone until you get what you want; I've got the results in my office. I take it Helsing officially told Göttingen she'd do the America jaunt?"

He set off walking briskly, without looking back to see if Fastitocalon was following. "I think I overheard someone in the canteen mention that External Affairs was using up a lot of etheric bandwidth all of a sudden."

"Yes," said Fastitocalon, mildly irritated at having to catch up. "At least I gather she must have, since no one has so far come banging on my door to demand that I intercede on our behalf to make her do so."

"Splendid," said Faust, leading the way into his office. It was still early enough in the morning for the lake to give off a visible glow, spread like a vast moving dance-floor of crushed opal in the early light. It was incredibly beautiful; Faust gave it a cursory look and dimmed the windows with a wave of his hand, settling down at his desk. "You wanted the pneum-spec results for that metal residue," he said, typing rapidly. "Here you go."

Fastitocalon came around his desk and looked at the giant central monitor with its spikes and valleys outlining the pneumic signature of the combination of elements found in the recovered debris: not just its physical ingredients, but the origin of those ingredients as well. Nothing in it looked to him like the characteristic pattern associated with Heaven.

"So—it's *not* angelic," he said after a moment, and a lot of the tension drained out of his shoulders. He pinched the bridge of his nose. "That spares us the infernocelestial politics. But it's nasty, nonetheless."

"Oh, its nastiness is not in question. Cocktail of heavy metals and white-magic herbs. Didn't you say that business a few years back with the thing, the remnant, involved blades with a sort of compound poison on them designed to drop your standard supernatural with a single graze?"

"I did," said Fastitocalon grimly. "I thought we were *done* with that. Everybody thought we were done with that. God, I hate copycats." The time he had spent under the city fighting with blue-lit madmen puppeteered by a ravenous fragment of creation was not one of his personal favorite memories.

"Looks like they hate you back," said Faust. "I'd warn any other demons in London not to go walking down dark alleys until we figure out what's going on, yes?"

"Yes," said Fastitocalon. "I wonder how they *knew* he was a demon. If they knew him already, and weren't just extremely lucky to hit the right mark. Can you tell from this sample's signature what other creatures are likely to be significantly vulnerable to it? Because while we're not overstaffed with demons in London, there are a large number of other unaffiliated but supernatural beings who might catch the eye of whoever's behind this."

"Give me—half an hour," said Faust, "no, forty-five minutes, with the scanner archive, and I can probably get you at least a basic list of species who'd react badly."

"Right. I'll go and see if Harlach's awake, shall I?" Fastitocalon pushed back his hair. Despite the rumpled shirtsleeves
and loosened tie, he still gave off the air of a slightly glum but
well-dressed banker, and Faust had to smile a bit.

"You're not to tire him," he said. "And absolutely no cigarettes anywhere in the hospital, by the way."

"Of course not," said Fastitocalon, with a vaguely credible
expression of innocence. "Thanks for your help. Really."

He asked the nurse at the central station where he could find
Harlach, and put some effort into his smile; he hadn't been an
archdemon for very long at all, but people respected the office,
and the hospital staff knew Fastitocalon quite well from any
number of previous admissions. The nurse on duty was clearly
aware of who he was and apparently well-disposed toward
him, with the same warning not to tire the patient; yes, Harlach was awake and could have visitors. He was directed to
one of the nicer rooms, one with a window looking across at
the next tower over and two beds, one of which was occupied.
"You can have twenty minutes," said the nurse. "That's quite
firm, sir."

"Understood," he said, feeling every second of six-thousand-
some, and came over to Harlach's bedside. It was strange being
on this side of the equation, as it had been sitting behind the
director's desk instead of in front of it; more than once the
London operative had come to see *him* in hospital during one
of his various indispositions. Harlach looked bad, but not as
bad as Fastitocalon had feared: very pale, with a white square

of gauze taped to his chest just under the collarbone—this last gave him an uncomfortable ripple of memory, Sir Francis Varney half-delirious with a poisoned wound in *his* shoulder, years back—and still visibly feverish, but not deathly ill. There was an IV tube in one arm and a pulse oximeter clipped to his finger, but there didn't seem to be much *more* medical paraphernalia involved. He opened his eyes as Fastitocalon sat down by the bed, and the surprise in them was unmistakable.

"Fastitocalon?" he asked, slightly wheezy. "How... aren't you running the whole Monitoring and Evaluation department these days?"

"I am indeed running M&E," said Fastitocalon, "which means I get to allow myself the personal time to come and visit a friend in hospital, especially a friend who is *also* M&E, without having it signed off in quadruplicate. I'm so sorry this happened to you—how are you feeling? Is there anything I can have sent over? Lavish fruit baskets?"

"I'm all right," said Harlach, and had to shut his eyes for a moment: clearly even he couldn't really justify that with any honesty. "I'm *embarrassed*, more than anything—please tell me someone has taken over transporting Lady Varney to work? I hate so much to leave her without a reliable ride. I don't remember much after taking her to Dark Heart, honestly. Someone said she took bits of whatever-it-was out of my shoulder, and then it gets a little confusing."

"She did indeed," said Fastitocalon. "And then since you were spiking a fever and she wasn't at all sure what was likely to happen and how much help she could be, she rang down here and had you transferred to hospital like a sensible clinician. Whom you shouldn't call Lady Varney if you don't want her to look at you funny; it's just Greta."

Harlach looked rueful and caught himself just before his hand reached up to touch the square of gauze covering the wound. "Greta," he repeated. "I gather that her decision to move me was...somewhat important, and that I gave everyone a lot of worry overnight. I can't remember much other than it hurting, and feeling extremely strange."

"That would have been the fever," said Fastitocalon. "And they're doctors, they're meant to worry. Practically a professional requirement. Anyway, Faust seems to think you'll be all right now, even if he's probably going to keep you here for a little while longer."

Harlach's eyes—brown, a rich but unremarkable color, under the faint orange iridescence that went along with his unholy nature—closed slowly, reopened. "I really am so sorry about collapsing, and please tell me someone's taking care of her?"

Fastitocalon nodded. "I'll make sure of that, if it will help you rest and get yourself properly better. I don't exactly know what's going to happen with surface monitoring right now; I need to talk to Sam about it. So far it seems that whatever got you was interested in harming demons, and I'm not wild about sending anyone else up to London to collect the essograph traces and monitor activity until we, or rather I, have a better handle on things; we haven't desperately needed real-time monitoring around the clock since the reset fixed the hole in reality. But I can definitely spare someone to nip up twice a day and do the commute duty for now; that, I think, carries much less of a risk."

Harlach, too, nodded. "I really can't remember much of any use about what it was that attacked me. It might be easier if someone had a look inside my mind, instead of me trying to articulate what I do remember?"

"We might do that," said Fastitocalon. "But not until you're feeling better." He checked his watch. "I must go; that nurse with the very severe horns will be cross with me if I don't, but I'll be back when I can, all right? And do let my office know if there *is* anything you'd particularly like."

"Thank you," said Harlach, looking up at him as he rose. "I—it's—it's nice of you, Fastitocalon. I mean that. Thanks for—taking the time?"

Fastitocalon could quite clearly remember Harlach's generosity and kindness in any number of the bad Victorian London winters he himself had really only survived by luck and fortune; Harlach making sure he had *something* to eat, even if it wasn't very nice, Harlach introducing him to the vampire Edmund Ruthven and Ruthven's bottomless well of charity, Harlach once making him a present of a worn but wearable coat against the bone-deep chill. "You're welcome," he said with a tired, but genuine, smile.

Faust was waiting for him at the nurses' station with a piece of paper. "Preliminary analysis suggests this stuff is dangerous to quite a lot of supernaturals," he said. "Not all, but quite a lot of them. I suggest we work out who's playing silly buggers with poison darts sooner rather than later."

Fastitocalon took the paper and ran a glance down the list. Damn, damn, damn. Faust had cross-checked the sample's pneumic signature with the recorded archives of various species' signatures according to the mirabilic resonance scanner, and the results were pretty comprehensive: vampires, vampyres, probably nosferatu, were-creatures (some more than others, but all weres would respond poorly to the silver in the mixture), banshees, ghouls, most of the minor creatures including wellmonsters and hairmonsters, various types of revenants... according to this, practically the only supernatural beings commonly found in London who were *not* likely to be susceptible to this stuff were the mummies, because they were made of and subject to a different magical tradition. Barrow-wights were probably immune, but they weren't exactly thick on the ground in Kensington and Mayfair these days. Bogeymen tended to have thick enough pelts that the darts might not be able to penetrate, but if they *did*—well, hopefully Greta Helsing's friends were capable of keeping her clinic up and running to handle the results.

Fastitocalon sighed, handing the paper back. "I concur regarding the need to get this sorted sooner rather than later," he said, "and I am in fact going to go and see Samael about it, and make it *his* problem as well as everyone else's. And ask him what he thinks I ought to do about sending anyone else up there."

"You seem to lack the proper gleeful anticipation involved in such a task," said Faust. "I want you to get some proper rest soon, even if it's just a couple of hours on an office couch. No sense going into something like this with a sleep debt already racked up."

"I'll take that under advisement," said Fastitocalon, and sighed again.

On the way back to his office he passed through the Monitoring and Evaluation cube farm. The memory of being part of M&E's accounting department back in the beginning—*really* the beginning, he'd Fallen with Samael and the rest of the rebel angels and worked in M&E up until a management shake-up in the sixteenth century—was still vivid and clear to Fastitocalon's recall, even if he hadn't had a little grey carpet-walled enclosure around his desk when *he'd* been working down here. That had been something close to good, for much of the time: he'd done a job he was good at, in an organization that made use of his skills, in a realm suited to the type of creature he happened to be, and on the whole he thought he'd been whatever passed for *happy* among such beings. That he'd then spent five hundred years stuck on Earth in varying levels of abject poverty and chronic ill-health didn't matter very much in the greater scheme of things. He was back now, he was *in charge of* M&E instead of just being one of its thousands of employees, and under his oversight the department was actually doing what it said on the tin and keeping an eye on the Prime Material plane in order to prevent any further mucking about with reality, *so* things were really on the better side of all right just at the moment. Even if he did have to tell Sam about the latest apparent iteration of silly buggers being played on Earth.

Which reminded him.

Fastitocalon stopped outside his office and retraced his steps, leaning into one of the cubes nearest his door. The little nameplate hooked into the grey carpet wall said ORLAX on it, printed on office paper slightly off level and hastily trimmed to fit into the plateholder.

He knocked lightly on the plastic doorjamb, and the cube's occupant—a young male-presenting demon with complicated hair and casually but overtly expensive clothing—looked up from his phone. On the desk lay a scattering of the red-ink essograph trace printouts, and the double monitors showed what looked to Fastitocalon like a thoroughly neglected inbox with several pop-up reminders hovering, ignored, over the unread messages. The second screen was flashing with a messenger app.

Orlax jumped a little when he saw who it was and reached out to alt-tab his way to a spreadsheet that might as well have been titled *lookbusy.xlsx*. "Fastitocalon," he said, sounding like an undergraduate, which was in fact what he was: a senior at Erebus University, on a mandatory internship. "Was there something you needed?"

"Mm," said Fastitocalon. "Step into my office for a minute, would you?"

His own voice was completely expressionless, matching his face and completely hiding his internal grin. He detached himself from the cube doorway without bothering to make sure the demon was following, and stalked down the corridor. In his office he settled behind the desk and gave Orlax a flickery, there-and-gone-again smile, like a lizard skittering across a rock. "Orlax," he said. "How long have you been interning with M&E?"

"Um," said Orlax, standing awkwardly in front of the desk. "Six weeks? Fastitocalon, is something wrong?"

"Not at all," Fastitocalon said. "I've got good news for you, as a matter of fact."

Orlax wasn't stupid; stupid would have been easier to manage. Nor was he malicious, exactly; he simply didn't care about the work, or the importance of doing it, as far as Fastitocalon had been able to ascertain, and it had seemed so far impossible to explain to him why he ought to do so. Calm lectures hadn't worked; coldly incisive rebuke hadn't worked; actually getting visibly angry hadn't done anything as far as he could make out, and visibly angry was a vanishingly rare presentation for Fastitocalon. "We both know you've found it—challenging—to adjust to working in this environment," he said. Orlax's eyes—slit-pupilled, bright blood-red—flickered ever so slightly down and to the side. "And while I do appreciate that it's a bit of a change from the university, I have to take into consideration the smooth running of the Monitoring and Evaluation department. I don't believe we're a tremendously good fit for one another, based on what I've seen so far and on our previous conversations."

Another flicker. "I—" Orlax began.

Fastitocalon lifted a finger, and he shut up. "Thus," he said, "when a new opportunity presented itself I thought it would be to everyone's benefit if you were... reassigned. To which end, it's my pleasure to announce that you will be joining the first-ever joint infernocelestial field-research trip to the Prime Material plane. This coming Monday."

Orlax lost the practiced cool expression completely. "*What?*"

"You will be working with a human, Dr. Greta Helsing, an expert on supernatural medicine, who is leading this expedition to the United States on behalf of Göttingen University. You will also be working closely with an angel, name of Adariel, who is currently employed as an orderly in Heaven's version of an infirmary, and who I am told is tremendously *keen*."

The look on Orlax's face filled Fastitocalon with a pure, silent, poisonous kind of glee. "The purpose of this journey," he continued, "is twofold: to conduct research on the ability of angels and demons to work in sustained close proximity on the PM plane as opposed to in either Heaven or Hell, and to investigate various populations of supernatural creatures and gather data on their medical issues for the Göttingen research department." He didn't mention the reset, or Dr. Arne Hildebrandt's questions regarding reality discontinuities; that wasn't exactly Orlax's pay grade.

"But," said Orlax. "But I don't—I don't do research, I don't do science, that's—I don't *do* that kind of sh—stuff, it's not my scene—"

"It is now," said Fastitocalon, rather than saying *neither is office work, apparently*, and could not quite repress a smile. "Welcome to the future, Orlax. You will be representing Hell in this inaugural project designed to partly fulfill the Accords between Heaven and Hell, so I would caution you to think quite hard about your actions. Dr. Helsing will be providing regular reports on your and Adariel's performance to me in M&E down here and to our equivalent in Heaven. You'll need to prepare for two months' worth of fieldwork; a list of necessary items has been emailed to you. Any questions regarding the trip should be directed to External Affairs, who are handling this project in conjunction with Göttingen."

Orlax looked as if someone had possibly come along and struck him firmly on the back of the skull with a sockful of sand; he blinked stupidly at Fastitocalon, clearly trying to find something to say. "Um."

"I'm entirely confident that your skills will be up to this task," said Fastitocalon through the smile. It wasn't entirely a lie: the kid could probably be relied upon to take notes and label sample tubes without too much difficulty. "And you might find it less...dull...than your current internship. You might even find that you enjoy the work."

"Um," said Orlax again, and then appended a "Sir."

"Off you go," said Fastitocalon. "You've got a lot of work to do. No time like the present. Your things will be sent over to your quarters later this morning; don't worry about clearing out your desk."

"Sir," said Orlax again, and drew himself up, turned on his heel, and marched out of the office, eyes glowing ever so faintly scarlet.

Left alone, Fastitocalon lit a cigarette and reached for Greta. *Are you awake?*

Of course I am, she said, but there wasn't much asperity in the mental tone. *It's ten in the morning and I'm at work. What's going on?*

News from Hell, he said. *Harlach is much better. Faust says you were right to transfer him when you did and apparently his fever was quite bad for a while, but he seems to be mending. You did say yes to the Göttingen people?*

Yes I said yes, she told him irritably. *Arne called me this morning bright and early, and I reassured him I was entirely on board. Does anyone know what was on that stuff I dug out of Harlach's shoulder?*

It's not angelic. That at least is in everyone's favor. But it's pretty comprehensive—Greta, it's a bit like the—

The Gladius Sancti poison, she said. *Yes. So I gather. Do we know anything more useful than that?*

Not yet, he said, sighing. *Not really, other than that it's probably dangerous to a great many other sorts of supernatural creature, not just demons. Again, like the GS poison. We're working on it. But at least this* doesn't *look like anything political we'd have to talk to Heaven about, which is absolutely the last thing we need right now with this mess about the Accords. No sign of angelic contamination on the scan results. Incidentally, Harlach is being woeful and guilt-ridden over not being able to flip you to and from work. I said I'd appoint someone else as interim taxi driver for however long it takes. Do you want a locum, or are you going to rely on mundane means of transport until the expedition leaves?*

I very much want a locum, she said quickly. *Tell Harlach he's absolutely not to worry, but God do I hate the prospect of having to make this commute the hard way twice a day. I borrowed one of Varney's cars to drive to the Salisbury train station this morning, and it took forever, and everything about this is annoying. I've grown hideously spoiled since the spring.*

I'll have someone there to pick you up this evening, Fastitocalon said. *And take you either to Salisbury to pick up the car or down to Dark Heart directly, exactly as you wish.*

And you think they're not *likely to get shot or stabbed by horrible little poisoned blades while they're at it? I can handle the shitty commute, much as I don't want to, if the alternative's going to put your people in danger.*

I shall ensure that they are very nimble and waste no time, he said. *In and out, toes a-twinkle. Unless—*

Unless something's lying in wait for demons on their way to that particular city park, she said sharply. *No. It's too dangerous. Move the rendezvous point, or—hell, just have them meet me here, in my office at the clinic. I don't know why we haven't been doing that from the beginning. There's at least wards and things on the front door, and I don't think people with poisoned darts are likely to sneak in while I'm not looking, unless this is a lot worse than we've been given to understand.*

That's not a bad idea, he said. He could vaguely remember when Greta had started to commute via translocation; there had been some conversations about where she and her escort should meet each morning and evening, but he couldn't recall exactly why that particular park had been agreed upon. Still, anyone who was sufficiently perceptive wouldn't have had too much difficulty isolating the pattern: Dr. Helsing and the tall young man with the curly hair met one another there every evening at the same time, and presumably the tall young man with the curly hair was relatively easy to follow on his way there from wherever it was he spent his days.

And presumably also that meant it was pretty easy to lie in wait for him along his way, sharp pointy things in hand. *And that idea gives me another one*—he began, but she cut him off.

You should find someone who isn't *susceptible to that particular white-magic cocktail and have them hang around and watch* for watchers *along routes used by supernaturals*, she said. *See if anyone's lurking around who shouldn't be. Someone who can defend themselves but isn't vulnerable to this stuff. And—someone who isn't noticeable. Not, for instance, Nadezhda Serenskaya. You need an* unremarkable *magic-user, but God knows where you're going to find one.*

Yes, said Fastitocalon, sounding tired. *Exactly. It's a tricky problem. Let me think about it and I'll get back to you.*

Fass, she said. *Should we even go ahead with this whole America trip, while this is going on?*

Oh yes, definitely. If nothing else, it'll get you and Varney and the postdocs out of harm's way, and it'll get Arne Hildebrandt to shut up about discontinuities for a little while. Cheer up, Greta. Hell is not about to shatter into pieces because yet another individual is running around trying to kill monsters; we're rather used to it at this point. I'm going to go upstairs and talk to Sam, and be in touch about who to expect tonight to take you home. His computer screen flashed with an incoming meeting request; he crushed out the cigarette-end and clicked on it. *Oh, and can you keep your afternoon open after about 3:30? External Affairs wants to meet with you and Faust and apparently me as well to go over logistics for the trip.*

All right, she said. *And take care of yourself, while you're at it. You sound tired.*

I am tired, he told her, wry. *Talk later.*

Greta opened her eyes; it was sometimes less disorienting to talk to Fastitocalon this way, mind to mind, with them shut. The familiar view of Harley Street from her office window was unchanged, but it no longer seemed *safe* in its familiarity: something out there wanted to harm her friends, yet again, and yet again Greta didn't know what the hell to *do* about it.

Varney had been right last night, she thought: everything was always complicated.

She really *didn't* know why she and Harlach hadn't been translocating directly from her office to Dark Heart all along, rather than meeting up in the park; presumably they'd had a good reason for the arrangement, which she couldn't recall months later—except possibly that the protective wards on the clinic's front door might crack or fail with the sudden and repeated entry of a demonic entity. She'd call her witch friend Nadezhda, who maintained the warding spells, and ask if that was likely to be a problem.

There were usually two or three demons in London at any given time, she thought, including the surface operative; four or five vampires; assorted weres and banshees; God knew how many ghouls; a handful of bogeymen; three or four active mummies; and doubtless several more monsters she'd forgotten about for the moment. If this thing *was* a Gladius Sancti copycat, almost every one of those individuals was likely to be a potential target, along with humans whom the sect considered unclean—

Stop it, she told herself. *You don't know the scope of the problem. This could be one lone nutjob with a good handle on alchemy and a grudge against demons; there is absolutely no use getting all panicky about what you can't fix before you have more information.*

Yes, but what if it is *that bad,* she asked in counterpoint. Sometimes arguing with herself inside her own head felt weirdly cathartic. *What if it is exactly that bad, and I'm just about to set off for America, leaving everyone behind to deal with whatever this wretched crisis will turn out to be?*

Not everything revolves around you. Like Fass said, Hell isn't going to shatter because someone else is yet again running around trying to kill monsters. At least this isn't angelic, or they don't think it is, so the problem isn't political.

Something was kicking her brain. *Angelic.* Even before the Accords, both Heaven and Hell had always had at least one surface op in every major city at all times, as far as she knew.

Fastitocalon had explained the purpose of M&E's main task to her long ago: the idea was to keep the balance steady between Heaven and Hell, not push it in either direction, and in order to do that, both sides needed to keep an eye on who and what was coming and going to and from the Prime Material plane in case somebody was playing reality-destabilizing silly buggers. Thus the network of surface operatives tasked with monitoring the essographs, or reality-measurement installations, on Earth, not unlike bearded postdocs peering at seismographs to see what the local geological faults were up to.

The balance thing—as opposed to the universe being a sort of constant Heaven vs. Hell game of soul capture-the-flag—was the clearest and most common misconception people on Earth had about the whole business, of course, and for reasons of their own, both sides had clearly elected not to change anybody's mind about it. They just *got on with* the work, and the surface ops for both sides had mostly gotten along okay, at least as far as Greta was aware. It was only since the reset that this business of overt, deliberate, ostentatious collaboration had become such a touchy little problem.

Which led her to the obvious next question: had anyone bothered to get in touch with London's resident *angel* about all this, and if so, what did he think? She couldn't quite remember his name, something else starting with *H*, but Harlach had seemed friendly enough with him and it was entirely possible that he might have some useful input on the business at hand.

Maybe she'd suggest that, this afternoon, when she spoke to Hell's External Affairs people, a thought which struck her as absurdist even by her own somewhat rarefied standards. It made her smile, and she was aware of how stiff her face felt, as if she'd forgotten what that expression ought to feel like. God, she needed a *holiday*, not a six-week field trip, but maybe the America journey might help to recharge a battery or two.

Greta made a note on her desk blotter: *ask about angel*, and settled in to do her job while she had the opportunity.

Brighton Beach, New York City

Gideon Tremayne did not pray *in his closet*, exactly; he did not, precisely speaking, have one to pray in. His apartment was a second-floor studio off Coney Island Avenue, and most of the time he remembered to close the blinds when he knelt down to give thanks; today he was slightly distracted, and as the harsh light of the streetlamps faded with early morning, passersby on the street below wondered what that weird pale glow from the windows could be. It wasn't the blue flickering of a TV screen; it was white, almost completely steady except for when it moved a little. As if whatever was giving off the light had bowed its head.

Nor did Gideon pray out loud. He didn't have to. He knew perfectly well that God was hearing his prayers and was well pleased with the work of his hands; after all, God told him so. Sometimes in words dropped into the still waters of Gideon's mind; sometimes in simple love, a feeling of inexpressible sweetness, *rightness*, assurance. He walked with the constant awareness of the presence of his God with him, all around him, and it showed in his face. It was otherwise a perfectly ordinary sort of face, round, freckled, with a gap between the front teeth that spoke of a childhood innocent of orthodontia, but Gideon Tremayne could at times *shine* with beauty.

He was thirty-two and had only in the past year managed to

move up in the world from DoorDash delivery to a job night-managing a Taco Bell, and this was further evidence of the approval of God, since it left his days more or less free to move through the city and visit with his fellow believers, encourage them in their efforts to preach the gospel, support them when the world's crushing cynicism and mockery threatened to overwhelm their joy in Christ. To guide and guard them, to shepherd them, to channel through his own being what God had entrusted to him to do, spoken the words into his mind in these ecstatic sessions in his tiny apartment, dropped the knowledge into him thought by thought.

Now, this morning, he had come home from work with a wonderful kind of urgency in his heart, a *wanting*: it felt as if God had a *new* message for him. Despite his eagerness Gideon took the time to change out of his uniform into clean things that did not smell of oil and grease; washed himself to become fit for prayer; knelt down, closed his faintly glowing eyes, and opened his mind, receptive, yearning to know what he must do.

CHAPTER 4

Heaven

Raphael, in his small pearl-white office, was staring at his computer screen. On it Dr. Faust, looking tired, was finishing up a neat little clinical description of what had happened to their London surface operative, and what he and his staff had needed to do to fix it, and how long that had taken. "He's recovering now," Faust added, in a slightly different tone, "but I'm keeping a close eye on him. But the point is, your side's London op should be aware of this if they're not already. We're trying to work out the best way to determine who's doing it, if they're a lone zealot or if this is the start of a coordinated campaign, but in the interest of openness and clarity we want to make sure your people have all the information we do."

Raphael ran a hand through his curls, trying not to think of Haliel, a few days ago, showing him a little uninteresting puncture wound next to his left wing-root. Raphael's opinion then and now had been that he was fine, not suffering

76

from anything even remotely like what Faust was describing with his demon patient, but *could* it be coincidence? Two dart wounds sustained mysteriously in the same city, with a similar blade? "Oh *dear*," he said. "I'm so terribly sorry this happened. Is there anything we can do to help?"

"You've got someone on the surface in London, too, haven't you? Ask them to keep an eye open for unusual activity," said Faust. "Particularly among people who might not be entirely ordinary wildtype humans. There might be some sort of supernatural *influence* at play here, and I know angels can spot that as clearly as demons can."

"Of course," Raphael said. "I'll speak to him—to our operative about it. What, ah, what should the protocol be if he *does* observe any such thing? He doesn't report to me, but directly to Gabriel." And how Raphael didn't envy him that privilege, he thought, and felt himself blush faintly gold. He was *lying to Faust*—by omission, but it was lying, and none of this was *right*.

"Have him notify Gabriel at once, and then we can set up a special line directly into M&E down here. I don't see why he couldn't call us directly to report things, unless that breaks protocol on your end." Faust looked wry. "Or unless Gabriel objects, which I imagine comes to the same thing."

Raphael nodded, curls bouncing. "Are you assigning another demon to take Harlach's place temporarily topside?"

"Not until we get a handle on this thing," said Faust. "I don't particularly want to have to spend *another* five hours in the ER trying to keep another demon from febrile self-immolation." Raphael winced, and Faust gave him half a smile, quickly there and gone again. "Relax," he said. "We can handle it, if we need to. I just don't *want* to need to."

"Quite," said Raphael, his feathers slightly fluffed, rather aware that he didn't have anything like the same confidence in his own ability to handle a similar situation, thinking all over again of Haliel in his office giving a one-shouldered shrug and asking for a jar of something to put on the tiny wound if Raphael thought it was worth bothering. "And—pardon me, but you're *very* sure there's no trace of anything angelic in the substance removed from the wound?"

"Nothing whatsoever. We ran it through the mirabilic scanner and even had the scrying department have a look at it, and if there's angel residue anywhere, it's homeopathically undetectable. Whatever this is, it doesn't seem to be anything to do with *you*."

Raphael couldn't help a sigh of relief, and a lot of the tension in his shoulders released, making the feathers rustle slightly as his wings relaxed. "I'm so glad," he said simply, despite how many things were still terribly wrong. "I couldn't conceive of one of ours doing any such thing as deliberately trying to harm a demon . . . even before the Accords, we'd stopped doing that millennia ago, but I'm so glad to know it *isn't* one of ours. And you think Harlach will be all right, once he's over the fever?"

"I do. Talking of ours and yours," Faust added, "we've got the go-ahead on the research trip. Is your—we're calling them postdocs, it's easier, fits the cover—your participant ready to travel in the next couple of weeks?"

Raphael laughed, slightly startled. "Postdocs," he repeated. "That's good. That's rather good. And yes, my orderly Adariel can't wait to get started. He's terribly...keen."

Faust looked sympathetic. "We'll get him out of your hair as soon as possible, I can promise that. Him and Fastitocalon's sullen little intern Orlax, who's also been selected for the mission."

"Oh—it's not—he's not *in my hair*—" Raphael trailed off, faintly flushed with embarrassment. Adariel's keenness was to be encouraged! Really it was.

"It's all right," said Faust. "Trust me, I do understand. We've all had at least one of those, several times over, and generally they do settle down and stop being so exhausting, but they can be rather a lot to handle."

"Especially if they aren't always entirely sure where their wingtips are," said Raphael with just the slightest hint of acid, and blushed deeper gold. "I mean. Nothing *important* has been knocked over, it's quite all right."

Faust was evidently enjoying this, which didn't help. "Only a few elixirs you'd been working on for hours, I imagine," he said. "Nothing of significance."

"Not *hours*. And the burner only singed *one* wingtip."

That got an actual snicker out of Faust. "Good lord," he said. "I do not envy you, Archangel Raphael, but I am very pleased to remove this particular source of potential laboratory fires from your hands. So. If you could have a word with your London op, I'll ask External Affairs and M&E to set up a direct line into the M&E offices for him to use if he does come across anything unusual."

"Of course," said Raphael, thinking of how Haliel would likely react to the news of his counterpart's attack. "And you will keep me updated on Harlach's case?"

"Happy to," said Faust. "I'll be in touch."

The screen went blank, and Raphael sat back in his chair and ran his hands through his curls, eyes shut, taking a deep steadying breath; where his fingers intersected with the fine golden hoop of his halo, they simply slid right through. Talking to Johann Faust always made him feel slightly as if he were playing some sort of game without quite understanding all the rules, against an opponent who was smiling all the time. He was almost sure Faust didn't do it on purpose, but it was exhausting nonetheless.

Well. Adariel would be happy to know the trip was going ahead—he'd been so excited to be selected that Raphael hadn't had the heart to tell him to calm down before he knocked anything *else* over, and it hadn't been an elixir he'd spent hours on. Just half an hour. Really, it was quite all right.

He heaved himself out of the chair, feathers rustling; he'd finish his rounds before going to ask the Communications people to place a call to Haliel down in London. He never had *many* patients, but with the ongoing construction projects in Heaven there were always some minor injuries to treat, some dust inhalation—despite the masks—and some of the bad allergic reactions tended to spend a day or so in bed before Raphael cleared them to return to work. Right now he had a moderately serious inhalation (sapphire dust, not pearl), two cuts-and-bruises who had come in earlier, one broken metatarsal (dropped a block of sapphire on his foot), and one recuperating allergy case who kept asking if she could get up, please, she felt quite all right now and wanted to get back to her construction work.

The healing cuts-and-bruises he examined and released with an admonition not to get the dressings wet or dirty with jewel dust; the metatarsal was doing about as well as he could ask—a few more days, angels healed fast—and the allergy case he finally relented and released: "but you stay *away* from demons, all right, and come back at once if you start to feel short of breath."

That left Nithael, who had gotten a faceful of sapphire dust a few days ago by accident: someone had carelessly been sweeping off a roof without looking to see if anyone was passing underneath, and his surprised gasp had taken in quite a lot of it. He was improving, but not as fast as Raphael would like. There simply wasn't a lot he could *do* for this sort of case other than empirical treatment and prayer; he didn't have any of the technical things, equipment, pharmaceuticals, modern technology, that Dr. Faust's hospital took for granted. More than once over the past couple of days Raphael had seriously considered calling Faust to ask if he might possibly borrow a bottle of oxygen; he was fairly sure it would help Nithael at least a little, but that was entirely the sort of modern-convenience, relying-on-tawdry-worldly-trifles thing Gabriel really didn't go for. In the chief archangel's world, ambrosia and nectar and prayer *should* be all the medicine anyone in Heaven could possibly need. That is, if they were *doing it right*.

Obviously.

Nithael was lying propped up on a heap of pillows with a chair on each side of the bed to rest his wings on, taking the strain off his ribcage. He looked half-asleep, his lips slightly blue; his breath was rustling audibly in his chest. Raphael had heard him coughing while he'd been on the phone with Hell, and had winced internally; he winced again now, taking in the slight extra movement of the shoulders and wings as Nithael used more muscles to breathe than he should need to. His mental assessment of the case shifted a little from *improving*.

He sat down on the edge of the bed and took Nithael's wrist between his fingers, feeling the angel's pulse: yes, still high and fast—and a moment later had to steady him as Nithael woke all the way, caught a breath wrong, and doubled over in a helpless, violent fit of coughing. Raphael slipped his arms around him, letting Nithael lean on him for support, rubbing his back firmly between the wings, which had helped before. The angel clutched at him, panicky-tight fingers curled around folds of his robe, like someone drowning. Previously Raphael's touch had been able to soothe the paroxysms to some extent; this time the fit just went on and on, the coughing desperate and hysterical, no room for breath between each awful spasm; went on until Nithael simply *could not* get enough oxygen past his own respiratory tree's attempt to expel itself, and he collapsed against Raphael's shoulder in a faint.

Raphael held his patient gently for a few moments, his own heart racing, before settling him back against the pillows. Nithael was still unconscious, limp and heavy as a sick child, breathing shallowly with effort, that rustle in his chest now a definite wheezing crackle.

Raphael's hands were trembling slightly, all the tiny golden hairs standing up at the back of his neck. That had been... *bad.* (It was *still* bad, even after the fit had passed: he knew now, after the war and its aftermath, that the crackling meant *fluid in the lungs*, and he also knew very clearly how little he could hope to do about it.)

This had been very probably the worst thing Raphael had seen since the battle for Heaven itself; it had frightened him quite a lot.

He didn't want to think about what his other patient, down at the far end of the infirmary tent, had made of the whole business; couldn't think about that right now. He'd deal with it in a minute.

Moving quietly, he returned to his office and placed a call. He wasn't paying any attention to anything but the screen, tapping his fingers impatiently while the infernal switchboard transferred him, and so he was entirely unaware that his orderly Adariel had crept to the door of his office, white-faced and shivery; had, in fact, overheard the entire miserable sequence from the little dispensary next to the main tent, and wanted very much to ask some questions.

When the hospital receptionist appeared on the screen, Raphael asked them quite politely, but with the least diffidence he'd ever shown, to be transferred to Dr. Faust, please. Now.

"One moment, please," the receptionist said, a little startled, and then the image of Faust's office replaced them. Faust was busily scribbling something in a notebook and looked up with obvious irritation at the phone chime; the expression slipped into surprise.

"Oh, it's you again," he said, straightening up. "What do you want?"

"Oxygen," said Raphael without preamble. "Bottled oxygen. With a...a mask, to inhale it. We don't have any up here."

Faust frowned. "I thought you didn't go in for that sort of thing—what's happened? What do you need it for?"

"One of my dust-inhalation patients is...not doing well," he said. "And no, we don't ordinarily go in for that sort of thing, but this is—I *need your help*, Dr. Faust." It was a lot easier to say than he'd expected, with the echoes of that awful crackle still in his ears.

"Shit. What was *in* the dust? How long ago?"

"Sapphire, and about three days. He just coughed himself into a faint and his breathing's worse, I need to get back to him, but if you could have someone send up a bottle—"

"I can do better than that," said Faust. "There any overt sign of infection yet?"

"I wouldn't be surprised if I've missed it. There's definitely fluid now, but no fever so far, and he stopped bringing anything up sometime yesterday. Right after it happened the cough *was* productive." This part hurt a bit to admit—*sin of pride*, he thought—but if he was going to do this, he'd do it properly: "I just don't have the...the diagnostic tools to know what's really going on. Or any clear way to manage it, even if I did." And this was probably the worst case of this kind he'd ever seen, he didn't add. Since the reset it had seemed to Raphael that they were all ever so slightly more *human*, with greater human frailties; he didn't know if that was fanciful, but he couldn't help thinking it nonetheless. He had a brief, impossible vision of an infirmary up here that *was* stocked with all the supplies and technology and medicine that could make something like Nithael's case *tiresome*, rather than terrifying, and pushed it away. *One thing at a time.*

Faust nodded briskly. "You lot are entirely AB-naive, aren't you? Right. I'll have some things sent up right away that ought to help, Raphael, and let me know if we can do anything else. Sorry you're having to ask us, glad we can be of help."

"*I'm* not sorry," said Raphael, surprising himself with the words. "I'm engaging in *collaboration*. Thank you."

He ended the call, closing his eyes for a moment. A tiny sound behind him made him jump and turn to find Adariel leaning in the office doorway, huge-eyed and pale.

"What are you doing?" Raphael demanded. *Other than eavesdropping on people's private phone conversations.*

"I—I couldn't help hearing—I tried not to but I couldn't help it—Raphael, is he going to *die*? I've never seen anyone cough like that, he couldn't *breathe*, is he dying? *Can* we die?"

Oh, dear, thought Raphael, so as not to think *oh, hell.* He got up and came over to put a wing around Adariel, remembering that the new angel had been created *after* the war and hadn't seen the piles of dead angels and demons strewn about

85

the place, the pools of blood, the golden viscera. "No, he is not going to die, not if I can help it, and yes, under some circumstances we can, if we are sufficiently hurt. But I don't intend to let that happen, and so I've asked for some help."

"From Hell?" said Adariel with a sniffle, huddling against him.

"From *our partner in the Accords*," said Raphael, still astonished at how easily those words came. "And I imagine that Gabriel won't be terribly happy about it, but we all have our roles to play and Gabriel is not the physician among us, mmm?"

It felt a bit like stepping out over some vast unknowable precipice without his wings to steady him, saying these things out loud, but... he had to. There wasn't another way. If there was, he'd have found it already, because God knew—oh, God knew—how much Raphael didn't want to deal with the inevitable results of defying Gabriel's will.

He sighed and gave Adariel's shoulder a squeeze, pushing away the mental image of the precipice and the unknowable gulf waiting below. "Make yourself useful, Adariel. Go and mix up some more of that nectar-honey syrup, that seemed to help Nithael a bit before, and then go check on Azakiel at the other end of the ward. Make sure they're all right after all this excitement." That would at least give Adariel something useful to do while Raphael dealt with whatever form of supply delivery Dr. Faust had in mind. He wasn't at all confident in his ability to *use* Faust's paraphernalia, but—he'd try.

Because it had to be done.

Hell, Monitoring and Evaluation Staff Canteen

"You would not *believe* what I just did," said Faust, sitting down at Fastitocalon's table with a tray. The Director looked up from a sheaf of papers, grey as ever, and Faust noticed he'd at least taken the time to tidy up and change out of yesterday's crumpled clothes; good. He was also apparently remembering to eat; the plate at his elbow held the remains of a sandwich. Also a good sign.

"Wouldn't I?" said Fastitocalon. "I've just spent two hours closeted with Samael not just going over the week's M&E work but trying to decide what to do about this damn demon attack business in London, so my capacity for disbelief is somewhat low at the moment."

"*I* just," said Faust, "put together a nice little somewhat-comprehensive pulmonary care support package, the sort one might dispatch to a Doctors Without Borders encampment, with instructions on what to use when and how, in handwriting that I took actual effort to make legible. And then I sent it up to *Raphael*. As *requested by same*."

"*Our* Raphael?" Fastitocalon blinked. "I mean, their Raphael?"

"The one I talk to occasionally. Turns out he does have a spine under all those lovely snow-white feathers; it just took a serious enough case for him to ignore Gabriellian disapproval and ask for some actual *useful* assistance. I'm kind of proud of him, in a way."

"You can condescend like absolutely no one else I know, other than Samael," said Fastitocalon. "It's impressive. So…"

what, one of the angels is deathly ill? I didn't know that was really a *thing* for them. I thought they went in for vocal strain or possibly calligraphy-hand cramps at the very worst; admitting to anything more would be letting down the side."

"Inhaling a lungful of crushed sapphire dust would spoil *anybody's* day," said Faust, and appeared to remember his salad; he applied himself to the arugula and beetroot and pomegranate while Fastitocalon winced a very sympathetic sort of wince. "Anyway, all they've got up there to treat something like acute inhalation injury is pretty much spoonfuls of honey and positive thinking and the odd hosanna, and this does not so much *work* as *not do a damn thing* when what you actually need is oxygen and inhaled steroids and beta-agonists and prophylactic antibiotics and so on, and our Raphael has apparently hit his limit for ignoring this point. It's—I hope the stuff works on angels, don't see why it wouldn't if it does on you lot—it's actually not a bad way to start off this official working-together lark: they asked for my help, I was very happy to provide same. Let's hope it sets a precedent."

"I am having so much difficulty seeing actual medical equipment and supplies *in Heaven*," said Fastitocalon, although he sounded as if he was enjoying the effort. "If it works, though, I don't see where Gabriel will exactly have a wing to fly on with regard to Not Using Modern Technology. And of course it directly fits into the whole Accords business." He leaned back in the chair with a sigh, working his neck and shoulders. "In any case, we're supposed to meet with

External Affairs in about half an hour to talk about logistics for the American trip. I'm surprised that Varney lobbied so hard to go with her; I'd have thought it was exactly not his thing."

Faust shrugged. "Who knows why vampyres make the choices they make?"

Fastitocalon *looked* at him, and spoiled it by snickering. Faust quirked an eyebrow. "Who've you picked to go fetch the Helsing to and fro while Harlach's laid up?"

"I hadn't, yet. Got any suggestions?"

"Asturel's a good reliable sort. Under-Duke of the Somethingth Torment, like most of you, but he never uses the title. Used to be M&E in Rome, got fed up with it, came back down here, works for me as a liaison and general sort of secretary. Should I instruct him to come poke his head into your office sometime later this afternoon?"

"By all means," said Fastitocalon, making a note and closing his leather portfolio. Faust wasn't wrong: for a while there hadn't been a demon in Hell who wasn't a Duke or Earl or Prince of something. He thought it probably had to do with demonologists on Earth wanting to summon *classy* demons rather than the rank and file, which told you rather a lot more about demonologists than they might strictly prefer. "If he can work as your liaison and not throw himself regularly off the tallest tower in Dis, he can certainly handle a bit of light transportation work with relative grace and tact."

"Precisely my thought," said Faust, chasing down a last scrap of lettuce. "Shall we?"

Harley Street, London

After the somewhat-disturbing conversation with Fastito-calon she'd had that morning, Greta had thrown herself into work, deeply grateful that she had a fairly full schedule of patients to see. And a nice variety, as well: things got a bit repetitive in years with a particularly bad strain of flu making its rounds, but today she'd seen a banshee with strep throat, a young were-something in search of birth control, a bogey-man with mange, two scheduled vaccine visits, and a glum-looking creature of indeterminate species with a nasty cold that was trying to turn into bronchitis. This last reminded her sharply of Fastitocalon as he had been years ago, before his renovation, and she was both very glad he was quite well again and doing a useful and important job back in Hell—and also *missed* him, cough and all.

Her nurse practitioner Anna brought her a much-needed cup of tea in the afternoon, just before the call she was expect-ing from Hell. She'd never talked much with the External Affairs people; they were Belial's department and handled all sorts of official interactions with Earth and Heaven, so she wasn't entirely sure what to expect when the phone rang. A pleasant, cultured voice said, "Dr. Helsing? Please hold for your conference call," followed by a click, and then the ines-capably awkward bit where she said hello just as someone else was asking "Greta?"

"I'm here," she said. "Who am I talking to?"

A smooth voice said, "Hello, Doctor. I'm Belial, with EA;

I've got Dr. Faust and Fastitocalon with me. This shouldn't take very long, I think."

"Faust?" she said. She hadn't expected him to be present.

"Since this whole thing was in fact the good doctor's idea, we felt it appropriate," said Fastitocalon's voice, veiled with amusement. She could picture the scowl on Faust's face and had to smile.

"Mine *and Archangel Raphael's*," Faust said. "To be scrupulously accurate. Anyway, getting on with it, Belial, this is your meeting."

"Indeed," said the smooth voice. It was the sort of voice that went along with slinky well-cut suits and five-hundred-quid haircuts. "Well. First of all, transportation..."

Half an hour later, with her notebook considerably fuller of details regarding the bus and its various amenities and offerings, Greta sat back. "So when do we start?"

"You will be flying into LaGuardia," said Belial, "in five days' time. Your—postdocs—will meet you at Heathrow with their convincing luggage. My people will arrange the buying and packing of said convincing luggage, because frankly none of us trust either one of them to manage it themselves. I'm afraid the angel Adariel is—what was it you said, Faust?"

"In need of professional supervision," said Faust delicately. "And not all that great about remembering not to knock things over with his wings. I do hope they are being very careful up there to make sure he understands he can't have visible wings or a halo in public."

"And the demon?" she asked.

"A sullen little bastard," said Belial. "Name of Orlax. He's an intern, been getting up Fastitocalon's nose in M&E, and it was judged best for everyone if he were to be reassigned. I'm not sure which of them you will find more trying."

He didn't sound as if he were tremendously cut up about it, either. She heard someone snicker in the background, and thought it was probably Fastitocalon. "Well," she said, with acid, "think of the fun we'll all have together, finding out. Faust, what am I supposed to be looking for in them?"

"Potential?" he said, and then relented: "Watch for signs of allergic reaction. How close together can they get before the reaction is noticeable, and can they in fact work side by side without it being intolerable? What *level* of reaction is it—an immediate emergency, or coming out in hives, or just sneezing and sniffling a lot?"

She was taking rapid notes in her personal shorthand. "What happens if it looks like an immediate emergency? Will epinephrine be enough, or is there some other thing I need to have on hand to deal with anaphylaxis?"

"For the demon? Concentrated lake water, intramuscular injection, after the epi. I'll make sure you have enough doses on board to handle a whole series of emergencies, and a couple of cases of the regular water just to have on hand as a general remedy. Don't worry too much about running out of things; we can always have someone flip stuff up to you if necessary."

"I have an entire cube-farm full of people who would love the opportunity to pop up to America, with or without supplies," put in Fastitocalon.

"I imagine so," she said. "Okay, but what about the angel? I can't go around shooting *him* full of Lake Avernus in the middle of an allergic emergency, it'd probably finish the job."

"Good question," said Faust. "I'll ask Raphael, but I have a feeling holy water's probably going to work much the same. You'll have to keep it safely stored, though. That stuff won't do vampyres and demons any good at all."

"Where do I get hold of it?"

"The angel can probably just bring down a couple of bottles when he joins you at Heathrow, or we can ask Heaven to flip it over once you're settled on the bus."

"Fair enough," said Greta, underlining *holy water* twice. "Is there anything else?"

"Not from me," said Fastitocalon. "Faust?"

"If I think of something I'll give you a call, Helsing."

"Splendid. I'll email you the complete schedule, Doctor, and give you the names of some of my staff who could help you work out what you'll need in your wardrobe." There was the sound of papers being shuffled and stacked neatly. "I won't keep you any longer. Thank you, Doctor. Gentlemen."

"Thank *you*," said Greta, and meant it. She hung up and looked down at her notes. Belial might give her a mild case of the creeps, but he was certainly an *efficient* creep.

It was becoming harder and harder not to get excited about this, as it became more and more real and concrete.

She finished her cup of tea, which had gone cold, and called her friend Nadezhda to ask her once again to take over the clinic for a couple of months. Between them, Anna and

Nadezhda were perfectly capable of running the place without her, and had done so for several months last year while Greta was away in Marseille at the mummy spa. Greta's patients knew them by now and were quite happy to have the witch and the nurse practitioner provide the majority of their care; any surgery that needed to be done was referred to the other supernatural GP in Hounslow, Hal Richthorn.

True to his word, Belial had emailed her the schedule along with some notes on what sort of clothing she would be likely to need, and the contact information of some of his staff; after a moment of thought Greta simply forwarded the list to Edmund Ruthven with a note saying *Help, I need your shopping expertise, call me.* Ruthven loved shopping. Even if he couldn't be here to do it in person, she thought she'd rather have *his* help in the matter than that of some complete stranger employed by Hell's Office of External Affairs; she wasn't at all sure she could live up to Hell's idea of style.

She spent the rest of the afternoon catching up on charting and dealing with her various inboxes, which were as usual overstuffed, and it wasn't until night had fallen and she felt the faint pressure-wave made by a body popping into existence that she remembered: she didn't have to pack up and go to meet Harlach in the park, because—*that* had happened. All of that. There was a horrible cascade of stacked concern that she'd just about managed to shelve for most of the entire day, which all came crashing down at once: Harlach was ill, Harlach had been attacked by something mysterious and horrible that seemed to be targeting demons, and therefore the person who had just appeared in the corner of her office was going to be a total stranger.

Greta turned to find a tall young man with dark curly hair, a rather nice cable-knit sweater, and an apologetic expression standing in the corner. He looked as if he could be Harlach's cousin: similar but not identical. "Er," he said. "Lady Var—I mean Dr. Helsing? It's a pleasure to meet you. I'm Asturel; Fastitocalon asked me to take over your transportation while Harlach's not well—I *am* sorry about just appearing like this with no warning, but I was told to meet you in your clinic office rather than a prearranged external location?"

"It's quite all right," said Greta, now that her heart was slowing down again. She vaguely recalled seeing a text message earlier, something along the lines of *transportation associate Asturel will meet you in your office this evening*, and pushing it right out of her mind. "Nice to meet you, too, Asturel. We very much don't want you to be put in any danger while helping me out, so us meeting somewhere outside seemed like an unnecessary risk. Thank you for doing this, by the way, it's deeply appreciated."

"It's no trouble at all," he said, and offered his hand; she shook it firmly. "Are you ready to go, or...?"

"Yes, let me just shut the computer down and pack up," she said, suiting actions to words. She was hell on handbags; this one was falling apart already, possibly because its designers had not intended it to be filled with mummy-bone castings and enormous reams of printouts and bound journals *as well as* her battered laptop. "Right. Let's go?" She could retrieve Varney's car from Salisbury tomorrow; she wanted to get home and tell him about the plans for the trip.

Asturel took her hand again, and immediately the bright blank whiteness of translocation was replaced by the familiar facade of Dark Heart, its windows bright against the chilly night. Either he was exceptionally good at this or she was getting so used to it that the disorientation passed almost at once.

"Thank you," she said, and squeezed his hand before letting go. She was very determinedly not thinking about Harlach, or whatever was out there in the world that wanted to harm demons, because there was simply nothing she could *do* about it right this minute.

Except—be hospitable to the ones putting themselves at risk for her sake.

"Would you like to come in for a drink?" she asked.

He blinked down at her—very large dark eyes, she noticed—and then smiled. "If it's not too much trouble, that would be lovely. Thank you."

"Varney will be pleased to meet you," she said, smiling back, and led the way inside.

Heaven

Hours later, hours after the evening prayers had been sung and the crystal bells rung in their endless silvery chime to mark the passing of time in a realm where dark never fell, the archangel Raphael sat in his tiny office and tapped his fingers on the white surface of his desk, looking through the empty computer screen rather than at it.

In the main ward Nithael lay propped up on a much more ordinary number of pillows, breathing more easily than he had done in days, the narrow snaking clear tube under his nose providing oxygen with an almost imperceptible hiss. When Faust's supplies had arrived, Raphael and Adariel had taken the preliminary precaution of spraying down the packages with holy water, not entirely sure if the Hell-sent substances would burst into flames or dissolve on contact, but nothing had happened—and nothing untoward had happened to either of them when they unpacked the supplies and read the (surprisingly clear) handwritten instructions on how to use them. No allergic reaction that Raphael could detect.

And the stuff had worked. It worked *fast*. Nithael had begun to improve immediately when they started the oxygen, and even more so after being given Faust's various medications. Raphael hadn't had to start an IV since the war, but you didn't forget how, and soon he and Adariel had various things dripping into the sick angel's veins and the improvement was astonishing.

He didn't want to think about what Gabriel was going to say. It didn't *matter* what Gabriel was going to say, except in the million ways that it really, really did, and Raphael could only hide behind the stupid Accords for so long, woodenly repeating himself, because the argument he was appalled to find he wanted to make was even more blasphemous: *if God* didn't want *this stuff to work on angels, it wouldn't, but it* very obviously *does work, so perhaps we ought to be thankful.*

That sort of thing didn't matter, up here, or it certainly shouldn't be allowed to. Evidence-based medicine was a thing that happened *on Earth*, not in the empyrean.

Raphael ran his hands through his curls, disarranging them further. He needed to go and request that Communications relay a message down to Haliel on Earth about the attack on his counterpart and ask him to keep an eye out for any further developments, and he needed to do any number of other small housekeeping things around the infirmary, and—all of a sudden he wanted very badly *not to be here*, which was a terrible thing to want for any angel but particularly for someone like himself—

—and with the same sort of oddly frictionless, freeing sensation that had accompanied his request for Faust's help, he thought, *I could just…go.*

Without telling anyone he was going—no. No, he couldn't do *that*.

Raphael hauled himself to his feet and went to knock on the little dispensary door. Adariel was asleep with his head pillowed on his folded arms, and very nearly knocked over the inkwell and the bottles of whatever he'd been working on when he jerked awake. Raphael didn't hide the wince. "Um, sorry, sir," Adariel said, pushing his own curls out of his face. "Is something wrong?"

"No," said Raphael. "I'm just going down to talk to Haliel for a few minutes, that's all. Keep an eye on everyone for me."

"To talk to Haliel?" he repeated. "On Earth?"

"Mm. I won't be long."

He tried quite hard not to notice the shock on Adariel's face turning into wonder and then into something like admiration, even as he gathered his robes around himself and folded his wings neatly and reached for the thread of reality that would take him from Heaven to the Prime Material plane. He hadn't translocated like this in—oh, must be years and years now, but you didn't forget the knack of it.

The white dizziness faded out to reveal the inside of a small, cheerful little flat stuffed to bursting with books and framed maps and charts; a kettle was beginning to boil on a tiny three-burner stove and a young man in a soft grey cardigan was sitting at the kitchen table looking at several strips of paper marked with red-ink graph markings and a black pen trace. He looked up as Raphael's vision cleared all the way, and dropped his pencil, getting up in a hurry. "My lord? Archangel Raphael?"

Raphael supposed Haliel's superiors didn't tend to come down to check on him in person; Gabriel certainly wouldn't sully himself with the mortal realm if he could possibly help it. "It's all right," he said hurriedly. "I'm not here for any terribly dire purpose."

The kettle shrieked, and Haliel stopped staring at him and went to make the tea: pale straw-colored tea in a glass pot, smelling pleasantly of chamomile. "It's a pleasure to see you, my lord," he said. "Unexpectedly. What can I do for you?"

"It's about that wound you received a few days ago. The... you said someone hit you with a dart?"

99

"Oh, *that*," said Haliel. "Yes, it's fine, quite healed up now. The stuff you gave me made it stop itching, thanks for that, but you needn't worry about me."

"I'm not," he said. "Or not exactly. There's been another attack. This one was rather worse, apparently."

Haliel was stirring the glass teapot; now he put down the spoon and blinked at Raphael. "Another dart?"

"Another poisoned dart, and this time it wasn't an angel who was wounded," he said. Haliel's eyes widened. "This time it was a demon. Your counterpart."

"*Harlach?*" Haliel said, staring. "Harlach's been hurt? Is he all right? What happened?"

"He will be," said Raphael. "I had a call from Dr. Faust. Harlach was hurt on his way to meet a human he's apparently been tasked with translocating to and from her job in the city, and she happened to be a doctor and got him transferred down to Hell for proper care, and Faust says he *will* be all right but he's apparently had a very nasty fever as a result of the wound—watch out—"

Haliel was just in time to set the drooping glass teapot back on the counter before it spilled over. "Oh *no*," he said. "*Harlach*—you're sure he'll be all right? It hurt a lot but I was all right as soon as I got the thing out, I didn't get *ill* because of it—"

"Sit down," said Raphael, not unkindly, and propelled him to one of the kitchen chairs, taking a mug from the cabinet and pouring Haliel some tea with quite a lot of sugar briskly stirred in. "Here. Drink that. Yes, I'm sure, Faust is a bit—more than a bit—off-putting in his habits, but I do trust him." He had to laugh a little at himself, pushing back his curls; he was still in angel-shape, his wings folded tightly against his back so as not to knock over Haliel's bookcases. "Rather more than I thought I could trust him, in fact. But he wanted me to ask you to keep an eye out for anything out of the ordinary. Anyone hanging around places where you know Harlach spends his time, or looking suspicious, or—" He waved a hand. "You get the idea. Faust wants to request that any such information get passed along to Hell's Monitoring and Evaluation department if doing so won't get you in trouble with our lot."

"I'm sure it would," Haliel murmured, hands wrapped around the cup. "Oh, Harlach. Who'd want to hurt *him*?"

"Who'd want to hurt *you*," Raphael said, wry. "Everything's gone all...*political*, I'm afraid. I've had to ask for Faust's help with my patients, and while he's been more than generous with his supplies and equipment, I am not looking forward to the fallout, which is actually why I'm here, I think. To let you know what's going on." He was very much aware of the fact that angels, especially archangels, didn't generally make statements implying they needed to think about why they'd done something. Angels didn't *think* much at all; it wasn't really what they were for, or at least it hadn't spent much time at the top of their list of purposes.

Hitherto, Raphael thought, despite himself, aware he was doing it, and pushed the thought away.

Haliel swallowed half the contents of the cup, and some

color came back to his face. "I don't...suppose I could see him. I mean. Of course I can't, there's no way I could go down to Hell even if I had permission—"

"I think Faust might let you call him, at least," said Raphael. "Shall I ask?"

"Would you?"

"Yes, of course," said Raphael, more briskly. "And—just to satisfy medical curiosity—may I have a look at your back?"

"It really is just a scab," Haliel said, but he was already wriggling out of his cardigan and unbuttoning the shirt underneath it. Revealed, the little wound beside his shoulder blade was barely noticeable, no redness visible in the milk-pale skin around it. Raphael ran a gentle fingertip over the little scab and felt no swelling or heat whatsoever; it was quite hard and nearly ready to come off.

"That's healed very nicely indeed," he said, taking his hand away to let Haliel put his clothes back on. "I'm quite pleased." He was: whatever else it meant, this suggested that the darts didn't pose much of a danger to Heaven's people even if they did send demons to hospital with raging fevers, which was useful to know. And he could now—at least inside his own head—make the *argument* that he'd had a good clinical reason to make a house-call to the Prime Material plane, although he knew perfectly well it wouldn't stand up for very long. "I'd better be going, but I'll ask Faust about the possibility of you talking to Harlach on the phone, and if you like I'll keep you updated with any news he gives me on Harlach's recovery."

"Thank you, sir," said Haliel, looking more composed. "And thank you for your time. I appreciate it very much."

He walked Raphael to the door. Once it shut behind him, on a rather uncharacteristic whim, the archangel reached back into his memory and pulled on the human-seeming he'd worn the last time he'd been down here, now hilariously anachronistic—double-breasted pinstripe suit, felt hat—and walked out into the night of Earth. Just for a few minutes. Just because.

Not because he didn't want to go home. Not that *at all*. Just because the night chill felt nice against his human-shaped face, and because it was *dark*, the way Heaven never truly was: dark enough to see the stars like a scatter of diamond chips across the vault of the sky.

CHAPTER 5

New York City

"You know what really gets on my nerves about this kind of shit?" said Aurelio Contini, lighting a fresh cigarette off the butt of his previous smoke, and gestured to the black-and-white security-cam footage running on the laptop on his desk. "These guys. They're not only *in my way* and they don't apparently realize this is a thing they should not be, but what really pisses me off here is the fact that *they can pass.*"

In the darkness of his shuttered office, the glowing cherry of his cigarette and the twin sparks of red light in his sunken eyesockets looked almost the same, except that the eyes stayed steady rather than flaring and fading in a rhythm. "They can fucking *pass.* This guy, whatever his name is, because I *know* it isn't "Kraven" with a *K*, he gets to stay on the surface, sleep in the nice hotels, own a fancy condo, drive around in a fast car like a goddamn *hume* right out there in public, and nobody pays any attention. How well you think that'd go over if you or I tried that kind of shit in this day and age?"

"It's bullshit, boss," said the lieutenant who was watching the footage with him: not Mario this time but one of Contini's old guard, the creatures who had come out of northern Italy with him to find a new life, back in the eighteen-whatevers. His name was Francisco and, like Contini, his looks would very definitely have turned heads on the streets of New York: high-shouldered almost to the point of deformity, he had tall pointed ears, a high forehead and slicked-back hair, and deep-sunken eyes above a great blade of a nose. All of that might have been dismissed as unfortunate genetics or possibly special-effects makeup, but the most remarkable and unignorable feature he and his employer shared were the elongated, pointed maxillary central incisors that had occasionally (and briefly) given the *nosferatu* subspecies the nickname *Bunnicula*. The fangs meant that both he and Contini lisped slightly, and when they and Contini's other nosferatu employees did have to venture abroad where anyone might actually see them, they had to bundle up in hats and high-collared coats and scarves to hide the ears and the lower half of their faces, huge sunglasses to camouflage the sunken red-glowing eyes, pulling don't-notice-me influence around them like a shroud so as not to attract attention. Meanwhile, classic-draculine assholes like this kid calling himself Kraven could simply bop down the street exactly as they were, passing as nothing more than weirdly attractive human, no effort required. Didn't even have to bother wearing shades; people just assumed the strange eyes were colored contacts.

Francisco checked his watch. "Should be any minute, boss."

"I know," said Contini, and lit another cigarette, putting his feet up on the desk. On the laptop screen, a static view of what appeared to be an underground parking-lot elevator bank hadn't changed for the last five minutes; now a group of three figures came into the frame from the lower right corner, one of whom pushed the elevator call button.

Contini sat up again to get a closer look at the figures. Two appeared to be male and one very obviously female, all of them apparently dressed for a Goth party. On the black-and-white footage it was impossible to tell their hair color, but he happened to know that the tallest of the males had dyed his flowing locks a fetching shade of dark magenta that did not at all go with the bright red of oxygenated blood.

Pity, really.

He waited as the elevator approached, the numbers on the little board above the door changing, and as the three figures stepped into the car and the door closed behind them. He counted down under his breath—

—and right on time there was a visible puff of some kind of smoke or vapor around the edges of the elevator door, and some slight movement as if whoever was inside was banging on the door trying to get out again. There was no sound on the security footage, so he couldn't hear the muffled screams, but then again he didn't need to; they wouldn't last very long.

One of his phones rang, buzzing on the desk; he picked it up. "Yeah."

"It's done, boss," said the voice on the other end. "Went off just like it was supposed to. Enough pure allicin in aerosol

STRANGE NEW WORLD

form to fuckin' melt their lungs to goo, not to mention every inch of exposed skin." In the background someone said something about popping eyeballs, snickering, and gave an *oof* as if being elbowed silent.

"And the note?" Contini asked.

"Just like you wanted it, boss, on the inside of the door. It's kinda a mess on the floor in there right now, but you can still read it just fine. Should still be there when they find the bodies."

"Good work," said Contini. "Go on, get out of there, make sure you cleaned up real good, I don't want any of that shit on you guys."

"You got it, boss," said the voice on the other end, and he dropped the phone back on the desk.

"We good?" said Francisco.

"This time next week," said Contini, and lit another cigarette, "the smart money says that the Hellcat Club will be *unexpectedly back on the market* due to unforeseen complications, and my organization will be *surprised* but quite *happy* to take it off the hands of the late Mr. Kraven's remaining idiot hench-vamps. Not to mention my social plans for the season will be cleared right up. Warm fuzzy feeling of a job well done—"

One of the *other* phones on the desk buzzed, and he took his feet down and squinted at it before thumbing the screen. "What?"

Mario, this time. "Sir, it's happened again."

"*What's* happened again?" Contini snapped.

"The, uh. The thing that got Radu? That dart thing? We got another one."

"*Fuck*," said Contini. "Who is it now?"

"Donnie B. He's sick but less sick than Radu, I guess maybe this one didn't have so much poison shit on it or something—and he *did* grab the fuckface who shot him with it."

Contini sat up straight, squashing out his current cigarette. "Still alive?"

"Breathing *and* conscious," said Mario. "*And* lucid, far as we can tell. Even got most of his teeth left. Little skinny hume, had a crucifix on him but Donnie got a handful of his shirt around it and ripped it off, he wasn't carrying anything else dangerous. No garlic, no Host, no holy water, nothin'. You want I should ask him some questions right now, or wait for you?"

"Wait for me," said Contini. "You're at the restaurant?"

"Yessir. He's all ready for you."

"I'll be there soon," said Contini, and got up. "Frankie, you stick around here in case anyone calls in about the Kraven job, but I got a feeling this shit's more important. I'll be in touch."

"You got it," said Francisco, and waited until his employer had departed through the window on bat-wings to slide the laptop computer over and smile at the narrow, but growing, stain of dark fluid seeping under the elevator door.

Erebus General Hospital, Dis

"You're sure this is *allowed*?" said Harlach for the second time, sitting up against his pillows and trying not to fidget while the IT people set up a laptop on the bed-tray. Faust stood back, arms folded.

"If it wasn't," he said, "we wouldn't be doing it, would we? All Raphael said was he wants to talk to you, not 'he wants to talk to you *and* is going to get in lots of trouble about it.' I don't see Raphael as the type to leave that sort of thing out, or to recommend something that's officially verboten, even if he *is* showing the odd sign of independent thought these days. All we're doing is calling your colleague's phone from this end so you two can have a brief natter, not asking him to do anything particularly untoward."

The techs had stopped fiddling with the computer; now one of them opened the video-call software and typed in some codes. The screen went black and they could hear the phone ringing on the other end. Faust nodded and swept out of the room, techs in tow, leaving Harlach staring awkwardly and apprehensively at the computer, wishing he'd had the presence of mind to ask for a mirror and a comb to try to make his hair behave—even assuming Haliel was *there*, or wanted to pick up the phone—

The black screen flickered and resolved into the familiar face of the angel in his human seeming, the one he used all the time on Earth, first absurdly close and then at arm's length as Haliel figured out the proper focal length for FaceTime. "Harlach!" he said, beaming, and then the smile slid off his face in favor of the sort of concern that hurt Harlach's chest. "Oh dear, are you—you look *dreadful*—I mean, sorry, that was rude of me—are you all right? How bad is it? What happened?"

Harlach ran a hand over his untidy curls self-consciously, aware that he was blushing. "I'm fine," he said. "I mean—okay, I've been better, but it hardly hurts at all now and I don't have much of a fever, so don't worry?"

"Of course I'm going to *worry*," said Haliel. "The *Archangel Raphael* came to my actual flat, in person, to tell me you'd been attacked and were in hospital, how am I supposed to *not* worry?"

"Well—" Harlach said. "I mean, don't worry *now*? I gather I wasn't doing so well when I got transferred down here, but I'm much better now—wait, Raphael came to see you?"

"*Yes*," said Haliel. "So you didn't get any kind of look at whoever shot you with the thing, either?"

"Not even a glimpse, it happened much too fast—I was passing an alley and this thing just came out of the blackness and got me—" His hand had risen to the square of gauze taped over the wound involuntarily, and then he blinked. "Wait, what do you mean *either*?"

"Oh," said Haliel, blushing faintly. "I...it's nothing, but a few days earlier something similar sort of attacked me? A little metal dart thing? It poked me in the back."

Harlach stared at the screen, his stomach dropping. "Oh fuck," he said. "Oh God. Fuck. Haliel, it got *you*, too? Are *you* okay?"

"I'm totally fine," said Haliel earnestly. "Really. Please don't worry? It healed over almost at once and Raphael even had a look at it while he was here, he says it's nothing. I wasn't ill at all, I promise—"

"Who would possibly want to hurt *you*?" Harlach said, still sick with horror. "You're an *angel*, it makes no sense—people don't like demons, that's fine, it's part of the whole, you know, idiom, but who would try to hurt an angel?" Especially one like Haliel, who enjoyed his job and loved the city, who'd never harmed anyone?

"I don't know," said Haliel. "It doesn't seem to have worked on me, though? They can't have mistaken you for me and tried again; we don't look at all alike, you're dark where I'm fair, and I don't wear long black coats with little *Armani*s woven into the lining." He tilted his head, thoughtful. "Actually the only real similarity is that neither of us is human."

"I know they ran some tests on the stuff the doctor took out of my shoulder," said Harlach. "To see what sort of creatures it might be dangerous to. What happened to the dart that hit you?"

"Gabriel took it," said Haliel. "When I went to him to report the attack—he's my supervisor for the surface-operative work—he took it. I don't know what he did with it."

Harlach closed his eyes, feeling dizzy all over again. As far as he knew Heaven didn't exactly have a well-appointed laboratory available to analyze trace toxins on blowdarts, and his general impression of the Archangel Gabriel's attitude toward all things surface-related suggested that the dart was probably now in some sort of celestial incinerator, beyond any hope of use. "I can ask Dr. Faust about the results he found," he said, sounding exhausted even to himself.

"It doesn't seem to do angels much harm at all," said Haliel.

"It did hurt rather a lot at first, but as soon as I pulled it out and got myself back to Heaven, I seemed to get on with healing just fine... Harlach, are you sure you're all right? You don't look at all well."

"I wish there was something I could *do*," he said, opening his eyes. Haliel was closer to the camera now, his own eyes vivid clear blue, wide with concern. "I hate just—lying here helpless while something up there is running around with poison darts."

"Poison darts that don't seem to be very much of a problem for angels," said Haliel thoughtfully. "Hmm."

"What?"

"Nothing," said Haliel. His face had taken on the expression Harlach associated with the angel's occasional attempts at *craftiness*, not that he'd had a lot of basis for comparison. "I ought to let you rest," he added. "But it's lovely to see you, and if they let us, I'd very much like to talk again soon?"

"As long as you don't get in trouble for it," Harlach said. "Haliel—don't do things that would get you in *any* kind of trouble? Please?"

"That would be irresponsible," said Haliel, angelically, which did nothing to reassure him. "Get some sleep and feel better, Harlach, and don't worry about me, I'll be quite all right."

"I—" he said, but the screen had gone black again. He lay back against the pillows, eyes shut, the mostly-healed wound in his shoulder throbbing, and tried not to think of someone or something having another go at the angel with their blowgun. He could so clearly picture the shocked hurt on Haliel's face when the dart had struck him, the *confusion*: he wasn't the sort of creature that had experience with sorrow and pain and the grief of a wound, it must have been so frightening for him to be hurt out of nowhere—

—yes, but he'd *healed*; it hadn't done him this kind of damage, like he said, it wasn't much of a problem for angels—

—*That would be irresponsible*—

Cool fingers took his wrist, pressed gently over the pulse. He opened his eyes to find Dr. Faust leaning over him. "My," said Faust. "*That* doesn't seem to have done you any good at all; perhaps I ought to forbid any further calls—"

"No," Harlach said, hurried. "Please, I *need* to be able to talk to him again, I don't know what he's planning to do and it's probably dangerous, *please*, he's already been attacked once by this thing—"

"What?" Faust said sharply.

Harlach gave him what details Haliel had shared, including that the wound had healed very quickly without incident, talking while Faust scribbled rapidly in a pocket notebook. His shoulder was really throbbing now, as if the conversation with Haliel had woken up the wound.

"Well," said the doctor, underlining something twice. "It might have been helpful if my colleague Raphael had seen fit to mention this to me before, but at least we know now—"

"What are you going to do?" he said.

"Tell Fastitocalon, for one thing," said Faust. "And then tell Samael. This has gone rather comprehensively political. *You,*

113

my friend, are staying right where you are and not worrying about it for the time being."

"I don't know how I'm supposed to not worry," said Harlach, "and I think he's planning to do *something* and I'm pretty sure *he's* not supposed to—"

There was the tiny flood of coldness in his arm he'd grown very used to during his time in Erebus General, and he opened his eyes to see Faust removing a syringe from the lock on the IV. "You are *supposed* to not worry," said the doctor, "and I have just made that physically possible for you. I'll be back in a couple of hours to see how you're getting on and let you know if anything's changed, all right? I promise."

The sedative was both officious and deeply welcome, wrapping around Harlach's hindbrain with a wonderful kind of numbness, and he didn't even try to fight it as sleep rose up and claimed him like a tide.

Hidden Castle, Romania

It took four rings and one sleep-vague nudge in the ribs before Edmund St. James Ruthven roused sufficiently to roll over and reach for the phone on the nightstand by his bed.

It was a very nice bed: about sixteen feet tall, richly carved dark wood hung with deep red brocade curtains that matched the bedclothes as well as the rest of the chamber's furniture. The room itself was full of the blank sourceless light of a snowy midmorning, the air chilly since the last embers in the fireplace had died out hours ago.

Ruthven struggled far enough out of the bedclothes to peer at the phone, and then flopped back against the pillows, thumbing the screen. "Greta?" he said, still half-asleep. Beside him the hummock under the covers that was Grisaille curled up tighter, grumbling.

"It's me," said the voice on the phone. "Good lord, Edmund, did I wake you? It's got to be getting on for eleven in the morning where you are."

"Mmh," said Ruthven, eyes shut. "Unlike you, the Voivode keeps his household to a *civilized* sort of schedule that is largely crepuscular. Was there something in particular you wanted?"

"I'm assuming you didn't get my email," said Greta Helsing. "I need your help, Ruthven. Specifically your help *shopping for appropriate clothing for a journey*. And I need it in something of a hurry."

He squinted at the screen. "What on earth are you talking about? What journey? Why?"

"Six weeks' worth of fieldwork in America," she said. "For research purposes on behalf of both Göttingen University and the infernal civil service. Leaving early on Monday."

"Wait," said Ruthven, emerging sufficiently to sit up and reach for his laptop, also on the nightstand. "Start again and use small words and simple sentence structure, will you?"

There was distant laughter down the line. As she talked he opened up his email and skimmed the list of requirements and the planned schedule for her trip: okay, mostly just the sort of thing she wore every day, jeans and decent sweaters, the odd tailored piece, a couple of semi-dressy outfits for the receptions on the list, maybe one really nice thing in case she and Varney wanted to go out somewhere decent in an actual city—

"They did say we'll be staying in hotels where we can, and that limited laundry facilities will be available, so I won't have to pack an entire six weeks' worth of knickers and socks and so on," she said. "I'm still not entirely clear on who is running this jaunt on the American side, but presumably all will be made clear once we get there. Nor am I looking forward to watching over this angel and this demon with unqualified joy, but at least Varney's going to be with me and he's a lot more impressive than I am when it comes to intimidation."

"I find it desperately difficult to believe Varney volunteered for this gig," Ruthven said, balancing the phone between ear and shoulder as he typed rapidly. "I wouldn't have thought he'd have the slightest interest in visiting America, not since the Voivode's people took care of all that unpleasantness—he's got good thrall, though. I suppose if called upon to do so, he could look sufficiently quellingly at an obstreperous demon. You haven't changed shape much since the last time I bought you new things, have you?"

"Not that I'm aware of," said Greta. "How *is* the Voivode and his lady wife and Lucy? Wolf lessons proceeding apace?"

"Wolf and bat and *mist*, would you credit it? Grisaille was right: that kid is already better at vampiring than the rest of us put together. And the Voivode seems more content than I've ever known him in the past several hundred years—you'd hardly believe how little silver there is in his hair now, and the Countess looks practically forty at the absolute outside."

"Any sign of aging in Lucy herself?" Greta asked. He could hear the faint tone of anxiety under the words.

"Grisaille and I haven't been here long enough to really make a study of the matter," said Ruthven, carefully, "but from what I *have* been able to observe, she does appear to be growing, ever so slowly. The things I bought for her when she was staying with us are just a little bit too small now; you wouldn't notice if you weren't paying really close attention, but I do think she *is* changing at least a tiny bit. Vlad's been keeping an eye on it; he says he wants to take her to come see you when it's convenient, hopefully in the spring, partly to visit and say hello and partly so you can take a proper look at her and see what *you* think about it."

"I'd love that," said Greta. "Tell him so, I'd be thrilled to see all of them. Hopefully this nonsense will be over and done with by the end of the year—we're supposed to get back just before Christmas—and then I'll be able to focus properly again."

"I'll let him know. Anything interesting going on in London I should pass on, while I'm at it?"

There was the faintest hint of hesitation. "Not really. My demon friend who takes me to and from work is a little under the weather and someone else is handling the job for now, but that's not really your jurisdiction."

"Harlach, right?" said Ruthven. "Tell him I hope he feels better soon. And do let me know if anything *does* turn up that I—and the Count—ought to know about?"

"I will," said Greta. "Nadezhda and Anna will have the

clinic while I'm gone; you know how to get in touch with them, right?"

"Of course," he said. "Let me break out the black card and do some retail-therapy-by-proxy, and I'll have these things sent to you hopefully by tomorrow morning so you can manage any exchanges before you have to leave. I promise I won't pick out any *terribly* avant-garde looks."

"You are the only person I know who uses *look* as a noun who isn't on the telly," said Greta. "I love you anyway, Edmund. Say hello to Grisaille for me and give the Draculas my best?"

"Of course," he said, and hung up. After a moment Grisaille poked his head out from under the scarlet brocade covers and squinted at him.

"What on earth was all that about?"

"Our Dr. Helsing's headed to the New World," said Ruthven. "Taking her husband with her. I wonder what Sir Francis Varney wants to find in the land of opportunity—"

"Mmh," said Grisaille, and reached for Ruthven under the covers, insistent and sleepy, and shortly afterward whatever he'd been about to add was entirely lost.

Brighton Beach, New York City

Aurelio Contini had been *in New York* since the late eighteen-hundreds, one way and another; hounded out of his own country by tiresome and officious interference, he had made his way to the New World and found it offered him far more

varied opportunities than he'd expected. By the time the
stock market crashed he had settled into the city like an inva-
sive spore, developing a deep-underground mycelium network
of influence that sprouted a variety of fruiting bodies. For a
while Contini had held all of New York in the slightly-hairy
palm of one white hand: he knew what came in and what went
out, who was owned by whom and for how much. Nobody
so much as ran a Find the Lady game anywhere in the five
boroughs without Mr. Contini knowing about it—or at least
they didn't for very long, and the examples Mr. Contini made
of people who *didn't* follow his very simple and straightforward rules were hard to forget.

He'd been on top of the world, and the money had been
roaring in, and—he'd had a premonition. Sometimes he got
them: strange dreams that grabbed down inside his hindbrain
and tweaked like a meathook might if it was extra-gentle:
dreams he couldn't, wouldn't ignore because he was who he
was and he'd lived this long by not being really fucking stupid. This one had said: put the money somewhere safe, set
up your organizations against disaster, and go underground,
because bad times are coming. Bad times for everyone, not
just your kind, but bad times your kind can survive if they are
smart about it.

So he'd done a thing few people understood at the time, and
shut it down—but built the keys of starting it up again into
the act of shutting his operation down. Parking the money in
places where it would be safe while he slept, like grave-goods
in a royal tomb, waiting for their owner to wake again to the

next world. Putting things away carefully so they could be picked up, including the command structure of his organization. The last thing he'd done was give the keys to his most-trusted lieutenants, tasking them with staying awake, keeping it silent, keeping it secret, keeping it safe, against his eventual return.

And this spring he had woken up again, entirely of a sudden, not sure *what* had woken him but unable to get back to sleep, and had crept back up into the waking world, and found that everything had gone directly straight to *shit* while he'd been away.

Since then he'd been tidying up the mess. Since then, systematically, he'd been cleansing the city of the upstart idiot vamps and other assorted monsters who'd filled the vacuum of his leadership with their own poorly-advised organizations. Since then, his influence had been increasing—gradually at first, and then beginning to snowball faster and faster as word of mouth spread and brought with it sufficient fear of retribution to send some of the upstarts running, even before he'd come along to say hello and tell them to fuck off out of his city if they knew what was good for them. Throughout the summer and into the autumn he'd tightened his fist again around New York, feeling it settle once more into a thing he knew the shapes of, where very little could surprise him. He had *plans*, both short- and long-term plans, and on his dance-card the city's autumn social life was beginning to take satisfying shape.

Which was why he'd been the bad kind of surprised to find

out what was behind these fucking poison-dart attacks. At first, anyway. It had been clear to him reasonably quickly how they could be put to his advantage.

In the noisome back-room of the Bowery restaurant, he'd gotten information out of the captured assailant rather the way a veterinarian gets poisoned bait out of a very stupid dog: once regurgitation was initialized, the flow sustained itself without much external influence. The assailant didn't know how many of them there were. The assailant knew only that he, like his fellow street-preachers, was called to share the word of God with the mortal city (Contini liked that phrase) and that he and his fellow preachers had been meeting up together in the company of Brother Gideon for—a little while now, he wasn't sure how long—

Who is Brother Gideon? Standing back, out of the way of the dripping blood from the man's wrecked nose, out of the range of the worst of the stink.

No one seemed to know—

A brief interlude, in which parameters were reset: now the prisoner had a clearer understanding of the fact that his captors could and would break all the bones in his hands one by one, even the very little ones at the ends of the fingers, which weren't actually all that easy to do. Brother Gideon—last name Tremayne—night-managed a Taco Bell over in Brooklyn. On Coney Island Avenue. Brother Gideon Tremayne got off work at five a.m., lived within walking distance, and probably went straight home to change after his shift because none of them had seen him in his uniform during the day.

What does Brother Gideon Tremayne look like?

Average height, early thirties, nondescript medium-brown short hair, freckles, gap between his front teeth. Kind of glows with holy light?

Holy light?

Another distal phalange and another high bubbling scream, but all the man would say was *holy light*, over and over again, until Mario hit him hard enough to make him stop saying anything at all.

And so, now—in a clean shirt, his fingernails once more innocent of human blood—Aurelio Contini leaned against a honey-locust tree on the other side of Coney Island Avenue, wearing don't-notice-me like a muffling cloak, and watched a figure move inside the brightly-lit restaurant. There was nothing visible from across the street that suggested a holy glow, but nonetheless he was fairly sure he was watching the right person; after a couple of centuries you developed a pretty sensitive ability to read human body language.

A few phone calls had produced Gideon Tremayne's mailing address, not quite a mile south of the restaurant, and Contini pulled the don't-notice-me tighter around himself—barely necessary at half past four in the morning, but again, one did not take unnecessary chances—and sauntered off down Coney Island Avenue. He would wait for Brother Gideon to get home, and then he would ask the good brother some simple questions about his operation with the street preachers and what he hoped to achieve thereby, and very probably make him an offer it would be highly imprudent for him to refuse.

And then the party Contini had been planning for his own people, where he'd make known his own plans for the immediate future, would go off without a hitch.

Contini didn't *mind* other people operating in his city, exactly. He just minded when they got in his way. As long as they could be maneuvered into doing what they wanted to do in a way which did not interfere with what *he* wanted to have done, he was all for free enterprise and the pursuit of happiness. Wasn't that the American Dream, after all?

Behind the upturned coat collar and the scarf, behind the influence making himself as unremarkable as possible, Aurelio Contini's unbeautiful mouth was stretched in a deeply satisfied grin.

Hell, Monitoring and Evaluation Director's Office

Fastitocalon woke with a start to the sound of somebody banging on his office door.

It was hardly the first time he'd fallen asleep on the couch in the director's office, but he did *try* to make a point of sleeping in his actual bed from time to time, both for the principle of the thing and for the sake of his back. He sat up and muttered a couple of imprecations in Enochian as he shoved a stack of paperwork slithering off his chest to the floor—yes, right, he'd been looking at esso traces from London—

"Yes, all *right*," he said as the banging recommenced, and stacked the piles of paper into some semblance of order on his desk before opening the door. Faust stood there, fur-trimmed robe and beard looking more incongruous than usual against the aggressively ordinary backdrop of the M&E offices. "What's the matter?" he demanded.

"Guess what," said Faust. "No. Don't guess, guessing is for amateurs; just listen. Harlach's not the only one who's fallen afoul of mysterious blowdarts in the rainy streets of Soho, or wherever it is he dwells. There's been another attack."

"Fuck," said Fastitocalon in good old Anglo-Saxon. "Asturel?"

"No. Much worse. *The angel.*"

Fastitocalon stared at him. "What angel? You can't mean London's operative, what's-his-name—"

"Haliel," said Faust. "I can and I do. He got shot with one of these pigstickers several days *before* our Harlach, and Raphael didn't see fit to share that with me; apparently he and Harlach are the sort of friends where they get touchingly worried about one another, and when Haliel heard about Harlach's attack, he wanted to call him and so on and so forth." Faust waved a hand in a dismissive sort of way. "Turns out Haliel seems to have shrugged it off as nothing particularly troublesome, *unlike* our Harlach, so it looks like the scanner was accurate as far as that goes: it hurt him a bit when it went in but there was no serious reaction to speak of, so whatever's on the blades really is calibrated to harm the naughty rather than the nice. And now I've got to tell Sam about it, and he is not going to be a *happy* devil when I do."

"And you want moral support," said Fastitocalon. "Ugh. Yes, all right, this is my business as well. Can it wait long enough for me to wash and change and find a different tie?"

"If you hurry," said Faust. "Stay not about the manner of your going."

Fastitocalon glowered at him, but grabbed his wrinkled suit jacket from the back of the couch and vanished with a faint collapsing pop of air.

He couldn't remember the first time he'd seen Samael's white office. It had been so many different versions of itself over the millennia: there had been white marble and crystal mosaic floors, the sort of curtains that anywhere else would have been edged with tyrian purple, pure-white fleeces draped over inlaid benches; there had been highly intricate carved-stone archways and pillars; there had been delicate rococo embellishments, spindle-thin exquisitely carved furniture, decorative plasterwork, all in white, lacking only the gilt. At one point Samael had gone in for crystal-clear furniture and floor tiles that glowed faintly with an inner light, but that phase hadn't lasted very long.

The current white-on-white office appeared minimalist only in color; objects thronged the shelves, the occasional tables, Samael's vast white-wood desk. Three huge white monitors stood on one end of the desk, and a much larger display hung on one wall, plain white when not in use. The view beyond the balcony doors overlooked the plaza and the opal surface of the lake, shimmering gently in the morning light. Fastitocalon, in his hastily-pressed 1958 double-breasted suit, looked inescapably rumpled and out of place; somehow Faust's fur-trimmed dark velvet and floppy hat didn't seem quite so starkly mismatched with his surroundings.

The Devil was in white linen this morning, collarless shirt open at the throat, sleeves rolled up, trouser-pleats immaculate. If the white were a more comfortable ivory, he would have looked perfectly at home on a veranda in the tropics sipping something with an umbrella in it; as it was, casual but snowy, he looked almost as dangerous as Fastitocalon knew him to be.

Part of that was the expression, of course. As soon as he and Faust had been shown into the office and explained the reason for their visit, Samael's butterfly-blue eyes had gone blank scarlet from lid to lid, cabochon rubies that gave off faint but visible light.

"And Raphael didn't see fit to mention this initial attack in his various conversations with you," he said, sitting down behind the desk. "Despite—*how* much of our equipment and supplies did you send up there?"

"Enough to run a small Doctors Without Borders clinic for a few days, which technically is sort of what he's got going," said Faust, arms folded. "The fact that he could bring himself to ask for my help at all is, in my opinion, a significant step forward. And the further fact that he's apparently now making his own house calls *to the Prime Material plane* should perhaps not be overlooked in its turn."

"It's very unlike an archangel to take a personal interest in anything on the surface," Fastitocalon murmured. "I gathered from Asmodeus's records when I took over that *their* surface operatives never seemed to have a great deal of contact with whoever was in charge of them; it sounded rather as if they sent in reports and went about their daily business and didn't hear back from Heaven about much of anything, although of course that's just the impression our M&E people reported. Raphael's not only *asked for Hell's help* but also apparently taken it upon himself to get involved in Heaven's own surface-operative organization, and—well, it isn't like them."

"*And* I want a clearer clinical picture of the actual course of Haliel's injury and recovery," said Faust. "Furthermore I *definitely* want to have a look at that inhalation injury and how they're getting on. In the spirit of the Accords, et cetera, and not just out of clinical curiosity."

"And I would like to get a *clearer picture*," said Samael, enunciating, "of what the hell they're playing at up there. It's all very well for an archangel to shriek for our help, I vividly recall them doing exactly that in the middle of the attack on Heaven, but it sounds as if Raphael may have gone behind Gabriel's back on this one, and that I *do* want to know more about. Ring him up, Faust."

"What, right now? Here?"

"Ring him up," Samael repeated, and slid the white-on-white keyboard across the desk to Faust, who glanced up at Fastito-calon and then bent over to type in a series of commands. The big wall display lit up with a desktop background and then the black screen of an outgoing video call.

Three rings. Four. Five—and there was a click, and another white room sprang into view on the screen, tilted, and straightened itself. This white was the severe lack-of-color of an ascetic's whitewashed cell rather than the high-ceilinged monochrome of Samael's office. An angel's head came into the shot, looking anxious and much more exhausted than any of them were used to seeing angels look, but it definitely wasn't Raphael. The halo was much smaller, and the lovely nose was slightly but noticeably snubbed.

"Um," said the angel, biting its lip. "Can I help you?"

"Who are you?" Samael asked.

"Adariel—oh. Oh. *Samael.* Your Majesty. I didn't realize it was you—"

"Never mind that," said Faust. "Where's Raphael? What's going on up there?"

"He's—um—he's busy right now?" said Adariel. "Can I take a message?"

"Busy with what, exactly?" said Samael. His voice was gentle, but underneath the smooth surface there was a core of steel. Adariel winced, and they could all see just how worn the angel really was; Fastitocalon didn't think he could remember *ever* seeing one this visibly tired except in the immediate aftermath of the attack on Heaven. It was not a comfortable sight.

"Um," said the angel. "It's—it's Gabriel, Your Majesty. He's here."

Fastitocalon thought, absurdly, *My God, man. Does he want tea?* Beside him, Faust said, "Would it be reasonable to infer that Gabriel is having somewhat heated words with your supervisor regarding medical supplies and equipment and the correct angelic and medical protocol for standard-of-care in Heaven?"

"Um," said Adariel again. It seemed to be something of

a tic. "I think you could probably say that, sir. It's all gone rather complicated."

He looked so wretched that Fastitocalon, uncharacteristically, wanted to put an arm around his shoulders. He glanced at Faust, and saw a similar hastily-squashed instinct flicker across the human's face.

"Right," said Samael, coolly, with the air of someone who has made a decision. "Put him on."

Fastitocalon flicked a glance at him: he was being extremely inhuman at the moment, distant and statue-like, and despite recognizing the tactic and its purpose, he couldn't quite help feeling a faint wash of awe flood over him. The wings were slightly visible, slipping into and out of reality, and Samael seemed to have grown several inches in height.

"Y-Your Majesty?" said the angel.

"Go and fetch Gabriel," said the Devil with awful patience, "and put him on. Raphael, too. Right now, please, Adariel. This is important."

"Yes, Your Majesty," said Adariel miserably, and vanished from the shot.

Fastitocalon looked over at his boss. "What are you planning to do?"

"Remind our esteemed colleague the Archangel Gabriel of the contents of the Accords," said Samael delicately, and took a cigarette from the inlaid box on his desk; it lit itself. "In case the detail escapes his memory for the moment. He seems to be more interested in yelling at his colleagues for doing their job than, I don't know, doing *his own* job. Like taking care of his surface operatives and finding out everything he could about the apparent attack on Haliel. I don't have time for this, Fass. None of us do, not when somebody's running around playing silly buggers with poisoned darts."

"At least there hasn't been anything inexplicable on the esso traces," said Fastitocalon, wanting a cigarette of his own. "Last night I thought there might be something going on, but I'm pretty sure that was just Raphael nipping down to Earth to have a chat with Haliel in person, exactly the way neither he nor the rest of the host of Heaven normally do. Might be nice to clear that up while we're at it."

Heaven, Raphael's infirmary

Raphael was wondering whether he *was* in fact going to be sick in the near future, and if so, how much warning he could expect to have before the unhappy event itself. He'd been unable to sleep after the visit to Haliel: he'd drunk too much of Heaven's limited version of faintly-stimulant herbal tea over the course of the night, watching over his patients; that plus nothing to eat and vicious anxiety had combined to make him feel thoroughly unwell, and Gabriel's presence—and his lecturing—was making it worse. When Gabriel was displeased with you, being near him, within the influence of his pneumic fields, was like having some mildly corrosive liquid trickle over your brain; it acted as a force multiplier for preexisting misery. It was making him feel not just sick but *dizzy*, which did not help in the slightest.

It also didn't help that Gabriel was doing that opera-libretto thing where he'd make a point, then make another point, then circle back and make the first point three more times in case you hadn't got the message yet. Raphael didn't know whether he was doing it on purpose, and didn't know if it would be better if he *was*.

"—and so it puzzles me, Raphael, it really puzzles me, why you thought this was in any way appropriate or acceptable, given your presumable breadth of knowledge and understanding," he was saying for the nth time when Adariel poked his head around the doorway.

"Um," he said. "Sir? Sirs?"

"What is it," snapped Gabriel, interrupted in mid-repetition.

"S-Samael's on the phone. His Majesty. From Hell. He, um. He wants to talk to both of you."

Raphael closed his eyes, swallowing hard. Beside him Gabriel made an annoyed huffing noise through his nostrils. "This is not a good time, Adariel. I'm having a conversation with Raphael, if you hadn't noticed."

"He, um. He wants to talk to both of you *right now*, he said."

Dimly Raphael was slightly proud of his orderly, who was clearly terrified but holding his ground. All at once things started to feel slightly hilarious: what *else* could possibly go wrong? They hadn't even begun to cover the subject of his own unscheduled and uncharacteristic departure from Heaven the previous evening; all Gabriel had addressed so far was his decision to seek assistance from Hell for his desperately ill patient.

Raphael didn't even know if he *knew* about the visit to Haliel, and if so, what he planned to say about the matter.

Aloud he said, "Well. Mustn't keep the Devil waiting, Gabriel. After you."

Gabriel gave him the most disdainful look he could remember seeing on an angelic face, but said nothing, merely huffing again as he led the way back to Raphael's little office. On the computer monitor they could see a large white desk with a thing that looked like a marble statue of an angel behind it, flanked by Dr. Faust in fur-trimmed velvet and a tall thin demon in a suit, and again Raphael's mind gave a horrible little off-kilter hiccup of mirth. He gave Faust and his colleagues a little wave, aware of the doctor's horrified expression; he didn't know what he must look like at the moment, but it probably wasn't reassuring. "Good morning," he said. "Sorry about this."

The statue-being was all white save for the bright red glow of its eyes. "Raphael, can you give me an update on your most recent patients, please," it said, and the archangel wondered if he'd ever seen Samael manifest quite like that before. It was undeniably effective. He wished he could think better past the dizziness.

"—I—"

"Excuse me," Gabriel cut in. "This is quite frankly *not* a wonderful time, politically speaking, for you to poke an inquisitive nose into the way we run any aspect of our Heaven, *Samael*. It's bad enough your dead human doctor Faust down there got involved with the treatment of an angel patient; now

I have found Raphael's infirmary *full* of inappropriate and mortal-based contamination—"

"They still alive?" asked Faust.

"What?" snapped Gabriel.

"The patient treated with our stuff. Corundum-dust-inhalation injury, critically ill. Still breathing?"

"Of course. I am not speaking to *you*, human."

"'Cause I'm willing to put significant metaphorical cash on it that he had a good chance of popping his angelic clogs without the O_2 and drugs we sent up. Based on what Raphael told me, you were starting to get fluid filling the lungs, and you can't fix *that* with hymns and daisy-chains and nectar, no matter how holy you are." Faust shrugged.

"He's not wrong," murmured Raphael, trying not to sway, and unobtrusively wrapped his fingers around the edge of the desk to steady himself, eyes closing for a moment. "The oxygen was—like magic, Gabriel. That and the medicines to reduce inflammation and keep his airways open, I've never seen anything like it that *wasn't* a miracle. The other drugs, the antibiotics, I don't know if that's done anything or if the oxygen and medicine just helped keep his body from drowning itself long enough for him to begin to heal on his own, but the improvement is amazing."

"I'd say you have a *succès fou* on your hands up there, Gabriel," said the Devil, steepling very long fingers on the white desk. He was still the remote marble statue, but slightly less so—slightly less Mannerist and more Baroque. "You will of course recall last year the historic moment when you and

I together signed the infernocelestial Accords, on the plains of Purgatory, with the massed hordes of Heaven and Hell as witness. Article seventeen, section C, subsection three of the Accords states *all available aid and support is to be provided by either side to a being in extreme danger or need, regardless of infernal or celestial origin or allegiance; there is to be no partisanship in the provision of care.* It is right next to the one that says angels and demons are to work together on collaborative projects to further the joint interests of the infernocelestial world, which is what's been giving everyone hives for months now, but I would draw your attention to the *all available aid and support* bit."

"Looks to me," said Faust, chiming in, "as if what you got there is you had a being in need of assistance, you did not have the necessary equipment to provide the care this being needed, so you asked us for a loan *since we have the stuff.* That makes it *available aid and support,* even if you did have to ask first. From our side it's even simpler: you need the stuff, we have the stuff, we send it on up there, your guy keeps breathing, everyone goes home happy."

"What a remarkable illustration of Heaven and Hell working together for the common good," said the demon standing beside Samael, bland as milk. Raphael couldn't remember his name. He ought to know it: the demon was something to do with their surface-operative department, in charge of Harlach; probably he was concerned about his employee… Raphael really *should* have told them about Haliel's attack, shouldn't he…

Gabriel's golden eyes narrowed, and he had drawn breath to say something probably everyone was going to regret when Adariel piped up, out of frame from the demons' point of view. "Um," he said. "Sorry to interrupt. I don't—know anything about, well, anything really, I'm too new to have any real experience with how things worked before the Accords, but—I'm supposed to be going on this trip to Earth with a demon to work together and do research for a human doctor? And this is maybe one of the kinds of thing that the trip's designed to find out, like, can collaborative patient care work, or can supplies and equipment from Hell work on angels? I think—um—based on what we've just seen, they really kind of *can*, and I'm pretty sure the doctor is going to want to hear about it."

"And how," said Faust with satisfaction. "She's going to want to know *everything*, Raphael. Pump you like a stomach. And it's all entirely in the service of the Accords."

"Isn't it," said Samael. "So perhaps on the whole it might be as well, Gabriel, to allow Raphael to continue doing his job to the best of his ability, even if that includes the occasional use of modern technology?"

Gabriel was seething; being near him, inside the influence of his fields, was making Raphael's dizziness enormously, sickeningly worse. He wished Faust hadn't mentioned stomachs, even if everything they'd said was encouraging: Gabriel really *didn't* have the moral high ground here, for once, and he thought all of them knew it.

"Very *well*," the archangel snapped, all his feathers fluffing out like an angry bird's. "Your point is taken. However, I am—*requiring*—that all equipment and supplies from Hell be decontaminated fully with holy water before any further use. I am further requiring that they are to be used *only* in cases where all normal acceptable methods and techniques have not produced satisfactory results. They will *not* be the first line of care. Am I understood by all present?"

"It would be difficult to mistake you, my lord," said Samael. "Very good. And, Raphael, do try to keep Faust better updated, will you?"

"Of course," said Raphael through his teeth. That had been a barely veiled accusation that he'd lied by omission, not telling Faust about Haliel's attack, but he couldn't think about that now. The screen mercifully cut to blackness, and Gabriel— wings mantled, halo glowing brightly enough to leave actinic afterimages floating in front of their eyes—turned on his heel and stalked out of the infirmary.

"Is he gone," said Raphael, eyes squeezed shut, still clutching the edge of the desk. Closing his eyes didn't help: the room was still swooping and tilting crazily around him, the floor bucking under his feet like the deck of a ship in heavy seas. *Please let him be gone*, he thought, as fervently as any prayer. *Oh please let him not see this, please—*

"Um. Yes?"

"Good," he said, and let go of the desk, fell heavily to his hands and knees, and was violently, helplessly sick for the third time in all his millennia of existence.

CHAPTER 6

Dark Heart House, Wiltshire

Greta Helsing had spent much of the afternoon tidying up in the clinic and updating her inventories, making lists, organizing, and generally preparing the place for her friends to run in her absence. She'd only had a couple of walk-in patients all afternoon, which had made this possible, and was beginning to feel the crawling agitation of *oh let's get on with it* that tended to show up in the last stages of preparation for a journey. Ruthven had forwarded her a slew of emails promising delivery of various packages. The journey up to the airport was clearly marked on everybody's schedules. Everything was going as smoothly as she could have hoped, so far.

Now, in her bedroom at Dark Heart, glowering at her battered suitcases and the stacks of books and journals she was somehow supposed to fit in them along with all the idiotic clothing Ruthven was having delivered, she was extremely glad when her phone rang and the caller ID showed simply H E A V E N, annoying kerning and all. That was clearly a *lot* more important than the topological challenges of packing. She grabbed the phone and picked up on the second ring. "Hello?"

"Um. Dr. Helsing?" said a voice that was thoroughly unangelic in its diffidence. It was beautiful, the way all angels' voices were beautiful, but it definitely lacked the standard angelic certainty. "This is—um—Adariel. I'm the angel you're supposed to take on the America trip?"

She sat back on her heels. That did not sound like an angel who was either terribly keen or very sure of itself, although *in need of professional guidance* did seem to fit. "Hello, Adariel," she said, with her calming talking-to-patients filter halfway in place. "It's nice to speak to you. Is something wrong?"

"Um," he said again. She got the idea that that particular vocal tic was going to become annoying very quickly. "Sort of? And—sort of not? We're supposed to, to work together on this trip, right, angels and demons and humans? And see how we can collaborate on projects?"

"So I gather," said Greta. "They're particularly interested in seeing how you and the demon Orlax react to one another on the Prime Material plane in terms of allergy, since it's been such a continuous and fundamental problem in both Heaven and Hell." Fastitocalon had told her a little more about Orlax via email earlier in the afternoon, including an estimate of how much product he put in his hair every single day and how long he was therefore likely to take in the bus's limited bathroom space; she managed to keep this out of her tone.

"Right," said the angel. "Um. So—we've—we've had some incidents. In Heaven."

"Incidents," she repeated. "Should I be talking to Raphael about this?"

"He's, um. Not feeling very well right now. It's—well, one of the angels who was in the infirmary for dust inhalation got *very* ill, frighteningly ill, and Raphael made the decision to, um. Call down to Hell for help."

"Help from Faust," said Greta, blinking. "Voluntarily?"

"I don't think he was at all *happy* about it, but—the patient wasn't responding to anything we were doing, he could hardly breathe, and Raphael—he managed to get him through the worst of the attack and then as soon as it was over he just went to his office and rang down for Dr. Faust to ask for help." There was more than a little awe in the angel's voice. "I don't think it was easy for him. At all. But he was still shaking from the—the strain of trying to help Nithael through his fit, and he said something about how there wasn't any point in denying the patient effective treatment even when that treatment didn't—um—fit with the aesthetic?"

Good heavens, Greta thought, revising her mental image of both this unknown angel and the rather exhausted-looking archangel she'd only seen once or twice on official videos. She knew Faust talked to him on the phone from time to time, but hadn't really spared a lot of thought for what kind of clinical challenges must be facing the angels in a post-reset universe. This was—rather huge. She'd never heard of angels ill enough to need that sort of help, and certainly not angels *asking* for it. Out loud she said, "And Faust sent up some supplies?"

"What he called basic supplies and medications. The sort of

things you use in Hell and I think on Earth as well. Chemicals and—machines, and things."

As opposed to holy water and milk-and-honey and nectar and ambrosia and the power of positive thinking, Greta thought, remembering the high-tech surgical ward in Erebus General, the dispensaries brimming with every sort of medicament imaginable, glittering equipment standing by, a small army of highly-trained medical staff on call to manage any emergency. The contrast between that and the one or two images she'd seen of Raphael's nearly-empty ascetic tent infirmary was vivid. "Did it help your patient?"

"It really did. Like, *almost at once* helped. Once we gave Nithael the medicine and started him on the oxygen, he was so much better, it was like a miracle," said Adariel. "Raphael knew Gabriel wouldn't be happy about it, but the patient was so sick and nothing we could do would have helped him, we *needed* the stuff from Hell, and he said something about how we've all got our jobs to do and Gabriel wasn't the physician here. Um."

"Good for Raphael," she said, and recalled not just the exhausted look but Adariel saying *he's not feeling very well.* "I'm getting the idea that wasn't the only incident, though. What else has happened?"

"Um. Apparently there's been—some attacks on Earth. A demon was wounded—"

"I know," she said. "I was the one who transferred him down to Hell."

"You were? —I mean, um. Dr. Faust says he's doing better,"

said Adariel. "But—um—he's not the only one. There's an angel assigned to London, Harlach's counterpart—Haliel—"

"*Haliel?*" Greta said, sitting up straight. "He was attacked?" Christ, was it just yesterday she'd been thinking about the London angel, wondering if anyone had bothered to get in touch with him, to warn him about Harlach's attack, to let him know he should watch out? "When did that happen?"

"Yes," said Adariel, sounding exhausted himself. "Before Harlach. Days ago. It didn't do him anything like as much harm as Dr. Faust said the other dart did to the demon—he reported it to Gabriel when it first happened, and then came along to the infirmary for Raphael to look him over, but it just looked like a very minor puncture wound that was already healing. I don't think Raphael gave it a second thought until we heard that Harlach had been hurt with a similar weapon and was in much worse shape."

"And then Raphael *did* think twice?" Greta asked.

"He, um. Went down to Earth to talk to Haliel. In person."

"Went to *Earth*," Greta repeated. "I'm—forgive me if I'm completely ignorant of Heavenly protocol, but is that exactly the sort of thing the archangels *do* on a regular basis?"

"No," said Adariel, sounding both worried about it and impressed. "It really isn't. He just—told me to keep an eye on the place and that he'd be back soon, and off he went. He was gone for maybe half an hour, and he looked very tired when he came back, but not unhappy." The angel sighed. "That was yesterday evening, and then he didn't get any rest watching over Nithael—he's so much better now, but not *well*, despite Dr.

Faust's medicine, and Raphael did have to submit a report to Gabriel about it, and Gabriel...wasn't very happy at all. He came down to the infirmary to, um. Lecture. About the inadvisability of going behind his back and asking for Hell's assistance."

This she could picture, without much pleasure. "I thought archangels didn't—disagree much. In front of other angels."

"The Archangel Gabriel has very distinct and specific preferences," said Adariel, and for the first time she wondered if there weren't a flicker of sarcasm under the innocence. As far as she could recall from the briefing notes, he was a brand-new angel, having been made since the reset, and had no personal experience of how nasty the world could get. "He was extremely disappointed in Raphael for making a decision to sully Heaven with non-celestial things."

"And for tacitly acknowledging that celestial medicaments and therapeutics are perforce somewhat *limited*," said Greta, and sighed. Poor bloody Raphael; angels didn't do well with any admission that they weren't entirely in charge. "Okay. Where's this going, Adariel?"

"Well," said the angel. "Gabriel was sort of...repeating himself, again, and Raphael really didn't look at all well, and I didn't know what to do, and just then, um. Hell called."

"Hell," she repeated.

"His Majesty the Lord Samael and Dr. Faust and, um, a demon in a pinstripe suit," said Adariel. Distantly Greta was aware of a subtle difference between his tone and that of other angels she'd encountered when referring to the infernal hierarchy: Adariel didn't sound any different saying *Lord Samael* than he did pronouncing *Archangel Gabriel*, as if top brass were top brass no matter which side of the serpent they represented. It was oddly refreshing. "His Majesty wasn't very happy, either. There were... words."

She just bet there were. Samael when displeased was capable of radiating icy chill like nothing she'd experienced outside a liquid-nitrogen dewar. Adariel gave her a quick rundown of the conversation, ending with Gabriel's furious acknowledgment of the wording of the Accords and instruction to leave the modern technology as strictly last-resort: "But he didn't forbid its use either to Samael's face or after he hung up."

"Well, good. That makes sense," she said. It did; for a lot of the ordinary, minor illnesses and injuries Raphael saw, standard celestial therapeutics were perfectly effective, and there was no reason to use up finite supplies of pharmaceuticals when a good dose of honey-nectar syrup and some solid prayers would do the trick. "But clinically speaking it's extremely important to know that the medicine and oxygen from Erebus General *worked* on an angel *in Heaven*. We know they work on angels in Hell, based on what we observed in the midst of the emergency response during the attack, but this is entirely new information." She pushed away a mental flicker of the emergency-surgery ward splashed with golden angel blood, her own voice snapping out orders to try to stabilize patient after patient. "Did you do anything to contain any potential allergic reaction before you used them, given the origin of the supplies?" Greta found a notebook and pen, scribbling down some rapid shorthand.

"We swabbed the outside of the packages with holy water," said Adariel. "I didn't feel any kind of reaction and I don't think Raphael did, either."

"No itching or hives, no watery eyes, no difficulty breathing," she said, still writing.

"Nothing. And the holy water didn't seem to attack the surface, either. I was sort of frightened that it might dissolve the wrapping?"

"I would be, too," she said, underlining something and shoving the notebook back into her handbag. She had a *lot* to think about. "But it is fantastic to know that isn't a problem. Thank you very much for calling me, Adariel; this is all extremely useful information—"

"I—um. I know you're very busy but I was wondering if you could tell me what to do for Raphael," he said in a rush. "He really doesn't seem to be feeling well at all after Gabriel's lecture, and I've given him ginger and nectar but it didn't help, and I don't want to keep bothering Dr. Faust for advice—"

"Yes, of course," she said, focused again. "Unwell how?"

"He was dreadfully sick after Gabriel left," said the angel. "I think he was feeling dizzy? He was sort of hanging on to the desk with his eyes squeezed shut, and then as soon as Gabriel was gone, he just sort of collapsed and was sick all over the floor and *went on* being sick even when he didn't have anything left to be sick with. Do angels do that? I don't think I've seen one do that before."

"I certainly haven't," said Greta, frowning. "I've never seen an angel so much as hiccup other than during the attack on

Heaven and the immediate aftermath, but as I mentioned my experience is limited. Was he feeling ill before Gabriel arrived, do you know?"

"Maybe," Adariel admitted. "I know he didn't get any sleep. He didn't say anything about feeling sick, but he looked awfully pale—but it got a lot worse once Gabriel started lecturing?"

Greta narrowed her eyes. "Did *you* feel any different while Gabriel was there?"

"I—" he began and then stopped, apparently thinking. "I don't know. I was—upset, I suppose, and worried, and Gabriel really is very *good* at lecturing and you feel about six inches tall when he looks at you and...well, maybe I did feel a little peculiar."

She filed that one away. "Well," she said. "I expect Raphael will be quite all right after some rest and fluids, but if he's feeling really awful, you can go into the stores Faust sent and see if there's any dimenhydrinate pills." She spelled it for him. "Might be labeled for motion sickness; I've no idea how Hell's pharmaceuticals are packaged." She didn't think Gabriel needed to know about this particular instance of infernal medicament—and anyway, Adariel *had* already tried the first-line remedy without effect. Nor did she think Faust was likely to have sent up any prochlorperazine or ondansetron, but if *she* were supplying a clinic with truly basic pharmacopoeia, she'd definitely have included the common antihistamine antiemetics.

It would be fascinating, she thought, to know to what

145

extent angels were subject to bodily infirmity, how much of their lack of overt weakness was entirely show, and how much of their general state of health was influenced by the sheer power of suggestion. For the first time she found herself honestly wanting to get a firsthand look at Heaven's infirmary and chat with its medical director; for the first time she was actively looking forward to spending some significant amount of time in an angel's company and asking them a great many very curious questions.

"Di-men-hy-drinate," Adariel repeated half to himself, the way one does when writing something down. "Thank you, Doctor. Um. I appreciate your time. We're supposed to meet at the airport?"

"That's right," she said, trying to remember Heathrow Five's layout. "Sir Francis and I will be there early to watch out for you. The packet from External Affairs says they're going to bring Orlax up to meet us, and presumably your people have been instructed to bring you down?"

"Um. I think I was given a picture of a building to translocate myself to?"

Oh, for crying out loud, Greta thought. "I'll have a word with my contacts in Hell; I'm sure someone can come and fetch you and make sure you and your luggage get there safely. Has anyone given you our pictures so you know who to look for?"

"No," the angel admitted. "I was going to ask about that but then this... business with Gabriel and our treatment of the inhalation patient came up and—"

"Quite," said Greta. "Well, I can email you some bad but useful photographs and a map of the airport, if you like. You're *adariel at heaven dot he*, right?"

"Adariel-five-two-four-seven," he said. "I'm not sure what the numbers mean. I was given the address when I went through orientation?"

"I see," she said, writing it down, her voice carefully even and without expression. "Well. I'll send you those pictures. Go ahead and give Raphael a dose of dimenhydrinate, and if he's not feeling any better in an hour or so, ring me back?" There wasn't necessarily a lot she could *do* for the archangel from down here, but she knew from experience that being given instructions was helpful at least for Adariel's peace of mind.

"I will," he said, sounding deeply relieved. "Thank you, Doctor."

"Of course," she said. "And please don't hesitate to call or email if you have any other questions or concerns. I look forward to working with you, Adariel."

"You do? —Um. I mean. Thank you?"

"You're very welcome," said Greta, and hung up the phone.

Hell

Fastitocalon was finishing up his evening rounds of the M&E offices, a thing his predecessor, Asmodeus, had never bothered with. A few of the longer-lived employees grumbled about it when he'd started up with the practice, but most of the people who missed Asmodeus's hands-off management style had self-selected out of M&E after the reset. Most of Fastitocalon's employees, in fact, got an obscure sort of comfort out of the sight of the tall thin figure threading its way through the cubes, past the individual offices, pausing to chat briefly with someone here and there. As long as Fass was on the job, things couldn't go too badly wrong, was the general unspoken consensus.

The fact that he knew the *names* of everyone who worked for him, from the most junior of the cleaning staff to the chief of information technology, did not surprise anyone who'd known Fastitocalon in any of his previous roles. The fact that he knew not only their names and titles but also what they were working on was a little more unnerving, given the fact that M&E employed over a thousand analysts. His promotion from ex–disgraced accountant to archdemon had been seen by many as high-handed on the part of the Devil, at least until they had need of M&E's services and discovered that the famously dysfunctional department not only now functioned but approached *efficiency*.

Approached being the appropriate word, Fastitocalon thought as he eyed their latest innovation without a great deal of love, leaning against the doorframe of the dedicated server room that housed the surface-monitoring essographic compilation system. On paper it was a great idea—a combined computer-aided analysis of all the individual surface-monitoring essograph stations in a particular location, functioning as a backup to the surface operatives' daily reports—but in practice the damned thing worked about half the time and spent much of the rest either frozen or truculently refusing to disgorge useful analytic parameters.

They'd come up with it after the events leading up to the reset, to ensure that never again would Hell lack vital information about the state of reality due to any one individual operative's failure to do their job. The ECS was designed to receive real-time feeds from all the essographs in a city—in this case, Paris—and not only combine them into one easily-read output format but conduct analysis on observed trends that would theoretically act as an early-warning system for any instability in the fabric of the universe. Paris had been chosen as the location for the prototype ECS because it had been the Paris surface operative who had so comprehensively failed to report the repeated interference patterns that had destabilized reality to the point where Fastitocalon had had to expend a great deal of energy welding it back together—energy he hadn't had to lose. That ex-operative was now working in a bakery on Plutus Boulevard making quite excellent croissants, and Paris was currently being watched over by a much more efficient individual who submitted their daily reports on time *and* correctly spelled, much to Fastitocalon's quiet satisfaction.

At the moment the ECS terminal screen was in sleep mode; if Fastitocalon wanted to wake it up, he could request a report on activity in Paris over the past seven days and compare it to the surface operative's individual reports, but at the moment his desire to do so was nil. He was more interested in what the hell was going on in London; he'd give a lot to have an ECS set up for *that* particular location, so that the fact that his surface operative was still in Erebus General didn't mean he was without eyes and ears in the ancient city. It didn't come as a great deal of comfort that the angel Haliel was apparently quite recovered from his own dart wound and presumably back at work keeping an eye on London; Fastitocalon had absolutely no illusions regarding the intrinsic value of angelic data-gathering, even if Gabriel would *let* the angel pass on information without vetting it first.

Everything appeared to be in order; he hadn't turned up any issues on his rounds that needed his personal attention. Those of his people who were working the overnight shift were quietly settled in with coffee and pastries, equipped with paper and pens and printer cartridges and anything a well-appointed analyst's cube could possibly require. The ECS computers were quiescent, without a single blinking red light to complain of some malfunction. *Ten o'clock and all's well*, he thought, smiling to himself.

He closed the door to the ECS server room, which was kept cold by the same mechanics that chilled the seventeen cold hells, and returned to the comfortable clutter of his office. The mental image of Gabriel, this morning, white with fury— even the rims of his *nostrils* had been white—returned despite Fastitocalon's attempts to push it away: of course he'd known the archangel wouldn't take kindly to his people using Hell's medical technology, but the *extent* to which it had bothered him was in Fastitocalon's opinion excessive, especially since it sounded to him as if the equipment and supplies had been very obviously needed.

He lit a cigarette. Gabriel had looked infuriated, the new angel—Adariel—had looked terrified, and Raphael had appeared frankly unwell. He wondered what was going on up there, and what, if anything, JHVH thought of the current situation.

Fastitocalon was so very *glad* he'd Fallen, what with one thing and another. He woke up his computer and had a look through the emails that had accumulated over the past couple of hours: nothing from Faust, nothing that needed his immediate attention. There was the official notice from Personnel that Orlax's internship with M&E had been terminated and a group of potential new interns was being gathered for Fastitocalon's review; there were five meeting requests, two of which he could dismiss out of hand and the other three could wait until morning. For once nothing was on fire that wasn't *supposed* to be—

His phone rang. He crushed out the cigarette butt and picked it up; the screen said SAM. "Fastitocalon," he said. "What's on your mind, my lord?"

"Lose the 'lord,'" said the Devil. "Are you tremendously busy about my affairs?"

"Not at the moment," he said. "Why?"

"Come up for a drink." The voice was amber-golden, warm and pleasant, as unlike the ice-edged marble of this morning as could be imagined, and yet recognizably *the same*. Samael's ability to turn into whatever version of himself was most appropriate to a situation was unequaled by any creature in Fastitocalon's acquaintance other than the octopus. "I'm bored," Samael added on a faintly plaintive note.

"That I can't allow," he said, "I'm on my way," and shut down the computer, hooked his jacket from the back of his chair, and locked the office door behind him.

There were always people out and about in the towers, no matter what time it was; M&E and the hospital weren't the only divisions with overnight shifts. Still, Fastitocalon only passed a few demons on his way to the glass elevators, and no one at all was in sight on Samael's office floor. It was both delightful and slightly eerie to see the place *so* empty of demons bustling about; apparently Samael's civil service was running efficiently enough to prevent issues from becoming crises of the sort that involved actual work at odd hours.

Samael himself was still in the white linen he'd worn that morning, standing at the floor-to-ceiling windows of his vast office, glass in hand. He turned when Fastitocalon came in, and smiled: the real smile, not the press-conference version most people would recognize. "Fass," he said. "All quiet on the earthly front?"

"So far," said Fastitocalon, helping himself to whiskey and joining the Devil at the windows. "Even the machine seems to be blamelessly asleep. No unexpected incursions to report."

"Good," said Samael. "Did anything about that conference call this morning strike you as odd?"

Fastitocalon eyebrowed him. "You mean the bit where Gabriel clearly wanted to say *Bother the gosh-darned Accords, adhering to them does not make me a happy little archangel* or words to that effect, or the bit where the Archangel Raphael looked as if he was about to either faint, be sick, or possibly both?"

"Or the bit where the baby angel was clearly scared out of his tiny little mind but tried to be helpful nonetheless," said Samael, and snickered. "Poor baby angel. Do you *remember* Gabriel being that—I can't select the appropriate word, I'm afraid; there are so many."

"I could recommend *bitchy*," said Fastitocalon. "*Snippy* doesn't really convey the depth of his feeling. *Incensed* might be closer."

"Are archangels supposed to be incensed?" Samael sipped his drink. "Except in the fumigation sense, of course."

"Of course," Fastitocalon echoed. "No, I don't honestly believe they are. I wonder how that sort of thing squares with the Lord their God."

"Far be it from me to speculate on the feelings of the Almighty," said Samael, demure. "It's a little odd, though. I do wish we had an unbiased viewpoint on whatever's going on up there."

"So do I," said Fastitocalon. "Ordinarily I'd have one of my surface ops talk to their divine counterpart and ask some questions, but I don't think at the moment any of *their* surface ops are going to be cleared to tell us anything they don't absolutely have to. I thought we were supposed to be doing the whole *glasnost-and-perestroika* bit post-reset, and honestly I think it might be *worse* now than before the war in Heaven."

"So do I," said Samael, sipping whiskey. "So do I."

Brighton Beach, New York City

Gideon Tremayne watched the coffee mug circle slowly in the microwave, hypnotic in its rhythm, intrinsically *ordinary* and without paranormal significance.

He liked paranormal significance, normally. Paranormal significance, if it was of the correct and respectable type, was just fine with Gideon. He was more than happy to believe with his whole heart that his visions and his dreams were genuinely touched by God, that he had been given the vast and ineffable gift of communing with the divine, and that he was following its instructions to the best of his ability.

The mug stopped its measured dance as the microwave beeped for his attention: *I have done your bidding and made thermodynamics happen.* Gideon took his coffee out and fetched a container of nondairy creamer labeled HONEY FLAVOR from the fridge. It didn't taste a lot like honey, to his personal experience, but then again the mug said WORLD'S BEST GRANDMA! on it, so maybe he didn't have to worry too much about accuracy in labeling.

There was sugar in the HONEY FLAVORed creamer, but after a sip Gideon lost a brief argument with himself and added the contents of a single-serve sugar packet to the mug. People were supposed to have sweet things after they'd experienced a shock, weren't they? He was sure he'd read that somewhere.

And it had *been* a shock. He held out a hand and peered at it: yes, he was still trembling a bit, his heart beating too fast. First the physical shock of *assault*: hard, cold hands out of nowhere, hands as yielding and gentle as steel cuffs, slamming him up against the wall of the alley behind his apartment with enough force to send sparks across his vision, shove air out of his lungs—and then the *secondary* shock that had come with the realization that the creature who had him in its grasp was very much not an *ordinary* sort of mugger. It had still been fairly dim even with the sun above the horizon; the sky was solid grey with cloud from rim to rim, and in that dimness Gideon had seen the red glow of the creature's eyes sunk in deep pits. The glowing eyes and the stink of it, musty-mildew and a lower, sweeter reek like meat going over, had told him quite clearly that he was in the grip of something unspeakable: one of the things he had sworn to drive out of the mortal city, one of the things that should not be, that were sin and stain and filth and wickedness.

Gideon sat down on his futon, absently shifting sideways to avoid the most egregious of the mattress lumps, and wrapped both hands around WORLD'S BEST GRANDMA. His hair was still slightly damp from the shower—he'd stayed under the hot water until there absolutely wasn't any left, and he still felt *sullied*, unclean—and the apartment seemed colder than usual. He didn't want to lose any of the heat the microwave had lent his coffee. He didn't want to go out on his usual daily rounds today, either; he wanted to crawl into bed and pull the covers over his head and maybe try to sleep a little—but he was pretty sure that the thing with the red eyes would find its way quite easily into his dreams. He'd had his people, his *children*, the street preachers, tasked with finding such things and putting an end to them to cleanse the city of evil, but until now Gideon had not actually seen one close-up himself, or smelled one, and despite himself he had known fear.

The fact that it sounded like a person—like a New Yorker, in fact—should have been absurd, laughable, but it had somehow made the whole encounter *more* unsettling. When he'd taken the first step into the strange, exciting, dangerous world he was beginning to explore, he had expected the monsters to be…well, *traditional*. To speak in foreign accents and wear capes, or at least something more sinister than ordinary dark well-cut outerwear. This one had sounded not exactly ordinary, but if Gideon hadn't *seen* those glowing eyes, he could have easily mistaken it for any middle-aged Italian-American man. Possibly one you didn't want to cross, but just a man for all that, and instead it had had *teeth* that should have been funny and very much were *not*…

"Gideon Tremayne," it had said. "*Brother* Gideon, I presume. I got some questions for you," and while it had let go of him with that steel-cuff grip, and while Coney Island Avenue was maybe twenty feet away, busy now with the morning's traffic, Gideon had been entirely sure that trying to get away from this creature was both impossible and a *really* bad idea. And then it did something with those red-glowing eyes, something Gideon couldn't quite remember clearly, and after that the sequence of events got a little hazy.

The next thing he *could* very clearly remember was standing at his front door, keys in hand, at the top of the poky little staircase, and letting himself into the apartment. By the clock on the microwave he'd lost something like half an hour that he simply could not recall in detail, only that it had been lit with red eyes and they had talked about very important things and he had been told what it was he must do; *that* part he remembered, at least. He needed to go out, to talk to his people, to pass on the instructions he had been given, and he needed to do it before they went out tonight. Because if one of them made a mistake on this, Gideon was not sure what the creature would do, but he knew for a fact he did not want to find out.

I don't have a problem with your people taking down these motherfuckers, it had said. *Hell, you're doing me a favor getting rid of 'em. I'll even help you do it. But there's some ground rules you gotta follow, in return for my help, and one of them is that you stay the fuck outta my way. You understand?*

Gideon had nodded. That much was clear.

Good. How this works is simple. You stop your *people shooting* my *people with fucking poison darts, we won't have a problem, everybody gets along. Your guys drop anyone on my payroll, or you get involved in my social event–planning process, what do we have?*

A problem?

Right with Eversharp. So you're gonna wait for my guy to get you the list of names and places, and your people can go tidy up the city for us, and my big shiny party will go off without a hitch, and everything'll be just…peachy…keen. Yes?

Yes, he had said, fervently. *Yes, of course. I understand.*

Now, still trembling as he sat on the edge of his futon,

wondering if the pink marks on his shoulders where the creature had slammed him against the alley wall were blooming into bruises, it was still true: he did understand. Very well.

Gideon just wasn't sure what to *do*, exactly. Not without putting his soul, and more importantly his people's souls, at risk. When he'd begun this quest, this crusade, he'd been *sure* of himself and his righteousness. He was still fairly sure of that part. It was the bit where he and the creature with the red eyes were now at least sort of *on the same side* that was giving him mental vertigo.

He tried another sip of the coffee and made a face, putting down the mug. Waste was sinful, but he wasn't completely sure he could stomach any more of that cloying sweetness.

He had to talk to God.

All at once, and very urgently, he had to talk to God.

It wasn't his usual time for prayer, but maybe God wouldn't mind, and Gideon needed it badly: needed the comfort and reassurance of his God's presence, needed to feel clean again, freed from the sullying influence of the creature in the alley in a way that scrubbing himself in the shower hadn't begun to touch. Needed the guidance of his God's word, like a bellows blowing the guttering flame of his certainty, his true belief, his determination, back to its white-hot glow.

Gideon slipped to his knees, eyes closing, his hands folded before him, and reached for the quiet echoing space within himself where that still small voice had always been found before. He refused to let himself entertain conjecture that the touch of the creature could have defiled him sufficiently to make this communion impossible, because if *that* were true—no, he couldn't think about it, because despair was a sin as well—*the spiritual state of unbelief is desperation*, he'd read somewhere, and it had been true then as it was true now...

Our Father who art in heaven, he began inside his own head, lips moving silently, and by the time he had reached *for thine is the kingdom and the power and the glory, for ever and ever*, he knew he was no longer alone, in his mind or in his heart: beyond any doubt, his God was with him.

North Kensington, London

The angel Haliel had been assigned to London for long enough that he had moved several times in order to maintain the polite fiction that he wasn't an angel at all. He'd rather enjoyed living in Covent Garden because it was handy for the theater; his current flat in Portman Square was considerably nicer, if more of a walk from the nearest tube.

It was raining a little as he climbed the steps of the Kensal Green station, and he turned the collar of his overcoat up, wishing briefly he'd dared to wear the hat that really went with it. He *liked* the hat, especially when he had the coat collar up and the belt tied tight and his hands shoved into the pockets. Wearing the hat made him feel as if he ought to be smoking a cigarette, or at least be the sort of person who might have a packet of cigarettes and a lighter about himself in case he decided that he wanted one.

(Haliel had tried cigarettes, and decided after nearly making himself sick several times that they were probably wicked and therefore insalubrious for angels to partake of, but sometimes he very nearly *envied* people who weren't intrinsically holy and could have vices.)

He hadn't quite had the nerve to wear the hat, and so he just hunched his shoulders against the chill of the rain and hurried, head down, like any other person with places to be on a night like this, across the road and into the gateway of the West London Crematorium. Past the glow of the streetlamps into the darkness of the Kensal Green cemetery proper, the locked gate opened at his touch and closed behind him without protest. This entry led to the cemetery's Anglican chapel, familiar to Haliel as any of his other essograph emplacements, but tonight he did not so much glance at the dark shape of the chapel building as he hurried past it, past avenues of little houses of the dead, past weeping trees and lichen-crusted gravestones, toward the much smaller structure at the far end of the cemetery. The rain intensified as he walked, trickling down his neck, and he wished again that he'd had the nerve to wear the hat.

There it was: the Dissenters' Chapel, a low neoclassical building with two curving colonnaded wings, one on each side, looking both forbidding and slightly dangerous in the yellow-orange light from the streetlamps beyond it. A shiver touched the base of his spine at the awareness that he *should not be here* after dark: unlike the Anglican chapel, this was not one of his places, consecration notwithstanding. It wasn't one of *his* places, it was one of *Harlach's*, and that meant Haliel definitely should *not* be here when it was nominally closed to the public.

He smiled, aware of how wrong it was to be smiling, and felt a little flicker of excitement follow the raindrops down the back of his neck.

Haliel's own essograph emplacements were fine; he'd checked them earlier today, as he always did. Here, in Kensal Green; Westminster Hall; St. Paul's; the Tower; and St. Peter and St. Paul at Greenwich, all neatly recorded with his fountain pen in the notebook he always carried with him; he would pull the week's worth of esso traces tomorrow and have a closer look, but none of the essographs had shown anything remarkable for that day's recording. Which was *probably* also the case for Harlach's essographs, if they were still running without his regular monitoring.

Probably hadn't quite been good enough. Earlier this evening, sitting at home with a mug of tea, Haliel had started to wonder: what if demons' essographs picked up things his own couldn't, and vice versa? What if Harlach's emplacements were recording something Hell ought to know about? And then, hard on the heels of that particular question, *what if I could read his just as well as mine, while he's out sick?* It would save time and effort, and it'd be just the sort of thing to hold up as an example of fulfilling the Accords. And maybe—he wasn't sure of this, but maybe—Heaven ought to know about things Hell was interested in.

And if it turned out he couldn't read Harlach's machines, if the demonic essographs were somehow unreadable to angel eyes, or gave him a painful shock or something, well, that would be useful information, too. Wouldn't it?

The chapel's door opened for Haliel the way the locked gates had done, sweetly and easily, and he passed through into the main chamber. To human eyes it would have been nearly impenetrably dark, but he could clearly make out the little door to the left of the pulpit that led to the crypt below the chapel.

Haliel crept down the narrow stone stairs, moving with surety in the darkness, his eyes glowing faintly golden, unlike the dim scarlet of a demon's eyeshine. Nor did he need to search for the essograph; Harlach had mentioned where it was, he thought he could remember that conversation, but he could *feel* the machine's weight on reality perfectly well without being told. It was in one of the farthest loculi, the little stone apartments meant to accept a single coffin, along the far wall of the crypt, and to his vision it was in fact glowing very faintly red.

He approached it carefully, not sure whether to expect a warning spark or some other indication that this was a demon's machine and did not welcome angelic interference, but nothing happened. It looked exactly like the essographs he used, the same metal cover over the active guts of the machine, the same little window showing the black ink-trace on the red graph-paper drum. Very cautiously Haliel reached out to lift the cover off and examine the day's trace more closely, and could not help feeling a faint sense of letdown when this produced not so much as a flicker of static.

Well, he thought, *that answers several questions*, and took out his notebook and pen to write down the day's readings and the essograph's coordinates. No, nothing seemed to be happening that Hell's machines could pick up but his own could not; yes, he could read a Dis-built machine; no, it didn't appear to mind him doing so. He put the cover back on and tucked his notebook away in his messenger bag, and was about to leave the machine in peace when a sound in the chapel above made him freeze, eyes wide.

Two voices, the sound carrying clearly through the barred gap in the chapel floor through which coffins would have been lowered when this crypt was in active use. Young, by the sound of it. One high-pitched, breathless with excitement, female; the other trying not to be quite so excited, deeper in tone, probably male. Haliel stayed where he was, listening hard, and belatedly shut his eyes tight in order to cut off the dim golden glow. He doubted they could see the light from where they were, but a light where no light should be was exactly the sort of thing that people felt they had to investigate.

"—never tried sneaking in here before," the girl was saying. She sounded human enough, but there was a definite smell not unlike wet dog permeating the air of the crypt that Haliel thought he could recognize. "Luz always said not to, said we'd get in trouble, but I don't see anyone hanging around. Just smells like church." There was a soft glassy *ching* sound and a slosh of liquid, and Haliel could hear swallowing. "There supposed to be a big bad watching over all the cool graveyards, or what?"

The bottle changed hands, followed by the unmistakable snap of a match, and then a bout of coughing; Haliel could clearly smell what they were smoking even over the damp-werewolf reek, and it wasn't cigarettes. "Shhhh, fuck," said the male voice. "Keep it *down*," and that apparently struck both of them as hilariously funny. "Supposed to be some old vampire who's been here for forever," he added. "Nobody's seen him or heard of him for a while, maybe he's fucked off back to Transylvania. Who cares?"

"Not me," said the girl, and took another pull at whatever they were drinking, and shortly afterward Haliel found himself wishing very *much* that he could translocate himself out of the crypt without the collapsing air making a sound that even intoxicated youthful werewolves wouldn't be able to ignore.

Heaven

There was no nighttime in Heaven, exactly; there were prayers to be said at certain times, and some of those were *evening* and some were *morning* prayers, and the crystal bells should be rung, and the various ranks of angels would sing their endless praises as prescribed, but it never exactly got *dark*.

Gabriel, sitting at his white desk in his white office (he and Samael might disagree utterly on most things, but they were of one mind regarding the appropriate color for office furniture), caught himself feeling as if it ought to. As if he should be able to look up from this desk, from the pool of lambence cast by the white-shaded lamp, and find the windows turned to dark mirrors, see himself reflected *alone* with the heavy weight of his duty—

No. That was a bad sort of thought to have; angels weren't good at thinking at the best of times and Gabriel had never made much of a point of it. Nevertheless his wings shivered, once, hard, the pinions rattling together like a peacock's display.

There was so much to do. There was always so much to do, and that was right and proper, and Gabriel had been hard at work all day, and *that* was right and proper, too. And if he had spent some time with his office door shut, not entirely *present* all the way, focusing on something else—anyone looking in would have been able to see through him like an angel made of gauze—well, that was right and proper, too. He was the Archangel Gabriel, and what he did was right and proper because he was the Archangel Gabriel, and there was an end of it. When he was angry, he had good reason to be.

(He had been righteously angry at Raphael, who had defied his direct orders, and never mind what meddling nonsense Satan and his hangers-on had to say about the Accords—)

(—no, he did not think about the Accords, not unless he had to. His lovely mouth turned down in a moue of distaste, as if something small and dead had been placed upon his desk.)

But Raphael had *defied* him, and Raphael was actively welcoming into his infirmary *chemicals* and *machines* like the ones the demons used in Hell and the humans used on Earth, as if they needed any such nonsense up in Heaven where everything was white and gold and perfect and very, very *simple*.

He wasn't sure when *simple* had become something to strive for instead of something that just happened all around him, the way it was meant to. He was trying not to be sure, at all, that thinking about Earth, and the problems of Earth, was rapidly becoming simpler than thinking about Heaven and the things about it that were... new. Since the reset. Because things that were new did not have clear answers, and he liked knowing the answers before the questions were asked; it was right and proper that he should. New questions were not *simple*.

Gabriel had never felt quite this way before the universe had changed around him. It wasn't just the crawling sensation of things *not being the way they used to*; that had been bad enough, but now that discomfort was sometimes accompanied by physical distress. The first time it had happened, after the reset, he'd been astonished and a little alarmed at the sensation, and he'd gone to Raphael to see what had gone wrong, why his halo felt so tight, a band around his temples that was *physically uncomfortable*, and Raphael had told him it was a *headache*. That it was possible for his head to ache, for no good reason, when there was nothing whatsoever wrong with him.

It had *offended* Gabriel. And so had Raphael's matter-of-fact approach, with none of the holy dread he felt was indicated by the level of discomfort he was experiencing. *Don't look at bright lights, lie down in a dim room with a cold cloth over your eyes*, as if he were just any angel who had somehow malfunctioned. The fact that it had gone away after he'd—somewhat resentfully—tried adopting Raphael's advice had not gone very far to assuage his feelings.

Now, though. Now he had become *used* to the experience. Especially since he'd begun paying more attention to the foibles of the mortal world. It seemed to him that while being righteously angry at something that was clearly wrong and required adjustment seemed to bring on the headache, expressing that righteous anger *at someone else*, whose fault it very well might be, seemed to soothe it. As if the pain were somehow transferring itself to whoever he was talking to, slipping its way across like smoke on a breeze.

(The other thing that helped was the time he spent not quite being *here*, locked in his quiet white-on-white office, talking to something no one else could see that occasionally asked him questions of the sort Gabriel knew he *could* answer. Was *sure* of the answers. That surety felt like—oh, like the crystal chimes, ringing on and on, pure and aching sweet and clear inside all the hollows of his bones. He knew the answers, and therefore when the questions were asked, the questions themselves were correct, and right, and just. In a Heaven that sometimes now felt to him almost as alien as the *other* Heaven from which the endless boiling army of hostile angels had erupted, Gabriel had found that being asked the right questions by something that wanted the right answers, that *believed* in him unquestioningly and wholeheartedly, was very simply a balm. Even if he had to think about them rather more than was his wont, and even if he had to do a bit more complex mental footwork to justify those answers, it was a balm.)

167

Gabriel rose from his desk, settling his wings, painless and serene. *He* was correct; the guidance he had given to the asker of questions was both righteous and true, and *that* was correct, and its correctness settled into him as smooth and as soothing as milk flowing over marble. The little moue of distaste on his face had been replaced with an expression of such utter peace he appeared to be faintly lit from within: an archangel entirely sure of what and who and where he was, who simply never had to entertain conjecture of questions such as *why*.

CHAPTER 7

Carlyle Hotel, New York City

Greta Helsing lay flat on her back on the hotel bed, feeling the anesthetic of being managed by other people ebbing slowly away and wishing she felt energetic enough to get up and do anything other than investigating room service. Varney had disappeared into the shower as soon as they'd arrived, with the air of a cat wishing to clean itself, and while Greta also felt thoroughly grubby after the eight-hour flight, she couldn't really dredge up the willpower to care very much.

It was the first time she'd ever been to New York, and she felt the niggling edges of awareness that she ought to be taking advantage of their extremely limited time in the city. According to the schedule External Affairs had provided, they were supposed to meet up with the people handling logistics the next day and finish any last-minute shopping in preparation to board their luxuriously (and possibly magically, she wasn't sure) appointed bus the following morning, and trundle off to start the job of conducting research into infernocelestial working groups, with no appreciable pause for NYC sightseeing.

Greta was not quite the sort of person who cringed at the very thought of sightseeing; she rather *wanted* a look at all the New York landmarks, if it could be done without wearing glow-white sneakers and a fanny pack and following a tour guide with a group number on a stick. It seemed a little unfair to have parked them here and not even allowed time for a quick jaunt round the Metropolitan Museum of Art, which was just a few blocks away in Central Park, as Greta knew perfectly well; she'd sent Grisaille and Cranswell off to case said museum the year before from this very hotel. *At least they got to have a look at some pretty things before having to commit major antiquities theft*, she thought sourly. Of course they'd then encountered the late Leonora Van Dorne and her own priceless collection of antiquities, who'd thrown a Middle Kingdom wrench into their plans.

After Van Dorne's mysterious disappearance Greta didn't know what had been done with the woman's collection— whether it had been broken up and returned to the museums where it ought to have been in the first place, or disappeared into the underworld entirely to grace individual collectors' crypts. She couldn't quite hide a smile, thinking of some of her own pieces at home in Dark Heart which the curators at the Met would have salivated over, wedding-gifts from Greta's mummy friends after the averted apocalypse. It would have been nice to have a look at the Metternich Stela in the museum and remember the second greenstone stela that had once stood next to it, the one that had stopped existing when the world had started itself up again, leaving no trace behind. A great many things about that time had been terrible, but the memory of the god Djehuty stepping out of a haze of ink-strokes in the air, summoned by a mummy priest with the help of the apocryphal second stela, was not one of them.

Greta Helsing, the god had said, the warmth of his stylized hand still shocking—like sun-heated stone—against her chest, *your heart does not rise up against you as a witness, nor does it make opposition against you in the presence of the keeper of the balance.* Back then she'd rather badly needed to hear it.

She sighed and sat up, pushing back her hair. At least at the moment she didn't have to hope for godly assistance in figuring out anything particularly dire; all she had to worry about was the welfare of an angel and a demon. Oh, and six weeks' worth of road-trip logistics that had been preplanned for them by Belial's Office of External Affairs. *Infernal* external affairs, she thought, squashing a desire to snicker.

Quite a long time ago Greta had decided, consciously, not to think too hard about some of the aspects of her life which were particularly unbelievable, since they weren't about to stop being either true *or* unbelievable, and for the most part had been relatively successful in doing so. She looked at her watch, which she had only just managed to remember to adjust when they landed, and reached for the Carlyle's room-service menu. Outside the greyness of late afternoon had turned into a cold blue, and soon it would be full dark.

By the time Varney emerged, neatly combed and swathed in

the snowy-white of the hotel bathrobe—he still looked rather more like an aging rock star than a vampire, shoulder-length hair and all—she had ordered a selection of things designed to tempt uncertain appetites without asking too much courage on behalf of the diner. "Hello, darling," she said. "I'm going to invite the postdocs for an informal bite to eat. I haven't ordered you anything, but the minibar's got some decent single-malt to offer."

"I think I'll go out," he said, coming over to drop a kiss on the top of her head. "You don't *have* to be the gracious hostess, love. You got us all here in one piece, without anyone losing anything important or taking on other forms; I think that's enough superhuman achievement for one day."

Greta smiled, taking his hand and kissing the fingertips. "One feels responsible," she said. "And I've got to work with them for the next several weeks. I might as well try to start things off on a decent note. How's the shower?" She just about had time to wash and change before the food arrived.

"Splendid," said Varney. "Leave the window open for me?"

"Of course," she said, and got up, shrugging out of her jacket. "Have someone nice to eat, darling, and don't stay out too late."

In the end she'd asked Fastitocalon for his help in transportation, and she was fairly sure that without it the angel Adariel would not have been able to join their little traveling party without drawing at least minor attention to himself. Fass had gone to lean in Belial's office doorway and drawl at him, which was presumably the means of communication to which Belial most reliably responded, and thus an External Affairs demon had been dispatched to Heaven with neatly packed luggage and a garment bag. Said demon, clutching a handkerchief to her face, had deposited the newly dressed Adariel and suitcase on the Wellington Road pavement outside Terminal Five and promptly disappeared again, muttering things about *other duties as assigned.*

Greta had to give Belial's people credit for attention to detail, though. The newly minted Adam Riel, PhD, looked *exactly* like a somewhat-shabby and very awkward young human male of extraordinary physical beauty (that was sort of impossible to avoid with angels, she'd found), complete with the right sort of battered but good-quality Briggs & Riley luggage, and shoes that showed both wear and careful repair. From what Adariel had told her on the phone, it hadn't been Heaven's version of External Affairs who'd achieved that particular sort of patina, or bothered to trim the golden curls as if they were the result of a decent haircut grown several months out; all Heaven had been willing to do was give Adariel a picture of Terminal Five to use as a translocation anchor.

(Orlax, whose human name—"J. O'Lack"—was considerably less successful, had managed his own transportation. External Affairs had supplied him with a beat-up black Samsonite hard-shell case covered in band stickers, and either he or they had selected a corresponding wardrobe of black jeans, boots, and sweaters that stopped just short of actual frayed holes. *His* hair fell carefully over one eye and smelled strongly of the sort of product Ruthven deplored in the young undead community, but at least he had left off the eyeliner and facial piercings Greta was fairly sure he affected in everyday life, and his eyes appeared to be a reasonably human shade of brown, the pupils unremarkable. He had acknowledged Greta and Varney with a brief handshake and retreated into monosyllables, staring at his phone, and she had thought briefly and miserably *Six weeks of this, on a goddamned bus?* before marshaling her businesslike pleasant mood back into place.)

There were several very good reasons why Greta Helsing was never, ever going to have children, and by the time she'd gotten the little party through check-in, through security, and down several levels to the walkway leading to the B gates, any last remaining hesitation in the matter was driven completely out of her mind. Adariel wasn't *difficult* to manage, exactly, but he was broadcasting a kind of helpless, confused desire to please that Greta could watch having its exact opposite effect on the demon, and had to squash her own instinctive desire to snap at the angel not to be so *wet*. There wasn't an easy way to ask Orlax to be nice to him, and she could clearly see that Orlax knew it, and it made her want to give him a smack, and all in all she was more than glad to see the sign for the British Airways first-class lounge in 5B with its full bar facilities. She'd never flown anything other than bare-bones economy before, and there was a certain exhausted sort of glee in being allowed to use the rich-people bits of the airport, particularly when she so bloody well deserved it.

Things got a little easier once Varney absently but lavishly tipped the staff—he came by the air of a very rich person not *trying* to point out how much money he had quite honestly— and in fact the rest of their journey was conducted with obsequious care on the part of British Airways, which left Greta some mental space to try to reassure the angel that everything was going to be all right. She was particularly grateful to Varney for silently volunteering to sit beside Orlax while she and Adariel took the other two seats across the aisle, and very consciously decided not to mention it when she noticed Orlax unsubtly charming the flight attendant into bringing him several more rum-and-Cokes than she thought he strictly needed.

The angel had told her a bit more about working for Raphael, but not much by way of detail, and she'd been able to reassure him regarding the prognosis for their inhalation-injury patient. Nithael had been so much better by the time Adariel had had to leave: he'd been off the oxygen entirely, able to breathe without assistance, and he'd regained enough strength to start asking when he could leave the infirmary because he wanted to get back to work. The change was nothing short of miraculous, according to the angel, and Greta had told him that as long as Nithael was careful and stayed far away from anything that was likely to cause irritation in his air passages, and rested properly and had all the ambrosia and nectar he needed, that he was very unlikely to relapse. And that Raphael had done exactly what was needed for him. That she'd have done just the same had she been the physician on duty. That seemed to comfort him more than anything else she'd said, which was perhaps a bit strange, but Greta was just glad he seemed happier about things after they'd talked it over.

Adariel had fallen asleep somewhere south of Iceland, and she'd been afraid of that, in case he lost the tight control over his seeming and manifested a halo and enormous snowy wings; even in first class that would probably attract attention. He didn't seem to have a problem with it, though, merely shifting fitfully from time to time and whimpering something she couldn't quite make out. That he was worried about his superior angel was obvious; that he wasn't sure he was either supposed or allowed to be worried, especially in front of *mortals*, was just as clear, and despite her tiredness and general inclination to snap, Greta couldn't help feeling sorry for him: he was by all methods of accounting so very *young*.

(It wasn't his fault, of course, that they ran into turbulence coming in over Newfoundland, and he certainly wasn't the only passenger to experience *distress* due to the rough air. She was just glad she'd bothered to check the seat-back pockets for sick bags before they became necessary, and deeply appreciated the flight attendant's patient and sympathetic assistance in tidying up afterward, as well as her own foresight in tucking some scopolamine patches into a pocket of her enormous handbag. By the time they came in to land, the angel's physical misery had been replaced with simple embarrassment, which was a different kind of difficult to manage.)

She was out of the shower and properly dressed when the room-service waiter arrived. Belial's people had given her an envelope containing a truly ridiculous amount of cash in dollar form for tipping various people, which had come in handy once already in paying off the taxi from LaGuardia. She signed the room-service slip and handed over another twenty, and tilted her head at the expression on the waiter's face.

"Is there something wrong?" she asked.

"Oh! Um. No. Excuse me, ma'am," said the waiter, and hastily finished setting out dishes—and hesitated. "Um."

"What is it?" She was getting heartily sick of that particular non-word.

"Well," said the waiter, and sighed. "Um. Pardon me, ma'am, but is the gentleman with you...the tall one, with the hair...is he, uh, of alternative vital status?"

She looked at him. Young, neatly groomed, but perhaps slightly longer facial stubble than was strictly expected at this hour of the night on a five-star hotel employee, and the eyes were a yellower shade of brown than was entirely common, plus he was wearing very *nice* white gloves firmly buttoned in place against the brightly polished metal cloche he'd taken off a dish. "He's a vampyre, if that's what you mean," she said, taking pity, and the young were's shoulders slumped a little in what looked like relief.

"Is he, uh. Out to eat?"

"He went out a little while ago; I expect him back in a couple of hours," said Greta. "Why?"

"It's—pardon me, ma'am, but I'm real glad he's a vampyre. That means he's less likely to run into, uh, trouble. And he's probably more *careful* about where he dines?"

"What do you mean, *trouble*," said Greta sharply, but the waiter's walkie-talkie crackled, and he gave her an embarrassed look of apology and wheeled his cart out before saying anything else. She let the door close before grabbing her phone and texting Varney:

Word to the wise, apparently, be careful out there? Ominous but not very specific warning from a were-something on kitchen staff.

There was a pause, then: *What warning exactly?*

Greta reproduced the conversation as closely as she could remember. *He seemed relieved that you're not a classic draculine?*

My palate is indeed of a more discerning nature, Varney replied. *Don't worry, love. I'll be very careful. And keep my ears open in case anyone else says anything interesting and cryptic.*

See that you do, she told him. *Love you. Wish me luck re dinner.*

All the luck, said Varney, and she could so easily imagine the warmth in his voice; she couldn't help smiling even as she texted Orlax and Adariel to invite them over. Yes, okay, the vague warning had been unsettling, but she knew Varney *could* take care of himself, New York or no New York, and right now her responsibility was here.

Orlax had thrown himself on the bed and stared determinedly at his phone as soon as they'd closed the hotel room door behind them, ignoring the angel with every fiber of his being. His expectation of how the next six weeks were going to go—never tremendously high—was at an all-time low after the experience of the flight; he wondered if they were going to have to pull the

stupid bus over every half an hour so the angel could puke. It...
he...had seemed a lot better after the doctor stuck some little
adhesive patches on his neck, but the general air of confused
misery was still coming off him like a smell, and Orlax didn't
do sympathy all that well even at the best of times.

At least so far they didn't seem to be allergic to each other.
He hadn't noticed any itchy or watering eyes, no sneezing or
congestion, and from what he'd observed, the angel didn't
seem to be manifesting symptoms either. On the one hand
that was good, and on the other it meant they had to *do* this
stupid research project, since evidently they could.

He had lost three browser games in a row when the doctor
texted them to come get dinner, and looked over at Adariel,
who was sitting unhappily at the hotel room desk reading the
Gideon Bible and not looking the least bit hungry. It wasn't
clear even to Orlax why this should be so damned annoying,
but it was.

"C'mon," he said, getting up. "The doctor wants us. You
can read about begats and things later."

"I know it already," said Adariel. "Um. I mean, not this version. This one's very...Earthly?"

"What version *do* you guys use?" he said faintly, interested
despite himself. "I mean, is the King James the official transla-
tion of Heaven, or what?"

"It's complicated," said the angel, but looked slightly less
miserable. "It's—we don't really have a single one, since it's
all sorts of different bits in different languages, but we *like* the
King James?"

179

"Makes sense," said Orlax, ushering him out into the hall-way. The doctor's room was next door, slightly larger than theirs, and she'd had a whole table set up with plates and cut-lery and everything; there was even a vase of flowers in the middle. Despite himself he was slightly impressed; beside him the angel was staring in awe. "Hey," he said, as noncommit-tally as he could.

The doctor got up, smiling tiredly. "I ordered a few different things, and there's fruit and bread and butter and so on. Do sit down."

He gave Adariel a nudge. "Thanks," he said. "It's cool of you."

"Least I could do," said Dr. Helsing. "Adariel, how are you feeling?"

"Um," said the angel, sitting down. "Not great? But not awful. I think I'm just tired. The...the patch things you gave me really worked. Was that the same medicine you told me to give Raphael?"

"Not quite," she said. "Yours is a bit stronger. I'm glad the other stuff helped him, though."

"Me too," said Adariel, and picked up a bread roll with what Orlax considered excessive trepidation. "I've never seen him like that before. I mean...of course I haven't, I'm new, but—"

"You said it was because of Gabriel's—what, influence? Being near him when he was so angry?"

"I think so? He didn't look well before Gabriel got there but it was very noticeably worse afterward." Now the angel was actually *buttering* the bread.

"Is that a thing that happens often? One angel's mood influencing another's so strongly?"

"Again, I don't really know," said Adariel. "But I do remember being near Raphael when he was doing patient care sort of made me feel calmer, like everything was going to be all right?"

"Fascinating," said the doctor, selecting bits of fruit and cheese from a platter. "I wonder if it works on people. And if demons can do it, too."

"Why?" said Orlax, actually faintly curious.

"Because it might be jolly useful, that's why," said Greta. "If you can project a sort of calming field that affects someone while I'm doing something unpleasant or painful to them, it would be of considerable help. At the moment I've got the option of having Varney thrall them, but that's a lot of effort on his part and can be upsetting to the patient in itself."

"Huh," he said. It did make sense, although he hadn't heard of demons being able to influence people with their fields; maybe it was a thing they didn't do on purpose. He looked over at the angel, who was now consuming the bread carefully, and—before he could think better of it—*thought* calm-serene-happy at him. It felt a little like leaning on something with his mind.

Adariel's eyes went wide and he dropped the bread roll onto his plate, with a faint gasp. Orlax drew back hurriedly.

"Adariel?" said the doctor sharply. "Are you all right?"

"…Yes," he said, blinking in apparent surprise. "I feel better— was that *you*?" He looked at Orlax, pupils slightly dilated.

"Uh," said Orlax. "Maybe? I wanted to see if I could."

"It might be better to ask first," said Dr. Helsing drily. "Adariel, can you describe it?"

"Not really? It's—I just feel *better*, I'm sort of hungry, and I don't ache anywhere now?"

"Huh," she said. "Can you do it to me, Orlax?"

"Maybe," he said, not sure, and half-closed his eyes, feeling the weight of her on reality, and *leaned* again. There was the clatter of a fork falling on a plate, and he opened his eyes to see her sway and clutch at the edge of the table with one hand, eyes unfocused, and thought *oh, fuck, did I break her* before she shook herself back into full consciousness.

"Jesus," she said. "That's—remarkable. I think maybe you can step down the gain a bit when you do it to humans— I wouldn't let me operate heavy machinery for a while—but yes, it works. I don't hurt anywhere, I'm less hideously tired, and I'd bet the worst of the jet lag is probably gone as well."

Adariel was looking at him with wide, very blue eyes. Orlax tried to ignore the expression in them, which was a sort of dawning wonder. "That's amazing," said the angel.

Orlax shrugged. "Didn't know I could," he said. "Cool, I guess."

"Very cool," said the doctor. "I may ask you to do that to people from time to time, if you don't mind."

He shrugged again and picked up a sandwich, took a bite before saying "Sure" with his mouth full. *I wonder if all demons can do that*, he thought, *or if it's just me*, and had a sudden unexpected flicker of memory: a couple of weeks ago he'd been at work, in a foul mood because of a combination of busywork and a nasty headache, and Fastitocalon had come to stick his head into Orlax's cube and asked him some question or other—and then narrowed his eyes at him. Orlax had been about to say *What?* when a sort of wave of calmness had flowed over him, like being touched with a cool hand, and the headache had receded to an ignorable throb. At the time he'd shrugged it off, but Fastitocalon's eyes *had* flickered orange just for a second, hadn't they?

He wondered if his did, too. The orange thing was kind of cool, actually, when he came to think about it. And this sandwich was pretty okay, for Earth food. Maybe this wouldn't be a completely shitty six weeks after all.

Orlax was ignoring Adariel and therefore didn't notice the angel's briefly intent expression before it faded back to his usual vague wonderment, or the split-second glance he and the doctor shared.

Heaven

Raphael had seen off his orderly with firm instructions to listen to the human doctor and do his very best to be helpful, useful, and informative (and to get on with the demon as much as possible), and had spent the rest of the day in a kind of fretful inability to *settle* to anything. Nithael had insisted he was well enough to get up, and after several hours Raphael had let him briefly putter around in the garden, and then been glad when the slight exercise had exhausted the convalescent angel to the point where he drifted off to sleep immediately upon returning to bed.

And then Raphael hadn't been able to settle, again. He had changed all the beds, folded linens, checked on the inventory of ingredients in the dispensary, made some syrups and tidied up the workspace, looked at his blank inbox, and finally gone for a brief walk in the gardens himself... but couldn't shake the feeling that he ought to be back in the infirmary *in case* something went wrong.

When he got back to find an angel waiting for him, looking mildly uncomfortable, Raphael had to work hard at keeping the self-castigation out of his own expression. Then he got a closer look at his patient and blinked.

"Haliel?" he asked. "What brings you here? Not another attack?"

"No, no," said Haliel, waving away the concept of attacks. "Um. It's—well, I'm glad you're here. I—think I have a bit of a sniffle?"

"Come sit down and tell me about it," said Raphael, very grateful to be able to slip back into his usual role. "How long have you been feeling ill?"

Haliel followed him to his office and stifled a sneeze on the threshold. "—'Scuse me. Actually it's—I didn't really know who else to tell, but... I might have, um. Maybe gone to look at one of Harlach's essographs. While he's out sick."

"Did he ask you to?" Raphael said, blinking.

"No. No, not at all. I haven't... actually told him about it yet?"

"Why, then?"

"I was curious?" said Haliel. "I wanted to see if I *could* read an infernal machine. Like, if it'd let me? And I wanted to know if anything had registered on it, in case Hell needed to know. While Harlach's away from his post."

"And did you see anything of note?"

"No," said Haliel. "The machine looked just like mine do, except it glowed a bit red, where mine are gold? And it seemed to work just the same, same rate of recording and amplitude control and so on. I looked at mine in the nearest location earlier that day and didn't see anything there, either." He cleared his throat. "Mostly it was...curiosity, I think?"

"I see," said Raphael, who didn't, really. "So then what?"

"Well," said Haliel. "I was in the chapel where his essograph was located, and I was just about done and ready to leave when...well, when some other people showed up. Young people. Young *not-human* people."

"Not human," repeated Raphael.

"I'm pretty sure they were were-somethings," said Haliel. "Young ones. Luckily they didn't seem to smell me over the general smell of *church*. But—well. I overheard them talking, and they were saying something about—oh, a vampire, a sort of guardian in the city of London who kept an eye on certain places. An old vampire. Someone who frowned on people, especially supernatural people, breaking into these places and, um. Engaging in behavior."

"Behavior?"

"I think they were *drinking alcohol*," said Haliel. "And

consuming illegal drugs? And quite possibly *carnal knowledge* was being had? And they definitely shouldn't have been in there at night. The doors were all locked to stop people getting in." People other than him, of course, Raphael thought.

"I see," he said. "So you heard these young people discussing this vampire guardian, when they weren't too busy with carnal desire?"

"And they said that *no one's heard from him* in a while," said Haliel, and sneezed again, more forcefully. "Excuse me. And that…didn't really sit well with me? That a vampire who's supposed to be keeping an eye on the city *isn't*? It's not like them, Raphael."

Raphael narrowed his eyes. "I'll take your word for it," he said. "And you haven't told Harlach yet?"

"Not yet," he said. "Last time I spoke with him he didn't look at all well and I really don't want to worry him, but— I thought perhaps since *you* sometimes speak with Dr. Faust you might…well, find out if Harlach is well enough to talk? Or, um. If he's not, maybe you could pass on the message and Dr. Faust can decide what to do with it?"

Raphael was faintly aware of a sort of excitement he certainly shouldn't be feeling. "And you came to me, instead of Gabriel, to report this?" It was, after all, exactly the sort of thing Faust *had* asked him to let them know about, but Raphael was still a little surprised.

Haliel nodded, earnestly looking at him, and Raphael could clearly remember the moment when he had decided to visit this angel in person to talk with him. "I see," he said. "Well.

I'll ring up Dr. Faust, yes, and let him know what you've said, and—" Haliel interrupted him with another sneeze, looking embarrassed. "Bless you," said Raphael. "And I'll make you something for that cold. Did you get caught in the rain after looking at demonic essographs?"

"Er," said Haliel, and cleared his throat. "Not exactly. More sort of—inadvertently compelled to remain in a very damp and chilly chapel, against my personal inclination, for some time?"

"I see," said Raphael again. "Well. Some honey-nectar syrup and a nice cup of chamomile tea ought to help, and you can keep me company while I'm making it."

Haliel beamed at him, not entirely unlike the way Adariel had done, and the archangel felt a kind of warmth easing the *unsettled* restlessness that had plagued him all afternoon. "Thank you, sir."

"Not at all," said Raphael. "I probably *ought* to tell Gabriel about this, but—"

"Oh, I don't think it's important enough to disturb him," said Haliel in a hurry. Raphael raised an eyebrow. "I mean...um. He seems to be very busy at the moment, I gather, and I don't have anything real or concrete to report, just a thing I overheard that may mean nothing at all and wasn't for my ears in the first place?"

Because you shouldn't have been there, Raphael thought. "Well," he said, conscious of balancing on a very narrow edge. "When you put it like that. Come with me, we'll get you sorted out, and you must go right home afterward and stay warm properly, all right?"

"Yes, sir," said Haliel, and it really did feel as if the world was ever so subtly *right* in a way it hadn't felt all day.

Sir Francis Varney rather liked cities, when he was in the right mood.

London would always be a bit fraught for him, of course, what with the whole confusing and confused history he shared with that particular metropolis—his brief stints as a hangman *and* as a condemned highwayman didn't help—but New York held no particular horrors for Varney, and he let himself enjoy the evening. It was nice to stretch his wings after the long flight, and while he was not unsympathetic to the postdocs, being as new and wet behind the ears (possibly wet behind the horns and halo, he added to himself) as they were, he'd had *enough* of them for the time being. And he did want to find dinner.

The lunar-sensitive subspecies of sanguivore, as Greta Helsing had so often lectured, was subtly different from the more common classic draculine, so-called due to its members sharing traits with the Voivode Dracula himself. The lunar sensitives, vampyres with a *y*, were extremely and inconveniently sensitive to certain metaphysical aspects of human blood, such as *virginity*, and imbibing the blood of someone who'd passed that particular one-way gate would result in violent, extended sickness on the part of the importunate vampyre. In particularly bad cases it could lead to total prostration and collapse, even fatality, but the other interesting trait of vampyres was their propensity to be brought back to life by the rays of the moon, for a certain value of *life*. You could kill a vampyre with a stake, or with garlic or holy water or the Host or any of the other fairly standard methods used to great effect on the classic draculine, but all the vampyre's friends had to do was drag the body out into moonlight and sit around waiting for a while in order to resurrect them. Bringing a dead vampire back to unlife took a lot longer and involved the application of blood from another full-strength vampire, but vampyres just needed some moonlight and a bit of patience.

Because of the sensitivity of their systems to virgin vs. non-virgin blood (and Greta had very definitely been working on figuring out what the hell actually triggered that reaction, but so far hadn't come up with anything concrete), vampyres were also blessed with a highly specific sense of smell, which meant they rarely made stupid mistakes in terms of whom they chose to bite. It also meant that they were very much aware of *other* sanguivores in their vicinity, much more so than draculines; in fact, a vampyre's nose could make out quite a few types of monster with pretty good accuracy, although nothing on the order of a werewolf's nasal acuity.

Which was why, having had rather a nice time flitting about in Central Park on bat-wings and then making his rounds of the city to find himself a bite to eat, he'd fetched up in a bar somewhere in Hell's Kitchen nursing a glass of single-malt—and now sat straight up, eyes slitting as he sniffed the air. That was…familiar. That was a smell Varney hadn't come across for *centuries*.

Pulling his don't-notice-me fields tighter around himself,

Varney set his glass down and unobtrusively looked over his shoulder. The bar was dark, of course—bars like this were always very dark indeed, and red-lit—but he could see in near pitch-blackness, and it was very easy to make out the high-shouldered form of a creature sitting in the corner of the farthest booth: a creature with even stronger don't-notice-me than Varney himself, with eyes like little cigarette embers in the darkness of its shadowed face.

One of those embers went out, briefly, as the creature winked at him.

Varney had not been *winked at* in longer than he cared to recall, not counting Hell. He thought briefly of Greta's texted warning, and his own response: *I'll be very careful. And keep my ears open in case anyone else says anything interesting and cryptic.*

With that in mind, he made a decision, got up, dropped a couple of twenties on the bar, and sauntered over, glass in hand, to the booth where the creature was sitting. The smell of *nosferatu* was very strong, close-up: a salty sort of mildewed scent he didn't actually mind, and then underneath that a less-pleasant smell of decay, but Varney was used to smells. He'd spent the twentieth century largely asleep in the Dark Heart cellars among the cobwebs and the nitre, after all.

"A pleasant evening to you," he said, raising an eyebrow. The nosferatu nodded at the seat opposite them—*her?* Varney thought; *good heavens, a lady nosferatu?*—and he sat down.

"And what could a nice English vampyre be doing in a dive like this?" she said. She sounded both amused and entirely New York.

"Enjoying myself," he said, raising his glass slightly. "I didn't expect to meet such a rare colleague, though, I must admit."

She laughed, and he could make out the glint of red light on the central incisors, the bunny fangs that marked the sub-species. They ought to look comical, and possibly under other circumstances they might have done, but right now he was conscious of a healthy respect for them. "You *must* be new in town," she said. "We're not so rare anymore, me and my kind. You might say we've experienced a kind of *renaissance* just recently."

"Oh?" said Varney, sipping his drink. To his limited knowledge, the nosferatu subspecies was extremely rare everywhere except Eastern Europe, and even there it wasn't exactly thick on the ground. To find nosferatu in New York like this was— unexpected. "I'm only in town briefly, in passing. Francis Varney, by the way."

"Francis Varney," said the nosferatu, as if tasting the name. She had the slight lisp that came with the fangs; some of them went to more of an effort to hide it. "Now where have I heard that name before?"

"I devoutly hope you have not come across a terrible work of mostly fiction titled *Varney the Vampyre, or The Feast of Blood*," he said drily. "Hardly required reading on the order of Polidori or Stoker or Le Fanu, but—"

The nosferatu did not snap her fingers but rattled the tips of her very, very long nails together, an unsettling little clittering sound. "That's right," she said. "Weren't you part of some London group? Something to do with trans-Atlantic vampire shenanigans last year?"

"I suppose you could say that," he said, uncomfortable. "But I'm not here on any sort of personal business, just passing through to accompany my wife on a research trip."

"Your *wife*," said the nosferatu, with another glint of her fangs. "Does she know you're out on the town talking to strange bloodsuckers?"

"She does," said Varney, looking at her over the rim of his glass, and after a moment the fangs flashed again in laughter; he felt as if he'd passed some sort of obscure test.

"Fair enough," said the nosferatu, and offered him a hand to kiss. "Adriana Cenci. Buy me a drink, Francis Varney, and I might just find it in me to offer some advice about how to stay out of trouble as a bloodsucker in today's bustling and vivacious New York. And even how to have a good time out on the town, if you're so inclined."

"By all means," said Varney, and smiled over her hand.

Carlyle Hotel, New York City

Like many people whose jobs tend to require them to get up at odd hours and snatch sleep where they could, Greta Helsing had developed the knack of waking easily and just as easily sinking back into sleep. When Varney turned back the covers and slid silently into the bed beside her, she woke all at once, without alarm, and wriggled close to him. He was like a whole-body cool spot on the pillow.

"...Didn't mean to wake you," he whispered, but his arm curled around her waist, pulling her close.

"You didn't," she whispered back. "I did. Anything interesting?"

"I suppose you could say that," he said into her hair. "I ran into a nosferatu, of all things, and she told me some fascinating tales of what's been going on around here...I wish we could stay a few days, Greta. There's apparently a new underworld hierarchy in town that's preparing to solidify its control over the city, and I'd frankly love to stick around and watch."

"A new underworld hierarchy," she repeated, now fully awake. "A *nosferatu* hierarchy?"

"My informant didn't specify, but that's the impression I received," said Varney. "Apparently their leader's been here for simply ages, but he was off in hibernation for a century or so and just recently returned to power."

"How recently?" Greta asked, squinting at him in the dimness.

"I believe since the reset, but again, I didn't take detailed notes," he said. "He's back and he's tidying up the place, and that means clearing up some messes on the part of *less* well-organized sanguivores. Has very little patience for nonsense, apparently."

Greta's eyes were still narrowed. "Did you get the impression this person knew anything about the Pittsburgh coven that the Voivode's people got rid of?"

"She mentioned something about trans-Atlantic vampire shenanigans," said Varney. "I made vaguely affirmative noises but didn't offer specifics."

"Mmh," she said, and sighed. "I really *do* wish we were

staying longer. All of that sounds like the kind of thing I'd definitely rather know more than less about, and also possibly like the sort of thing the Voivode should know about if he doesn't already—"

"Based on what we know, he probably *does*," said Varney. "He's got absolute scads of spies all over the place, or at least that's the impression I received last year, and it's also not our business. I'm just curious, that's all. And I'd have loved to be a fly on the wall at this Contini's grand do tomorrow night. The nosferatu I met did very kindly extend an invitation, but I demurred on the strength of having to get up very early to get on our bus and trundle off in search of scientific discovery."

"Contini," Greta repeated, resting her cheek against Varney's chest.

"That's right. Does it mean anything to you?"

"No," she said. "If you really do want to go to the party, I'm sure we can request to stay in town another day—"

"And throw off Göttingen University's carefully prepared schedule for the sake of frivolity?" he said, and laughed; she could feel as well as hear it. "I shudder to think."

"Maybe we can stop in the city on our way back," she said. "Once we've done all the work and sent in all the samples. Have some time here for me to decompress and do touristy things and for you to hang out with nosferatu underworld kingpins." The smile in her voice was audible.

"We can at least ask," said Varney, and nuzzled her hair. "Did anything interesting happen *here* while I was gone?"

"I told you the werewolf waiter offered a somewhat unhelp-
ful warning about things that might be dangerous to you,
right? Presumably that bit's been covered." Greta had been
ever so faintly touched by the waiter's concern. "Oh, and
apparently our Orlax is capable of influencing people's moods
in a way I think is going to be of clinical significance. Adariel
had told me about how his boss got physically sick from being
within the influence of Gabriel's tantrum, and I wondered if
that could work the other way as well—making someone feel
better, not worse—and Orlax sort of hauled off and threw
some influence at Adariel, which apparently cleared up his
lingering airsickness malaise like anything."

"Fascinating," said Varney. "I wonder how much power is
involved?"

"Hard to say, but I told him to try doing it to me, and it was
like thrall, Varney. It was—untrained, uncontrolled, but very
definitely powerful. If he can do that to people while I'm taking their blood or doing minor uncomfortable procedures, I
think we'll all have a much nicer time."

"If he can learn to control it, I'm all for him acting as a sort
of bipedal sedative. Especially if he can calm Adariel down.
How *is* our angel?" Varney asked, absently stroking her hair.
He smelled of cigarette smoke and faintly of whiskey, which
she didn't mind in the least.

"Better now. He wasn't at all happy when they came to dinner, but after the fields of influence thing—I'm going to have
to come up with a better name for it—he did seem to cheer
up quite a lot. We'd talked on the plane: he's anxious not just

about his boss back in Heaven having to do the job without him, which is touching if slightly ridiculous, but also about what to expect during the trip. I think it's partly the unaccustomed awkwardness of being on the Prime Material plane and therefore subject to various experiences, such as motion sickness, that he's never encountered before. He's feeling a bit trapped in his physical form and not sure how it's going to behave, for the first time. On the plus side he's so damn new—less than a year old—that he hasn't had that much time to get used to being in Heaven, either, so I think he'll adjust well enough once the initial shock has passed. And neither he nor the demon seems to be showing any signs of allergic reaction to one another so far."

"That ought to please Dr. Faust," said Varney, and yawned hugely. "Did you send him an update?"

"I think it can wait till morning," Greta said, trying not to yawn as well; it was contagious. She could think about nosferatu underworld hierarchies *tomorrow*. "The day, my friends, and all things stay for me."

"Very appropriate," said Varney into her hair, and she closed her eyes and breathed in his scent, and let herself begin to drift.

Heaven

Raphael was making the beds again, alone in the infirmary with Nithael, who was at the point in his recovery where he was beginning to do the closest thing angels ever got to *complaining*; it was somewhat of a relief to the archangel that his patient was once more asleep. He'd seen Haliel back off down to Earth with a bottle of nectar syrup and some honey lozenges and an instruction to *take an aspirin* if he didn't feel much better by morning, and was still not quite able to shake a sense of letting the side down in some unexamined way. Surely he should have just left it at the syrup and lozenges and some good solid prayer. The fact that he was also fairly sure that the aspirin would help did not, itself, help Raphael.

Nor was he very clear on what he ought to do with the knowledge that Haliel was doing something utterly beyond his remit as Heaven's surface operative and actually *checking Hell's emplacements*. That felt like the sort of thing he ought to go and tell Gabriel, right now, but for a wide variety of reasons Raphael did not want to do so.

He smoothed down another pillow, moving without thought, hands doing their job with the ease of long practice. It was something of an adjustment not having Adariel there to do minor chores like this for him, and he tried not to think about that, either. He shouldn't *mind* in any way having to do the chores himself—

Raphael sighed. There had been a time, not so very long ago, when *should* and *shouldn't* were not anywhere near the top of his mental list of overused words. *Get on with it*, he thought to himself, much more viciously than he'd have said it to Adariel even in the worst of his recent moods. *Adariel is busy doing his work, my patients are much better—everyone but*

197

Nithael is back at their own work—and Haliel is just worried about his friend, that's all, and that's not a bad thing.

And it wasn't as if Haliel had even done anything *terribly* beyond the pale. He and the demon had their essograph emplacements close to one another's for reasons: the machines, which translated to something like *reality-meters*, measured disturbances in the fabric of reality that resulted from things moving between planes, and therefore they were located in bits of the Prime Material plane where such comings and goings were more likely to occur. Cities like London had several individual locations where the surface operatives measured disturbances; a smaller town might have only one or two, but Raphael thought Haliel had five or six of them scattered around the metropolis—so presumably Harlach did, too. And it made sense to check to see if Hell's machines were picking anything up, really. It made perfect sense.

Still, Raphael thought, he'd send Faust an email, once he'd finished his rounds for the night. Just to put his own mind at rest. He checked on Nithael, who was sleeping peacefully, made sure all the spirit-lamps in the dispensary were safely out, shut down his office, and was about to cross to his adjoining private quarters—and paused.

There was an angel sitting in the main courtyard by the infirmary, beside the shell-pink fountain, which was turned down now, quiet at this time of the never-ending celestial day, its faintly gold-dust-sparkling waters plashing softly. This wasn't one of the main courtyards of the white city, where angels came and went at all hours, hurrying about their business; ordinarily no one was about, and certainly no one with quite such vast snow-white wings, or a halo so intensely, vividly bright it threw rainbows in the falling jewel-drops of water from the fountain.

Raphael recognized both wings and halo and was horrified— mildly, tiredly horrified—to find in himself that his first instinct had been to dart back inside his own infirmary and hide from the light of Gabriel's halo, even tilted away from him as it was. His second, much less upsetting, instinct was to go to his fellow angel and see what was the matter; he knew Gabriel had been having headaches since the war, and the set of those vast wings was not *happy* or particularly peaceful.

His third instinct, warier, reminded him that Haliel had been to see him earlier this evening and specifically asked Raphael not to bother Gabriel about what he'd been up to.

He couldn't erase the vivid visceral memory of what it had felt like to have Gabriel lecturing him about the infernal supplies and equipment—over and over, repeating himself in endless self-referential loops of accusation, scraping away at Raphael's nerves like a diamond-burred file. He'd felt ill to begin with, but after ten minutes of Gabriel's focused disapproval, he'd been hardly able to see through the drifting sparkles of dizziness, aware that being sick was no longer a matter of question but of time and praying for the minor mercy that Gabriel would *go away* before he disgraced himself. He'd felt the archangel's disapproval before, all of them had, perhaps himself more than most, but never with such vicious, poisonous *force*, and when Gabriel had finally gone, it had taken him hours and some of Faust's worldly potions before Raphael had felt anything like equal to the challenge of *getting up*. He was very, very disinclined to revisit any such experience, and yet—

And yet his superior archangel looked *unhappy*, in a way Raphael was very much not used to seeing him. Unhappy and very far away, which was also unlike Gabriel. Or unlike the Gabriel he knew.

He sighed internally, settled the folds of his own white robes in decorous drapes, and silently offered a prayer for Nithael's continued slumber—hopefully no one, Nithael included, would need Raphael for anything else tonight—before padding silently in his sandals over the gemstone cobbles of the courtyard. For a moment, as Raphael hesitated, he was almost sure he could see the pink marble rim of the fountain *through* the snowy curve of Gabriel's wing; then he shifted slightly and blinked up at Raphael, and the illusion—if such it had been—was gone.

"What is it?" he demanded. Raphael could feel himself coloring faintly, a brush of gold high on each cheekbone.

"Sorry," he said. "I didn't mean to disturb you, Gabriel. Is everything all right?"

"Of course," Gabriel said, and got to his feet, pinions clattering as he settled them. "Why wouldn't it be?"

"No reason," said Raphael. "You just—looked a little tired, that's all."

"Well, I *am* tired," Gabriel said, and then clearly decided to change his tack. "I mean. We're all tired. We work very hard to make sure Heaven runs at peak efficiency. Being tired is correct and rightful and nothing for any angel to complain about."

"Of course," said Raphael. "I just meant—"

"I know that in your work you are required to deal with angels who have *difficulty* keeping up with their peers," Gabriel continued. "That does not mean that such weakness should be *encouraged*, Raphael."

"Yes, Gabriel," he murmured. "I'm pleased to be able to report that Nithael is nearly ready to be discharged back to his duties."

"Well, good," said Gabriel. "I'm glad to hear it." He settled his wings again and said in a different tone of voice, "And how are you getting on without your orderly?"

"Oh, fine," said Raphael. "One misses his enthusiasm, a little, but I'm glad for him to be taking on responsibilities of his own."

"One hopes he is equal to them," Gabriel said, looking down his nose. It was a very lovely nose, and very well suited to looking down. "He seemed—eager."

"Extremely eager," said Raphael. "But I have faith he'll not disappoint either me or his new colleagues."

Gabriel's nostrils flared briefly. "Yes, well," he said. "I believe I've made my opinion of the entire project clear."

"Yes, indeed," said Raphael. "I'll say good night, if you're sure you're all right."

"Of course I am," and there was the ice on the edges of every syllable, familiar and vicious. "Good *night*, Raphael."

He inclined his head, managing not to shiver *or* to hunch his shoulders, and walked away as if he could not feel the archangel's golden eyes boring two small holes in his back between the wings; and it was not until he was settled in his own bed, wrapped in a silk nightshirt, that the mental image of being able to see *through* Gabriel came back to him.

It was a while before Raphael closed his eyes, and a while longer before his breathing evened out into the steadiness of sleep.

CHAPTER 8

It's *worth it*, preaching in the city. Spreading the Word. It's worth it. It isn't supposed to be *easy*.

If it was easy, everyone would be doing it, instead of just people like us. People who have a call to the ministry. People who don't mind hard work and hardship when it's for the Lord.

And part of that call is not asking questions. Everyone is real clear on that. No questions. Shouldn't need to ask questions anyhow; anything we *need* to know we get told. At meetings.

It's okay that I don't remember where the meetings are held. I don't need to know that. I just need to know I'm chosen, that I'm part of something truly important. That I'm doing the right thing, doing His work, walking with Him. There's people down South who go into some kinda crazy trance when the Lord comes upon them, and they don't remember anything they said once the spirit passes, because it's not them saying it, it's the Lord, speaking *through* them, or that's what somebody said, early on—I don't know when, time's not important—and so when you don't remember what happens, that just means you were a *conduit*. Blessed and exalted.

Brother Gideon was there at the meeting. I do remember that, before it goes blank. Brother Gideon, pale as a sheet, his eyes burning—like the angel in the Christmas song, *his eyes aflame*. I never got what that meant before but I swear it looked like he had fire inside him and it wanted to come out. Brother Gideon preached to us, and that was good, that was like fire inside *my* bones, itchy and crawling like something wanted to get *done*. I remember him saying we were doing the Lord's work and the Lord had—that word, starts with a *v*, means *told*—told Brother Gideon that He was *pleased with us*, and I have been clean now for four months but you don't ever forget some shit, and I swear to you that, hearing that, it was like the fuckin' *bloom* of a shot, like he was pushing that into my veins, lighting me up from the inside, and—

—well, I don't remember anything after that, is all.

I was there and then I was here in the shelter, and it was morning, and I had blisters on my feet like I had when I didn't have anywhere to go so I had to keep moving all the time. Big ones, like cookies. Some of them had burst and there was blood in my shoes.

I went to the social worker lady who does mornings here and she helped me put some Band-Aids on them and asked me what I'd been doing to walk the soles right off my feet, and I had no fuckin' idea what to tell her. Not one idea at all.

It feels like we're getting closer to something, in the meetings, though. Like something's speeding up and up and up, and taking us with it like trash running down the gutter to a storm drain, like we can't stop even if we wanted to, and *that* is also the kind of thing we're not supposed to think, and it kinda makes me feel sick to my stomach so I'm gonna stop thinking now.

Thinking isn't what we're for. That's the best part of this. That we don't have to think.

Hidden Castle, Romania

Edmund Ruthven had been in many places as well-disguised and well-concealed as the castle of Dracula, but none of them had held personal significance even approaching that of this particular ancient fortification. The don't-notice-me spells on the place were about as powerful and well-maintained as those protecting the mummy spa in the south of France: only people Dracula and his family personally permitted to know about this place had any idea it existed.

(They were, for somewhat obvious reasons, perfectly happy to have the Dracula legend tied firmly and enthusiastically to any of the three *other* castles associated with the story—Poenari, Hunedoara, and Bran—and in fact the Voivode himself sent a yearly contribution to several of the societies responsible for Dracula tourism to encourage them to keep up the good work. Every little bit helped; now and then on a very clear day one could make out the twinkle of coach-windows from the distant parking lots associated with the other castles, and imagine the herds of happy tourists taking pictures of one another, and the deep peace and quiet of the forested valley felt all the sweeter for the contrast.)

Far, far below, the glitter of the Argeş against the fresh snowfall looked like a silver chain in a white-velvet lap. When the wind was just right you could hear it, faintly, rushing over its rapids; it was a very *long* way down, and Ruthven was entirely sure he'd not have had the courage to hurl himself from these battlements into the river, marauding Turk or no marauding Turk; the Voivode's lady wife was made of sterner stuff than he. *The dead travel fast*, he thought, smiling.

He lit a black cigarette and leaned on the ancient stone parapet, looking idly down into the valley. Now and then between the black trees it was possible to make out tiny moving forms, sleek and rapid, four-legged, and he could occasionally hear the echo of a howl.

Behind him the snow crunched softly, and he didn't have to look over his shoulder to know who was there; Dracula's weight on the world was slightly, subtly, unignorably heavier than that of anyone he'd ever known who wasn't an angel or a demon, and being near him always felt as if gravity's vector had altered just a bit.

"You're letting her run with the pack unsupervised now?" he said. Beside him Dracula leaned his own black-velvet elbows on the stone.

"She's fluent in wolf, if not grammatical, these days, and Yellowfang and his mate still have the *energy* to keep up with a young person," said the Voivode. "Running about on all fours is splendid exercise, and it tires her out so she can sleep soundly; she hasn't had nightmares for—oh, months now, I should say, since she started spending a lot of time down in the valley. When she first got here she was so cross with herself for waking me and Sofiria up."

"Poor kid," said Ruthven. "I don't blame her, but I'm glad it seems to be getting better now. This place is perfect for her."

"She does seem to enjoy it," said Dracula, with a smile in his voice. "Of course it's done us enormous good as well, having her here. One can neither achieve actual boredom nor become fixated on anything in particular with a young person tumbling around the place asking endless questions."

"Boredom is hell," Ruthven agreed, and tapped ash. The air around them felt like wine, cold and bracing and invigorating, and the scent of the pine forests was sharp and sweet to his senses; he could just about imagine what it would smell like to someone in wolf form. "It's lovely to get out of the city for a while. I'm telling myself that if anyone actually needed me they'd send a message."

"Of course they would," said the Voivode comfortably. "There's something to be said for organizing one's responsibilities well enough that other people can manage them neatly enough in one's absence, and your so-capable London friends know how to reach you."

"That they do," said Ruthven. "Greta's away herself at the moment, but her colleagues are running the clinic and keeping an eye on the place. I have every faith in their ability to keep the city from sinking underneath the wave for a little while longer without my presence."

"Quite right," said Dracula, and stretched, with a little sigh. "I was going through my cellars earlier and have discovered an as-yet-untouched little treasure-trove of very nice Tokay, of the sort that was utterly lost on that tiresome estate agent. May I tempt you to a glass?"

Ruthven pitched the cigarette-end over the parapet, watching as it caught the light on its long fall to the valley below. "That sounds remarkably lovely," he said, and smiled at his host. "Lead on?"

New York City

So this is what it means, Gideon Tremayne thought as the train swayed and racketed its way through the gathering darkness of Brooklyn. *This, at last, is what I'm for.*

This is what it means to be truly alive in the Spirit, to be one with God, to be the great sword in His hand, the scourging fire, the pitiless light; I am, oh, I am, and I know what I must do.

Since midafternoon he had been in deep meditation, kneeling in his little apartment, not aware that his knees were not touching the worn linoleum of the floor. He had had just enough worldly presence of mind to call in to his job, since there was no way he'd be showing up to work this particular shift, or possibly ever; ever might be the case, and Gideon was consummately okay with that. He had spoken with his people, his followers, the ones who had found themselves drawn to him, to what he had to say; conveyed to them what they must do, where they must go, and to whom they must do it, and when; and in his meditations he had been given his own orders, his own information. His own role and *mission* and purpose.

The evening before, he had gone out into the city to prepare for tonight. He wasn't entirely sure what it was he had done, only that there had been a great deal of walking involved, and subway trains, and bottles of something that clinked and smelled metallic. Where he had gotten them, who had given them to him, did not matter; nor did what he had done with them afterward, where they had gone. Not much mattered except for the fire inside him, the force, the *purpose* he had never realized he so desperately needed.

Tonight he knew exactly where he was going, and what he was doing there. As soon as dusk fell, he had left the apartment, heading for the B train into Manhattan. He carried with him a paper grocery bag—not the clinking bottles tonight, but something heavy and wrapped in rags, along with a roll of silver duct tape, and if he did not know where they had come from, that was unimportant compared with what he knew he must do with them. But those were not the most important of the things Gideon carried on this particular night unlike any other; no, the most important was a thing he did not hold in his hands but in his mind and in his blood and bones, a gift he had never hoped to pray for, a gift he was entirely sure he did not deserve—but a gift he carried with deep, deep joy nonetheless. To his eyes, that gift was faintly visible in the darkness: it glowed in a branching, laddering pattern, each vein and capillary under his skin faintly lit with gold. Everything he touched carried a faint fingerprint stain of that gold light: the subway turnstile, the pole he hung on to, the edge of a seat; all glowed as if smudged with luminous paint, invisible to other human eyes. If perhaps one or two people on the train stared and unobtrusively made their way in the opposite direction from Gideon Tremayne, he did not notice; neither did he remark on the fact that most of his nearby fellow passengers sniffed unconsciously at the air in his direction, the way people did when passing a honey-locust tree in spring, with a faint smile on their faces. All that most people on the train knew was that something smelled distantly wonderful, and that whatever they were particularly worried about right at that moment seemed briefly to matter less, as if the world was just for a little while a sweeter, kinder place.

Chelsea, New York City

The last time Greta Helsing had felt quite like this was probably back in Paris, stepping out of the taxi at the Palais Garnier on Edmund Ruthven's arm, very much aware that she was exceedingly small and unimportant and common and probably shouldn't be here *and* excited all the same. That she shouldn't be here was obvious; she had no business at a party like this one, and they had to get started with the actual *research trip* she was here to conduct first thing the next morning—and still, as Varney gave her a hand out of the cab, she couldn't help feeling glad that Ruthven had insisted on providing her with a couple of what he called *formal looks*. Tonight it wasn't the tight Madame-X black velvet thing she'd worn in Paris; tonight she was in a dark grey suit over a hilariously inappropriate embroidered bustier top and had let Orlax do her eye makeup, after some negotiation, and she felt completely unlike herself and rather good about it nonetheless.

The invitation had arrived midday, heavy cream-colored paper and raised printing with a personal note to Varney in beautiful copperplate handwriting: *Dear Sir Francis, I can find it in myself to forgive you the oversight of neglecting to mention your title if you and Lady Varney would be so kind as to join me for tonight's little get-together, Adriana C.* in dark-purple ink that glittered green and smelled faintly of perfume.

Adriana? she'd said, eyebrowing Varney, who had the grace to blush very faintly.

The nosferatu I told you about. Lord knows why she bothered looking up the title. We don't have to go . . . that is, perhaps I ought to look in but you needn't feel you have to—

Balls, Greta had told him. *How often does one get invited to exclusive New York parties by* nosferatu? *Especially lady nosferatu. I've never even met one before. Let me find something remotely suitable to wear and you can take me along as Lady V and I will try not to say anything too hideously embarrassing.*

You are not embarrassing, *Greta*, Varney had started to protest, and she'd told him to hush and went to go look through the garment-bags hanging in the hotel closet to see what Ruthven had decided well-dressed Gretas were wearing these days.

How often did one get invited to exclusive New York parties by lady nosferatu who were *pretty clearly hitting on one's lawful wedded husband*, she asked herself now, huddling a little inside the sharply cut suit jacket. It was cold without a coat, but the chill was more trepidation than temperature. *Brass it out, Helsing*, she told herself, *you'll have a nice time once you get inside*, and she met Varney's questioning look with a smile and a *lead on* gesture.

Behind them the angel and the demon were sticking close together, and Greta could spare a brief hope that they wouldn't get into too much trouble with the underworld hierarchy and that neither of them would say anything too unignorable, and then she was floating on Varney's arm in the faintest hint of his thrall—he did that sometimes for her to lean on, and it was deeply appreciated, like a tiny sip of anxiolytic—and they were inside the gallery, in bright light, surrounded by a thousand people talking at the top of their lungs. The heat inside was very welcome, and so was Varney's iron-bar arm—and then the crowd around them had parted and she was face-to-face with a creature in a van Herpen dress and a necklace of raw boulder-opal pieces the size of tangerines, whose exquisite makeup did absolutely nothing to hide the characteristic bone structure of a nosferatu.

But she's beautiful, Greta thought, *it goes something close to banshee, the pointed edges of the zygomatic arch and the ear and the sharp jawline*, and mentally scrabbled for some kind of composure, automatically offering her hand. The nosferatu took it in a dry, brisk shake. "Dr. Helsing, I presume," she said. There was the faint lisp that went with the fangs, but the only accent was Italian-American. "Adriana Cenci. Thank you so much for joining us on no notice. It's a pleasure to welcome you to New York."

"The pleasure's mine, Ms. Cenci," she said, taking in the expert, expensive hair color and lacquered claws. "I'm delighted to make the acquaintance of nosferatu again; it's been years."

"You and I must catch up," said Adriana Cenci, and gave her hand to Varney to kiss, and they were swept along into the crowd, pausing long enough to snag a couple of glasses of fizzy wine from a passing waiter.

The space was beautiful, very clearly a functional art gallery with a loft area where the open bar was set up, huge complicated canvases on the walls, and a couple of blocky sculptures on plinths here and there to help direct traffic. Across the room Greta could make out a couple of faintly familiar faces, and after a moment or two managed to place them: demons, the New York surface-operative demons who had helped Cranswell and Grisaille abscond with the Hermopolis Stela from the Met last year and brought it, and them, to the mummy spa in Marseille. Dimly she could remember that the woman was a gallery owner and the man a theatrical producer—how very New York—and therefore this gallery must belong to her: an entirely fitting sort of place for an underworld celebration, one way and another.

Varney had also recognized the demons, and both he and Greta belatedly looked around to check for their own angel and demon charges. Adariel was looking very anxious indeed, and Orlax had retreated into the kind of faintly sneering disinterest that Greta was fairly sure he thought looked sophisticated rather than sophomoric, but neither of them was doing anything too embarrassing just at the moment. She took a long sip of wine and felt herself beginning not just to relax but to *enjoy* the weirdness of everything around her.

Adariel had never been to a party before. Of any kind. Heaven didn't exactly go in for celebrations of the sort that involved spirituous liquors or cubes of cheese on sticks, and very definitely he'd never seen this many people wearing different shades of black in one space before now. He hadn't actually known there *were* this many shades of black. Nor that people could come in quite so many different shapes and sizes.

Dr. Helsing had told him this event had been organized on behalf of, or possibly by, an important personage in the monster world: a sort of blood-drinker called a *nosferatu*, not to be confused with either the *vampire* or the *vampyre* (like Sir Francis). To angel eyes the nosferatu looked extremely monstrous with their pointed ears and front teeth and deep-sunken eyes, but Adariel thought he'd managed not to look too obviously put off when introduced to the lady nosferatu who'd invited them. The rest of the crowd was made up of all sorts of people, most of whom clearly were not ordinary humans; he could identify two individuals who were definitely demons, presumably the New York surface operatives for Hell who were responsible for the city, a woman and a man both in unrelieved and complicated black who were smoking black cigarettes and exuding what he recognized after a moment as *cool* by its resemblance to whatever Orlax kept trying to achieve all the time.

There weren't any other angels. Or at least any other angels who were letting themselves appear as such to fellow angels: he could see colored auras around lots of the attendees, indications that they were various flavors of supernatural, but nowhere could he make out the clear glow of gold that meant angel stock.

It was very warm and quite bright in here and there were a *lot* of people, and Adariel found a handy alcove in a wall to lean into and tried not to make himself noticeable. He'd found himself missing Raphael more than a little over the past couple of days—missing not only Raphael but the simple, unquestioning comfort of being in Heaven, in a known place with known parameters—and he thought probably that wasn't going to go away. They had six weeks of work before he could go home. He'd just have to get used to it.

Orlax had slipped off as soon as they'd all been presented to the nosferatu host lady, and now Adariel looked around for him—ah, there, over by the refreshments table, talking to someone rather a lot taller than he was, with scarlet streaks in her waist-length hair.

The doctor and Sir Francis were...mingling. He thought that was what they were doing, anyway: drifting through the crowd, greeting and being greeted, engaging in brief conversations. Adariel found himself face-to-face with a waiter who had red pupilless eyes, who handed him a glass that *looked* like glass but was in fact lightweight plastic, full of something pale gold and fizzy. Belatedly he tried to thank the waiter, but they had already moved on, tray in hand, and he blinked into the depths of the glass.

It was probably *champagne*. He had never had champagne before, but it looked a little bit like nectar if nectar were somehow made fizzy, with sparkling lines of tiny bubbles rising in the clear liquid and popping effervescently on the surface. When he raised the glass to take a sip, the bursting bubbles tickled his nose, and the taste was very much *unlike* nectar— much sharper, hardly sweet at all, but after a moment or two he thought he could make out a sort of fruity, flowery taste that wasn't unpleasant so much as unexpected.

He took another, longer sip. Despite the fact that the liquid was cold enough to dew the outside of the plastic glass with condensation, he felt a sort of burst of paradoxical warmth in his midsection not unlike the one he associated with nectar, and found himself smiling a little. He didn't know anyone other than the doctor and her husband and Orlax, and he had no idea what to do, and he wasn't even sure if he was wearing the right clothing since it wasn't any sort of black at all but grey; but despite all that, Adariel was slowly beginning to think he might not have a terrible time tonight after all.

The first glass was hardly empty before another waiter came by and replaced it without Adariel having to ask, which was sort of like being on the plane and being brought things by the people in little vests and neck-scarves except very much more comfortable. He leaned against the wall of his alcove and listened to people talking.

"—could have knocked me over with a feather when Aurelio showed up bold as brass after a hundred years asleep and proceeded to pick up where he'd left off as if nothing had happened," someone was saying. "Of course it did take him a few weeks before people really twigged that he was back and he meant business, but the guy hasn't lost his edge. Did you hear about that thing with Kraven's people and the garlic?"

"In vivid detail, darling. Remember one of mine's in the medical examiner's office? I'm regaled with *autopsy reports* over the breakfast table. You do not want to *know* what pure allicin does to vampires when released in a closed environment. *Believe* me, you don't."

Someone else snickered. "They mention those fucking dart things?"

"Word is Contini's found out who was doing that and asked them all nicey-nice to quit it or he'd unscrew their head," said the first partygoer. "Not really a good fit with his idiom, randos running around his city with poison darts all willy-nilly."

"Not a good look," the third one agreed, at which point they moved out of easy-listening range, much to Adariel's chagrin. Dart things? Dart things like the ones that had hurt Harlach and Haliel back in London? It sounded like maybe he ought to know about it, or Orlax should, so that he could tell Hell... Wait, weren't there surface operatives from Hell already here, should he tell *them* or did they already know... were they the *same* dart things...?

Slowly Adariel became aware that he was thinking much slower than usual, as if wading through treacle, and realized the second glass of champagne had somehow emptied itself all the way down to the bottom. He felt slightly, pleasantly lightheaded, as if the pull of Earth's gravity had somehow slipped a little. He had thought he was hungry, when they'd arrived, and had definitely meant to work his way across the gallery to the table with the cheese on sticks, but right now he didn't want anything to eat at all. He was quite thirsty, though.

Darts. He should ask someone if they already knew about darts. Or *what* they knew about darts. And whoever Contini was. That felt like it might be important.

"Now what is a nice angel like you doing in a place like *this*," said another voice, this one quite close by, and he turned unsteadily to find himself being addressed by one of the demons he'd noticed earlier: not the very short dark-haired woman with the jeweled cigarette holder, but the taller man with artfully disheveled hair streaked with silver. "You're new around here."

"Um," said Adariel, and the man beckoned to a passing waiter. Without him paying much attention, a third glass of champagne somehow materialized in Adariel's hand, and he took a sip. That bloom of heat in his midsection was back. "I'm, um. With Dr. Helsing? And Sir Francis Varney, and— um, Orlax?"

The man snapped his fingers. "Of course," he said. "The very British delegation. Adriana mentioned something about you and some sort of famous vampyre, but I've never heard of you before."

"I'm new," said Adariel, and took another sip. The man smiled with pointed teeth.

"Of course you are. And I am Morax, not Orlax, and the lady who owns this benighted display-case for overpriced art is Glasya. What's *your* name?"

"Adariel," said Adariel, and found himself suppressing a hiccup. "I'm supposed to be working with Orlax on Earth to, um. To do research on, on the allergic reaction between angels and demons? As part of the Accords?"

Morax rolled his eyes and snagged a glass of wine for himself as another waiter passed. "How very laudable, I'm sure. Well, Adariel, how are you enjoying the party?"

He realized the third glass was now half-empty. "Um. It's very nice?" He was starting to think he might like to sit down, however. "I haven't been to many parties. Um. Heaven doesn't really do parties?"

"So one hears," said Morax. "And you're the *only* angel here. Presumably the only angel in New York, since neither Glasya nor I have seen halo or feather of the one that used to be stationed here for quite some time. I gather your side doesn't have quite such an assiduous approach to Monitoring and Evaluation as ours does?"

Adariel tried to think through the champagne bubbles. "Um," he said. "I don't really know? Gabriel's the archangel in charge of all of that and, well, I'm usually with Raphael in the infirmary?" He really didn't know what the situation was with regard to the other surface-operative posts, he realized; there was Haliel in London, but— "There used to be an angel stationed in New York?"

"There was indeed, but that was—oh, ages back," said Morax. "We didn't exactly *talk*, you understand. When they disappeared, Glasya and I thought presumably there had been some sort of shake-up and they were going to be replaced, but then there simply wasn't any sign of another angel, so we just got on with things. There *was* something odd last year with some individuals who apparently looked like angels but weren't, but it didn't seem to go anywhere. Figured it was, what's the word, ineffable."

Ineffable was a word Gabriel used a lot. Adariel was starting to feel decidedly odd: something was poking at his senses that he couldn't quite make out clearly past the growing sense of lightheaded disorientation. He closed his eyes for a moment—that helped a little; the edges of things had begun to go fuzzy—and tried to figure out what it was he was sensing.

"—Hey, are you all right?" Morax asked, sounding faintly concerned. Adariel opened his eyes again.

"Um. Maybe?" he said. "I might…I think I'd like to sit down?"

"Sure," said the demon. "Right over here," and he took Adariel's elbow and ushered him over to a black leather bench next to a sculpture on a pedestal. "Maybe take it easy on the bubbly—"

Adariel sank onto the polished leather, eyes closing again. He almost had it—something was kicking his brain—

"—sure you're okay?" the demon was asking. "I can go find your friends—"

"I'm *not* the only angel," said Adariel, eyes wide open. "Or... I don't think I am? Something *like* an angel's very close by."

"Where?" Morax was bending over him. "What do you mean, something *like* an angel?"

"I don't know," said Adariel. "Something that feels like one, anyway. I'm not sure; it's so confused... I think I might be *drunk*..."

"Tight," said the demon. "What you are is *tight*, and—can you tell me what direction this angelic thing might be?"

"Is that what *tight* means?" he asked. "Um. It's... I think it's that way?" He turned, very briefly losing the edge of the seeming he was using to cover his wings and halo; for a fraction of a second the white feathers flickered into visibility and were gone again. "That way," he repeated, and pointed: directly back toward the offices and utility closet at the rear of the gallery, away from the crowd. "That way, and *up*."

"Stay here," said Morax. "Stay here and keep your astral eyes, or whatever, open."

"Where are you going?"

"To find out if somebody's trying to crash the party," said Morax, and gave him one of those pointy-toothed smiles. When he was gone Adariel found he was still holding the half-empty glass of champagne, and peered into it vaguely before deciding with thoroughly unangelic fatalism *what the hell* and swallowing what remained; it didn't seem as if it would make much difference one way or another.

He could definitely still feel whatever it was. Quite close, and *like* an angel; it had a lot of the same golden tones to its pneumic signature, but there was a lot of other stuff as well, things Adariel couldn't identify. He wondered if the New York angel was back, or if they hadn't actually ever left, and realized all over again how little he actually *knew* about Heaven's surface-operative organization or the parameters of its mission, how little he knew about so *many* parts of Heaven. How little he knew if that lack of knowledge was due just to his own newness or the short amount of time since his creation, or if something or things had very deliberately chosen to keep that information from him for reasons, and what those reasons might be.

One of the major benefits of holding events at venues owned and operated by demons was the total lack of necessity, once inside, to maintain the individual don't-notice-me fields Contini and so many of his people relied upon in the rest of the waking world.

It had just gone ten-thirty. Outside Glasya's Gallery Sixty-Six, Twentieth Street was dark and empty save for drifting veils of cold rain, all the lights on the block either flickering-dim or out; from the outside, the huge windows giving on to the snowy interior were dark and empty, with a couple of posters up in the door and some large nondescript canvases dimly visible on the walls. Inside it was bright and warm and alive, for certain values of alive, and completely invisible to the sort of eyes who were not welcome within.

Aurelio Contini was pleased, so far: no one he'd personally

invited had failed to show, and the overall tone of the conversation was following the lines he'd designed it to. In about half an hour he'd tinkle an hors d'oeuvre fork against a glass for attention and begin the actual point of the evening's festivities; until then he could simply entertain himself by watching Adriana Cenci charm her way through the crowd. Adriana was undeniably useful, and he was pleased with himself for bothering to keep her around; she'd introduced herself to him shortly after his reawakening and made it clear she intended to latch her personal wagon to his rising star, and in fact had made this worth his while.

The unofficial leaders of the city's were population—all three of them—were getting well stuck in to the world-class charcuterie buffet Contini had had laid out for his guests (it was possible to source very good charcuterie without garlic contamination, but by Christ did it cost you), and the younger classic-draculine vamp couple who had mostly taken over their population's leadership in the past couple of years were clearly having a nice time as well. He'd seen Francisco unobtrusively escorting a human who looked quite happily drunk, if somewhat too pale, out the back way, and shortly afterward reappearing with a different human on his arm; Contini's approach to community engagement involved prearranged and consensual *refreshments*. It was easy enough these days to organize a nice supply of clean, nourishing blood to meet a variety of dietary requirements if you had sufficient cash to throw around. Not for the first time he pitied the creature he had been in his previous waking existence, before the advent of the Internet.

(One of the things he'd been working hard to do away with, in clearing the city of the amateur-hour monsters that had been infesting it, was active murder of humes. He didn't particularly care much if a bunch of random humes ceased to be; he did care quite a lot if monsters were messy and wasteful eaters in ways that might draw more attention than strictly necessary. Simpler and neater for everyone involved if no one got dead, or undead, and everyone walked away from the encounter in one piece.)

He swirled the blood in his glass and looked out over the crowd. The vampyre Adriana had invited, the one with a human wife, of all things, and a baby angel and demon tagging along for some truly improbable reason Contini hadn't paid much attention to, seemed to be enjoying himself. The little demon was trying to show off to a couple of vampire women, apparently failing to notice the fact that they were married to one another; the angel was...Contini smiled to himself...getting mildly squiffy on Dom Pérignon in an alcove by a Brancusi sculpture and being *talked to* by Morax.

He didn't envy Varney his companions. It had taken Contini a moment or two to place the name, when they were introduced; there had been a Varney among the vamps in England involved in tracking down that idiot coven earlier this year. Some kind of friend to Edmund Ruthven.

There was a name Contini had no difficulty remembering. He could very clearly recall Edmund St. James Ruthven and his hands-on approach to ridding London of the bloodsuckers Edmund St. James Ruthven *personally* disapproved of. How extremely fortunate for everyone that Ruthven had apparently stopped paying quite so much attention to his self-assigned guardianship of the city of London, now that he and the Voivode Dracula were *simpatico* after that business with the little girl. Every report Contini had received recently had suggested that if Ruthven was still active in London, he wasn't paying much attention to the place, and that he seemed to have fucked off to Romania to find his roots or something and hang out with the elder statesman of his kind. Contini was emphatically in favor of that particular development.

He was glad, too, that he'd found the bastard responsible for the attacks on his people, and that he'd had a chance to engage in deep, meaningful conversation with said bastard. The smell of abject terror coming off Gideon Tremayne when Contini caught him had suggested quite strongly that Contini had made his point, that Gideon Tremayne was not likely to break his promise and do something unspeakably stupid such as *continuing* to attack Contini's people, and that the problem of the street preachers and their poison darts was, if not solved, then placed on a very far-back burner while Contini solidified his leadership role.

He checked his watch. Getting on for eleven. Some of the people here had to do work in the morning; he didn't intend this to turn into an all-night orgy the way parties always used to do. Time to get on with it, he thought, looking around, and paused. The angel Morax had been talking to was looking rather like a freshman on the third ill-advised screwdriver, and Contini wondered if someone ought to escort them to the facilities before they could commit a party foul. He had Francisco and Mario in the gallery office and several more trusted people keeping an eye on the crowd; he could easily catch someone's eye and alert them to the need—no, the angel looked as if they were distracted by something rather than about to be sick, like they were trying to hear something above the sound of the crowd—

The noise, when it came, was so prosaic and familiar that Contini couldn't even place it for a minute. Then it came to him: the clank and rattle of water moving through pipework, like the steam heat in an old building, like the ones he'd known in the time before the big sleep. Water moving in the *ceiling*, not the floor or walls... the hell was going on, Contini wondered, was someone else in the building, this was an old subdivided warehouse; maybe there could be other people— someone sneaking in after dark—

He wasn't the only one looking up at the ceiling with *what the hell* on his face. Right before it happened, when the clanking and groaning sounds stopped completely, he met several of the others' eyes and saw the same dawning suspicion followed by horror in every single gaze.

And then the sprinkler heads popped open, one after another, with a spatter and hiss, down the length of the gallery chamber, cones of rust-colored water hazing the air; and a moment later, ragged and horrible, came the screams.

The first thing Greta Helsing thought was *but nothing's on fire*.

She'd been *in* houses that were on fire. Memorably so; she'd been in Edmund Ruthven's Embankment mansion while a bunch of madmen set it on fire with Molotov cocktails, for example, and since then she'd had a particularly sensitive nose for things that were hotter than they ought to be, as well as a twitchy near-panic response to smoke alarms going off. There hadn't even been a faint smell of scorching, let alone any suggestion of smoke. There had just been the bang and clank of water moving through pipes, a weirdly domestic sound, and then the pop-hiss of the sprinkler heads one by one, which made no *sense*, didn't they go off in response to heat? No one was burning anything—

Like everyone else her instinct was to duck, to cover her head with her arms, as the water rained down. It was *cold* and rust-stained and it stank; there went her fucking Donna Karan suit Ruthven had picked out—

—and all around her the yells of surprise and shock were turning to shrill, helpless screams of pain, what the *hell*, it was only water, gross and cold and stained, but *water*—

—and the penny dropped as she pushed dripping hair out of her eyes and saw welts and blisters rising on the exposed skin of everyone around her: not just water but *holy water*, and by the looks of it there was probably silver in there, too; the were-cat she'd been talking to five minutes ago was screaming as visible steam rose from her skin—

—and Greta and Adariel and the humans Contini had hired to be the open bar were the only people standing perfectly still in the middle of the chaos as everyone else struggled for the exits, staggering and falling and flailing in the effort to get out of the burning rain.

A door at the back of the gallery flew open and another couple of nosferatu took in the scene, frozen in horror. Greta fought her way through the crowd to grab Adariel by the wrist and drag him with her, struggling past the screaming guests to the office door. "Holy water," she said urgently to the nosferatu over the background noise. "Or something like it, something corrosive. There's got to be a valve somewhere; this isn't a normal sprinkler system—"

"In the back," said one of Contini's men, grabbing for a raincoat. The other snatched a tarp from a paint-stained stepladder, and then both of them were gone, pushing past her into the chaos that was the gallery, on their way to find their boss.

Greta pushed the wet hair out of her eyes again. Adariel was leaning heavily on her; as she straightened up, he let go, leaned over, and was sick on the floor, which seemed to help a bit. The two humans were staring at one another with the glazed look of people who had been given something to calm their nerves, and she dismissed them from immediate utility. "Come with me," she told Adariel, who was wiping at his mouth.

"Angel," he said, slurring a little. Greta stared at him.

"What is?"

"Feels like. *Feels* like angel, but isn't," he said, and seemed to pull himself together, nodding at her, and she stepped past the humans and the office desk and into the narrow utility corridor behind the office itself. Here there were old, paint-spattered, dusty iron water pipes, and *here* there was what looked like a valve body with a handwheel, and—

And on the valve, stuck on with prosaic, ordinary duct tape, was a silver crucifix. She reached for the wheel and Adariel grabbed at her wrist, shaking his head. She could see his halo faintly, a line of light in the dimness. "It's blessed," he said. "Let me?"

"What does it look like to you?"

"Lit up gold," he said. "Glowing. *Bright*. Don't touch it."

She wasn't an eldritch abomination, but Greta had to admit she wasn't exactly a vessel most pure, either, and stood back with her hands clenched into fists while the angel set his own hands on the wheel and spun the valve closed. Behind them the screams from the gallery began to turn into moans and whimpers.

Holy water, she thought, *blessed by something pretty significant, and I'm going to bet colloidal silver got in there somehow, and I wouldn't put it past them to have snuck some fucking allicin in as well. This wasn't even close to a random attack. This was a surgical strike, and apparently the nosferatu had no warning whatsoever.*

She wiped her hands on her hips and looked helplessly at the angel. There had to be what, sixty, seventy people of various species, *including her husband*, in that gallery and God knew how many outside in the street, with various levels of chemical burns and toxicity, probably some pulmonary injury, too, given how fine the sprinkler spray had been; almost certainly a couple of them had swallowed some of it. All of them needed to be decontaminated and treated for shock and injury. And what she had at her disposal was...whatever this fucking gallery had for a first-aid kit. At least it was raining outside; that would wash the worst of the stuff away.

And they had to figure out who was responsible for this and do something about it. That part she could happily leave to other people; the triage was going to be her immediate problem.

Greta rarely gave in to fits of despair, and it wasn't going to help if she started now, but *Jesus* did she wish sometimes that this kind of thing could happen to someone *else*. "I don't suppose you've ever done triage," she said to Adariel. "Since you were lucky enough to have missed all the fun during the war."

"No," said Adariel. "But I can follow instructions?"

"Good," she said. "Find buckets, cups, whatever you can that'll hold clean, fresh water, and follow me."

It had quickly become apparent, in the headlong rush for the exits, in the stampede of creatures fighting to get *out* of the burning rain and into the relative safety of the ordinary rain in the street outside, that the attack wasn't limited to those still inside the gallery: the first staggering rush of vampires, nosferatu, and were-creatures had met a hail of tiny poisonous dart blades that some of them barely even noticed under the agony of the holy water on exposed skin. As wave after wave of victims fought their way out into the street, the little blades found marks where they could, the guns and pipes responsible for sending them on their way retreating as soon as they had served their purpose. Some of those who had the presence of mind to notice the figures disappearing into the rainy night gave chase, but gave up after a block or two, wheezing and sick with the fumes they had inhaled.

By the time the killing rain inside the gallery had stopped, with the closing of the valve, the authors of the blowdarts were nowhere to be found.

Inside the gallery, it wasn't quite as bad as Greta had feared. It was bad, plenty bad, but a lot of the party guests had been able to scramble for cover underneath coats or cloaks, and some of the hanging mobiles in the middle of the gallery had blocked the worst of the spray.

In the middle of the worst moments of her life, Greta had encountered a strange and paradoxical phenomenon: the world went slow and very, very clear, and what she had to do was entirely self-evident. She had felt that weird, glassy clarity when a mad monk had held a poisoned knife to her throat in the dark; when she'd had to treat Grisaille for a sucking chest wound in the middle of a pitched underground battle; and more recently, in Hell, when she'd had to perform emergency surgery on a never-ending series of dying angels in the middle of the war in Heaven. She felt it close over her now, surveying the mess that was the art-gallery floor covered in collapsed, moaning people, stinking of rust and rot and not a little of blood.

Beside her Adariel was sick again, as quietly as he could, without spilling any of the water in the bucket he was holding; she appreciated that, distantly. What she appreciated more was the sight of first Varney and then Orlax emerging from underneath somebody's coat on the far side of the room.

Varney had some visible burns, but the way he waved to her
and then immediately bent over to help the person next to
him told her he wasn't too badly hurt; a tide of relief washed
through Greta, there and gone again.

Orlax pushed the ruin of his carefully styled hair away from
his face, saw her, and picked his way through the people on
the floor to join them.

"What do we do?" he asked. He, too, had some superficial
burns, but nothing Greta thought she had to worry about,
compared with most of the other injuries.

"We need to get these people decontaminated," she said.
"Adariel, take the buckets and go round sluicing off the poison. Get the ones who can walk to go out in the rain and wash
it off. Orlax, I'm going to need you to do your fields trick,
if possible." Across the room Contini's goons had emerged,
one of them carrying their employer, who was visibly burned
and semiconscious. "—He's first," she added, and gave Orlax
a questioning look. He pushed his hair away from his face
again and nodded.

"I can do it," he said, and she believed him.

In the gallery office Contini's bodyguards had laid him on
a couch, and one of them had the presence of mind to fetch
water from the cooler in the corner to pour over his burns.
They looked up as she and Orlax came in. "I'm a doctor," she
said. "Let me see, please," and despite her bedraggled appearance, there was enough authority in her voice to make two full-
size nosferatu obey without question. She knelt down beside
the couch. "Can one of you see if this place has a first-aid kit

anywhere, and the other one find the buffet humans if they're still around? He'll be better off with some fresh blood in him."

Contini first: with the contents of the first-aid kit she could at least cut away his clothing to reveal the worst of the burns, clean them, and apply antibiotic salve. He was still unconscious, under the watchful eye of one of the bodyguards, when she moved on to the rest of the victims.

Morax had been lucky enough to avoid the worst of the deluge, and he and Contini's other goon were running triage. Greta was glad of it, even as she knelt down beside a whimpering vampire and beckoned to Orlax, who joined her wordlessly and half-closed his eyes; when he opened them again they were very much not human, and she could feel the tension in her patient release with his influence. "It's going to be all right," she told the vampire, and got to work.

She was aware of Adariel hovering nearby as she finished salving and dressing the vampire's burns, and sat back on her heels, looking up at him. "What?"

"Um," he said. "It's...not just the water, Doctor. There's more of those—those dart things? The people who went outside seem to have run into them?"

"*Shit*," said Greta. "How many?"

"Twenty so far," said Adariel miserably. "On top of the burns."

"I hope to God I don't have to send a whole party's worth of monsters to Erebus General," she said, and pinched the bridge of her nose. "I need supplies. I need the *bus*, Adariel." She pulled out her phone, handed it to him. "Call them," she said, and shook her head before he could summon the presence of mind to object. "They're in my contacts under GÖTTINGEN AMERICAN LIAISON/EMERG. Call them and say there's been an attack on a number of supernaturals and I need the bus and all its supplies here and now along with any medically trained staff they have available. I'll talk to them when I'm not in the middle of handling an emergency; we can discuss everything else in the morning."

She turned away without waiting to see him place the call, and moved on to the next victim, a were-something in respiratory distress; they'd obviously inhaled some of the spray, and judging by the effects, there *had* been colloidal silver in the water. Orlax knelt beside her with a questioning look, and she nodded, and again felt the immediate change as his influence took hold, calming the fear and easing the pain, as she helped the were sit up to ease their breathing and administered albuterol, and on to the next victim, and the next, and the next.

At some point the bus must have arrived, because someone brought her the *big* EMT bag and a pallet-load of bottled Lake Avernus water, and after that it got easier. She gave orders to whoever was listening: lake water to anyone who could swallow, lake water on the burns, lake water to irrigate the dart wounds; oxygen and bronchodilators to the ones in respiratory distress; sedatives; high-octane painkillers. Blood to those who needed it, as long as supplies held out. Beside her Orlax pushed energy into his fields over and over, face grim and eyes glowing orange over their red irises, and every time she could feel it as the influence flooded over her patient, taking away the worst of their distress; she knew beyond the shadow of a doubt that without his help at least half of these people would be in deep shock. Without his help she *might* have had to call Hell for emergency medical evacuation; with it, she thought she might get everybody through the night.

He swayed as they got up from the latest dart-wound patient, eyes going unfocused, and Greta caught and steadied him. She'd been afraid of this since the beginning: how much energy was he really putting into this, how much did he have left, *could* he keep going without damaging himself—and was about to ask when he blinked hard and straightened up.

"I'm okay," he said, meeting her gaze, shock-pale, brown crescents under each eye. "I can keep going."

Greta looked at him hard and then just nodded. It was more trust than she'd generally display to someone she barely knew and had worked with for less than a week. "I have to," Orlax added. "It *needs* to be done."

It needed to be done, and there was not much left to say.

She had no idea how long it was before they ran out of people to patch up, before someone helped her to her feet and told her Contini was awake and asking for her. She had just enough presence of mind to tell whoever it was to give Orlax a stiff drink and find him somewhere to lie down, and then she was picking her way through the lines of people with rolled-up coats under their heads and feet, heading back to the little office.

*   *   *

"It had to be someone who knew this building," Aurelio Contini was saying for the third time while Greta dabbed lake water onto his pointed ears. "Ow. Someone who knew it used to be a hazardous-goods warehouse with a deluge sprinkler system."

"Someone who was able to *bless* the entire system, too," said Greta. "Hold still, sir. With some kind of really *intense* blessing. Not everyone can do that. I think you have to be ordained to bless stuff properly, don't you?"

"Officially," said Adariel from the doorway; he'd drifted over from the main room. "But I think people touched by God can do it even if they're not ordained?"

"God has a fucky sense of humor," said one of Contini's goons. Greta thought he was Frankie, but he might have been Freddie; she wasn't sure and wasn't about to ask.

"No argument there," she said, feeling a million years old. "So, someone who knew the building, or knew someone who did, who was able to get in here and stick that crucifix on the valve and do some blessing, who was able to get into the utility space and introduce the colloidal silver to the tanks for the deluge system before they activated it. Someone who knew what sort of people were going to be here and what they'd be vulnerable to. Who *did* know about the guest list?"

"Pretty much anyone who mattered in the underworld," said Contini. "Everyone who's anyone." He struggled upright on the couch, pushing away her hand. "Frankie, pull the security tapes. Mario, get me an idea of who's worst off and who

236

might need to stay somewhere safe for a couple nights while they heal up. You, angel. You said you sensed something right before it started?"

"I think so," said Adariel. "I was...um. Drunk. But I definitely thought I felt something *like* an angel's presence but not any angel I know of?"

Greta sat back on her heels, thinking very hard about a phone conversation she'd had with Faust the previous year, after Ruthven had contracted what was apparently disguised as an angelic curse. *An* angel *did this to Ruthven?*

Something that looks *like an angel to the MRI algorithms, but if it's an angel, it's a type we've never seen before.*

Faust had been as mystified as she was. And he'd gone on. *Gabriel and his bunch wouldn't go in for this sort of thing, anyway. It's politically unwise and they don't get involved.*

That had been before the Accords, before all this business with working together and collaboration. Before Gabriel had started lecturing his fellow archangels to the point of collapse.

She pushed the thought away. "What time is it?"

Adariel looked at his watch. "Four in the morning. We're supposed to meet up with the bus driver at eight-thirty. Or we were."

"Somehow I don't think that's going to happen," said Greta. She had no idea who had brought the bus here, with its loads of supplies, or where they were now, or anything.

"Bus?" said Contini, narrowing his cigarette-ember eyes at her.

"We're supposed to be on a research field trip, and I've

conveniently got this well-appointed luxury coach full of all kinds of first-aid stuff at my disposal, which I summoned to help treat people, but God knows what's going to happen to the field trip now, not that it matters a hell of a lot." She took his wrist very lightly, counting the pulse beats, and sighed. "You'd be better off with another half a pint in you, sir," she said. "We've run out of immediately available humans except me, but I promise I don't have anything untoward in my veins, just bog-standard O-neg and a glass of champagne."

Contini blinked at her. "You're offering?"

"You need it," she said, and held out a wrist faintly mottled with small white half-moon scars; she'd lost count of the times she'd done this for sanguivores in her care. "It's definitely not the first time I've obliged."

"—I appreciate it," said the nosferatu after a moment, and took her wrist in both cold hands. For once the sensation of her own blood running out of her veins was almost pleasant, as a distraction from the aching soreness of every muscle, the dragging, drowning fatigue, the remnants of sour adrenaline, and she closed her eyes and let him feed.

CHAPTER 9

Hell

Fastitocalon was not by *nature* an early riser; he had spent several hundred years on Earth holding down a variety of not-very-good jobs for not-very-worthwhile employers, and one of the things he loved most about being back in Hell was *not* having to get up at five-thirty in the morning, break the ice in the basin to wash, and make tea over a horrible little gas ring. Most of the time these days he even slept in a proper bed, rather than on his office couch, with a heap of pillows that made him feel *wealthy* with their luxurious multitude.

This didn't mean he was difficult to wake. When the knock came at his door, he sat up, squinting into the dimness for only a moment or two before calling out softly *Come in?* Nobody would bother knocking on his personal bedroom door at the hour suggested by the dim lake light through the windows if the matter at hand wasn't important.

His secretary poked her head in, tight-curled horns limned

by the brighter light in the hallway. "I'm sorry to disturb you, sir," she said.

Fastitocalon sighed, pushing back the covers and reaching for his dressing gown. "What's gone wrong now?" he asked.

"It's—well, External Affairs got a call from topside, the Göttingen liaison people in America for the research trip?"

He ran his hands through his hair. "Shit. What's gone wrong *with the research trip?*"

Greta hadn't called him, via either mindtouch or the cell phone; she was there in the back of his head, distantly present, the dim touch exhausted but not under enormous distress. Whatever had happened, it didn't feel like an *immediate* emergency, at least.

Fastitocalon tied the belt of his dressing gown tight and motioned for the secretary to lead on. Like most of the archdemons he had a well-appointed office in his private quarters, and it was to this space—neat, but stacked high with esso traces and typed reports—that she bustled with him in tow. She had a clipboard tucked under her arm; of the available sorts of secretary, Fastitocalon had chosen the middle-aged hyper-competent female with grey hair and sensible shoes, albeit one featuring tightly curled spiral ram-type horns, and she gave off the air of carrying a clipboard even when one was not in evidence.

She waited until he'd settled at his desk to continue. "External Affairs said on the phone that apparently there was some sort of concerted attack on a group of supernatural creatures in New York City last night and Dr. Helsing requisitioned the bus—the research-trip bus—and its supplies, to be used in treating the victims of the attack. We're not sure what this is going to do to the official schedule, and so far I think no one's informed Göttingen before they talked to you and Belial and got some orders?"

Fastitocalon rubbed at his temples. "Could you ask someone to get me some coffee? What sort of attack? What supernatural creatures? Has anything come through on any of the monitoring equipment?"

"They're checking right now, sir. From what I've been told so far, mostly vampires of various types and some werecreatures were at the event where this attack occurred, but it sounds as if it may have involved some of our personnel. The two New York operatives."

"Glasya and Morax," said Fastitocalon, wincing. "No calls from them? No contact?"

"Not so far, sir. And there's another thing. The *main* attack sounds to have been chemical or sacral in nature—apparently someone got holy water into a fire sprinkler system or something, I'm not entirely clear, but there's something about *darts* as well. Like…well, it sounds like the one that wounded Mr. Harlach up in London a little while ago?"

"Oh, *damn*," said Fastitocalon. "Damn and blast, I'd hoped we'd seen the end of that. Okay, have someone try to contact Morax and Glasya, see if they're answering any of their phones, and if not, leave a message to call down here as soon as they can. I'll get onto Dr. Helsing to fill us in on what actually *happened*. I want to talk to Belial and to Faust as soon as they can get vertical and caffeinated—give me fifteen minutes to get dressed and I'll meet them downstairs in my conference room."

In fact it was twelve minutes by his watch before Fastitocalon, fully dressed, his hair combed into its regulation part, settled into the chair at the head of his conference table. Faust arrived shortly afterward. The doctor looked rumpled and ill-rested in his scrubs, but then he always looked like that, Fastitocalon thought. "Good morning," he said.

"Is it?" Faust inquired, and watched as he lit a cigarette with his fingertip. "Any word from your chaps upstairs yet, or are they still on the casualty list?"

"We've left messages," said Fastitocalon. "Nothing clear's shown up on any of the neighboring locations' monitoring equipment. I've been on the phone to the Philadelphia and Boston operatives; they haven't seen any blips suggesting anything's come or gone from our side of the great divide, not that I really thought it might have done. So far preliminary reports I've seen suggest that the attackers used holy water, which isn't something our lot is likely to be playing with. What I'm concerned about is this business with the darts. I don't know enough about it yet to essay any conclusions."

"Can't be of much use myself without some data," said Faust, and looked up as Fastitocalon's secretary ushered Belial in and set down a tray of coffee. "Morning," he added to the archdemon as the door shut once more. "You got anything useful to add to this little confab other than groovy eye makeup?"

Belial sat down, glaring. He was immaculately put together in a dark red pinstripe suit, perfectly lowlighted hair draped over one eye; the other, thus displayed, was a masterpiece of smoky burgundy shadow. As Fastitocalon watched, a sparkly champagne-colored highlight brushed itself over his brow bone and his lips outlined themselves in shimmery cocoa. It was more than a little distracting, and he reached for a cup of coffee, looking into its depths instead of at his colleague.

"What the hell *time* is it," Belial asked while his face finished putting itself on, and picked up his own cup; sugar added itself. "No, never mind, don't tell me, I don't want to know, and no. All I'm aware of is that my nice, neat timetable is now comprehensively fucked. The goddamn field trip was *supposed* to start today—in fact it was supposed to have started already, Helsing and her merry men ought to be on their damn way to go bother some mine-dwelling knockers instead of dealing with a bunch of vampires with second-degree chemical burns."

"Don't forget poisoned dart wounds," said Fastitocalon. "Apparently."

"Oh, we don't want to forget those," Faust said sourly. "Well. You haven't got through to your people on the surface, you were saying."

"Not the ones involved," said Fastitocalon. "But I'm going to have a go at getting Greta on the phone, now that I've got both of you here to join in, unless you've got a better idea?"

"Not I," said Faust, yawning enormously and leaning back in the chair. Fastitocalon chained another Dunhill

243

and reached for the keyboard, waking the big wall-mounted screen and typing in Greta Helsing's number. He could vividly recall not so very long ago when such a thing would have been impossible, when telephones were large black Bakelite objects about as suitable for bludgeoning murder victims as communicating information, and was glad in passing that at least nobody in Hell had ever suggested they ignore technological advancement as it happened to occur.

Three rings. Four. Five. He was almost sure he'd have to leave her a voicemail when a very tired, raspy, low-on-patience voice said, "Helsing." The screen remained resolutely black: she wasn't going to let them see whatever physical state she was in, and Fastitocalon didn't entirely blame her.

"Greta," he said. "I've got Faust and Belial with me. I know you've got to be incredibly busy, but if you've got a minute—"

"Oh, Christ, it's you," said Greta Helsing. "Thank fuck. Fass, I had to use the field-trip supplies, I'm sorry about that, I know it's a logistical mess, but I absolutely didn't have a choice—"

"Course you didn't," said Faust. "What actually happened?"

"I can only tell you what I *saw* and what's possible to extrapolate from available data," she said, and then rattled off a brief overview of the previous evening's festivities, starting with the gathering of Contini's guests and staff members in the refurbished gallery space currently leased by the demon Glasya. Fastitocalon couldn't necessarily follow all the clinical details, but he watched as Faust scribbled rapidly on a yellow legal pad in the spidery shorthand of doctors everywhere.

"How many would you say are going to need significant clinical follow-up?" Faust asked.

"Of the—call it sixty-five people who were affected, the majority are walking wounded, they'll recover on their own with some rest and care, but there's a good ten patients I'm not happy with," said Greta. "And much as I appreciate the bus and its facilities, I don't have anywhere to *put* several of those for more than a couple of days. Happily Mr. Contini himself wasn't terribly badly hurt and will be back to his old self in a week or so, but I've got a couple of weres with internal silver burns and several patients with those goddamned dart wounds up here, and I don't know what the hell I'm going to *do* with them, frankly. Orlax's been a great help—did *you* know demons can do that thing with their fields to calm people down and ease pain? He's been working flat out since last night and he's exhausted. Glasya's in moderately poor shape; Morax has her and the rest of us staying with him for now, but I've used up all the stocks of lake water and Morax is not super great at applied clinical cursing, so we can't really make our own cursed-water supplies."

"*That* at least we can fix," said Faust. "I'll have a couple pallet-loads of the stuff sent up wherever you need it to go, and we do have the room down here to take some patients on a short-term basis if they need hospital care. You said it was fire sprinklers?"

"Must've been an old deluge system, all the sprinklers went off at once," said Greta. "I didn't see anyone holding a lighter under any of them; they all just went. And I didn't have the opportunity to grab a sample, but the water was *gross*—rust-stained, stank like it'd been inside the pipes for a hundred years, like draining an old steam-radiator circuit, and I'd swear to it there had to have been some kind of silver suspension in it as well as all the blessings. I've seen holy water do weres some damage in the past, but this stuff *burned* them as badly as it hurt anybody else." She sighed audibly. "And that blessing, that wasn't just some parish priest waving a hand and intoning, that was *hardcore*. The angel with me said he could see it even through the pipes, when we found the valve to turn the water off. Said the whole damn pipe system was glowing gold with holy influence. Who the *hell* is going about throwing old-school holy influence into fucking *fire sprinkler systems* in *Chelsea*, for God's sake?"

"Who indeed," said Fastitocalon. "Did anything happen to the angel when the water started?"

"No," she said. "He got wet, like me, and he was sick, but I think that was just the free-flowing champagne at the party; he didn't show any sign of skin irritation, no erythema, no blistering, and nothing systemic. He and I and a couple of volunteer buffet humans were pretty much the only ones who *weren't* suffering, which frankly wasn't all that great a look."

"I can imagine," said Belial, and reached over to commandeer Fastitocalon's cigarette case. "Well. It sounds to me as if the field trip is going to need to be postponed, at least, until we can find out what the hell is going on. If it were just one lot of supernaturals chasing after another lot, or even just human monster-hunters going monster-hunting, well, that's hardly our business, but if there's this *angelic* stuff going on as well—"

"If there's angelic stuff going on as well," said Fastitocalon with a sigh, "then it gets complicated, and all this business with the Accords comes into play, and everything gets a lot *more* complicated."

"What are we supposed to tell Dr. Hildebrandt?" Greta asked. "It was his damn curiosity about the reset and the discontinuity that gave this whole business its cover story in the first place."

"Hildebrandt thinks whatever my people want him to think," said Belial. "But if you believe he'd be easier in his mind with some more specific cover story for the trip being postponed or canceled altogether—"

"We...ran into some *unforeseen preliminary results* in our research," said Greta, with the air of one making it up as she went along. "Regarding the discontinuity. And need to do more investigation before we can set out on the trip as planned. Wrap that up in administrator-speak and send it to him; that ought to keep him happy for a while. I wish I *did* know what was happening up in Heaven, to be honest. It sounds pretty sketchy."

"So do we," said Fastitocalon. "Right. So what I'll tell Sam is—"

"—is that Dr. Helsing, with supplies furnished by yours truly, is providing follow-up care to the individuals injured in last night's fracas," said Faust. "And will be back in touch with her assessment afterward, which may or may not result in some patients being temporarily transferred down here for care. It's hardly the first time we've treated worldly monsters—think of your friend Ruthven, for example—and it won't be the last. Don't worry about the psych aspect of it, either. We're very, very good at managing expectations and memory. Meanwhile the archdemon Belial's office will handle all the logistics required for extending Dr. Helsing and her entourage's stay in New York until this business is cleared up. Yes?"

"Something like that," said Belial. "Doctor, is, er, Mr. Contini's organization going to be conducting an investigation into this incident?"

"I think you could say that," Greta told him. "I don't believe Mr. Contini took very kindly to having his party blown up by chemical attacks and his constituents injured, and I also don't think Mr. Contini or his organization are going to be all that subtle in their approach."

"I see," said Belial. "Well. Do convey to him our deep sympathies and a standing offer to be of help however we can?"

"I will," she said. "Dr. Faust, can I email you a list of the stuff I need most?"

"Do so," said Faust. "And also if you can give me some more clinical detail just for my own personal interest, I'd appreciate it. We don't come across colloidal silver injury down here too often."

"Or at all," said Fastitocalon, retrieving his cigarette case from Belial. "Thank you, Dr. Helsing. Be in touch, yes? And we'll get back to you as soon as Belial's people have found the correct spin for Dr. Hildebrandt."

"I will," said Greta, and the call cut off.

"Well," said Belial again, getting up. "That was informative. And vivid."

"Would have liked to've been there," said Faust. "Awful thing to have happen, of course, terrible shame, but it's not as if we've got reams and reams of clinical data on holy-water injury in different sorts of monster. Fastitocalon, walk with me. I want to pick your brain."

"Of course," said Fastitocalon, tucking the enameled case away in his breast pocket. "Are you attempting to figure out how best to inform Samael about this, too?"

"However did you guess," said the doctor sourly, and led the way out of the conference room. The M&E offices were busy even this early in the day, with demons bustling around carrying stacks of printouts and cups of coffee, and Fastitocalon was briefly very glad of his people and their commitment to *doing the job*.

At least a lot of the logistical bullshit of dealing with this mess could be handled over the phone, Greta thought as she slipped hers back into her pocket. The hotel room reservations at the Carlyle had been extended for another two days, just for the sake of having somewhere safe to fall back; the now-denuded bus, littered with the wrappings and peelings of God knew how many individual doses of Lake Avernus water and adrenaline and hard-core antihistamine, syringe after syringe, gauze dressing after gauze dressing, had been taken back to wherever important rich people parked their gigantic tour buses when they were not in use. After the worst of the triage last night, those of Contini's guests who had been in any shape to take care of themselves had dispersed to their own safe-houses, bolt-holes, or penthouse apartments, according to their predilections. After some conversation, Greta had had the rest of her patients, including Contini, Ms. Cenci, Varney, and the New York demons, among others, transported to Morax's Tribeca loft, and it was from the palatial living room of this loft overlooking Franklin that she'd been talking to various people in Hell. It wasn't the setting she hadn't felt like revealing to her colleagues; it was her own current bedraggled state. She was still wearing the stained and ragged trousers and bustier top from last night's designer suit, the corresponding jacket having vanished at some point during the excitement, and somebody had given her somebody else's suit jacket to put over it against the night's chill; the effect was not exactly what Greta might call polished and professional. She kept meaning to ask if someone could go and fetch her luggage from the hotel, or the bus, or wherever it was, and kept forgetting; this was the first real time she'd had to herself since they'd arrived at the gallery the night before.

She could at least *remember* to email Faust the list of supplies she needed most urgently, Greta thought, sour, and pulled out her phone again. It had been clinically interesting, past the immediate emergency, to see how well Lake Avernus water worked on people who *weren't* actually demons:

it was a panacea for anyone originally hailing from Hell, of course, but she'd been very pleasantly surprised to find that it worked remarkably well on skin damage in not just vampires but vampyres *and* nosferatu, not to mention weres. The only people to whom it posed any sort of danger were angels, and she only had one of those to worry about. At least one she *knew* of. She couldn't quite forget Adariel talking about the way the contaminated pipes had been *glowing* to his particular sight, lit up gold; couldn't forget him warning her not to touch it. That hadn't sounded like any old mutter-mutter two-fingers-gesticulation blessing; that had sounded rather more intense.

The holy water hadn't done her any harm, extremely blessed or otherwise, that she could detect; sure, she was still a bedraggled mess, but she'd sluiced herself off with fresh water to make sure she didn't contaminate any of her patients with the holy-water residue, and she hadn't found any damage whatsoever. God, she wanted a proper shower and some clean clothes, though. It was so hard to think of herself as any sort of competent professional with a strapless bustier top digging into her ribs (that part reminded her of Paris, in a way she'd rather not have recalled).

Everyone seems to be getting on well enough, she added to the end of her email, after the list of things she was requisitioning from Hell. *One of the surface-op demons managed to* swallow *some of the muck as well as get it all over her, and that's taking a bit of time to fix, but I don't think I'm going to need to screech for emergency medevac. Fingers crossed. I'll send you down one of*

*the dart-points I removed from a nosferatu in case you want to do
science on it. Thx, G.*

"Greta?" said someone in a raspy voice behind her, and she
dropped the phone back into her borrowed-suit-jacket pocket
and turned to see Sir Francis Varney in a similarly borrowed
dressing gown, leaning against the doorway. He looked...
well, terrible, of course, he was clearly *feeling* somewhere along
the lines of moderately terrible, and she didn't blame him...
but in the muted light of Morax's vast apartment, against the
sharp geometric lines of the demon's minimalist furniture, he
also looked faintly editorial. She hurried over to him, slipped
her arms around his waist.

"Should you be up?" she said. "You had a nasty time of it
last night."

"So did everybody else," said Varney dolefully, but there
was amusement in his eyes. "I'm all right, love. Or I will be;
I'm just a little foxed around the edges. Did you ring up Hell
and ask for some more of that very nice fizzy water?"

"I did, and quite a lot of other things besides," she said.
"Lots for everyone. As soon as Faust sends things up, I'll do my
rounds, and then people ought to be a bit more comfortable."

Varney had been rather badly burned down one side of his
face and one hand by the corrosive water and had then sustained further damage in the process of helping several other
people who were worse off to escape the gallery, and kept
quiet about it while Greta saw to the more emergent cases.
When she'd finally peeled away his sodden formal-wear to
see the angry red burn-marks he'd been hiding, she'd come

very close to screaming at him, or possibly just dissolving into tears, she wasn't sure, but it wouldn't have been helpful either way. Decontamination and irrigation with Avernus water had at least stopped the damage from worsening, and she'd slathered burn cream on his arm and shoulder and told him to have a very stiff drink and lie down, and moved on to the next patient waiting in line, Orlax in tow. Now, in the light of day, she eyed him critically: still favoring that shoulder, but the burns on his face and hand were mostly down to angry pink irritation that would fade over the next couple of days. *Good*, she thought, *I needn't worry* quite *so hard over him, at least*; she could spare that concern for Glasya, who had been among the worst of the casualties, and the two weres who'd been unlucky enough to inhale water vapor that contained colloidal silver. She could worry about them, and about Contini, who wasn't as badly hurt but was very clearly the most important person in the vicinity, and not about her husband quite so much.

Varney slipped his arms around her, rested his chin on the top of her head. She could feel as well as hear the slow, slow beating of his heart. "You haven't had any sleep at all, have you," he said.

"Sleep is for people who aren't playing first responder to a chemical disaster," Greta said into his collarbone. "What I could do with is a very hot bath in water that has absolutely no religious significance in any direction, and possibly something to eat. I wonder if Mr. Contini's people could oblige with either. Where are the postdocs, by the way?"

"Orlax is sleeping; he more or less fell over as soon as you stopped needing him. The last time I saw Adariel he was heading for the roof and looked as if he didn't want to talk about anything whatsoever. One has to wonder just how our hosts must view an actual angel in their midst, given the current situation."

"One does," said Greta. "I suppose I'd best go and find him, and possibly reassure Mr. Contini and his employees that while Adariel is indeed an angel, he isn't here to sabotage anything. I suppose I could dig out the official paperwork signed by both sides to show them he's here purely for research purposes. Do you think it'd help?"

"To be honest I get the feeling these people are not exactly the sort who can be easily convinced by reading bits of paper saying something is the case," said Varney, bone-dry. "I think they're slightly more hands-on about the burden of proof," and she had to laugh and squeeze him very gently, so as not to hurt his healing side.

"Do you know what we're supposed to be doing right this very second?" she asked, without letting go of him to do it.

"My mind's gone a complete blank," said Varney. "Do enlighten me?"

"Right this exact second, I believe," she said, "we're supposed to be on our nicely stocked enormous luxury coach being driven into the wilds of western Pennsylvania to do Doctors Without Borders at a population of mine-dwelling knockers who have no real reason to welcome such an intrusion. And I don't speak a *word* of knocker dialect."

"I see," said Varney delicately. "May I hesitantly infer from your tone that the current situation is perhaps in some ways preferable?"

"This joint has a much nicer coffee machine," said Greta, and kissed his throat. "God, though. I wish we hadn't had to go through that...I wish *everybody* hadn't had to go through that attack, that was *bad*...but I can't say I'm not just a little pleased to be sticking around New York for the immediate future. Or to have fallen into the hands of Mr. Contini and his associates, whom I have to admit I rather like."

"Ms. Cenci was very complimentary about you earlier this morning," said Varney, just as delicately. "Although I'm afraid she did have some critical remarks to share on the subject of your current attire? I'll refrain from repeating them, of course."

"My current attire is effectively Mayfair-meets-war-zone," said Greta, "so I can hardly disagree with her assessment, but I do wish I knew whose jacket this was and if he wants it back. Either before or after it goes to the cleaners. Could you possibly lean on your acquaintance with Ms. Cenci to so inquire?"

"I'll see what I can do," said Varney, and kissed her hair.

Up this high there always seemed to be wind, even on a calm day. That had been true in Heaven, actually, although the wind in Heaven was a soft, gentle breath faintly perfumed with myrrh and aloes that lifted one's feathers and ruffled one's curls; here on Earth, it wasn't quite so kind a touch, and it did not remind him of the scent of myrrh.

The city *smelled* in a way Adariel hadn't quite been prepared for, a sort of huge complicated nasal symphony that hit you with everything at once, awful and lovely: perfume and urine and garbage and frying onions and spice from street food carts; the warm, hollow, faintly sulfurous smell of the subway stations yawning with their promise, *come down here into the dark and be spirited away*. Unwashed human and oily machinery, roasting nuts, steam from the darkness underneath the streets. The city reeked and the city breathed, and he wasn't at all sure what he was supposed to do in return. He was sitting on the end of a bench next to a planter, close enough to the edge of the roof that the wind was unignorable, and he did not know what he was supposed to *do*. At least Orlax had been able to be useful, to help Dr. Helsing in her work.

The water had been blessed, last night. The water that burned people had been *blessed*, strongly enough for the holy touch to have glowed visibly gold to his eyes. That water had been touched by something that was *of God*, and he had watched it hurt so many people—he could still hear the screams, but worse than the screaming had been the sort of *sizzling*, bubbling, *cooking* sound the water made when it touched the skin of every single person there who wasn't angelic or human. Blessed things weren't supposed to *hurt* you; it was... blessings were supposed to heal, to be helpful, to take away sorrow and pain and the grief of a wound, and he'd *watched* the angry wheals rising on Sir Francis Varney's face, Sir Francis who had been kind to him, and Orlax, who hadn't really been kind but whom he was here to *work* with, side by side...it was the Accords, it was supposed to be right—

He felt abruptly sick again and closed his eyes, leaning over as his throat hitched, but after a moment his insides seemed to settle once more. He had no idea what to do, because nothing made any *sense*, and all at once very suddenly he wanted to go *home*. To go home and to never have left Heaven, or...thought about anything, ever, at all. Never to have been sent to work for Raphael in the infirmary, where he could see bad things happening to people, witness pain or injury or sickness, be aware that they existed. He could have been assigned to one of the construction details, stacking bricks of sapphire on one another, or polished the jewel cobblestones, or sent to do sums in the pearl warehouses, counting out sacks of black and pink and purple gems to fill the fountain basins with gravel. He could have sung and sung and sung, been a thing that was *for* singing, simple and unquestioned. He could have been anything at all, and he would have been *happy*, and it wouldn't have mattered that he would never have *known* he was happy at all, because he'd never have known anything else.

But that wasn't right, either, was it? The worst part was not *knowing* how much of the things he didn't know was just his own newness, simple ignorance, and how much was information that had somehow been kept from him, hidden away so he need never encounter it. How much he couldn't trust anything he'd instinctively, blindly, faithfully believed, and what it would mean if that belief had somehow been *wrong*.

There was no up or down anymore. There was no gravity

pulling in any direction that he could believe in, that he could trust.

Adariel hunched his shoulders against the wind, and he did not know that the outlines of his wings were visible, like ice seen underwater, a moving shimmer, or that the tears that traced themselves one after another down his face were ever so faintly glowing gold.

CHAPTER 10

New York City

I don't know where I was last night.

I do know not all of us made it back, but not where they didn't make it back *from*, or why, or what happened afterward. I remember *going to* the place we had been told to gather at, and being given things to hold, and I remember it all seeming very clear. And then we were outside, in the rain, and waiting for something to happen. That's it. After that it's...just jumbled.

I don't want things to happen that I can't remember. That was part of my bad life, my old life, the one I put away and walked out of when I found the Lord. Not remembering things means you did something bad, and maybe someone's hurt or maybe you're in trouble and you don't even know it yet, and maybe you kind of want to die because you said and did fucked-up shit and it doesn't seem like there's a lot of stuff there to balance out all the fucked-up shit you did, and maybe you just want to *stop* and be over and not have to try anymore when your whole stupid fucking life was the mistake, when nothing you ever did was ever worth anything at all—

—That's the bad thoughts. That's what they tell you won't help, that when the bad thoughts like those come, all you can do is just trust in God and ask Him for strength to bear your troubles. And hope He's listening, the way real people don't.

My feet hurt a lot. I think maybe some of the blisters are infected or something.

I think maybe I won't go out and witness today. I think maybe I might be done.

I'm so tired.

Gideon Tremayne woke, stiff and cold, and had no idea where he was.

It was dark, and he wasn't lying on either his bed in Brooklyn or a park bench or…some vague imagined white-and-gold echoing space that smelled warmly of amber and honey. It was the kind of thick, soft-furred darkness that came with being underground. Not complete; he could see his hand move in front of his eyes, and there was some kind of very faint yellowish glow in the distance.

He sat up, blinking, wide-eyed, straining for the edges of things, and after a moment or two could make out that he was in a tunnel with grimy tiled walls. Underneath him the floor shook briefly and stilled again, and some dust sifted down from the unseen ceiling.

Gideon had been in the city long enough to recognize the rattle-shake-rumble of a subway train, although he'd never encountered it from this particular point of view. He must be in the tunnels somewhere—not one of the active bits, and certainly not one of the transit bores; presumably there were access tunnels, or maintenance passageways for the people who kept the system running to make their way across the undercity without being seen.

That must be why he was down here, he thought muzzily. To *not be seen*.

He tried to remember coming down here. Or being brought down, but there was no sign of anyone else in the vicinity. Had he somehow sleepwalked himself underground? The last thing he could recall with any clarity was...getting on a train. With a paper bag containing something heavy and precious.

Gideon scrabbled around himself but could find nothing on the floor anywhere near him other than what felt like some ancient coils of cable or rope and the long-dead corpse of an electric flashlight. He shook it, hopefully, and flicked the thumb switch, but he might as well have been holding a piece of lead pipe for all the light it gave.

So he'd lost—whatever it was. Okay. Maybe that didn't matter. It *felt* as if it didn't matter much, for what that was worth.

He leaned back against the grimy tile and shut his eyes again. Behind the closed lids some flickers of image faded into visibility: he'd been on a train, and then outside, in the rain, at night—he could remember that, the rain touching his face with a thousand cold fingertips, how it had felt nice against his hot skin—and then inside, in some old building that he'd never seen before but somehow knew like the back of his own hand. Knew where to go inside the building's corridors, and what to do there, and... it had to do with water. Not rainwater, but *like* it: something that would rain *inside*, that would wash away iniquity and stains and sin and clean the space so that it could be made godly and correct once more. He was there to... wash away sin. With water.

All at once he could remember staring at his own hands glowing gold in the dimness of the corridor, glowing as if he'd dipped them in molten gold, as if it should *hurt*—it hurt to look at them, that light was so bright, but inside the brilliance he could almost see something, see a face—it was too beautiful to look at for very long, he shut his eyes and still could see the bright rosy golden glow through their lids, see his own blood vessels like the deltas of tiny rivers, feel his own blood drawn through them bathed in that light, that *light*, that golden perfect light, oh, he wasn't worthy of this, no one could be worthy of this, but he had been *touched by God* and knew what it was he must do—oh, it was ecstatic, that surety, that *knowledge*, that knowing—he must touch things and with a touch change them, render them different, pass on the gift he had been allowed so very briefly to hold, and then—get out of the way.

Get out of the way and let the light do its own work, because the purpose for which he had been chosen was complete and over and done with, and so was he.

No, he thought, *no, please, don't let it be over, please, let me serve You, let me be Your hand,* and heard only the echoes of his own voice, the juddering, fragile, fallible sound of his own heart beating in his ears. He had *been* the tool, the blade held in the hand, but he knew with the same certainty that he knew which way gravity pulled that it was over now.

He thought he had done a good job. He hoped he had. It had been the most important moment of his life, and now there was going to have to be the rest of his life, marked endlessly and inescapably with the absence of that purpose.

Alone, in the grimy tunnel, Gideon Tremayne covered his face with his filthy *human* hands, more alone than he had been in months, and wept for everything wanted and taken and lost, everything gone that could never be recovered, the light of a favor now and forever over and withdrawn.

Hell

It had taken the demon Harlach much longer than he'd personally have preferred to throw off the last of the effects of the poisoned-dart wound; even now, despite complaining enough to get himself discharged from the Tower Six hospital and released with a series of follow-up appointments at the Spa, he didn't feel entirely *well*.

Nor had this been improved by the phone conversation he'd had with Haliel after leaving the hospital. Haliel had sounded like he'd picked up a cold, which Harlach didn't really associate with angels, but that hadn't been the worrisome thing. Or not the *only* worrisome thing. The idea of the angel actually sneaking around and getting into his, Harlach's, esso emplacements at the direct contradiction of his express orders from Gabriel *and asking Raphael not to tattle on him* was rather dizzying in its sheer strange lack of balance: if Haliel was up to that sort of thing, the world was upside down, *and* Edmund Ruthven had apparently been gone from London long enough for people to notice.

He'd known the vampire and his unsuitable boyfriend were out of town, of course he'd known that—it was his business to know that sort of thing, as London surface operative—but it hadn't really occurred to Harlach to question how *long* Ruthven had been away and when exactly to expect his return. If young werefolk were doing stuff like sneaking into cemeteries to drink and smoke and fuck around a little with *impunity*, knowing that the London city guardian wasn't likely to show up to bust them, then…well. Maybe somebody who wasn't him ought to know about it?

And thus Harlach had passed a sleepless night, thinking about things, and presented himself first thing in the business-day morning at Fastitocalon's office in M&E to make his somewhat belated report and pass on what he had discovered. And been told: *wait, the Director was busy elsewhere.* The Director was on a conference call. Now the Director was with Dr. Faust. No, the secretary couldn't say when he would be free; did Harlach wish to leave a message?

It's important, he'd said, and possibly the Harlach he had been before the poisoned dart caught him under the collarbone would not have done what he did next: turn on his heel and stalk out of the M&E bullpen and hurry over to the hospital to demand to see Dr. Faust.

"I'm afraid you can't go in," said the nurse outside Faust's office. "He's with the Director—"

"Of M&E. I know. I need to see both of them, actually." Harlach gave the nurse what fraction of a smile he could dredge up and shouldered past them, knocking sharply on Faust's door. After a moment or two it opened wide enough for Faust to squint up at him through the crack.

"Oh," he said. "It's you. What do you want? I'm busy. Something's happened up on Earth."

"Not in London, though?" Harlach said.

"What? No. What's London got to do with it?"

"Haliel's been doing my job," said Harlach, "and while he didn't find anything that'd need me to report it through official channels, he did find out that the city guardian's been away from his post for long enough to upset the order of things."

Faust sighed and let the door open the rest of the way, revealing the mess that was his office with the M&E director leaning against the desk, arms folded. "Harlach," said Fastitocalon. "What goes on?"

"Haliel," said Harlach. "He's doing my job. Or . . . conducting his own investigations. And very deliberately *not telling Gabriel* what he's found."

"He didn't mention anything about holy water or more poisoned darts?" said Faust.

"What? No. Just—I *know* he's not supposed to be looking

at emplacements that aren't Heaven's own, on his own time. He's been *sneaking* around, and Ruthven's absence is apparently no longer news to London's monsters, which I thought you ought to know, Fastitocalon—"

"Never mind London," said Faust. "New York's been hit with some intensely weird shenanigans that may or may not be angelic in origin, I'm afraid London is going to have to wait. I've been trying to get through to Raphael for a while now but it just goes to a busy signal. I do hope Gabriel isn't doing anything particularly drastic; last time I saw him he seemed to be doing his best to give poor old Raphael a blinding migraine out of sheer angelic spite."

"New York?" Harlach repeated, rubbing at the barely healed wound in his shoulder. The idea of Gabriel acting out of spite was... not exactly difficult to countenance, he had to admit.

"Sit *down*," Faust snapped at him. "Since you're here you might as well stick around in case I do get through; you can ask Raphael some more useful questions. In the meantime we're waiting on the analysis of some *new* poisoned darts to see if they're the same thing that hit you, and if so, what we can possibly do about it."

"More darts?"

"More darts," said Fastitocalon. "Aimed at demons and various sorts of monster, apparently. Nobody shot an angel this time around."

"Yet," said Faust.

"Yet," Fastitocalon allowed. "Sit down and tell me everything you can remember about your last conversation with

Haliel. We may need to try to get in contact with him if Faust can't raise Raphael. I don't suppose you know what their schedule looks like up there in Heaven?"

"I don't," said Harlach slightly dazedly, and sat.

Tribeca, New York City

It had been a very long time since Aurelio Contini had been physically hurt. Scuffed up, perhaps. Bruised, cut about, ruffled, certainly. But not *hurt*.

When the burning rain had begun to fall he'd had a horrid, vertiginous moment of certainty that this was the work of his own people, or his guests, a Masque-of-the-Red-Death moment designed to put an end to Contini's organization and his presence all at once, the ultimate betrayal. Then he'd seen Adriana Cenci screaming with scarlet-white burns down her face and throat; he'd seen Elgin the wolf choking on thin air, Sarasti the vampire half-blinded and thrashing helplessly in pain, and realized: no, this was a betrayal, but not of himself alone.

A betrayal couched as an act of war.

In the worst of the chaos and pain Contini had lost the narrative thread, time slipping sickeningly past him the way it can in dreams, the whole world turned into a kaleidoscope of bright broken shards of image. The red-stained water pooling on the floor, dripping down the walls, matting people's hair to their burning faces. The screams, and worse than screams. The *stink* of it, copper and iron and heavy metals and the smell of blessing, which no sanguivore could ever quite forget once they'd encountered it. Holy water, blessed with an old blessing, one that was deeply powerful and very dangerous indeed.

The next thing he'd been clearly aware of was lying on the couch in Glasya's office with his bodyguards standing over him while the human dabbed at his wounds. He could barely even remember who the hell she was supposed to be, someone Adriana had invited at the last minute, some kind of monster-adjacent hume, but she'd taken charge in the middle of all that and she had done something that had *stopped* the lethal rain from falling, and then there had been—*real* rain, outside, the worst sufferers helped out into it to wash off the corrosive liquid, and then something the human had applied from unmarked bottles, something that looked a lot like Pellegrino if Pellegrino had crushed-opal shimmer in it. The relief when whatever that was touched his burns had been so startling it had *rung* in Contini's mind like a struck glass, clear and reverberating, a shock of coolness that had taken the pain away with it.

She'd gone away for a while, and he'd given a couple of orders but could already feel his body trying to repair itself, sending him into a deep shock-sleep, and there had been a solid slice of nothingness before he'd woken up in an actual bed, clean and bandaged, feeling deeply unpleasant but no longer as if he were in anything close to actual danger.

The human had been there when he'd woken, and told him what he actually needed to know—where he was, how many people were hurt and how badly, what she'd done with them—and he'd given her the orders he needed her to follow. They were in Morax's place, apparently. Morax had been badly hurt but not as seriously as his partner Glasya or a couple of the weres; Adriana was in worse shape than Contini himself but not by much, and both of them were supposed to heal without serious permanent scarring, due to whatever it was the human had put on their burns.

Now, waking again, he saw it was midday by the clock on the wall; the room he'd been given had its floor-to-ceiling windows blanked out with blinds to block the sunlight. His head was a good deal clearer. Clear enough for a couple more questions and their answers, Contini thought.

He sat up, wincing as the movement tugged against healing skin. Frankie had been sleeping in a chair by the side of the bed, looking somewhat battered but in one piece, and he, too, sat up once he saw his boss was awake. "Get me the doctor," Contini said, and was silently grateful in his choice of employees: Frankie said neither anything useless such as *are you okay* nor anything counterproductive such as *are you sure*, simply nodding and levering himself out of the chair to go and fetch the human.

In the light of full consciousness, without half a gallon of adrenaline sloshing around Contini's bloodstream, he was surprised at how unimpressive she actually was. In his memories she'd wielded the iron-certain command of an expert in her field snapping out orders; now he could see she was barely five foot five without her heels, narrow-boned, and that the blonde hair wasn't artistic enough to be from a bottle.

Vivian Shaw

Someone had found her some clothes that weren't the ones she'd ruined the night before, dark jeans and a V-neck shirt she kept tugging absently on as if trying to get its neckline to quit baring quite so much. Someone had also found her a stethoscope, which she wore draped around her neck and which Contini had to admit did in fact increase the visual effect of authority.

"Mr. Contini," she said. She had what he considered a basic British accent, neither snobby nor yobby. "How are you feeling?"

"Like I got doused with fucking holy water at my own shindig," said Contini, and sighed. "Could be worse. *Has* been worse, in fact. I got you to thank for patching us all up?"

"Me and a few assistants," said the doctor. "You'll be glad to hear Ms. Cenci's improved a lot, and I'm sure now that she won't scar. No one who was hurt in the attack is likely to need hospital care if current trends continue."

"I don't know if you noticed," said Contini, "but most of us aren't what you might call technically alive, so taking anyone to the hospital would pose some logistical issues."

"Not hospitals *here*," said the doctor. What was her name again? *G*-something. Glinda? *Greta*. With the world's least believable last name. "I rang down to Hell for emergency requisitions last night and again this morning, and if anyone does suddenly get drastically worse, we can transfer people down there to be seen to. It's not the first time I've had to do that, not by far."

"You talk to Hell a lot?" he asked, and coughed, wincing:

270

he hadn't swallowed any of the foul stuff, thank God, but he'd definitely inhaled a bit of spray, and his throat felt raw.

"I do," said Greta Helsing, rummaging in the bag she'd brought with her and coming out with several pill bottles; she shook a selection of capsules and tablets into her hand. "Here. Antihistamine, decongestant, painkiller. Frankie, can you get me a bottle of the lake water?"

Contini's lieutenant nodded and slipped out of the room; a moment later he returned with that opal-shimmery sparkling liquid he could vaguely remember having dabbed onto his burns the night before. "What is that stuff?" he demanded, taking the bottle and sniffing at it: faintly sweet and wild, pleasant-smelling.

"Lake Avernus water," said Helsing. "Fresh from Hell. It'll help. Works best on demons but it's still pretty much a panacea for monsters as far as I've been able to see; it's the exact opposite of holy water."

Contini eyed her over his handful of pills and then just gulped them down, squeezing his eyes shut as the fizz burned in his raw throat. The burn was over quickly, though, leaving behind it a gentle kind of spreading warmth in his throat and stomach, like a kinder version of strong liquor. "Okay," he said. "So what happens now?"

"Can you tell me everything you remember not just from the actual incident but anything significant leading up to it? We have evidence that the point of the attack was both to harm, possibly kill, guests *inside* the gallery and to drive them out into range of what seems to have been a large number of people with poisoned blowdarts. It's not the first time I've seen the darts, but I've definitely never seen anyone try anything like the blessed-water business before."

"Those fuckin' *darts*," Contini spat, and had to lean back against his pillows. "Christ. I thought I had that whole business sorted—how many of them were there?"

"I'm not sure," said Helsing. "I saw at least twenty people who'd been wounded, and as far as I *know* nobody caught any of the people shooting them. You've seen the darts before here in New York?"

"Yeah," said Contini. "Got a couple of my people over the past week, two weeks. Whatever's on them fucks us up pretty good, depends on how deep the thing went, I think."

"Let me guess," said the doctor. "Pain, fever, dizziness, sickness following the wound, resolving over a day to several days?"

"The worst one was three days before he could get up, but he's okay now," said Contini. "Fuck. I know who was *doing* that. I went and had a little chat with him and everything. Seemed to me like we had an understanding vis-à-vis the whole *him not having his people shoot my people* concept."

"Apparently he misunderstood," said Helsing, and if she hadn't been radiating *no sleep* on quite such a broad band, Contini might have had a problem with her tone. "Can you tell me what you remember?"

"I could," he said, "but I think I'm not gonna, actually. I think what I *am* going to do is go down to that guy's apartment and have *another* little chat with him, and this time I don't plan on leaving any room for *misunderstanding*. Frankie, where the fuck are my clothes?"

Frankie started to say something, but the doctor raised a hand to forestall him. "Mr. Contini," she said. "I get exactly how much you want to find that guy and remove his head and possibly do something unspeakable down the hole, *believe* me, I get it, but—you're not in any shape to go avenging right now. Give yourself some more time to heal and let us see what we can find out, because I'm thinking that this whole business is probably not limited to some idiot playing games of what-can-I-get-away-with here. I think in all probability it's on a larger scale than just New York, or the New York underworld."

Contini glared at her, and most people would have quailed from that cigarette-ember gaze, but maybe most people hadn't had the night and morning this woman had experienced. "Who's *we*?" he demanded. "You said *see what we can find out*. Who's we?"

"Hell, mostly," she said. "Bits of Heaven, too, but they're less helpful."

"You really do spend a lot of time chatting with Hell?"

"Quite a lot," she said, "one way and another," and took his wrist between her fingers. "How are you feeling?"

"Shitty," he said, "but also slightly intrigued."

"I suppose that's an improvement," she said, relinquishing his pulse. "Frankie, can you bring Mr. Contini a very stiff drink, please, and see if Sir Francis and Ms. Cenci and Morax are awake? I think it'd be a good idea to have this conversation once instead of having to repeat bits of it."

Frankie nodded without question. Apparently, while Contini had been out, his people had decided they were going to obey this human woman, and—well, okay. Maybe that didn't sound like the worst idea he'd ever heard of, after all. "Oh," she added. "And Adariel. If you can find him. I think he'd gone up to the roof earlier. I'd like him to be in here, too."

"The blond guy?" Frankie asked.

"The angel. That's him. Blond, blue eyes, extremely traumatized. I think he's having some difficulty reconciling *holy things* with the damage he witnessed last night."

"Did you already tell me how come you got an angel and a demon hanging out with you?" Contini inquired when Frankie had excused himself to fetch the others.

"I did, but I doubt it sank in," she said. "It's sort of complicated, but the quick version is that since a sort of political shake-up last year, Heaven and Hell have been more actively working together, or have been *supposed* to be more actively working together, not that this has been a roaring success, and since angels and demons are hideously allergic to one another's realms, they wanted to see if an angel and a demon could work together more effectively *on Earth*. And I happened to be available as a sort of supervisor, for unrelated reasons. We were supposed to be doing a research field trip in our great big shiny bus, and instead here I am wearing someone else's Armani sweater and hoping real hard that someone who isn't me can figure out what the hell to do about all this mess."

"Well," said Contini. "Since you put it like that. I guess we lucked out running into you, huh, Doctor?"

"I don't know about that," she said. "But I'm here now, so I'm going to do what I can to help."

Probably if she hadn't spent thirteen hours doing emergency surgery on angels in the Tower Six hospital during the height of the attack on Heaven, Greta Helsing would have been rather more unnerved by the prospect of dealing with a cranky underworld mob boss. As it was, she held a healthy respect for Aurelio Contini and his goons, but just at the moment she was rather too tired to be frightened. She'd at least been able to have a bath and put on some clothes that hadn't been soaked in various horrible liquids, even if the shirt displayed more of the front of her than was typically on view, and someone had even taken the time to fetch her bag and stethoscope from the bus.

She'd done her rounds before Contini had summoned her for an update, and was more or less satisfied with how everyone was getting on. The weres she'd been most worried about were responding nicely to a treatment of nebulized Avernus water, their O_2 sats back up to where she'd prefer to see them, with much less respiratory distress. Ms. Cenci was definitely past the danger of scarring. Glasya was probably the worst of the serious cases at the moment, having swallowed some of the poison, but Greta didn't think she'd need to have the demon transferred downstairs unless something unexpected happened; she was still sedated and on a drip, but Greta thought she could probably dispense with the sedation later that day if all went well.

Orlax was still asleep, and she thought he'd better stay that way as long as possible; she had no idea how much energy he'd used up the night before, or how long it would take him to recover—assuming that he *could* recover without being taken back to Hell—so rest was pretty much the best she could do for him. Morax was trying to entertain his guests and failing; she hadn't seen Adariel since that morning but was fairly sure he wasn't going to do anything too terribly stupid. Sure enough, it didn't take Frankie long to round up Varney, Morax, Cenci, and the angel and usher them all into Contini's room.

Greta adjusted her mental assessment of Adariel some-what when he came in: he looked *lost*, the kind of help-less, adrift, unmoored look she'd seen on the faces of other people in the middle of some deep personal crisis. She came over and put her arm around him, and the fact that he sim-ply huddled against her and rested his cheek on her shoulder, heedless of whoever was watching, did nothing to relieve her anxiety.

"It'll be okay," she told Adariel, giving him a little squeeze. "After we talk with Mr. Contini and get a better idea of what everyone's next steps are, I want you to lie down and rest for a bit. I'll give you something to help your nerves."

"I don't feel good," he admitted in a very small voice, and she nodded.

"I know, honey. It's not your fault, okay? I've got you. I'll help." Contini cleared his throat, and she looked up with a sigh. "C'mon, let's have a quick conversation," she said to the angel. "He probably has some questions for you, and then you can rest."

Adariel nodded against her, and she gave him another squeeze and let go, settling herself by the bed. "Right," she said. "Can we go over the events leading up to the attack last night, and what you all remember happening during it, please? I'll fill in what I can as we go."

Not much of it came as a shock. She'd thought all the way back in the beginning that the darts didn't sound like the work of a small, locally based, exclusionary group such as the Gladius Sancti had been back in London, especially since they apparently attacked angels as well as demons. That had suggested they were dealing with something rather wider-ranging than just the inhabitants of the Square Mile. Contini's reports of his people being attacked by the darts, and the clinical course that followed, had fitted neatly enough with Greta's medical understanding of what the dart poison was designed to do, and that it was effective against monsters as well as demons, though less powerful. Nor had the revelation that the people involved had been apparently nothing more than quasi-homeless religious zealots spurred on by some sort of charismatic leader come as a shock. The problem was, of course, *what was driving the leader*, and there Contini's account stopped making that much sense.

"But you said he was human," Varney put in, head tilted. "The man you accosted and threatened. He was human, and he smelled as if he believed you meant exactly what you said?"

"He was," said Contini. "Maybe *weird* human, but nothing more interesting than that. Just some random God-botherer with a more hands-on approach to cleansing the Earth of iniquity than most."

Varney and Greta winced, looking at each other. "What?" Contini demanded.

"It's not the first time something *else* might have come along and found a willing vessel for its influence," said Varney. "Stepping into the part, so to speak. Years ago something similar happened in London; a preexisting little cult sect that hadn't been doing anyone much harm got taken over by a malign entity, which then proceeded to channel actual power into it and make the cult members do its bidding."

"You think the zealot guy was being...what, ridden?" Adriana Cenci asked. "By something else?"

"Something that *unlike him* didn't get put off its goals by having a conversation real up close with Mr. Contini," said Morax, and swallowed a third of his drink, coughing. "It'd take quite a lot of power to be able to avoid obeying those instructions."

"Question is, do we think the asshole running the dart-blowers—Gideon was his name, Gideon something—do we think he's the same as whoever fucked with the gallery sprinklers, or were they working together, and if so, who's the other party?" Contini said, and held out his own glass; Frankie refilled it with the seamless smoothness of the trained butler. "'Cause I know where Gideon lives. Wouldn't be too hard to go pay him another visit, ask him some questions."

"Assuming he's gone back there after the attack," said Greta. "I think the . . . the *riding* hypothesis might be nearer the mark than him working with another saboteur. Whatever poisoned the water in the deluge system was powerful. Really powerful. You didn't sense any such power last time you encountered him, sir?"

"Nope. Weirdo, but just a hume. Not superpowered. He was into the whole cleansing-the-sinful-world bit, wanted to get rid of all the evil monsters. I said, hey, friend, you go right ahead and you do that, I don't want those monsters here any more than you do, but in order for me to help you out, you gotta be careful not to get *my* people in the crosshairs," said Contini. "Not a challenging approach, if you get my meaning. He wanted the city cleaned up, so did I, we could do business."

"Mr. Contini is rearranging the balance of power in the city," said Adriana, demure. "Tidying things up. It's been just such a mess for so long. People need to have a clear understanding of who's in charge."

"Quite," said Varney. "And the conversation you had with him ended favorably?"

"He was scared shitless," said Contini, shrugging. "Had enough sense to see I meant what I said and that it'd be the dumbest thing he ever did to get in my way."

"Which didn't stop him," said Greta. "If it *was* him, anyway: something apparently got to him between that conversation and the party last night and changed his mind. Or took over his mind. It seems more likely than there being a totally coincidental *second* person or persons unknown who really wanted to hurt monsters and used the same means to do so."

"I think we *should* possibly have a word with him," said Varney. "I'd be happy to help in any way I can, of course."

"Sure," said Contini. "You got hurt, too, it's your right to be part of this, but it's my operation, yeah? I say what we do and when we do it. You gonna be okay with that?"

Varney nodded. "Absolutely. I would suggest, too, that you consider taking Adariel."

Everyone turned to look at the angel, who hunched unhappily. "Yeah?" said Contini. "Why?"

"Because he's the only one of us who can see what's been touched by the blessing," said Greta. "He told me last night, when we were looking for the valve to turn the water off. Said the pipe was glowing gold, it was that powerful. I don't think it can hurt me, but we all saw last night what that blessing can do to demons and monsters. I think we need him to warn us, in case anything around this Gideon person is still active with that kind of power."

"She's got a point," said Morax. "I mean, I could probably make out some level of glow, but I certainly can't touch the stuff even if I can detect it. We'd need someone like him with us to be safe."

"Fair enough," said Contini. "You, kid. Angel. Sounds like we need you, but only if you've got the balls to make yourself useful instead of crying and puking everywhere. You think you can handle that?"

"Um," said Morax. "I believe Adariel's, ah, indisposition

280

last night was possibly my fault. I may have been overgenerous with the complimentary champagne?"

Contini snorted. "Okay, fine, so nobody give the kid alcohol. We good?"

Adariel wrapped his arms tightly around himself and nodded, without meeting anybody's eyes. "Good," said Contini. "Doc, when can we do this thing?"

Greta looked at her watch. "There's another good six hours of daylight," she said. "Rest, and let's make plans to leave after full dark. That should give all of you time to heal a bit more before you try to do anything too energetic. And Morax, we'll need more blood. Can you arrange for that?"

"Of course," said Morax, clearly happy to be able to play the capable host. "And food?"

"I suppose we ought to keep body and soul together," said Greta, who hadn't had anything to eat since a few *hors d'oeuvres* the night before; the thought of food woke a sudden clawing hunger in her midsection. "Am I imagining this or is New York actually the kind of place where you can get literally any sort of food delivered anywhere at all hours of the day and night?"

"I am so very pleased to assure you that you are right," said Morax, and got up, offering her his arm. "Whatever you desire."

Adariel was worrying her...hell, everything was worrying her...but Greta thought perhaps she might worry more effectively once she'd had something to eat, and she could at least coax him to try something light. "Lead on," she said, and let Morax help her to her feet.

*　　*　　*

Adariel didn't know why people being *kind* to him should make him cry. It didn't make any sense; it seemed totally backward. Still, he'd spent almost all day with tears stinging his eyes and he'd nearly spilled over completely when the doctor had put her arm around his shoulders and told him it was okay that he didn't feel good, that she'd help.

Maybe it was the world. Maybe being in the Prime Material plane *was* bad for him, after all. Maybe he felt so odd and unsettled and unhappy because he was finally having a reaction to being here, or being among demons.

Not that Morax seemed all that demonic, he had to admit: he'd honestly never have known their host wasn't just a very rich human who wore all black and had a very stylish haircut if he hadn't been glowing faintly scarlet to Adariel's angel eyes. He had ushered Adariel and Dr. Helsing into the huge kitchen with its polished-concrete countertops and wine fridge and three different sinks, and she had had an incomprehensible conversation with him while looking through a sheaf of printed menus, and presumably they had decided on some sort of food to order; he didn't know what *sushi* or *miso soup* was and had no appetite at all, but maybe it would turn out to be nice?

He was trying not to think about tonight, about what they were going to do, what *he* was going to have to do. He wasn't *sure*, which didn't help, but he couldn't picture the group of them coming up against a being who could have put that particular blessing on the water in those pipes, something *that strong* in the touch of God, and . . . not having it be something like an angel.

(He could have done it. He was trying not to know it, but he could have done that blessing, pushed that much holy energy into the steel pipe and water within it, made it glow that bright gold to his own angel vision. He could have done it. He *hadn't*, but he could have, and he did not know what *other* creature could be here on the skin of this world that could have done so, or why it would have done it, or . . . what it would have to say to something like him, in such a company. Or what he could possibly have to say to *it*.)

Adariel wanted so *badly* to be back home in Heaven, where the universe had been so incredibly simple, so straightforward and unquestioning and unquestionable, without any kind of need to *think* about anything other than the importance of doing just exactly what he was told to the best of his ability exactly when and how he was told to do it. He had never understood how much it was possible to miss a lack of something before; it wasn't a concept that would have made any sense to him, in the time before all this. He missed that, too, the version of himself who had never had to tackle any such thought exercises, never had to try, never had to push his own mind past the comfortable limits it had been designed to fit.

"Adariel?"

It was Dr. Helsing. He blinked at her, realizing he'd been hunched over with his arms wrapped around himself again, not listening to whatever she'd asked him: rude. "Sorry," he said. "I'm sorry. What were you saying?"

"Just that if you don't feel up to this, you don't have to do it," she said. Her hand was on his arm, warm and solid and real, and she was near enough for him to see the green in the blue of her irises. "It's all a lot to take in at once, I know that, and you haven't had the experience of a regular surface-operative angel."

"What?" he managed.

"This. If you'd really rather not come with us tonight, I can ask if maybe someone else can do it."

"There *aren't* any other angels," he said, sounding miserable even to himself. "I'm the only one here. Or I'm...supposed to be the only one here..."

"From what I've heard," said Dr. Helsing, "I'm pretty sure the London angel would be willing to lend a wing. He's been in the world for ages now, he's seen all sorts of things, he's got mental calluses you don't. He's shown himself willing to do things beyond the ordinary remit of Heaven if it's to help out friends of his, including the London demon."

"Haliel," said Adariel. "But wouldn't he get into trouble?"

"I think we're all a little bit beyond getting into trouble by now," said Dr. Helsing. "But I think if we asked him nicely, he might be willing to come over here and help out."

Adariel closed his eyes, picturing it. He knew Haliel, of course, but only a very little, only to recognize; in his human seeming he was completely convincing, but in Heaven he never wore that; he just looked like a proper angel. He could remember Haliel with the wound in his back, in the beginning of all this wretched confusion, and could quite clearly picture him popping into existence here in this expensive apartment to help Dr. Helsing and Sir Francis and Mr. Contini go to find who was responsible for all the pain and suffering he'd seen the night before. How easy it would be for him to welcome Haliel and thank him so much for being willing to help where he, Adariel, could not do the job he was supposed to be here to do. For being willing to put himself in harm's way where he, Adariel, could not go.

"Adariel?" Dr. Helsing was saying.

"I can't," he heard himself say. "I can't ask that of him, Doctor. Don't make me?"

"It's not for me to make you do anything at all," she said quietly. "I can't. That is, and always will be, your choice to make."

I don't want to make a choice, he did not say, but something seemed to feel easier inside his head, as if he'd finally let go of the edge of something and struck out past where his feet could touch the bottom. As if some choice had *been* made, without his conscious decision.

He opened his eyes, wiped them hastily, and took an unsteady breath, and then another, and slowly the look on her face stopped being quite so hard for him to watch.

Heaven

Unlike Samael's Hell, which operated largely as a well-oiled civil service bureaucracy, the corresponding Heaven was drawn on very simple lines. Hell's Council of Nine ran the underworld via eight individual departments, each overseen by an archdemon who reported to the rest of the Council and to Samael himself; Heaven technically had a council of seven archangels, but in practice only the four most important met regularly to discuss business. In the weeks immediately following the war and the reset, those four had spent a great deal of time together, hashing out their side of what would become the Accords, but in recent months there had been only a couple of meetings scheduled for all four of them.

Technically any one of the four could call a meeting. It was almost always Gabriel who sent around the summons, when he had something he wished to remind his colleagues about at length, but *technically* any one of them had the right and authority to request to speak with the others. Raphael was seriously considering it, depending on the outcome of the conversation he was about to have. He felt relatively secure leaving the infirmary unattended, since he'd given Nithael something to help him sleep; there were no other patients to demand his attention. And he wouldn't be gone *long*.

At this hour, roughly corresponding to midafternoon on Earth, the archangel Uriel often took the air in the formal knot-gardens on one side of the white gemstone citadel. Sometimes he had other angels with him, pupils who were following his lecture on some topic or other of angelic interest; inasmuch as angels went in for education, or the pursuit of wisdom beyond doing what they were told, Uriel was the archangel who oversaw that aspect of their existence. He looked like all the others; his skin and hair were dark, rather than golden-brown or fair, but he had the same blank golden eyes, bright halo, and snow-white wings—but the white robes he wore had a faintly professorial air, with a hint of velvet lapels and gathered bell-like sleeves, rather the way Raphael's own robes carried just the suggestion of a white surgical gown while remaining firmly this side of plausible deniability.

Their sandals made very little sound on the pearl gravel of the knot-garden's pathways, and Uriel was deeply engaged with the book in his hands; Raphael cleared his throat politely to get his attention, and he looked up from the jeweled miniature painting on the page he held.

"Raphael?" said Uriel, tilting his head. There wasn't really the suggestion of a mortarboard about his halo; one just had the vague sensation that there ought to be. "One does not often see you away from your patients at this hour?"

"My patients," Raphael said, "are now patient, singular, and he's having his afternoon rest. I wondered if I might speak with you briefly, if you have a minute."

"Of course," said Uriel. "Walk with me?"

There was something deeply restful about him, Raphael thought, falling into step beside his colleague. Being near Uriel felt a little bit like settling in a quiet, peaceful cloister away from all possible sources of annoyance. He couldn't help remembering what it had been like to have Gabriel's fields licking over and through him, Gabriel's anger and frustration like acid on every nerve ending: exactly the opposite of Uriel's calm peace. *Maybe I ought to ask him to visit next time I've got someone terribly anxious to treat*, he thought, and pushed the idea away: not important, not germane.

Uriel was looking at him curiously, he realized, and Raphael tried to school his features into the expressionless expression of all angels in Heaven. They had come to a little arbor, a white-wood scaffold over which palest blue and pink dangling flowers had grown in a delicate arch sheltering a bench, as if anyone in this garden could ever require shelter from the elements. He sat down, arranging his wings out of the way, as Uriel did the same.

"Are you quite all right?" his colleague inquired, and Raphael could very clearly recall asking Gabriel the same question and being shut down flat.

"I'm fine," he said, trying to push away the strong sensation that he shouldn't be doing this, the drawing weight of fatigue. "I'm...well, a little concerned, perhaps. About Gabriel. I don't know if you've noticed anything different about him lately?"

Uriel raised a dark eyebrow and looked at him for just long enough that Raphael was seriously reconsidering the wisdom of this particular conversation, and then he said, "As a matter of fact, I have. I've not mentioned anything to Michael, and I doubt you have, either, since Michael is not...shall we say... the most subtle of us, and he hasn't said a word."

"I haven't, no. I wanted to speak with you first." The relief of *not being the only one* was so vast it almost hurt, ringing in Raphael's mind like a struck crystal bell. "It's...he's been having headaches since the reset, definitely since the Accords were signed, and he seemed to have left that behind for a while, but I'm fairly sure he's in pain quite often now, and hiding it. And he's—distracted. And even more short-tempered than usual."

"*Short-tempered* is one way to describe it," said Uriel, mildly enough, but Raphael looked at him sharply. "I came across him chastising one of my scribal angels the other day and he was fairly *radiating* displeasure; it made me feel quite strange. He's never had much patience with things that don't go the way he wants them to, or with anyone who doesn't immediately agree with him about everything, but I would say it's definitely worse now. And he does seem *distracted*, which is very much not like him; sometimes he doesn't answer his door at all."

"I'm so glad I'm not imagining it," said Raphael simply. He sketched out in very quick terms the situation he and Adariel had been in and what Gabriel's lecture had done to him, leaving out a lot of the more clinical detail, but Uriel looked faintly appalled nonetheless. "He's *really* not happy with the fact that we had to use Hell's supplies and medicine, or that I'm keeping a stock of those supplies in the infirmary in case anyone needs them in the future. He's never liked me talking to Dr. Faust, but that's nothing compared to my using things from Hell on our patients. And he definitely wasn't happy with this business of sending an angel and a demon to work together on the Prime Material plane." Raphael sighed and ran his fingers through his curls. "He doesn't like *anything* that involves us working with demons, as far as I can tell."

"Wasn't there some sort of accident with demons volunteering for construction work up here?" Uriel asked.

"That wouldn't have been a problem except that the demons *and* the angels who were having serious allergic reactions were given the same remedy—I wasn't summoned in time to stop it from happening, and the demons were given something that contained nectar, which did what you might expect. I'd warned people against that, but Gabriel said that was a *xenophobic and defeatist attitude* on my part."

Uriel frowned at him. "That doesn't follow, though, does it? He had to *know* the demons would have a bad reaction to nectar, or did he really think it would somehow be all right after the Accords? He can't have done, can he, not when they were having allergic reactions to begin with?"

"I don't know," said Raphael. "I really don't know. Either he knew and he wanted it to happen, or he didn't know because he quite specifically didn't care to learn the first thing about them, and then took the opportunity to be cross at me for something I couldn't possibly change. One *does* have to acknowledge that the wording of the Accords is technically not one hundred percent feasible, no matter how good the political optics might be, but…a little bit of common sense goes a long way?"

"I was frankly quite glad to hear that you'd requisitioned medical assistance from Hell when it was needed, and that it had actually *helped*," said Uriel. "I try to stay out of things that aren't my concern, of course, but that did strike me as a sort of clear illustration of furthering the *intention* of the Accords in a way we hadn't been doing much of hitherto."

"Well, yes, that was rather how I felt," said Raphael. "I'm all for collaboration when it benefits all parties, and Faust's made no secret of the fact that he's more than willing to offer clinical advice and support." He looked around, hunching a little, and lowered his voice. "Honestly, if it weren't *acceptable*, or— or correct, at least to some extent—for us to use technology and supplies from Hell on our patients, it seems to me that those technologies and supplies wouldn't *work* on us. There were no thunderbolts; there was no sense of disapproval other than Gabriel's own."

"That's a very good point," said Uriel, just as quietly. "One hesitates to invoke ineffability; it goes all ontological. But I can't see how He would allow such a thing as the Accords to be drafted and signed if He did not at least in some fashion approve, or why He should allow Faust's medicine to work on angels if it were counter to His wish."

Raphael could not say out loud, even to Uriel, that the only alternative explanation he could see was that God was setting up some sort of elaborate trick, or trap, for His angels to fall into; even thinking it made him feel hot and cold and achy, as if he were spiking a sudden fever. That was the sort of thing a human or a demon would think, not an angel, certainly not an *archangel*, and he clutched at the bench's armrest through a wave of dizziness.

"—Raphael?" Uriel was saying, steadying him with a hand on his shoulder. "Are you all right?"

He fought for composure, managed half a smile; he was so *tired*. "Yes—sorry. This is all just rather a lot. Gabriel's acting so strangely, and now he's spending so much time in his office refusing to be disturbed, and it's not just me: even one of his surface-operative angels has noticed the strange behavior. I confess I rather hoped you might have some idea of what we ought to *do* about it."

Uriel nodded slowly. "I will give the matter thought," he said. "Considerable thought. In the meantime, Raphael, may I suggest you return to your infirmary and try to get some rest?"

"That's kind," he said. "Yes. I think I'll do that. Thank you, Uriel. It's at least eased my mind to speak with you about this; carrying it alone had become somewhat heavier than I had realized."

"Of course," said Uriel, and got up, offering Raphael his hands; he was glad of the support as he got to his feet. "You do not have to bear *everything* alone."

Just most things, he thought with an internal unsteady hiccup of laughter. "Quite," he said, and settled his wings. "Well. I'll be in touch?"

Uriel inclined his head—again, the halo was a *halo*, not a light-limned mortarboard, but the mind filled in what was missing—and turned to stride off down the pearl-graveled pathway, book tucked firmly in the crook of his arm. Raphael watched him until he turned a corner and the white-gemstone garden wall hid him from view, and then shook himself a little, pinions clattering, and set off back to the infirmary. It *was* a relief not to be carrying all the weight of concern about

Gabriel alone; at the same time, it felt as if he'd set something much larger than himself in motion and could not now halt its progress even if he'd wanted to, that the first pebble of a landslide had been sent bouncing down the slope, carrying with it the pregnant potential of something that might be unimaginably huge.

It was true, though, wasn't it? If He did not wish for angels to benefit from Hell's technology, then surely He would have made it so that the technology did them no good. Unless it really *was* the sort of test He had set for the humans, deliberately allowing them the chance to make the wrong choice and face the consequences—but angels weren't *like* humans, were they? Angels didn't *make* the wrong choice; it wasn't in their nature. Or it hadn't been. Who knew what changes had been wrought in the fabric of the universe with the reset? Hadn't he thought that angels seemed to be subtly more *human* since the ending of the war and the shock of His presence?

This was doing him no good *at all*, Raphael told himself firmly, and when he regained the familiar shelter of his infirmary, he took the time to check on Nithael and then fell headlong, drowning-deep into prayer, needing it as badly as ambrosia or nectar, needing it the way his patient had needed oxygen in the very worst of the attack.

New York City

Morax had offered to flip the whole group of them from his apartment directly to Brooklyn, avoiding traffic or having to wait for the subway, but Greta had vetoed that: *we don't know to what extent this person's been granted special powers by whatever touched him, he might be able to sense translocation taking place nearby, and why give him the warning if we don't have to?* This hadn't gone over tremendously well with Mr. Contini, but the nosferatu had accepted it with bad grace and had Frankie call up a car to handle transportation.

Greta was aware of having been spoiled in terms of what was and was not *a giant logistical problem* by her association with vampires and vampyres, both of whom could easily walk around in public—preferably not in direct sunlight, but they didn't burst into flame; they just went scarlet and got sun-poisoning about twice as fast as the palest possible redhead. Both lunar-sensitive and classic-draculine sanguivores could *pass* for human, without having to wrap themselves in so much obfuscating magic that it made you go numb if you got too close to them; Mr. Contini and his friends and relations were about as human-seeming as Greta's old friends the ghouls, and would attract about as much attention on the surface even at night. Contini was also clearly very aware of the tiresome issue of having to conceal his physical appearance to human eyes at all times, but just as clearly he found the blackout-tinted luxury SUV a deep and familiar relief to settle into. Greta supposed that there must be any number of luxury SUVs with black-tinted windows being driven around New York that *didn't* contain nosferatu, and that nobody was paying the slightest attention to one more. This particular Escalade was driven by someone who at least looked human enough to fool a casual glance through the windshield; back here in the rich-people seats the tint was so heavy it was hard to see anything at all outside the car, and nobody looking in would have been able to tell they were there at all.

Driving in New York was still, obviously, a nightmare, and Greta was glad she'd had the presence of mind to bring her beat-up bag with her; she was able to rummage around in its depths and find Adariel a Dramamine chewable before the stop-and-go jerking could have regrettable results. He was sitting beside her, quiet and drooping, and when this night's work was over she was going to see if the Archangel Raphael would consider taking her calls, because she wanted him to get properly *looked at* by someone who knew what they were doing.

Contini had his two bodyguards with him, plus Morax, and Greta had brought Varney and Adariel; she thought unless this Gideon person cut up extremely rough indeed they'd be able to subdue him without much difficulty. Part of the reason she had the bag with her included a chemical backup plan; in case he didn't respond well to being manhandled by nosferatu, Greta was supposed to shoot him full of the strongest sedative she had, and was really hoping that it wouldn't come to that.

Beside her, Varney's narrow, cold fingers tightened over hers. He still had some angry pink marks on his face from the holy-water burns, but he'd told her he was fit enough for this little escapade and she trusted him to mean it. She wasn't sure what the hell to expect, but she'd seen Varney tear hardened steel like paper and she was pretty sure the nosferatu had similar unnatural strength, so—as long as Gideon didn't throw *more* holy water on them or try to wrap his influence around their brains, this would probably be all right.

Probably.

They had a pallet-load of Avernus water in the back just in case he did have any more sacred munitions in reserve, and Greta really, really hoped she didn't have to use it.

"Do we know anything more about this person?" Varney was asking. Frankie had a laptop open on his knees and handed it over with a shrug; Greta peered at the screen. Not much she hadn't already heard: thirty-two, night manager of a goddamned Taco Bell, volunteered at several churches and church-associated homeless shelters and soup kitchens— presumably where he recruited his street-preaching acolytes— no criminal record other than one arrest for disorderly conduct, charges dropped after review of video evidence. Reading between the lines, that had been a case of trying to convince a cop not to arrest somebody *else* for yelling about Jesus, nothing more dire. Just another religious do-gooder, only this one had nearly killed several people and injured very many more, and in doing so had caused Greta Helsing to have to do a hell of a lot of *work* she wasn't expecting to; a small shameful part of her hoped she'd have the opportunity to kick him ever so slightly in the ribs. Not that she'd ever *act* on such an unworthy urge, of course. She was a *doctor*. And these shoes weren't pointy enough.

It took them so long to force their way through traffic that Greta wished she'd kept her damn mouth shut about the potential dangers of translocation; eventually Contini's driver pulled the SUV into an alley several streets north of the block they were looking for, though, and the group of them climbed out into the chilly night. "Let me go first," said Contini, and Morax nodded.

"I'm right behind you," he said. "And so's the angel. Adariel, keep your astral eyes peeled, okay? Let us know if we're about to walk into anything holy."

"Okay," said the angel, shoulders hunched, and the rest of them fell in behind. Greta's hand was tight in Varney's, their fingers laced together; she couldn't help thinking of him creeping through a different night to face a different kind of danger, under the city of London. That time she hadn't been with him; that time she'd stayed behind, and it was only after the first Molotov cocktail came through the window of Edmund Ruthven's house that she'd hurried to catch up. This time he wasn't facing danger without her, at least. This time she was present and accounted for and—for once—immune to the worst of the dangers that might be waiting for their little party up ahead.

Tribeca, New York City

For the first four rings Orlax couldn't quite tell where the sound was coming from.

It had woken him out of a deep, dreamless sleep, and he

rolled over and stared up at an unfamiliar ceiling, trying to work out what he was listening to. It sounded like a video call, and it sounded weirdly familiar, and when it kept *on* ringing he hauled himself upright and slid out of the bed, hanging on to the headboard while the room steadied itself around him, and went to go find what was making the noise. He felt—strange. Empty and hollow, as if something inside him had been used up, and also as if something very heavy had run over him a few times. His side itched a little under the shirt he'd borrowed from Morax.

What the fuck was *making* that noise—

Oh. The doctor had left her laptop open on the kitchen countertop. There was a note beside it: *I've gone to Brooklyn with Mr. Contini, his bodyguards, Adariel, Morax, and Varney to find the person responsible for this. If you can, please look after the others until I get back.*

The computer was still ringing. Not only was he not supposed to be looking at her personal computer, he had no particular *desire* to see whatever the hell was happening in her world. He'd had more than enough of it over the past twenty-four hours; if he never had to do the thing with his fields ever again, it'd be too fucking soon, and—oh. The screen said FAUST, J. G.

Maybe he was supposed to take a message.

Orlax subsided onto a barstool at the counter—polished concrete, very industrial chic—and poked at the trackpad until he could click *Accept Call.* The black square on the screen turned into the familiar yellow-edged rectangle of a video call, this one showing what was an office in what was undeniably Hell, judging by the view of Lake Avernus out the window. And that was Dr. Faust, all right, and Orlax's old boss beside him, looking rumpled in his shirtsleeves, cigarette parked in the corner of his mouth. The sight made Orlax want one, too, and he patted vaguely at his pockets before remembering that his clothes had been soaked in holy water and everything he had on belonged to somebody else. He hadn't had the chance to stop and think for hours after the attack; he'd been too busy helping Dr. Helsing out.

"Um," he said. "Hi? She's not here right now. Can I tell her you called?"

"*Orlax?*" Fastitocalon demanded, tinny over the little speakers.

"Yup," he said. "The mob guy and his goons and the doctor and Varney and the demon Morax, they're off to Brooklyn or something to go find the guy who did all this shit and, I don't know, murder him?"

"What the hell is the matter with *you?*" Fastitocalon demanded.

"Me?"

"Yes, you," said Dr. Faust, leaning closer to the screen. "When was the last time anyone took your temperature?"

"They didn't," said Orlax. It was true: he'd collapsed into bed pretty much as soon as they'd gotten here in the small hours, and nobody had woken him since.

"Listen to me," said Dr. Faust. "Were you hurt last night in the attack? Did you get burned, or swallow or breathe in any of the stuff, or did you get hit by one of the darts when you got outside the gallery?"

"I dunno," Orlax told him, shrugging, and wincing at the shrug: something down his side kind of itch-hurt. "I mean. I got some of the water on me but the doctor told me to just go wash off in the rain outside, and she put some burn cream on me and it's just like a sunburn now? Kind of peeling around the edges? We didn't have a lot of time to do anything other than try to help the people who were worse off; I don't even know how many people I did the fields for?"

"You're *sure* you didn't get hit by one of the darts?" Fastitocalon said, intent. "Even scratched? We've been running tests down here on what Dr. Helsing sent down this morning. It's the first time we've had a sample of the latest dart toxin to study, and it is *not* nice in the slightest."

"Um," said Orlax again. He was faintly aware that maybe it wasn't a hundred percent *normal* that the barstool he was sitting on felt like it was going up and down in a steady kind of swell, or that he'd been sweating in the borrowed shirt but felt like someone had turned the AC way up. His hand went back to the itchy place under his arm, and this time he rolled up the edge of the shirt to expose his ribs, peering down at himself.

"*Fuck*," said Fastitocalon. "Who else is there with you, if Greta and the others are off hunting the bastard responsible?"

He didn't want to say *um* again, and he *really* didn't want to do anything quite so mortifying as bursting into tears, which staring at the narrow puffed-up scratch down his side kind of made him feel like doing, so he just pushed his sweat-damp hair back and hung on to the edge of the countertop and tried to remember who else was still here. Dr. Helsing had told him to keep an eye on the rest of them, if he could. "There's—just me," he said. "Everyone else is in bed. She said I was supposed to watch them while she was gone?"

"She didn't get a close look at you, I'm guessing," said Faust.

"I didn't see her," he said. "I crashed pretty much right when we got here and I just woke up because the phone was ringing, but she left a note?" Wow, he was really doing *fantastic* on the sounding-like-an-idiot front tonight, he thought. "Did—did you find out anything about the dart stuff that I should know? Like, for the people here who got hurt by one?"

"Are they vampires?" said Dr. Faust, as if this was important.

"Yeah," he said. "Well, the weird kind of vampires. With the bunny fangs. Like the mob guy."

"Nosferatu," said Dr. Faust. "Even less vulnerable to it than boring old classic draculines. They'll be fine with rest and blood, don't worry about them, but *you* look like hammered *shit*, my young friend, and I'm going to countermand my fellow physician's instructions. Fass?"

"Yes," said Fastitocalon, "quite," and Orlax stared at the little yellow-edged square on the screen as he vanished—and appeared a moment later, sending a flicker of pressure-wave through the air of the room, behind Orlax's chair.

Wow, he was *tall*. Orlax hadn't noticed that before. Had he? *Fastitocalon is as tall as the ceiling*: he would have remembered that about his old boss, right? Also, what was he doing here? This was Morax's apartment, he shouldn't be here—

Fastitocalon was muttering something at the computer, talking to Faust, who was still on the call, and then there was a narrow hand cupping Orlax's forehead, shockingly cool, so cool it almost *hurt*, but he couldn't help leaning into it, not wanting the coolness to go away. He wasn't sure why everything had suddenly gone so confusing; it felt a little bit like being very drunk, but he hadn't had anything to drink since the free wine at the gallery last night, and—no one had slipped him anything, had they? He'd been *asleep* all day; how could he still be feeling like this? His side hurt like fire and Fastitocalon took his hand away and that was terrible; he wanted the coolness back and had no idea how to ask for it—

"Hang on," said Fastitocalon, close by his ear, "it'll be all right, you'll feel better soon," and then he wasn't sitting on the barstool clutching at the counter anymore; he was *lifted* into someone's arms like he was an imp, like he weighed nothing, and all the world went blank and blinding white.

Brighton Beach, New York City

There was something inescapably, embarrassingly *depressing* about the place Gideon Tremayne called home, Greta thought, following the others up the stairs. It wasn't as if the little poky staircase was particularly filthy; the neighborhood didn't feel that unsafe—there weren't vacant houses boarded up and stained with the evidence of fire—but being here somehow made her feel as if the very air itself were ever so faintly tarnishing everything it touched, including herself.

Adariel hadn't stopped them, or said anything, on the trip up the stairs. She hoped that meant he didn't sense anything particularly dangerous to this little group waiting in the apartment beyond. Contini paused at the top of the stairs, eyes half-closed, sniffing. "One person," he hissed. "Human, male, could be the one I talked to before, smells like stress and subways. One heartbeat. Can't smell anything particularly holy. You?" he asked Morax, who also shut his eyes to sniff.

"No. Just distressed human. No holy water."

"You?" Contini hissed at Adariel.

"It's...confusing," the angel managed. "There's *echoes*... but no, um, no artifacts? Nothing physical?"

"Then we go in," the nosferatu said, his cigarette-ember eyes glowing brightly, and Greta was glad of Varney's solid presence at her back: *God* but it was hard to look Contini in the face sometimes, especially when he grinned like that. "One, two, *three*," and he and Morax threw their shoulders at the door together, and it burst open with a clatter of broken chipboard.

Varney lifted her and set her aside effortlessly, as one might relocate something delicate one wished to protect from harm; he and Contini's two bodyguards forced their way into the room, shouldering Adariel aside with less delicacy. The angel stumbled and half-fell against her, and she put an arm around him, aware that he was trembling in a low constant vibration. She couldn't see exactly what was going on past the numerous male backs surrounding something, or somebody, on the floor; then one of the bodyguards produced plastic cable-ties, the kind the cops used to restrain people at riots, and a moment later the group parted to disclose—a man.

Just a man, on his knees, with his hands fastened behind him, his no-color hair hanging lankly into his face. He looked as squalid and depressing as his apartment had seemed to Greta on the way in, and it was almost impossible to connect this pathetic specimen of humanity to the extent of suffering she'd witnessed the night before. How the hell had *he* managed to cause so much damage? she wondered.

"How the fuck did *he* do that last night," Contini demanded, apparently sharing her train of thought. "It's him, it's the same asshole I talked to a couple days ago, but apparently he's not too good at *listening*, huh?" He punctuated this with a vicious kick to the kneeling man's midsection that folded him up, wheezing and retching. "Not too good at *understanding what the fuck he was told?*"

Now the wheezing had turned into sobs. She'd wanted to kick Gideon Tremayne herself, but the desire was running out of her like water from a sack. "It can't have been just him," she said. "Something else must have been…driving. Or riding him." She could remember Adriana Cenci saying as much, back at Morax's.

"Possession," said Varney, sounding very disgusted indeed; he and Morax shared a look.

"Well?" demanded Contini with another kick. Greta hid a wince. "What the *fuck* did you do, and how did you do it?"

The man on the floor looked up at them through the filthy tangle of his hair. Snot was dangling from each nostril in long clear runners as he hiccupped and sobbed; after a moment she could make out what sounded like *please*.

"Please *what*?" Contini snapped. "Please snap my neck nice and quick and get it over with? Not a fucking chance, Tremayne. I got a *lot* of shit I intend for you to experience live in Technicolor, but first I want to know *how you did that* last night. —*Angel*."

He snapped his fingers at Adariel and pointed at the floor: front and center. "You said you could see the blessing in the water pipes, right? Like it was glowing?"

Adariel stumbled forward. "Y-yes. It was *really* powerful. That blessing was—not something a human should have been able to do? Normally?"

"Lay your hands on that piece of shit," said Contini, "and tell me if you feel anything *else* in there that shouldn't be."

Adariel knelt down, and Greta could see him hunching his shoulders even tighter when Tremayne shrank away from him as if afraid his touch would burn; not for the first time she wondered, *how much damage are we doing to this brand-new angel, how badly will this scar?*

He reached out to rest his hand on Gideon Tremayne's head, and in that instant his wings flickered into visibility, huge and white; his whole body stiffened, head thrown back, the cords of his neck too visible, his eyes blank gold from lid to lid, mouth open in a silent cry. Greta could see him shaking, jittering, as if in the grip of some vast and mindless current. She reached out without thinking, wanting to pull him away from the contact, but Varney grabbed her wrist hard enough almost to hurt, and she was glad of it—and gladder still when Tremayne flinched away from the angel's hand and broke the connection. Adariel slowly toppled over onto his side, wings once more invisible, and lay still.

Greta half-expected to see smoke rising from his body. She was frozen for a moment longer, and then shook her hand free of Varney's grip and knelt by the angel, rolling him onto his back, reaching for the pulse in his throat.

"What the bloody fuck was *that*?" Contini demanded after a moment, fumbling his cigarettes out of his pocket. Both bodyguards offered him a light, and she looked up in time to catch that neither of the flames was completely steady.

"I don't know," she said, looking over at Tremayne, who was weeping in a kind of slow, infuriating grizzle. "I don't think he's going to be tremendously helpful, either…Adariel, hey, shh, relax, it's me, it's Greta; lie still for a moment, okay? Let me make sure you're not hurt." He had stirred under her hand and was looking up at her—or at least she thought he was, but couldn't be sure. His eyes were still blank golden cabochons from lid to lid.

"It's…bad," he managed, reaching for her hand. "Dr. Helsing. It's *really bad*."

"Can you tell me what you…saw? Sensed?" She ignored the others, all her attention focused on the angel.

"He didn't do it, or…not entirely," said Adariel. "I was

right: no human could have done that blessing. It's... it was an angel."

"Another angel?" she asked. "Do you know *who*?"

"Not just an *angel*," Adariel managed. "An... an archangel. The most powerful you can imagine. An *archangel* did that, and I—I wanted to go home, Doctor, I wanted to go *home* where it was safe and nothing ever hurt and no one was ever sad and now I know that Heaven *isn't like that*, and I *don't have anywhere safe left to go*."

There was silence in the little apartment, broken only by Gideon Tremayne's endless grizzling and the near-silent sobbing of the angel.

"Well, *shit*," said Aurelio Contini, and sighed out a narrow quill of blue smoke. "Let's blow this fucking dump and get back to civilization. Frankie, Luca, I'd say set fire to the place on the way out, but I don't think it's worth the gasoline. I guess this is now officially above *my* pay grade."

He spat expertly and swept out, followed by his bodyguards, one of whom had Tremayne draped over his shoulder like a sack of bad decisions. Morax looked down at the angel, who had curled up tightly on his side, and then at Varney and Greta, and sighed.

"I think the time for being circumspect about the arrival and departure of angels and demons has officially passed," he said. "Let's *all* get back to the car, and I'll flip us back and save us a forty-five-minute drive. How's *that* for good intentions?"

"You, sir," said Varney, scooping up Adariel as if he weighed nothing, "are a gentleman on this and any other plane."

Greta followed them down the stairs, taking the time to turn the lights off and pull the broken door closed behind her. She had no idea what Adariel's revelation would actually mean, but on the whole she thought if she'd been through *one* Armageddon already, a rogue archangel—while undeniably a problem—was going to be *someone else's* problem for once.

She was probably imagining it, but the air outside felt subtly sweeter, cleaner, than it had when they'd arrived. God, she was tired, though. She'd left the other patients without any supervision; she'd left the note for Orlax, but he'd been asleep when they left and she had no idea when he'd wake up, or what condition he'd be in when he did. That was another worry: what had they done to Adariel with this entire clusterfuck, yes, but also what had they done to *Orlax*, who was just a kid himself, who had spent the entire night grimly shoving energy into his fields to calm down victim after victim, to ease their terror and pain? She'd talk to Fastitocalon about it, along with everything else, but she was pretty sure Orlax had bought himself a trip to Erebus General and the mirabilic resonance scanner to check how much damage he'd taken.

Another thing to feel guilty about, she thought, even though she knew they hadn't had a choice; Orlax had said it himself, *I can do this, it needs to be done, don't worry about me*, and she'd done him the courtesy of believing him. She only hoped they'd both been right.

She was glad to see the SUV and frankly wouldn't have minded the drive back into Manhattan for the chance to grab half an hour's shut-eye, but at least it was comfortable and had more than enough room for them and their unlovely passenger. She'd sleep...at some point. When and if it became feasible to do so. That was the ticket.

She was asleep before she'd fastened her seatbelt, her head drooping against Francis Varney's arm.

CHAPTER 11

Hell

H arlach had been hastily roped into helping Faust's people with the research they'd been doing on the dart poison, after Dr. Helsing had sent down a sample of the latest
version from New York in return for the supplies Dr. Faust
had flipped up to her. He'd lost count of the number of times
his blood had been sampled and the entire history of his own
experience with the poison taken down, and he wasn't even
slightly sorry to have the latest iteration of that interview
interrupted by a clamor down the hospital hallway and the
recognizable bellow of Dr. Faust calling for assistance.

Harlach got up and looked out of the little office just in
time to see Fastitocalon, in shirtsleeves, looking ever so faintly
disheveled, carrying the limp form of a young demon in his
arms; after a shocked moment he thought he could recognize
that obnoxious little twerp his boss had been bearing with bad
grace in the weeks before Harlach's own attack, the one who'd
apparently got himself reassigned to some project involving

Dr. Helsing. The look on Fastitocalon's face was only briefly visible, but it wasn't one Harlach had ever expected to see pointed at that particular demon. Faust preceded them into a treatment room, still shouting; clearly whatever was wrong was fairly seriously wrong.

"What the *hell*," he murmured, and rolled down his shirtsleeve over the little pad of gauze taped to his elbow; nobody was going to get any *more* blood out of him for at least a little while. He followed the knot of nurses and doctors surrounding Fastitocalon down the hallway, and wasn't entirely surprised when a large orderly barred his way at the door of the treatment room.

"No visitors," said the orderly.

"What's going on?" Harlach asked.

"Casualty from topside," said the orderly. "One of them dart things. Hey, aren't you the first one who got hit with them?"

"I am," said Harlach, wincing. "Is he going to be all right?"

"Dunno," said the orderly. "No visitors."

Harlach sighed. "Can I wait to talk to the doctor?"

"'S a free underworld," said the orderly, and he sighed again and straightened his shoulders. If it was anything like his own course, he had no idea when the doctors would be done with their latest patient; probably he ought to go home and wait to see if anyone bothered to update him via email.

Instead, he took out his phone, sloping off down the hall to the nearest waiting area, with a glimpse of the lake view beyond the curve of the next tower. He had no idea what time it was in London and thought probably it didn't really matter, in the wider scheme of things; Haliel would almost certainly want to know about this even if it *did* end up waking him out of a blameless angelic sort of sleep.

Three rings. Four rings.

"...Hello?" said Haliel's voice, blurred by congestion. Harlach winced again.

"It's me," he said. "You sound awful. Should I let you get back to sleep?"

"I wasn't asleep," said Haliel. "What's happening?"

"I'm not exactly sure," he said, flopping into a pink vinyl waiting-room chair and wincing yet again; it was clearly designed to be uncomfortable for anybody, no matter what their physical body type might be. "But I'm down in the hospital— I'm okay, don't worry—and I just saw the head of Monitoring and Evaluation translocate himself down here with that demon who got himself sent off to the Prime Material plane with Dr. Helsing, and *he* didn't look well at all. Dr. Helsing's demon, I mean, not Fastitocalon. Apparently the dart things have made it to New York now, and one of them got him?"

"Oh, good grief," said Haliel. "I haven't seen anything going on up here in London other than that it's *snowing*, if you can imagine, but...something's not right, Harlach. I think something's not right *in Heaven*."

"How can you tell?" he asked.

"It's more a feeling than anything," said the angel. "But the last two times I went up there it felt *off*. The first time I sort of snuck up there to see Raphael, and the second I actually tried to make a report to Gabriel, because it's overdue by now and I'd rather not get myself in more trouble than strictly necessary...and he was *unavailable*. Not to be disturbed. I think the angels up there are a little weirded out, too, and we don't do weirded out very well."

"They wouldn't tell me anything about how the demon got hurt in New York," said Harlach. "Wouldn't tell me much of anything at all. I don't suppose you have any way of trying to contact the *angel* who was with them? Started with an *A*, I think. New chap. Worked with Raphael?"

"Adariel," said Haliel. "I can try, I suppose? Doesn't Dr. Helsing have a way to talk to Dr. Faust? She had you transferred to Hell when *you* got hurt by one of the darts, right?"

"So I'm told," Harlach said, passing a hand over his face. "Wait. I think *I* have her number somewhere—I must have it, she gave it to me in case I needed to call and tell her I'd be late picking her up or something—"

"Call her," said Haliel. "Call her, and ask her what's happening, because something *isn't right* and I can't tell what it is. Nothing's pinging on any of our essographs—yours or mine—in London, and Gabriel's not answering his office door and Raphael wasn't in *his* office—"

"I'll call," said Harlach. "Um. Stand by? I have no idea what's happening, but—"

"I'm right here," said Haliel. "Safe in my flat. Not going anywhere right now."

He ended the call and flipped hurriedly through his contacts, dialing the doctor. Outside the sunless sky of Hell had clouded over slightly; the weather down here was directly connected to Samael's current mood, and Harlach really hoped he'd stubbed his toe or something, that the shift in atmospheric connections wasn't an omen that something more comprehensive had gone wrong.

This time the phone got picked up on the second ring. "Hello?" said a voice that very definitely wasn't Greta Helsing's. "Harlach?"

"Sir Francis?" he said. "Can I speak with the doctor? Is this a bad time?"

"Yes, no, and yes, in that order," said Dr. Helsing's husband. "What is it, Harlach? We're a little busy up here and nobody has had much sleep in the past couple of days."

"I just saw the demon who got sent up to join Dr. Helsing on her research trip get transported down here," he said. "He didn't look great, they said he'd got hit by one of the dart things like I did, and Haliel thinks something weird is going on up in Heaven—"

"I believe he may be right about that," said Sir Francis. "Damn. Is Orlax badly hurt? He must have been taken ill before we got back just now. Greta said she'd left him asleep; he was working with her to treat the victims pretty much the entire time we were there, and he just went straight to bed, but he didn't *seem* ill, just exhausted."

"I don't know, nobody would tell me," said Harlach, "but he was unconscious, or he *looked* unconscious, and Fastitocalon was carrying him?"

"Damn and *blast*," said the vampyre. "Right. Well. I'll let Greta know about that, but at the moment we're a little more worried about Adariel here and what's going on upstairs; just judging by what he said, something has gone badly wrong up there—"

"You mean in Heaven?"

"I do. We found the human who's responsible for both the darts and a very serious terrorist attack on the supernaturals in New York, and Adariel says, or said, before he collapsed, that this human's been touched by not just the power of an angel but the power of a very *significant* angelic being, which made it possible for him to do this much damage."

"A very significant angelic being," Harlach repeated.

"Such as an archangel," said Sir Francis. "Can *you* come up with a mental situation in which one of the archangels from *this* universe, not the smity sort that tried to invade and caused the war in Heaven, would not only actively take part in human affairs *on Earth* but deliberately influence and incite humans to a violent attack that nearly killed a large number of beings, *including* demons?"

"Fuck," said Harlach, shutting his eyes.

"Yes, rather," said Sir Francis. "I think your Accords might possibly be put to the test here, Harlach. Do *you* have any idea what we ought to do next?"

"We need…a meeting," Harlach said, eyes still shut. "A conference. Between Heaven and Hell, or at least people who can make decisions on their behalf? Held somewhere both sides can safely be?"

"Not here," said Sir Francis. "We've trespassed far enough on the hospitality of the New York operatives. But presumably somewhere on Earth?"

"London," said Harlach. "If I can get hold of Lord Ruthven, maybe he'd agree to let his mansion serve as neutral ground?"

"That's a damned good idea," said the vampyre. "What about the Heaven contingent? How are you going to get them to show up to such a meeting?"

"Leave that to me and Haliel," said Harlach, sounding more confident than he felt, but not by much. He was relatively sure that if he made *enough* of a commotion, either Fastitocalon or Faust would have to listen to him, and then it was up to them to have a conversation with Samael. And if any angel was determined and experienced enough to *force* other angels to pay attention, well, Haliel was that angel, after who knew how many years not just surviving on Earth but passing as a human. "We'll figure it out." And it was so, so much better to be doing something, instead of sitting around wondering what ought to happen next.

"I am inclined to let you," said Sir Francis, sounding faintly impressed. "And to stay out of your way."

Harlach couldn't help the edges of a smile as he hung up: it was nice, even in the middle of something going rather more wrong than anything had done since the reset itself, to have a vote of confidence in one's own ability to organize.

New York City

Adariel floated, somewhere near the surface of consciousness, out of time; his whole body still rang with the memory of that awful shock-touch. He was aware of pain somewhere a long way away, pain he wanted to put off as long as possible.

It's... bad, he had managed, reaching for her hand. *Dr. Helsing. It's really bad.* He could hardly make out her face through the drifting veil of sparkles, barely feel it when her fingers closed around his. He felt as if he'd been made entirely of thin-blown crystal that had been dealt a crushing blow, crazed all over with cracks, but not yet falling apart in a final unmusical collapse; he hung on through the dizziness, intent on making her understand. *Not just an angel. An... an archangel. The most powerful you can imagine.*

Being here was bad for him; being here might have *destroyed* him, the way he felt. Clearly angels were not built for this, not made to withstand revelations like this; he wasn't strong enough. He'd give anything to turn back the clock, make none of this have happened, find himself back in the familiar safety of Raphael's dispensary where he didn't have to *think*, where nothing was terrifying or strange or impossible at all. Everything was *wrong*, everything was broken and over and backward and shattered, perverted like the reflection in a broken mirror, distorting and distorted. He hadn't been created at the time the interreality septal defect had opened up and let a flood of invading angels into Heaven, swords aflame; he'd been told about it, but being told and witnessing were not the same thing, and he thought now that maybe he could understand a little of just how appalling that had been for the angels of his own Heaven to witness: a thing that clearly *was*, and just as clearly could not, *should not*, be. A thing that shattered narrative and expectation and turned laws and rules upside down, leaving nothing at all certain other than terror and vertigo as solid stone beneath their feet fell away like wisps of cloud, like lies.

He hadn't known he was crying almost soundlessly, hadn't even really known it when the vampyre bent to lift him from the floor, carrying him away from that place. Everything was made of moving stars, sickening in their frictionless slide across his vision; he had not felt the distant prick of a needle in his arm but was dimly grateful when the shifting sparkles began to be irised in by blackness, and when that blackness rose up to claim him and closed over his head; and now he clung to that blackness, to its sheltering oblivion, trying not to let himself resurface. Whatever was waiting for him beyond the black was nothing he wanted to know.

"No," said Greta Helsing, pinching the bridge of her nose. "Believe me, I understand exactly why you want Adariel to give evidence in person, but right now that isn't *possible*, Haliel. He's in no shape to talk to anybody, let alone archangels; I've had to sedate him. You're going to have to get Raphael to agree to this meeting on your own."

She could hear the angel's sigh on the other end of the phone. "Raphael I'm not too worried about, at least not in terms of him listening to me; he's more likely to want to see Adariel in person, to do whatever he can to help him—but, well. Uriel's different. Ordinarily I'm not under his immediate oversight; he's got no reason to talk to me." Haliel paused. "Then again nothing about this situation is *ordinary*."

"Well, just so," said Greta. "You did say he's the other reasonable one, after all, and I'd honestly have to wonder if he hasn't noticed something's amiss before now." Neither of them was saying the name of the other two archangels; neither of them had to.

"I didn't say *reasonable one*," said Haliel. "Did I? He's... sort of in charge of wisdom and education, all that sort of thing?"

"I'd start with Raphael," she said. "He at least sounds like he's willing to skirt around what's traditional in pursuit of what makes clinical sense, so he's got my vote. Start with him and hopefully between the two of you Uriel will agree to at least hear this out. I wish I *could* just send Adariel over there, or up, or whatever, to give his evidence in person, but he's not at all well and I doubt it'd be tremendously helpful."

"I understand," said Haliel, and sighed again, slightly raspy. "Well. I'll be in touch to let you know what's happening, Doctor. Could you call me if there's any change?"

"Of course," said Greta. "Good luck?"

"Luck isn't something we *do* much," said the angel, and hung up. Greta dropped the phone back into her pocket and came back to the bed, where Adariel was stirring a little, making soft unhappy sounds. She rested her hand against his forehead, and he turned his hot face against her palm, seeking the coolness of her touch. Again she wondered about just how much damage this, or rather *she*, was inflicting on such a brand-new angel, and how much of it might have been avoided.

He had woken up twice, or at least partly woken, since

they'd gotten back to Morax's flat; the first time he'd had what looked like a full-blown panic attack, and the second he'd simply cried himself sick. He was also running a fairly significant fever. If they weren't in the middle of dealing with a larger crisis, she'd have been fascinated by the somatic manifestation of spiritual distress; as it was, she'd simply given him another dose of high-proof ibuprofen and sedated him again, trying not to notice how gladly he slipped away from consciousness. What she'd said to Haliel hadn't been hyperbole: he wasn't in any shape to tell anyone what he'd sensed.

"You *could* take him down to Erebus General," said Varney from the doorway. Greta took her hand away, sitting back on the edge of the bed.

"I could," she said, "and if he gets noticeably worse, I may yet, but I don't want to do that until I absolutely have to; I'd say a good two-thirds of the physical insult here is due to *spiritual* injury, and I don't want to compound that by moving him to an environment that's diametrically opposed to his pneumic signature in every way. It isn't just that he's had a shock; it's that the shock is to the very central core of what he *is*, and that's thrown everything out of alignment, poor creature."

"They had angels transferred down to the hospital in Hell during the war, though," said Varney. "I mean. You did surgery on them. Lots of them."

"We did *emergency* surgery on angels, and that didn't do Faust's demonic staff any good whatsoever, which was why he had to ask me and Anna and Nadezhda to scrub in to help;

the allergic reaction in the angels just got overshadowed by the major traumatic injuries they'd sustained." She shoved her hands through her hair, remembering how it had felt to be slimed to the elbow with the golden ichor that was angel blood, and pushed the memory away.

The rest of her patients were progressing acceptably. Gideon Tremayne had also required sedation, understandably—she wasn't sure what his ultimate prognosis would be after brief but significant possession by a rogue archangel, and someone would have to deal with that sooner or later—but the rest of Morax's guests who were recovering from the holy-water attack were nearly at the point where she could in good conscience tell them to go home and take it easy for a few more days. She'd been very careful in going over everyone's injuries since the revelation of Orlax's wound, and was pretty sure no one *else* was hiding anything important.

(It would take a while before she forgave herself for failing to notice the demon's hidden injury in the middle of all the rest of the immediate work they had to do, or bothering to follow up with him other than simply leaving him to rest after such a prolonged, exhausting task; she'd assumed his mild surface burns were the extent of his physical damage since he hadn't complained of any other injury, and worried more about what potential damage he'd done himself with the field-influence work. She recognized that, and while she thought it was a *reasonable* oversight under the circumstances, it was not an acceptable one. He was much better now, according to the latest report, which salved her conscience a little.)

"So now what?" Varney asked. Greta smoothed the covers over Adariel and stood up.

"Now—I *think*—we can get our damned heads down for a couple of hours," she said. "While everybody else organizes things for a change. I don't envy Fass and Harlach and the rest of them the business of preparing and transporting everyone up to London to have a chat with half of Heaven's leadership. That's assuming Haliel can *get* the two least unreasonable archangels to agree to the meeting of infernocelestial stakeholders."

She was not one of them. She was just the sawbones who made it possible for various people to be present at such a gathering, and in a suitable condition to give evidence. There was a certain kind of exhausted exhilaration at *knowing* something was this far above her pay grade, that it was in no way going to be up to her what the respective powers decided must be done.

It made sense to have the meeting occur on Earth, and it made more sense to have it occur in London, where she had access to her clinic in case anything serious went wrong with anybody and where Ruthven's Embankment house could offer suitably luxurious surroundings for the various delegations. From what she'd been told so far, the meeting was to take place midmorning London time; it was midnight here, which meant—she counted on her fingers—they had at least a *couple* of hours in which to get some goddamn *sleep*. "I'm going to worry about everything else in the morning," she said. "Come to bed with me?"

"Your wish is my command," said Varney, and tipped her chin up to kiss her properly.

Hell

Samael's white-on-white office felt quite a lot less icy-cold and impersonal when its owner's mood was on the amiable side; even the *tone* of the whites felt slightly warmer, sweeter, less like ice and more like nacre.

Fastitocalon and his boss had worked through breakfast, preparing for the meeting to come, and the tray of coffee and croissants lent the surroundings a faintly domestic and less awe-inspiring air. Fastitocalon stacked their empty plates and took the tray over to the sideboard, returning with refilled coffee cups.

"Do you know," he said, settling back into the chair facing Samael's desk, "that this meeting is probably going to be the *least* believable thing I have ever witnessed you do, and I've been around since we all Fell."

"You've seen me dealing with the Harrowing," said Samael, "and with Asmodeus, and with a war in Heaven—don't imagine I've forgotten you quoting *Henry V* at me in the conference room while the world was ending—"

"You said, memorably, *don't chop logic with me in the middle of the bloody eschaton*," said Fastitocalon, and took a green cigarette from the mother-of-pearl box on Samael's desk, lighting it with a fingertip. "I thought that showed admirable presence of mind."

"One tries," said Samael. "One does one's best—Christ, the last time I was actually in London I was tidying up after that remnant tried its best to rampage, and *you'd* just gone and died on me. How the time does fly."

"The world was rather different then," said Fastitocalon. "So were we, for that matter." Back then he'd been an Earth-bound exile with chronic bronchitis and a terrible accounting job; back then the thin places in reality that would come to be torn wide open had not yet become self-evident. He *had* died, yes, that was true, one of the many casualties of the hungry remnant of creation that had taken over the minds and hearts of a small sect of slightly mad monks and twisted them into monsters, but he thought that particular death didn't really *count* if the Devil showed up to renovate him within half an hour of his giving up the ghost.

Greta had been extremely cross with him about that, but perhaps not as cross as Fastitocalon himself regarding the destruction of an irreplaceable 1958 double-breasted suit. He still thought it was unkind of the Gladius Sancti assassins to have stabbed him in the back, completely ruining the jacket.

Samael selected a bright pink cigarette for himself—they were in fact Sobranie Cocktails; Fastitocalon happened to know that one of the London surface-operative duties had for the past hundred years or so included regular visits to a St. James tobacconist to secure a constant supply—and lit it, looking up at Fastitocalon through the raftering smoke. "So we were," he said. "I think you're right, actually: this has to be the strangest thing we've done in recent memory. Signing the Accords was...well. That felt revolutionary, but *believable*. This I'm not sure how to take."

"Signing the Accords had the echoes of His active involvement still ringing in everybody's heads," said Fastitocalon. None of them had known it at the time, but the tipping point that had finally paused the apocalypse and gained not just the attention but the *intervention* of JHVH had in fact been the act of Sir Francis Varney daring to pray; in that incredibly volatile and chaotic situation, something about the vampyre's audacity, or possibly the *simplicity* of his request—*is this what you want*—had gotten through when nothing else seemed to, and had received an answer: *No.* Just the word, only the word, but He hadn't needed anything else: that single response had echoed and re-echoed around the farthest corners of the universe, and in that endless instant had *undone* all of Armageddon. There was a good reason most people on Earth, of most species, could not actually *remember* the aborted ending of the world: that *no* had undone memory as well as damage. There was, in fact, a good reason it was called *the reset*, and Fastitocalon was still going to have to come up with some sort of explanation that could put Arne Hildebrandt in Göttingen off its scent.

But after that single intervention He had said nothing more, withdrawing again into wherever His attention had been focused. Fastitocalon didn't know if He was asleep or had simply changed the channel and gone back to watching whatever other cosmic streaming series He was into this particular eon, but if He *was* still paying attention to this particular universe, He wasn't letting on. "I don't think it's really been all that fair to the angels, honestly," said Fastitocalon, blowing one smoke ring through its predecessor. "The whole dramatic *here-I-am-again, pay-attention, do-my-bidding* bit, followed by this conspicuous silence. Angels don't *do* well when they aren't entirely sure what they're supposed to be doing, and they tend to try to hide that by acting as if asking any questions is in the worst possible taste. Having Him back with them, having His presence, even for a tiny flicker of recorded time, must have felt like an impossible relief, and then—"

"Then the poor things discovered they had to soldier on and keep doing their jobs even *without* the ongoing moral backstop of His active presence and approbation," said Samael acidly. "I suppose it isn't terribly kind to them, no, but then again *some* of us have taken pride in managing exactly that, day in, day out, for several thousand years. It does explain why Gabriel agreed to so many clauses at the time, *which he subsequently clearly disagrees with*: he and all the rest of the angels were still riding a wave of euphoria when we drew up and signed the treaty."

"Well, yes, exactly," said Fastitocalon. "It's classic 'seemed like a good idea at the time' regret; I don't think Gabriel thought through all the ramifications of what *implementing* the Accords was going to involve. Like I said, thinking's not his thing."

"Which makes him ever such a pain to argue with," said Samael. "The only time in recent history when he *hasn't* looked at me like something nasty discovered on the bottom of his sandal was in the middle of the attack on Heaven, when he screeched for our help."

"Which if he'd listened to you in the first damn place he might not have had to do," said Fastitocalon. "Thinking *and* listening clearly pose a challenge."

"I suppose it must have been fairly awful for him," said Samael. "Having to do what is so clearly the opposite of all his instincts, and encouraging others to do so. Still doesn't mean it's in any way acceptable for him to experience some sort of psychotic break and go mucking about on Earth trying to, what, cleanse the world of evil one city at a time?"

"That's about as far as I could get in trying to understand this," Fastitocalon said. "He certainly managed to do quite a lot of damage in not very much time at all. I'm a little impressed at the creativity behind that holy-water stunt, and the poisoned darts were damned effective, if a trifle unoriginal. Faust tells me Orlax will be all right, but he's had a nasty night of it." He sighed. "One gathers that Gabriel would really rather have a do-over of the whole Armageddon thing with a somewhat different ending, or possibly just another great big Flood, and hasn't the slightest ability to either acknowledge this to himself or make the request to his God."

"Do you think that's it?" said Samael. "He wanted a different resolution than the one he got, so he's trying to push the edges of things into a more favorable conformation?"

"I doubt he's thought of it in so many words. I think possibly he might want to *know more than what he's been given to understand,* which to an angel is sacrilege," said Fastitocalon with a sigh. "They're no good at asking questions of anyone, let alone of the Almighty. But yes, I suspect Gabriel of secretly desiring a second go with the Flood to tidy up the universe a bit."

"I do not envy a latter-day Noah trying to work out how to fit two of every creature on the planet, even the very small ones, onto an *ark nouveau,*" said Samael. "There are so many sorts of beetles, for instance. Although with the size of some of those delightfully vulgar cruise ships they've been coming out with, he might come close—oh, hell, Fass, what's the right diplomatic attitude to take here?"

"For my money, simplicity's probably best," said Fastitocalon. "So sad to hear of colleague's recent indisposition, sympathize re: pressures of work, agree that the previous wording of the Accords has caused difficulties and needs to be reexamined, look forward to working together to come up with a more mutually suitable arrangement taking into account new information, et cetera. I don't think it'd be a bad thing in general if the other arches were to take over a more, shall we say, equal role in the organization and running of the celestial realm, instead of it largely being *Gabriel, who does the telling* and *everybody else.*"

"It's a very simple organogram," said Samael with a straight face, and then snickered. "Poor old Gabriel, it can't be much fun to hate everything so *much* all the time, and he hasn't even got the option of Falling to go split off and create his own realm to his personal preferences. I can honestly say that

I have not regretted the Fall since it happened, even the bits of it that hurt rather a lot at the time."

"I remember," said Fastitocalon. "How terrifying it all was, and then how terrifying it *wasn't*, because you knew what questions to ask and what to do with the answers. I think I was second-guessing myself all the way down, and I definitely questioned the wisdom of my choices while we were lying about on the lake and having our feathers burned white, but... once we got to shore, and you started *organizing*, I don't think that many of us ever looked back." It was true: he could remember the panic, the uncertainty and the pain, and then the dawning pleasure of *believing*, of realizing that Samael had meant everything he had said, and that the person he, Fastitocalon, had chosen to follow had in fact been someone worth the Fall.

"Good," said Samael with a crooked smile. "I'm glad; I've tried to be a decent boss, to run this place as efficiently and sanely as possible, and I suppose having only one Asmodeus situation over this many millennia isn't too dire a track record."

"Not too dire at all," said Fastitocalon. "Well. Shall I go and fetch Faust and Belial, if he's coming, and meet you there?"

"Probably you'd better," said Samael, and yawned, crushing out his cigarette. "I am so tempted to do this as the giant snake, Fass, you've no idea."

"I think that would be deeply unkind," said Fastitocalon. "Especially if you waited until the conversation was underway and then turned *into* the giant snake without a single word, and everyone just kept on talking as if nothing whatsoever had changed."

Samael snickered. "It'd probably drive the other three arches into psychotic breaks of their own," he said, "and be thoroughly counterproductive and so on, but thank you for that mental image nonetheless."

"One tries," said Fastitocalon, demure. "One does one's best in the infernal civil service, don't you know."

London, Embankment House

"I could be cross with you," said Edmund Ruthven, "for your wanton destruction of quite a nice Donna Karan suit and the loss of several more personally curated wardrobe pieces, but I think on the whole I'll just be quietly glad *you're* safe, even if everything else is a gigantic mess."

"If it helps, I did get quite a few compliments on the outfit from New York people of a chicness sufficient even for your taste," Greta told him, shelving books with businesslike speed. They were in Ruthven's drawing-room in the Embankment house, which had been hastily emptied of squashy armchairs and TV; the long mahogany dining-room table had been brought in to take up the center of the room, and she and Ruthven were putting away the stacks of books that gathered like dust on every available surface. "Then it all got drenched in holy water. But right up until that point people definitely thought I'd been well-dressed."

"I'll take it as a personal achievement," said Ruthven. "What's happening with the rest of your trip?"

"Not sure yet." She sighed. She'd had time to change into a different suit; someone had been back to the Carlyle for their luggage, and Ruthven had done her makeup, but the stress of the last several days was clearer than Greta might have wished. She'd got in from New York with Varney and Adariel half an hour earlier to help Ruthven set up the house, via supernatural travel organized by Harlach and Asturel instead of British Air. "I suppose everything rather depends on the outcome of this particular meeting, since it's really the Accords and how best to implement them that's at the bottom of it. I'm betting the research trip is canceled, though, and that means Fastitocalon or Belial or someone is going to have to come up with a way to make *that* make sense to poor old Arne, along with some answers for him on the explanation for the reset discontinuity."

"Seems to me like the easiest thing is to admit what happened," said Ruthven, running a duster along the edge of a bookshelf and following it with a fingertip to examine for any residue. He looked very much the better for his weeks in Romania, sleek black hair sleeker than ever, rubies in his earlobes. His partner Grisaille was still back there with the Draculas and their ward Lucy; it had been agreed that Ruthven would come on alone to open up the house and prepare it for this particular conference. "Just say something like *hello, Arne, old chap, you know about that odd discontinuity you mentioned in all your records? Yes, turns out that was due to the fact that the world sort of very nearly ended and then restarted itself—oh, and angels and demons walk amongst us and apparently occasionally have the odd complete mental breakdown, who knew?* and leave it at that."

"I'm tempted," said Greta. "Hell, it'd mean there could be scope for active study of mirabilics on Earth, which would give quite a lot of people more useful work to do. There's already ample precedent in terms of the study of *other* magics; all it'd really be doing is offering a more scientific framework in which *to* do the studying. I know Nadezhda would love to get stuck in to an applied-mirabilics course so she can use the right words to describe why her hair happens to be prehensile and too curious for its own good." Her best friend, the one whom Greta and her nurse practitioner most often begged for help to run the clinic, was an accomplished witch; a lot of the things in Faust's mirabilics textbooks would merely offer Nadezhda Serenskaya a new vocabulary and some useful equations to describe what she already knew. "It isn't up to me, of course, very little is, but if they get this talk over with and we don't find ourselves in the middle of *another* Armageddon, I might put it to Fass that the time for secrecy in such matters has well and truly passed."

"And just think of how *much* material would suddenly be available for the pyramidiots and crystal-woo enthusiasts to study," said Ruthven, dry. "Hell, some of them might even decide to stop mucking about with nonsense and try to actually get something right for a change."

"I think they'd probably expire if they tried it," said Greta.

"That sort's allergic to reality." She straightened up, hands pressing the small of her back. "Right. Chairs, and lots of expensive water and your nice crystal glasses, and I'll go and put several kettles on. They ought to be here in about twenty minutes."

"We've got what, Haliel and Harlach, Samael and Fastitocalon and Faust, and Raphael and Uriel?" said Ruthven.

"That's my understanding," said Greta. "I have no idea whether we ought to expect Gabriel himself at all, with or without Michael, nor in what sort of state. All I know is I told Haliel that he couldn't take Adariel with him to try to arrange this meeting, that he'd have to rely on his own means to convince Heaven it was in their best interest to discuss the matter on neutral ground."

Ruthven looked up at the ceiling. "How is he, anyway?"

"Adariel? Better, I think. A little bit. Harlach stopped in to see him briefly when we got here. I wish I had a scanner of my own; I'd love to know what his signature is up to, and I'm entirely sure Faust will want a look at him. I brought Gideon along with us in case anybody wants to examine *him* for permanent damage." She tucked hair behind her ear. "And so that Contini and his people have a chance to cool down a little more. I might not like the little worm but it wasn't entirely his fault he got used as a blunt instrument by the Archangel Gabriel in mid-psychosis, and I'd rather not see him murdered in cold blood, you know?"

"Right," said Ruthven. "You manage the tea and so on, I'll nip round the corner to fetch some nice pastries, and then I think you and Varney and I stay the hell out of everybody's way while they play *Paradise Lost*: Potsdam?"

"Something like that," said Greta, unable to repress a bit of a smile. It was *good* to have Ruthven back, good to have this *house* back as a safe place to welcome friends and allies and conduct business; it made her feel less weirdly adrift than she had for the months of Ruthven's absence, even if she had no idea what was going to happen next.

Heaven

Without Nithael there the long stretch of the infirmary tent felt too large, an exaggeration of itself, almost a caricature: surely nothing in Heaven could ever require *this many* beds for angel patients. Nothing ever went wrong in Heaven, after all.

That's how you knew it was Heaven.

Raphael had been very glad to see his patient go, of course, now recovered past the need for inpatient care. And he had made up the bed and tidied the whole infirmary and gone to measure all his stocks and make sure that his notebooks were all up to date, and then gone to sit in the little garden where his patients... when he had patients... took the air, and almost immediately come back in again to find something else to do.

It had almost been a relief when Haliel had arrived, even though what he'd had to say had been terrible. It was better to have it out, hanging in the air, than festering inside his own mind and heart—or at least partly. The revelation of how *much* damage had been done in the world, and that it had hurt Adariel, felt like a blow so sudden and profound that Raphael was still waiting for the ringing shock to resolve itself into pain.

He was glad he'd gathered the courage to go and talk with Uriel once already; however, following Haliel through the quiet peace of Heaven's gardens to find the other archangel, Raphael was a little surprised at how sure of himself *Haliel* seemed: tired, resigned, not particularly happy, but confident he was doing what ought to be done. More confident than Raphael himself. There was none of the hesitation or fluttering he'd have expected from an angel of Haliel's rank requesting audience with an arch whom he did not regularly work or speak with; he could only surmise it was the length and breadth of Haliel's experience on Earth that had lent him such remarkable self-possession. That, and Raphael himself was so *tired*: bone-deep fatigue.

He let Haliel lead the conversation for that reason, and because Haliel frankly knew rather more than he did about what had just occurred, rank notwithstanding. Uriel had led them to his office, a graceful white-and-gold space with arched diamond-paned windows overlooking the gardens, and Raphael had drifted to the window, looking out, as Haliel outlined what he personally had experienced and then what he had gathered from his conversations with Harlach and the human doctor.

"It can't go on, sir," Haliel was saying. "For everybody's

sake. I do know it's been difficult since the Accords, but it's difficult for everyone, and this is...not supportable. I've talked to some of the other surface-operative angels and they haven't had any meetings with him at all recently; either he's been unavailable when they showed up to speak with him or report, or he's canceled everything without giving a reason why, and...well. No one's quite dared to ask."

"I see," said Uriel. "When was the last time you met with him?"

"Back when this dart thing began," said Haliel. "I reported the incident to him, gave him the dart blade, and he said he'd handle the matter, and that was it."

"That was before this business with my patient and my request for help from Hell," said Raphael. "I believe that may have...distracted him, somewhat."

"And resulted in him losing his temper with you," said Uriel. "With somewhat dire results?"

"Regrettable results," said Raphael. "He was—I've been around him when he's displeased, dozens of times, we all have, but I don't recall him being quite like that before. He wasn't in control of his fields at all, or he was deliberately choosing to use them to affect me. I don't know which."

"Quite," said Uriel. "Neither is precisely to be desired. And this business on Earth, Haliel, with the darts: do you believe it to be entirely his idea, or...?"

"For my money, sir," said Haliel, "I don't think it *started* as his idea; I think my giving him the dart might have been a form of inspiration."

"You think he saw that and thought, *Ah, I can make use of this*?" said Raphael, a little surprised at himself. Haliel nodded.

"I do. I think it struck him as...well, as a useful sort of way to cause damage to monsters," he said. "Monsters and demons. Anyone he thought to be an enemy. And having *humans* do the attacking was just a sort of added bonus, as well as a way to maintain plausible deniability."

It was very, very strange to hear the term *plausible deniability* in this particular rarefied atmosphere, Raphael thought, feeling a little unsteady. "I see," said Uriel again. "And having tried this to good effect in London by causing someone to attack your counterpart, he then decided to try it elsewhere. How *did* he cause Harlach's attack?"

"I'm not entirely sure that *was* him," said Haliel. "I've been unable to find any clear evidence one way or another. I think possibly whoever was shooting people in London was unrelated, and he thought the idea had potential and went to find somewhere else to implement it."

"But why *New York*?" Raphael asked. "What about that particular city made it so, ah, attractive?"

"It's generally known to be a fairly naughty place," said Haliel, and Raphael shot him a look. His expression was unreadably demure. Astonishingly enough, Uriel smiled a little.

"I suppose it is," he said. "And also full of madmen."

"Exactly," said Haliel. "Madmen who would be more than willing to do what they were told by a...shall we say *charismatic* religious leader?"

"Who was being visited by a divine influence that told him what to do," murmured Uriel. "It's not without precedent."

"It's appalling," said Raphael. "It's exactly, completely counter to everything we've held dear. It's so much worse than any kind of demon-mischief *pretending* to be divine."

"I think, based on what I was told by people who were there—I didn't get to interview the angel Adariel; he was too ill at the time—I think that he may have gone so far as to either state or allow these people to believe that he *was* the actual voice of God," said Haliel. "I know he's—well, he's *Gabriel*; in the absence of the Metatron he's a very high-placed authority—"

"But he is not, and his is not, the voice of God," said Uriel with a sigh. "No. You are quite right, Raphael, it is appalling." He pinched the bridge of his lovely nose. "And you wish me...us...to speak with the leadership of Hell on the subject, to determine what must be done about it."

"Yes, sir," said Haliel. "I don't know to what extent the Archangel Michael knows about any of this, but—"

"Leave the Archangel Michael to me," said Uriel, rising from his desk. "This has very definitely gone on long enough, and I am slightly embarrassed to say that I had some inkling that things were not right, but failed to take any action to correct them; it is obvious that he has strayed from the path, but none of us are without blame. I will speak with Michael, and then I will go with you to London and put this matter to an end."

"What about him?" Haliel asked, and flushed faintly

golden. "Forgive me, sir. I meant to say, do we even know where Gabriel *is* at the moment?"

"As far as I know," said Uriel, "he is in his personal quarters, and has not emerged despite several attempts to see if he is quite well or requires anything, but if anyone knows more about his whereabouts, that angel will be Michael."

Haliel glanced at Raphael, who nodded slightly, and both of them bowed.

London

Greta wasn't entirely sure what she was expecting. She'd *seen* angels by now, lots of them, mostly in an emergent clinical setting; she hadn't *officially* seen archangels in any capacity. It wasn't much of a surprise when Fastitocalon and Samael arrived first, in beautifully-cut suits—Fass in his ordinary charcoal pinstripe and the Devil in his ever-present snowy-white—followed by Faust, in fur-trimmed velvet rather than scrubs and lab coat, and Harlach, looking neat in a dark suit of his own.

She and Varney were hanging back, unobtrusively, in Ruthven's kitchen; Ruthven had swung into action as homeowner and host, and had turned the charm on with full force. Greta watched as Fastitocalon and Samael took their seats at the long mahogany table, and wasn't entirely surprised when Faust set his floppy hat down beside them and came over to join her. "Helsing," he said by way of greeting. "I'm keeping your baby demon for a few more days, but he'll be all right. What's up with the angel?"

She shook his hand: warm and hard with calluses. She wasn't sure exactly *what* his vital status was at this point, but presumably he'd been granted some sort of quasi-demonic visa in order to travel outside Hell. "A hundred years ago I'd call it nervous prostration," she said. "As far as I could tell, he was having a sort of slow-motion panic attack brought on by Things Not Being as Expected, and then he touched our Mr. Gideon and got a solid whack of Gabriel's influence straight to the spiritual solar plexus, which resulted in a sort of brief seizure. I've had to sedate him quite heavily, but he seems to be feeling a little better now."

"Febrile?" Faust asked.

"Initially, but it's gone down a lot. If you want to see Gideon Tremayne, I've got him here as well, partly as physical evidence and partly to prevent a bunch of justifiably irked New York nosferatu turning him into zealot sashimi."

"I'll have a look," said Faust. "Might be interesting to run *him* through the scanner, see if his signature's been permanently altered by the angelic influence. Could be a paper in it."

"Be my guest," she said. "There's tea and pastries and so on, and the angels ought to be here any minute."

A shifting of chairs and a faint chime, like crystal bells being struck, suggested they had just arrived. Faust gave her a wry look and straightened his robes, going through to the drawing-room. There was Haliel, looking almost but not quite excruciatingly public-school with his golden curls and fawn-colored sweater-vest; Raphael, in what Greta realized must be his default Earth-seeming, which apparently dated back to the fifties—Ruthven was offering to take his very MI6 trench-coat and hat—and a tall dark-skinned person in something reminiscent of a dove-grey doctoral gown, who had to be Uriel. The human effect wasn't even slightly convincing, but she thought probably he wasn't trying very hard. She watched as they took their seats.

Varney came up behind her and rested his hands on her shoulders, and she reached up to lace her fingers with his. "Should we retreat?" he asked.

"Probably," she said. "I'd better keep an eye on Adariel, anyway. Edmund?"

"I'll stay," said Ruthven, hanging Raphael's coat and hat on the coat-tree in the corner of the kitchen. "Go on, you two, go play cards or something. Stay out of trouble."

Greta rolled her eyes at him, but led the way upstairs.

"Let us dispense with the standard pleasantries," said the Archangel Uriel. In the warm light of Edmund Ruthven's drawing-room he appeared to be faintly iridescent, or possibly covered with a fine layer of something shimmery. "The angel Haliel has brought to our attention the recent...*behavior*... of our colleague, and the injuries resulting from his activities. On behalf of Heaven I must apologize for the bodily harm done to your colleagues—"

Haliel whispered something in his ear. "—Orlax, Morax, and Glasya," Uriel finished. "I trust they are recovering?"

"So I gather," said Samael. "Orlax is in Dr. Faust's care in hospital, and Morax and Glasya are remaining in New York while they recuperate. One of yours, the angel Adariel, also suffered some ill effects from the experience while working with Dr. Helsing, but I am told he is improving; when our business is concluded, of course, you must feel free to take him back with you for the proper angelic care. The project for which he and Orlax were tasked to work together is on indefinite hiatus while we address these issues."

Uriel inclined his head. "Very well. My understanding is that while our colleague's dissatisfaction with the Accords practically dates back to the signing of the Accords themselves, his *actions* interfering with the stated priorities and goals thereof only began within the past—what would you say, Raphael?"

"That I'm aware of, perhaps the last month," said Raphael, "but it could very well be longer. Haliel?"

"It's difficult to say, my lord," said Haliel. "Personally speaking I would say that the Archangel's attitude toward the surface-operative program in general has always been somewhat dismissive, but yes, within the past one to two months I believe he has been more distracted?"

"I have spoken with the Archangel Michael," said Uriel "and he, too, does not have a specific timeframe of reference, but he does agree that Gabriel has been more *distracted* of late. While he does not feel this is alarming *per se*, he is concerned for Gabriel's well-being and its influence on his work as a celestial administrator."

"We have the human he was using in New York," said

Faust. "Gabriel's human. The one who did the dirty work for him. I mean, if you want to be sure how long he was rootling around in that particular brain and telling it what to do, that should be pretty straightforward to find out, but can't you just *ask* him?"

Raphael winced, and Samael reached over to place a hand lightly on Faust's. "Perhaps in a few minutes I'll request that they bring down Mr. Tremayne for examination," he said. "But let's assume for the moment that this is the extent of your colleague's rogue activities. While considerable suffering has been caused, there have been no deaths that I'm aware of. Do you have reason to believe that Gabriel is likely to continue to behave...erratically...or can you provide an assurance that this situation will not recur?"

"It's clear that the problem really lies in the changes outlined in the Accords as signed," said Fastitocalon. "Up until then I don't think I would have ever said he was *thrilled* with the state of affairs between Heaven and Hell, but I believe he was less unhappy with it?"

"I would agree with that," said Raphael. "Prior to the Accords—well, prior to the war, and to the reset—I believe he felt toward the infernocelestial relationship as two nations might feel toward a long-standing treaty that did not require anything beyond mutual tolerance?"

"I think so," said Samael. "I do know he was not happy with having to request Hell's aid in fighting off the invasion."

"Which he might not have had to do if he'd done a bit more listening to advice he didn't want to hear," said Faust, and got a glare from the Devil. "What? It's true. And it's also true that this business with the Accords was frankly never going to work the way it was written. It's just physiology. I don't care about the deep meaningful political angle here; I mean the wording simply ignores that angels and demons *cannot* work together as written because the way they are *made* means that they react *predictably, strongly, and negatively* to one another under *known parameters*. I said so at the time and I've said so who knows how many times since and *not once*, gentlemen, not once has a single decision-maker *listened* to a damn word of it."

He subsided, breathing hard. Samael redirected his glare to the ceiling and then shut his eyes for a moment, pinching the bridge of his nose; to everyone's surprise it was Raphael who broke the silence.

"I've thought the same," he said, sounding both weary and resigned. "At the time and ever since. And I believe I may have said it as well, but as my colleague points out, it isn't something people have wanted to hear. I don't agree with Gabriel's actions at all, I find them regrettable in the extreme, but… there really never was going to be a *good* way to implement the Accords as written. The only circumstance under which it could really work is, well, either virtually or on the Prime Material plane. Angels in Hell and demons in Heaven are just not at all suited, and the sooner we all acknowledged that, the better."

"That's what *I* said," Faust agreed.

"Ever so many times," said Fastitocalon delicately, "graciously waving your tail, yes, and while impolitic, you had the general virtue of being right. At least we can have that out in the open, and perhaps take the one positive result away from this entire business of *rewriting* that bit of the Accords to take out the physically impossible requirement."

"Hear, hear," said Faust. "A lot of the rest of it is jolly laudable, and I have to point out the recent collaboration between my hospital and Archangel Raphael's practice, which, despite Archangel Gabriel's profound distaste, seems to have had concrete positive results."

"I've never seen anything like that clinical progression," said Raphael. "I've never had to treat a patient in anything like so bad a condition before, but as soon as we got the oxygen and medication started it was like, well, a miracle. Nithael's quite recovered now and back at work; you'd never know he'd ever been so ill."

"And *I've* got a hell of a useful case study to add to the literature," said Faust. "We now know that therapeutic interventions that work on demons not only work on angels *but also* work *in Heaven*, which leads to the conjecture that you lot could set up your own fully stocked and fully equipped hospital with all-celestial tech modeled on Hell's."

"And that's not all," said Haliel, and they turned to look at him. "I mean. If Hell's medical technology works in Heaven, why shouldn't Hell's communications and monitoring technology? Why shouldn't we have a properly equipped facility to watch what's happening on Earth the way Hell does?"

"Because monitoring and evaluation in Heaven is run by

Gabriel," murmured Fastitocalon. "Who does not believe it to be worth angels' while, in general."

"That, I think, is another change that needs to happen," said Uriel. "It is obvious that Heaven is lagging behind in technological advances because Heaven has for too long assumed it is unnecessary to pay attention to anything outside itself."

"Or to question anything," said Raphael. "Questioning things has historically not gone over well. Which I think may have…set us up to fail, during the lead-up to the war."

"The impression is that whatever questions may have been asked, the answer is *because that's how it's done*," said Samael. "Which is, of course, an understandable response, but my realm is based on a rather different answer to that question, and therefore the society that developed in Hell is one where asking questions is celebrated rather than firmly discouraged. I think it is possible that both of our realms could learn from one another."

"It seems to me," said Uriel, "that we have been given a chance, with the reset, to begin again, using information gathered from everything that has gone before. Including this rather regrettable mess with the Accords. I believe if they were to be rewritten to acknowledge realistic limitations, there would be no hesitation in re-signing them, at least among myself, Raphael, Michael, and the three other arches; furthermore, I do not see a problem with potential future expanded collaborations regarding technological advancement."

"Which leaves the main problem," said Faust. "What if you

get everything all neatly set up and a brave new Heaven raring to go and a month later there you are with Gabriel pretending to be the Voice of God and sabotaging everything behind your backs all over again?"

Samael sighed. "Forgive my colleague's phrasing," he said, "but his point is valid. Do you have reason to believe that the Archangel Gabriel *will* agree to . . . well, stand aside?"

Uriel, too, sighed, and pinched the bridge of his nose. "We will have to find a way," he said. "There is no justification for one archangel to defy others, even if he does hold traditional authority over them, when the others have agreed on a course of action. I do not look forward to the conversation I will have with my colleague, but it is one I do not believe I can avoid."

"*Have* you talked to him?" Harlach asked unexpectedly. "I mean really talked? Not just, I don't know, shouting through a door?"

"Attempts have been made," said Uriel. "To my understanding he has not left his personal quarters despite those attempts."

"Does he have any friends at all?" said Faust. "I ask because he does not strike me as the type who has a wide and comfortable acquaintance."

"He does not seek out the company of other angels," said Uriel. "I believe he has stated that needing companionship is a sign of weakness."

Harlach and Haliel looked at one another across the table. "I think it's possible that he might really *need* a friend to talk to," said Harlach. "Would it be possible to pause the conference for a few minutes, my lords?"

"I suppose so," said Samael. "Have you got a friend in mind?"

Harlach looked at Haliel again and nodded. "Yes, sir. I think I might."

They had, in fact, been playing cards. Or attempting to, badly; sitting at the little table between the great windows of Adariel's room in the Embankment house, Greta had apparently forgotten all the rules of anything more sophisticated than Go Fish. She glanced up from her cards at the knock on the door, meeting Varney's embarrassed expression, and sighed, putting down her hand to go and see who it was.

"Oh," she said, looking up at Haliel and Harlach, who were utterly dissimilar except in their standard physical beauty: one tall, one short, one dark, one fair, one in a decent suit and one in a baggy fawn-colored sweater-vest and corduroys. That neither of them was human was, currently, quite noticeable. "What can I do for you?"

"Can we see Adariel?"

"He's not in any state for visitors—" she began, but a little voice from the palatial bed interrupted with "Who is it?"

"It's us," said Haliel. "Me and Harlach. Can we talk to you for a moment?"

"I said he's not in any state for visitors," Greta repeated crossly, but again the little voice overrode her: "Please let them in?"

She looked over to see Adariel struggling upright against the pillows, and had to go and help. Over her shoulder she glowered at the surface operatives. "You can have five minutes," she said. "Adariel, you don't *have* to talk to them."

"I know," said the angel, and there was a certainty in his voice that had been missing since before the party. "Please."

"Fine," said Greta. "Varney?"

He rose, gathering the cards, and joined her to watch Harlach and Haliel hurrying over to the bedside, both their wings flickering in and out of visibility for a couple of fractions of a second: they were both clearly very intensely excited, and by the visible glow of Adariel's halo so was he.

"To be a fly on *that* wall," said Varney under his breath as they passed out into the corridor. "Do you want me to be a bat and see if I can listen through the windows?"

"It's tempting," she said. "But no. Let them have their talk. And if they've set Adariel back, I will rip each of them a new one, celestial being or no celestial being."

"That seems reasonable," said Varney with a sigh.

This time when Adariel had woken it had not been inside a cloud, but in a high many-pillowed bed in a room he'd never seen before, but which was definitely still on Earth. It didn't smell like New York; it smelled like old wood, polish, books, and faintly of what he was coming to think of as *vampire*.

He felt odd, but not *bad*, exactly: empty, like a blown eggshell, like he imagined someone coming out of a sharp attack of fever might feel, burned clean and white like calcined bone, like salt and ash; *light*, as if he might rise from the bed and float in the air were it not for the duvets covering him.

Somewhere in the tumbled mess of the past however-many-hours, the hideous uncertainty that had given him such vertigo on the roof of Morax's building seemed to have dissipated, or possibly found a seed of solid reality and crystallized around it into something bearably believable, and that was: *I am.*

Whatever Heaven was, whatever right and wrong were, whatever knowledge and lies might be, Adariel knew that *he was*, and that felt like something relatively steady on which to stand and observe the rest of the universe. Possibly he'd never *had* "I am" before, in his short career as an angel; he'd been around for so few months compared with most of them that he'd simply not had time to consider it in any detail, even if Heaven had encouraged such consideration. But if nothing else, he'd thought, blinking sleep from his eyes, watching the doctor and her husband play cards at the table by the windows, if nothing else, being on the Prime Material plane had given him *I am.*

When the knock had come at the door he'd roused a little further, pushing himself upright, and asked for her to let the surface operatives in; another thing of which he was suddenly quite sure was that he very much wanted to talk to them.

He'd met Haliel before, of course, but he'd never been introduced to Harlach—taller, darker, wavy dramatic hair, faintly giving off red light to angel eyes. Both of them sat down on the edges of the bed, one on each side, moving easily with each other, and Adariel thought, *But they never needed to do the research project at all, did they? It's obvious angels and demons* work just fine *together here on Earth; these two are clear and present proof.*

"How are you feeling?" said Haliel. He was, in his human seeming, just a somewhat-frumpy graduate-student type, frizzy pale curls, spray of freckles across his nose, inelegant clothes, but Adariel could see through that to the thing he actually was. It took some effort to *stop* seeing through it, and after a moment he gave up; Haliel's wings were reassuring. So were Harlach's, vaguely visible past his sleek dark suit.

"Strange," said Adariel. "Better, I think. But strange. I don't know anything, Haliel. Anything except one thing."

"You know that *you are*," said Haliel, and from his other side Harlach nodded.

"You know that you are *Adariel*," he said. "It's sort of up to you to find out what that means, but at least you know that much. It's a place to start."

"I'm an *angel*," said Adariel, "but...does that mean I'm *good*? That I don't...go around harming people? Or is harm good when an angel does it?"

"Harm is never good," said Haliel. "Sometimes it's inevitable, inescapable, and then I think the thing to do is work out what possible choice to make involves the *least* harm."

"One thing I've learned over the course of the war and the reset and this miserable business is that *what* you are does

351

not necessarily have to determine *who* you are," said Harlach. "And I think that's not necessarily frowned upon by God, because, frankly, if it were, you'd think He'd have something to say about it."

"It took me a while to sort of wrap my head around that," Haliel admitted. "But I think we're made to do our jobs, first and foremost, and if doing that job means having to think sometimes, or make decisions of our own, well—that might be part of what we're for."

Adariel closed his eyes, reopened them. "Orlax helped Dr. Helsing save the people. At the party. I saw him. I saw how much energy he was putting into it; it lit up the whole room bright scarlet to angel eyes. And he didn't even want to be there. He didn't care about the project, or—or about any of those people, he just *did it*."

"Because it needed to be done," said Harlach. "Yes. That's sort of what Samael said about sending help up to Heaven in the war: because it needed to be done. That's not part of being *a demon*, I think. That's not—he didn't do that *because* he's the Devil. He did it because, well, he's also a person?"

"Things seemed a lot more simple in the very beginning," said Haliel. "We didn't have to think much, because there weren't many things to think *about*, and then He made the world, and suddenly there were so many things. I don't think we were really people back then."

"You weren't," said Harlach, with a smile Adariel classified after a moment as *fond*. "You weren't; *we* were trying to become people, and that's why we Fell. But you're people now, Haliel."

"It makes everything so much more complicated," said Haliel. "You know that much. But... I think it's possible that Heaven can learn to be a place with people in it, Adariel. I really do. We've got archangels and archdemons talking to each other about the problem right now, downstairs, and it sounds to me like there's a good chance of reevaluating some of the things that have been going wrong and trying to find a way to make them go *better*."

"Gabriel," said Adariel, and closed his eyes again, feeling that awful ringing shock when he'd touched Gideon Tremayne's head and felt the unmistakable signature of the archangel still lining the man's pneumic signature with gold.

"Yes, Gabriel," said Harlach. "It sounds like he's... unhappy. Like he's *been* very unhappy for a while now, and it's made him do some things he wouldn't have thought of doing before the reset."

"He hates the Accords," said Adariel. "Or what he thinks they mean, even if they're not supposed to mean that. Even though he hates the sin of hate."

"And that's the problem," Harlach agreed. "He's tied himself up in knots with it, and this time there isn't going to be a divine intervention to untie everything and reset it once again. It's up to him. *He* has to do the work."

"And he doesn't know how," said Haliel. "It's evident that he doesn't know how."

Adariel looked up at him, and then at Harlach on his other side. The demon smiled at him, tired and pale and not tremendously well, but very warm nonetheless. "Who can tell him?" Adariel asked.

"Well, we were rather thinking *you* might," said Haliel, just as warm, and met Harlach's gaze. "Since you've already just done it yourself. You worked it out, Adariel. You know the important thing, and that is that *you are*."

"I am," said Adariel, and again, wonderingly, "I am?"

"You are *Adariel*," said Haliel. "That is the foundation to stand on while you work out the rest. Gabriel doesn't...have that. He has what he *was*, which is a name and a shell of epithets and descriptions, but..."

"But he doesn't know what the bit inside really is?" Adariel asked.

"Precisely," said Harlach. "Do you think you might be able to help him find out?"

"How?" he said.

"By meeting him where he is, inside where he's locked himself, inside his mind," said Harlach. "To paraphrase, *il faut que tu cherches l'ange là où il est*, and I think between us and Raphael and Uriel we can probably get you there."

"Will it hurt?" He hated the sound of the words as soon as they were said.

"Probably," said Haliel. "But a lot of things worth doing are painful while you're doing them, and it would be the kindest thing anyone has ever done for Gabriel. Will you help him find his way back?"

"I'll try," said Adariel, excitement rising inside him with fear: *can I do this, will I let everyone down, am I good enough, am I strong enough?*

And inside his mind, warm and echoing each other, two voices, Haliel and Harlach together: *You can, and you are.*

Greta watched as the most unlikely collection of beings she'd ever seen in one place crowded around the bed, Samael and Fastitocalon and Harlach standing a little farther back while Raphael and Uriel and Haliel leaned in to lay their hands on the diminutive form of her postdoc. All of them had lost the seeming by now, and Adariel was completely hidden from view by the overlapping curves of vast white wings.

Beside her Varney and Ruthven watched, arms folded, and Faust had poured himself a stiff drink on the way up to join them. "You think this is going to work?" he said.

"I have no idea," she told him. "At this point it's all up to the angels to, well, angel at one another. We can hope that Adariel's up to the task."

"The others seem to think so," said Faust. "Beyond *my* pay grade, that much I can tell you. Angels in my experience aren't too great at the whole working-together, independent-thought business."

"I gather that may be changing," said Varney. "I happened to overhear a little of the conversation the surface operatives were having with him—a few words only, you understand, and through the *door* rather than the window at my wife's request—and the gist I was able to make out was that perhaps the modern angel is changing its worldview slightly to include independent thought as a Good Thing rather than an abomination."

"Gabriel isn't going to like *that*," said Faust.

"My own impression from the conversation downstairs is that Gabriel is going to have to lump it," Ruthven put in, "and also that Gabriel has been driven into a sort of profound psychological crisis that will take considerable effort to winkle him out of again, but may *be* winkle-able. Thus the…group effort."

"What's going to happen to the human Gabriel was using?" Varney asked.

"For my money, you should've left him where you found him," said Faust. "Or just let the nosferatu snap his neck and be done with it—oh, all *right*, no, I know you couldn't do that, don't glare at me. I suggest you ask Hell to take him back to New York and dump him on the doorstep of some psych hospital or other along with a hefty check made out to that institution for his long-term care, and not have to think about it anymore."

"That could work," said Greta, hoping she was right. "What about the street preachers *he* was using to shoot monsters with blowdarts? And was it even Gabriel who gave him the darts and told him what to do with them?"

"It had to be," said Varney. "I think you were right: the first attacks here in London were unrelated, and it caught Gabriel's attention as a good way of getting rid of unclean monsters?"

"The poison on the first couple of darts and the stuff from

the attack on the gallery weren't exactly the same," said Faust. "Close, but not identical on the mass-spec. I'd say New York was a copycat. A well-designed, deeply effective copycat with a lot of resources behind it."

"I think probably the street preachers are no worse off than they were before Gideon," said Greta. "Certainly no better off, but I don't think they were under his influence deeply enough or for long enough to cause lasting damage beyond what they're already carrying. But taking Gideon back and depositing him in the care of some institution capable of providing that care, along with enough cash to keep him there, seems like the kindest option available."

"When this is over, assuming it *can* be over without stopping the universe again," said Faust, "I'll get External Affairs on it. And don't worry about Hildebrandt. Either we'll tell him or we'll come up with some good fake answer, and I'm leading toward telling him. I've read some of his papers and the man's got a brain; it'd be no loss to have someone like him working on applied mirabilics on the Prime Material plane. Him and his colleague Klein."

"Dez would love that," said Greta with a sigh. "She'd jump all over the first course available, and smoke everyone else with her encyclopedic if completely untrained knowledge. God, it'd be nice *not* to have to constantly self-censor."

"Have Fastitocalon talk to Sam," said Faust. "If this mess ends up favorably, he might be willing to listen, especially if the Accords do need to be rewritten."

"Which it sounds as if they do," said Ruthven. "And when

this is over I'll be in touch with the Voivode to discuss how best to approach the *new* vampire political landscape in the New World. Are we going to know when—"

All of them felt the psychic shock-front as the figure on the bed blazed blinding white, visible even through the overlapping curves of angel wings; three of them thought, in dazed fragments, *it's like it was under Paris, the rip in reality,* before they stopped thinking completely and entirely for the moment.

CHAPTER 12

Heaven

White upon white; white as dismissal of darkness, but also of depth; white as the bounds of infinite space, the shell of a pearl, the hollow heart of a bone. White as a prison and as a refuge; white as the walls of a cell.

The Archangel Gabriel had closed the door of his office and rendered it no longer a portal at all, canceled his windows with a wave of his hand, dismissed his desk and his chair as if they had never been. He was alone, as he was always alone, as he always had been and always would be, and that was as it should be, for he was the Angel Gabriel, and therefore his being was correct, for it was his. Nothing else was quite as sure as that, so he could rely on nothing other than that, the familiar ontology, self-referential loops of it all the way down, receding into endless formless white. He was alone, and he was the Archangel Gabriel: those two things he could be sure of.

Time was not a variable that meant anything. He had

no real idea of how much time had passed in the world, on the Prime Material plane, since he had been *inside* his servant and then *not* inside, since he had withdrawn from that servant and left them in the cold stinking darkness of their world's underground burrow. He had ridden in that servant, in the corrugations of their brain, the clear jelly of their eyes, the stinging discharges of their synaptic clefts as they *did his bidding*, did his will, carried out his commands; he had been there in them, with them, and then with the job done he had withdrawn, shutting down and coalescing himself back into himself, on this and no other plane. He wanted to be alone with what he had seen and heard and felt and *done* through the body of his servant, and with the bright vicious satisfying pleasure of that sensation, and with the sure and certain knowledge that he was not supposed to see or hear or feel or do any such thing, that doing so had been what he was *not* supposed to do. That he had broken some fundamental connection between parts of himself and was not sure how to put them back together, or if they could *be* put back together even if he could find the pieces; if some intrinsic force of the universe would prevent it, repel each individual shard from its fellows, send him sparkling and expanding like glass in a vacuum.

He had harmed. He had felt the harm as he had done it, and in the instant of doing it had *loved* it: had reveled in it, been full of a true and vicious and bright joy of doing it. He had harmed mortal creatures, not invading angels from a monstrous Heaven intent on destroying his own. He had harmed creatures *on Earth* that were *of Earth*, and meant to do it, and known he was doing it, and *wanted it*, because the creatures were filthy and vile and unclean. He had harmed mortal creatures and he had *prepared* to harm them and he had *planned* to harm them and had laid those plans over time, had thought about it, decided on this course of action, knowing and deliberate, and now he was alone inside the whiteness and the knowledge of what he had done was the shattering blow that had broken him from the inside out. Gabriel was waiting for the pain, because maybe pain might mean that he was *not* alone entirely. That perhaps the pieces of himself might somehow be gathered up and stuck together again by something with power far greater than his own—

—Gabriel?

It was a very small voice, echoing in all the vastness of the white, and it was not his own; it was not even a voice he recognized. *Gabriel?*

Who are you? he asked, and heard his own voice echo as well.

I was lost, said the voice. *I was new and I was lost, too, and I thought everything was broken because it didn't make sense.*

Who are you? he asked again.

I didn't understand. Because everything I thought was right wasn't right at all, up and down didn't make any sense, holy things were wrong *things at the same time, and you thought that, too, didn't you?*

Who are you, but this time it felt as if he knew the answer,

361

fumbling inside himself for a name. Who gave them names; did they come into existence with names or were they given, bestowed, like any other gift? This one he thought he did remember, *so* new, barely fledged; he could remember this one *looking* at him while he excoriated...who had it been... Raphael, flayed him open with the acid blade of his anger and disgust, wanting to *hurt*, wanting to cause pain, wanting the satisfaction of it—this one had been, had been—*Adariel?*

Yes, said the little voice. *I am. It was me. I felt you in him afterward.*

In who?

Your servant, said the little voice. *The human who did your work. Afterward. I touched him, and I felt you in him like a fire, like a flame.*

Gabriel stared into the whiteness, horrified. *You felt me?*

I saw what he did. I was there when he did it. When you did it through him. I saw what you *did.* The little voice was implacable. *Would you like to see it, too?*

I—

But there was a tiny hand on his, out of the white void; he could not see it but he could feel it, and then he could see *everything*, could see it through this angel's eyes. Every drop of poison, every scream, every runnel of blood and bubbling blister. The *confusion* in the angel's mind as he watched, the shock of it and then the confusion, as everyone but him writhed in sudden agony. The little fingers laced with his were determined, so small and so strong, and Gabriel stopped trying *not* to watch and simply let go of everything and let the memory flood through him, over him, a torrent of pain and fear and sickness and confusion that rolled him helpless as a drowning man in an undertow and fetched him up gasping and shuddering and blinded with his own golden tears—and still not alone.

I was there, said the angel's voice. *I saw all of that and then I touched him and I felt you in him and I knew it had been you, and then the world closed like a lady's fan, Gabriel, because how could both of those things be true?*

I don't know, Gabriel sobbed, soundless.

No, you don't, it said, softer now. *Because you didn't know how any of it could be. Because the Accords said impossible things, didn't they?*

What? he managed.

The Accords were God's will because they had to be God's will, because why would He ever have let them be drawn up and signed if they were not His will . . . but they said things that made no sense to you.

I—

They said you should work with *the demons. That all the differences between you and the demons didn't matter now, that they should be washed away and forgotten, and you should forgive evil and not mind that it existed. That anything else was against God's will. That the unclean was clean and the filthy was chaste and right was wrong and up was down.*

I— he tried again.

And none of that was true but it all seemed *as if everyone else believed it to be*, said the angel. *Didn't it? As if you were the only* one who still understood what was real, and everything new was just a false dream sent to fool you.

I—

The Accords were wrong, Gabriel, said the voice, even softer now, tiny but somehow ineffably kind. *They were written badly. It was impossible to comply with them because they were written badly. The fault was not in you, it was in them.* The hand in his tightened. *You did something wrong, but you are not wrong. There is a difference. And you are needed.*

I am?

You are, said Adariel's voice. *That is the first thing you must understand, Gabriel. You are. Once you understand that, everything else becomes possible to countenance.*

I am, said Gabriel again, slowly.

Yes. Things will be different than they have been. This is the future. I think, anyway. It's strange, and it's frightening, and I'm…not sure what is going to happen, and it's going to be strange and frightening for you, too. Probably even more than me, because you know more, you've seen more, you've been more. But I think it's worth it? I think it's going to be worth it. If you can hold, be true, be faithful, be kind, Gabriel, for you are, and you are loved, and you are needed, no matter what you have done.

And then a pause, and the voice sounding older now, a little, more confident:

Come home?

Help me, he said, and the little hand squeezed his. *Help me, I don't know how.*

You are already here, said Adariel, and around him the whiteness opened like a door, and on the other side were many hands reaching out to touch him, to draw him through, to welcome him home, at last, where he belonged.

THE END

EPILOGUE

London, one week later

"Well," said Sir Francis Varney, folding his arms. "I suppose that counts as a successful, if somewhat unexpected, conclusion to an international research expedition?"

Greta closed the video-call screen and shut her laptop. "It'll have to. I do not at all envy Ruthven putting up Arne Hildebrandt and a handful of his colleagues for a week while Faust gives them the world's quickest 'Welcome to Mirabilics' lecture course, but he's one of Nature's gregarious host types and I am emphatically not. It'll be nice to go over to New York in the spring, though; Mr. Contini says the park is absolutely gorgeous with all the trees in bloom."

"I gather the Voivode is pleased to have reestablished diplomatic communications with the Contini family," said Varney. "Now that it's all sorted who's in charge of whom and where. I am very happy to stay the hell out of vampire politics, my darling, and I am so glad you agree."

"Utterly," said Greta. "I could not care less which clan is in ascendance and what group or court or coven has to tithe to whom; the whole international business of Vampire: The Eternal Hassle just seems so unnecessary. I *am* going to put *Lady Varney* on the brass plate just to stick it to the rich and famous medical men of Harley Street, though."

"I'm thrilled to hear it," said Varney, and kissed her. "And what odds do you give this business of Orlax and Adariel continuing their internships with you here at the clinic?"

"Orlax I'm pretty sure has at least the beginnings of a vocation," she said. "Which surprised him about as much as it did me. I've rarely come across someone with that amount of applied clinical empathy who doesn't have a hell of a lot of *emotional* empathy to go along with it; it's sort of refreshing. I'm fairly sure he's so effective because he gets a kick out of the power-trip aspect of the field-influence trick, but it works so well I can't bring myself to mind. Adariel, I think, is going to finish out the six weeks here and then flee back up to Raphael's infirmary, where he is going to be a lot more help. He'll have a solid clinical basis and he's a sponge for information; plus he hero-worships Raphael and wants to be in on the ground floor of the new era of celestial medicine, and I don't blame him." She shrugged. "I definitely get the feeling that Orlax and Fastitocalon will be getting along rather better now than they were before this whole adventure."

"And Heaven's really going to be expanding their M&E department as well as their infirmary," he said, sounding dubious.

"That remains to be seen, but I think it's *possible*," said

Greta. "One wishes to remain positive, you understand. One does not wish to dismiss it out of hand."

"One wishes to give good old glasnost and perestroika a fighting chance," he murmured.

"Precisely," she said. "In the spirit of openness and sharing and generally dragging everyone into the next century by whatever portion of their anatomy happens to be close at hand. I *do* love the idea of not having to constantly self-censor among my colleagues regarding the science of magic, and it would be *amazing* to have a proper mirabilic-resonance-imaging facility on Earth; if anyone can afford it, and has the space, Göttingen's a prime candidate. Who knows, in fifty years there might be MRIs everywhere."

"Who knows," said Varney. "For now, though, unless you've got more work to do, let's go home?"

"That sounds like a wonderful idea," said Greta. "Do you want to page the on-call demon or shall I?"

"Oh, let me," said Varney, taking out his phone. "The gentleman should offer transportation to the lady, I'm sure of it."

"Then as a lady, *technically*," Greta said, smiling up at him, "Sir Francis, take me home at once."

There was a line she'd read in a book about a thousand years ago, drawing a conclusion at the end of a deeply complicated, terrifying, deadly, heart-wrenching adventure, that came to mind even as the demon arrived and took both their hands in his: *we have reached the open sea, with some charts; and the firmament.* Maybe the sea still held unknowable, dangerous shoals, or currents beating onto deadly rocks; maybe the charts were out of date and the skies too cloudy to steer by, but for now, just for now, Greta Helsing thought they had reached open water, with the promise of clear sailing ahead.

The world went its familiar blank and blinding white as their hands closed around one another's, and she closed her eyes and slipped through reality one more time, on her own way home.

ACKNOWLEDGMENTS

Like I said in the dedications: none of this would have happened without a bunch of people's care, companionship, guidance, effort, creative input, and ability to tell me to fix things that needed fixing. All of you who made Greta a thing in the real world, and all of you who helped me develop her as a concept, years ago, I want to thank you for helping me make an idea into a person into a story into a series. I want to tell everyone reading this what Laura told eleven-year-old me, centuries ago, when I was first writing books: *don't stop*. Just that. If you want to tell stories, tell stories, tell *all* your stories, no matter who gets in your way or who informs you not to bother; tell your stories, and don't stop. Don't ever stop.

Thanks to everyone who made this series possible. Every last one of you, over the years. Thank you. I see you, and I'm grateful, and I hope you'll come with me where I'm heading next.

extras

orbit

meet the author

Emilia Blaser

VIVIAN SHAW wears too many earrings and likes edged weapons and expensive ink and, as an expat Brit born in Kenya, is not actually *from anywhere*. She has a BA in art history and an MFA in creative writing and publishing arts, and makes jewelry for fun. She writes about monsters, both in and out of classic horror literature; medicine, in its many forms; machines, extant and fantastical; disasters and their causes; and, perhaps most important, found family. She is the author of the Dr. Greta Helsing contemporary fantasy series and the sci-fi/horror novella *The Helios Syndrome* (Lethe Press). She reviews for the *Washington Post*, and her short sci-fi/horror fiction has appeared in *Uncanny* and *Pseudopod*.

Find out more about Vivian Shaw and other Orbit authors by registering for the free monthly newsletter at orbitbooks.net.

375

if you enjoyed
STRANGE NEW WORLD

look out for

BITTER WATERS
A Dr. Greta Helsing Novella

by

Vivian Shaw

*Relaxing at the country estate of her husband, Sir Francis Varney,
Dr. Greta Helsing has more than work on her mind. But before
she's had the chance to properly put her feet up, a barrow-wight
appears on their doorstep carrying a newly turned vampire child.
Turning a young adult is a grave transgression; to do it to a
ten-year-old is nearly unheard-of. Who could possibly commit
such a sin, and why would they abandon her?*

*Dr. Helsing and her vampiric friends will travel across the United
Kingdom and to Hell and back to find the answer.*

CHAPTER 1

Evening at Dark Heart: soft and slow, blue dusk rising out of the parkland little by little, drawing color out of the world. The long avenue of copper beeches that gave the house its name turning from deepest purple to black; over the ornamental lake a faint haze of mist, drifting on the slow night breeze.

Greta Helsing had been down at Dark Heart for a week now, and had spent every evening sitting on the parterre with a drink, watching the slow changing twilight, enchanted by it every single time. Nightfall in London just *happened*: here it was a process, a kind of tide one could observe going out, and the old parklands were at their most beautiful in the blue deepening dusk.

It was late spring, and still chilly enough once night had properly fallen to send her inside, shivering, to warmth and light and the welcoming scent of a cheerful applewood fire. Sir Francis Varney, draped in a chair by the hearth with a couple of hairmonsters at his feet, looked up and smiled. "Still satisfactory?" he asked.

"Deeply," said Greta, and set down her empty sherry glass. Stacks of veterinary textbooks everywhere indicated that Varney's unofficial ward, the young vampire Emily, was studying hard for her latest exams; Greta carefully moved several out of the way to sit on the arm of his chair. "I could watch that every night for a *year* and not get bored. It's so—peaceful."

"There are certain advantages to having a country house," said Varney. "One cannot order takeout at all hours of the night, nor nip round the corner shop for a packet of fags, but there are nevertheless certain advantages." He curled an arm around her waist. "You're not missing the city too much?"

"The only thing I miss is the clinic," Greta said. "And that is in good hands while I'm down here. I keep meaning to do something about my flat in Crouch End and I keep not getting around to it."

"Such as *moving out*," said Varney. "I can't think why you lived there to begin with; it's a wretched place and a long way from your work."

"Money," Greta said, wry. "Up until recently I didn't have any of it, and trying to find a flat anywhere near Harley Street is a thing that normal people cannot actually do—but I'm staying with Ruthven and Grisaille so much of the time now that keeping the Crouch End place is getting a little ridiculous."

"You know you have access to all the money you want, darling," said Varney, giving her a little squeeze. "Along with a somewhat absurd but genuine title that you are entirely allowed to use."

"I'd have to have the brass plate redone," she said. "*Greta Helsing, MD, FRCP, Lady Varney*. The idiom's just wrong."

"I don't know, I think it has a ring to it," said Varney, and leaned up to draw her into a kiss. This was sufficiently distracting that Greta didn't notice Emily come through from the library with yet another stack of books until she shrieked and dropped them on the floor.

Greta startled, turning to see Emily staring at the French doors onto the terrace with wide horrified eyes. "*What the fuck is that?*" the girl demanded.

"Good God," Varney said, following her gaze, and Greta had to admit she might have lost her grip on the books as

well. Standing on the other side of the glass was the figure of
a woman, skeletally—almost ghoulishly—thin and pale, long
hair in green-gold braids hanging over her shoulders, her eyes
nothing more than two cold points of greenish light in hollow
dark pits. She held in her arms the limp figure of something
bundled up in blankets, the size of a child.

"What *is* it?" Emily demanded, still frozen in place, and that
was enough to get Greta moving; she stepped over the fallen
books and went to unlock the doors and let the barrow-wight
inside.

"Thank you," said the wight, in a voice like cold stone echoes
in the dark. This close, the chill she was giving off was enough
to make Greta shiver despite the warmth of the room. "I'm so
sorry to barge in like this, but I didn't know where else to go."

"What's—what happened?" said Greta, and the wight pulled
aside a fold of cloth to show her what it was she was carrying.
Varney was beside them now, and both he and Greta sucked in
their breath at the sight.

A child. A *young* child, no more than ten or eleven. Asleep,
or unconscious.

And very definitely a vampire.

"I found her wandering in the fields," said the wight, whose
name was Sigyn, sitting by the fire with a glass of syrup-cold
vodka in her hands: frost was forming on the outside. "My barrow's a few miles from here. We have a lot of—well, sort of
ward-spells woven around each individual barrow, to warn us
if someone's trespassing, and ours went off. I thought it had to
be teenagers on a dare, but when I came out to run them off, I
found this little girl just sitting on the barrow, crying."

The child had been wrapped up in warm blankets and laid
on the couch, still unconscious; after a brief exam, there was

nothing physically wrong with her that Greta could discern other than the puffy eyes from her earlier tears—and of course, the single greatest and most irrevocable problem of her new nature.

"I knew this house was here," Sigyn continued, "and—that it was owned by a vampyre, so I thought it might be possible to take her here for help. I couldn't think of anywhere else to go, and she couldn't stay in the barrow, she'd freeze to death—" She stopped, winced. "Not to death. But—"

"I know," said Greta. "I'm glad we were here, and that you thought to bring her to us. Did she say anything about what happened to her?"

"Not much that made any sense," said Sigyn, looking over at the couch. Emily was sitting on the arm of it with a totally unreadable expression on her face. "She cried herself sick and said something about getting separated from a school group and a stranger talking to her, and then waking up in the darkness alone like—well, like this."

Greta reached out sharply to put a hand on Varney's arm, just in time; he made himself *not* snarl viciously with all his teeth bared. She knew this was the thing he hated most, that Ruthven hated most: the unethical, nonconsensual, irresponsible, and effectively homicidal turning of a human. It had been bad enough when they first encountered Emily, and she'd been nineteen when she was turned: this little girl's entire *life* had been stolen from her, childhood and all.

"I am going to find who did this," Varney said very carefully. Greta could feel the fine tremor running through him, the effort he was putting into keeping his rage in check. "I am going to find who did this, and I am going to *end them*."

"*What can I do to help?*" said the wight, staring at him with her cold-glowing eyes, and the deathly chill in her voice—frozen stone echoes, deep underground—made Greta shiver all over again.

Her name was Lucy Ashton, it turned out, and she was just short of eleven years old.

After Varney and Sigyn had departed in search of the creature responsible for her condition, she'd woken up and immediately burst into tears all over again, terrified and in shock, and it had taken a while for Greta to calm her down enough to give her name and age. Her vitals weren't settled into normal range for a classic draculine yet, and Greta knew perfectly well that the worst physical effects of the rapid transition were still to come.

Huddled on the couch, still wrapped in blankets and sniffling miserably, she was still not making eye contact. Greta was using all her encouraging and reassuring bedside manner, kneeling in front of the couch and looking up at her, and it was slow going.

"Sigyn said you'd been on a school trip," she said gently. "Where was the group going?"

"S-Stonehenge," said Lucy. Greta winced: that was miles away. Either she'd walked all that way herself in the dark, or whoever had done it had carried her.

"And you got separated from the others?"

"I wanted to see closer." She sniffled. "When the teacher wasn't looking, I—sneaked away and hid behind a stone."

Greta had to wonder why the whole of Wiltshire wasn't crawling with police searching for a missing child, and speculated darkly on the capabilities of the teacher involved. "The stones *are* really interesting," she said. "I've often wanted to go see them close up myself."

"How did they *get there*?" Lucy said, for a moment sounding like an ordinary curious kid, and Greta's chest hurt sharply.

"People dragged them a very long way," she said. "Very clever engineering. So you were inside the stone circle? What happened next?"

"I don't *know*," Lucy said, and broke into fresh tears. Through the sobs she added, "It was—there was a man—he seemed nice, he asked if I was lost and—and said he'd help me f-*find* the others and then it's just—"

She was crying too hard to speak, and Greta simply put her arms around the girl and held her close, only briefly surprised at Lucy's strength when she clung and buried her face in Greta's shoulder. None of the things she wanted to say were true: *It's okay, you'll be all right now, you're safe, it's over.* The worst was very much still to come.

"I've got you," she said instead. "I've got you, I'm going to help you, Lucy, I'm so sorry this happened to you but we're going to help."

"W-what did happen?" Lucy asked when the sobs let go somewhat. "I don't—know what he *did* to me."

Christ, Greta thought, shutting her eyes tight. At least there was absolutely no sign the attack had been sexual in nature. "Well," she said, "he did something bad to you, but it wasn't—the sort of bad thing kids get warned about in school."

"I don't... it doesn't hurt," said Lucy, sounding uncertain. "Not *there*, anyway, but my *neck* hurts?"

"That's because I'm afraid he..." Greta swallowed. "He bit you."

"He *bit* me?" Lucy uncurled enough to stare at Greta, eyes huge in her tearstained face.

"Yes. And the bite has done some things to you."

"Do I have AIDS?" she asked without hesitation.

"No. You don't. You do have a—a sort of disease, however." *Fuck*, she wished Ruthven were here, he could do this so much better, he could thrall her into understanding—

No. Not thrall. This kid had had enough of being mind-controlled for a damn long while.

"What *kind* of disease?" Lucy insisted.

"It's rare and inconvenient, but you can learn to live with it. What happened when you met Sigyn? Were you afraid of her?"

Lucy blinked at the sudden change of subject. "Y-yes? Her eyes glowed?"

"But you let her help you?"

"She was—nice," Lucy said. "I was too tired to run away and she talked to me, and she wasn't—like—*trying* to scare me? And she was wearing a sweater and jeans like a normal person even though her eyes were weird?"

"That's right," said Greta. "She's a special *type* of person, but she's just a person. She's actually a barrow-wight. Do you know what they are?"

Lucy stared at her.

"They get a bad rap because an author called Tolkien wrote about them being horrible ghost creatures that want to hurt people, but really all they are is a sort of very old magic being that lives inside barrows. That's why she has the funny glowing eyes and why she's so cold."

Lucy blinked. "I know who Tolkien is, everybody knows that, but—barrow-wights aren't real. Magic isn't real."

"That's what *most* people think," said Greta, letting a hint of conspiracy into her voice. "Most people don't know that it's been real all the time, all around them."

Lucy paused, and then, hesitantly, said "Like in *Harry Potter*?"

"That's *right*," said Greta, enormously relieved. "Like how the Muggles have no idea about the magic world, but it's right there nonetheless."

Lucy pulled the blanket tighter around her shoulders, taking some time to process that. "Are you a witch?" she asked after a while, looking up at Greta.

"Nope," she said. "I'm absolutely bog-standard ordinary human. No magical powers at all. I'm a doctor who treats magical people, and I have friends who are witches, but I'm not one of them."

"What kind of magical people?"

"All kinds. Mummies, bogeymen, ghouls, vampires, werewolves, you name it."

Lucy narrowed her eyes. "Those are all *real*?"

"Every last one of them," said Greta. "I know, it's a lot to take in, especially when you're scared and feeling awful, and I'm sorry it's happening to you."

"But *what's* happening?" Lucy asked. "Is it gonna get worse?"

"For a bit, yes, but once that part's over, you'll feel much better. When the bad person bit you," Greta said with a sigh, "he turned *you* into a type of magical person, which he should not have done *at all* to someone your age, but certainly not without your fully informed consent. That means that you would have known about it, wanted it to happen, and asked him to do it, none of which are true."

Lucy's hand rose to the wound on her throat. "Oh my God," she said, sounding both terrified and fascinated. "Am I gonna be a werewolf?"

Greta had to laugh a little. "No," she said. "You're going to be a vampire."

The girl's eyes went wider still. From behind Greta another voice said, wry, "It's a lot to get used to, but it's not all bad. I promise."

"That's Emily," said Greta, turning to see the vampire leaning in the doorway, wearing a Royal Veterinary College sweatshirt. "She got turned into one by a stranger, just like you. She might be able to answer some of your questions."

extras

Emily came over and knelt down by the couch. "Hey," she said. "I know how gross and scared you feel right now, but it does get better, and these people will help. The really hard part is that you kind of can't really go back to live with your mum and dad anymore."

"I don't have a mum or a dad," Lucy said. "They died when I was two. I'm a foster."

Emily and Greta shared a look of profound relief.

if you enjoyed
STRANGE NEW WORLD
look out for

THE SCHOLAR AND THE LAST FAERIE DOOR

by

H. G. Parry

Camford, 1920. Gilded and glittering, England's secret magical academy is no place for Clover, a commoner with neither connections nor magical blood. She tells herself she has fought her way there only to find a cure for her brother Matthew, one of the few survivors of a faerie attack on the battlefields of WWI that left the doors to faerie country sealed, the study of its magic banned, and its victims cursed.

But when Clover catches the eye of golden boy Alden Lennox-Fontaine and his friends, doors that were previously closed to her are flung wide open, and she soon finds herself enmeshed in the seductive world of the country's magical aristocrats. The summer she spends in Alden's orbit leaves a fateful mark: Months of joyous friendship and mutual study come crashing down when experiments go awry and old secrets are unearthed.

Years later, when the faerie seals break, Clover knows it's because of what they did. And she knows that she must seek the help of people she once called friends—and now doesn't quite know what to call—if there's any hope of saving the world as they know it.

1

In the end, it was four words that changed the course of our lives and the history of the world. Perhaps it wasn't really so surprising. They were, after all, the most important words in any language.

"What are you reading?"

At first I didn't think the words were addressed to me. To begin with, in those days people didn't speak to me without reason. In the week since I had come to Camford, I could count on one hand the number of conversations I'd had with the other students; if I counted only those unprompted by myself, I was down to one finger. That had been on the first day, when somebody had asked who I was. After that, everyone knew, and there had been no more questions. They all pretended not to understand my accent anyway.

For another thing, I was tucked away in a corner of the library where nobody ever came, in the depths of one of the oldest stack rooms, where the shafts of sunlight were clogged with dust and the air had the sweet, stale smell of old paper. The library was the heart of Camford, a great sprawling structure so labyrinthine it was rumoured to be larger inside than out. Some of the students preferred to steer clear of it entirely, not only for the usual reasons students avoided libraries but because they claimed that if the library took a dislike to you it would swallow you up and you would never be seen again. But I never felt the library disliked me—on the contrary, it was the only place among the crooked towers of Camford where I felt instantly embraced. It gave me the books I'd yearned to read since I had first learned of the magical world, and it did so readily, as if they were nothing. It hid me from unfriendly eyes, and admittedly from friendly ones as well. I could hear only the occasional murmur of student voices in the corridors, and I had been confident none would come near.

Most important of all, the voice that had asked the question belonged to Alden Lennox-Fontaine.

Back then, I knew very little of the aristocratic magical Families whose sons inhabited Camford. They blurred into an endless parade of pale faces and well-cut grey suits, smooth accents and smooth haircuts, motorcars and cigarettes and showy spells. I used to tell myself I didn't care about them, when really of course they didn't care about me. Still, I couldn't help knowing, against my will, about Alden. He was the golden child of our year: heir to some vast estate up in Yorkshire, blue-eyed and blond-curled, well-dressed and well-shaped and effortlessly charming. I couldn't even pretend he wasn't clever, because he was. I would hear him behind me before class started, halfway up the stadium seating: laughing with his friends, quick

and disarming, the kind of verbal thrust-and-parry the magical Families seemed trained in from infancy. And yet once the
lecture began, he would stop laughing and listen; if he spoke at
all, it was to ask sensible questions, all trace of irony bled from
his voice. A deft, supple intellect, unafraid to want to learn
from his teachers yet too full of wit and mischief to be teased
by his peers. I had never expected to see him up close, much
less to speak to him.

But here he was, so close I could see each strand of artisti-
cally tousled golden hair, and he had in fact, despite all logical
reasons to the contrary, spoken to me.

He must have thought I hadn't heard him, because he
repeated his question again, in exactly the same tone, with
exactly the same important words. "What are you reading?"

I found my voice at last. "A book," I said. These were important
words too, but in context they were a little lacking in specificity.

Alden laughed his easy laugh. "I didn't think you were reading a map. What book?"

If my cheeks hadn't flushed already, they certainly had now.
"Cornelius Agrippa."

"Interesting," he said. "You must have gone quite deep into
the library for that."

I couldn't tell if he was teasing, so I chose not to reply. I
looked at him and waited for him to move away.

Instead, he looked back readily. I couldn't help noticing, as if
it were important, that his eyes had little amber flecks in them.

"I've seen you in here before," he said after a while. I wondered if he was telling the truth: Certainly he had been in the
library at the same time as me, but he never had any reason to
notice my existence. "What's your name?"

I wished, not for the first time, that I had a name I didn't
have to steel myself before declaring. My father had chosen it,

liking plant names for girls in general and thinking it would bring me luck. I loved my father, from whom I had inherited my mousy hair and my talent for drawing (my stubbornness came from my mother, according to him). He had died in the Spanish flu outbreak two years ago, and I missed him more than I could say. But honestly.

"Clover," I said. "Clover Hill."

His mouth quirked, as I had feared. "The scholarship witch. I should have guessed."

"What does that mean?" I asked before I could stop myself. "You should have guessed?"

"What do you think it means?"

"It could mean a lot of things." My voice was tight. Tears had pricked my eyes, unexpected and mortifying. I wouldn't normally be so sensitive. The truth was I had been sitting at the desk aching with homesickness. It didn't help that Alden's vast estate was really not so very far from my Lancashire farm. His public school upbringing had smoothed away most traces of an accent, but the vowels held just enough touches of the north to reach my heart. "It could mean that my clothes aren't fashionable enough for me to come from money. It could mean that the work I'm studying is obviously outdated, and that indicates I'm not Family. It could mean that I'm in a library on a Sunday afternoon, and that means I need to study to keep my place here."

"You give far too much credit to my powers of observation," Alden said. "I just meant that you looked clever. I don't even know why I thought that. Probably it was the glasses."

I took them off, and managed to wipe my eyes discreetly in the process.

"As I thought," Alden said with a satisfied nod. "Positively thick-headed now. I'd have taken you for a duchess."

I smiled, shamefaced. God, what was wrong with me? I'd been lonely for days and pretending not to be; I'd been aching for the sound of a friendly voice or a kind word. And the moment someone had stopped to give me one, I'd bitten his head off.

"I'm sorry."

"Not at all. I should apologise. I was being thoughtless." He slid his long limbs into the seat opposite me. I felt his proximity like heat on my skin; suddenly, it became a little harder to breathe. It wasn't purely attraction—though he was undeniably attractive. It was the world he represented. Wealth, breeding, and glamour radiated from him. He was like a burning sun. In my experience, you sneak looks at the sun, careful not to get blinded; you don't expect the sun to look back at you. You certainly don't expect it to pull up a chair, reach across the table, and take up your book with long white fingers. "I *won't* apologise, of course. I was raised badly, and it's far too late to reform now. Still, I'll certainly concede that I should. I'm Alden Lennox-Fontaine."

"I know," I said, and wondered if I should have admitted it. It might have been better to pretend I had no idea who he was. Then again, that might have made me look unsophisticated. The Families tended to know one another.

He smiled, as though he saw full well both halves of my mind. "What do you think of Agrippa?"

It could have been polite conversation. But Alden Lennox-Fontaine had no need to be polite to me. More importantly, I recognised in his face a gleam of real interest, not in me, but in what I was studying. It set me at ease. I couldn't talk about myself; I could certainly talk about Agrippa.

"His theories are terribly old-fashioned," I said. "I know that. They're inaccurate too, which is worse. I think he might be on to something with his binding rituals, though."

"Yes," he said. "Yes, I think exactly the same."

"You've read Agrippa?" I flushed again, realising how that sounded.

He laughed. "We do learn to read at public school, you know. We don't leave all the intellectual activity to those far from the madding crowd."

"I didn't mean that. I just meant—as I said, he's terribly old-fashioned. I know he isn't taught anymore. I only know him because I was taught out of a lot of books that were—well, out-of-date. I grew up in a small village in Lancashire. Even when I found out magic existed, there wasn't a lot of new scholarship."

"He's not on the curriculum," he conceded. "But old houses, like small villages in Lancashire, tend to accumulate old books. I read Agrippa when I was fifteen. Until I met you five minutes ago, I was the only person I knew who had. I came to the same conclusion you just did."

"What conclusion?"

"That he might be on to something with his binding rituals. Now, I've just said that you look very intelligent, and I'm sure you are, but I at fifteen was a relative clod. And yet we both saw that there was something worth pursuing in Agrippa. Why, then, do you think there hasn't been any work on it?"

"Nobody works on faerie magic anymore." My heart was beating fast, and I didn't quite know why. "It's illegal."

"Perhaps. Still, it's interesting, isn't it?" He checked his watch before I could answer and made a face. "I knew it. I have to go to a luncheon. Whenever I start an interesting conversation, I have to go to a luncheon. It's an eternal curse."

I had never been to a luncheon—not a real one, the kind he was talking about. I hadn't thought I wanted to. But I wanted to keep talking to him about Agrippa, so I felt a pang of disappointment.

"Perhaps that curse is Agrippa's influence from beyond the grave." It was my best attempt at Camford student banter. "And that's why nobody's followed his work."

"Hm. But you clearly had no distractions until I came and provided them. The luncheon curse has no power over you. Unless you'd like to join me, of course. Or would that make *me* the curse?"

I blinked. "I'm sorry?"

"You're welcome to join us, if you're not busy." He sounded casual. Surely he could not be. Surely he knew that scholarship students, particularly the only one from an unmagical family, did not attend the same parties as Alden Lennox-Fontaine. "It's just a few of us—a tiresome crowd, for the most part, but one or two good sorts. Hero will be there, if you're worried about being in a room with too many men."

"Hero Hartley?" I asked, trying to match his careless tone. There were few female scholars at Camford, even by the low standards set by Oxford and Cambridge. Of the three hundred undergraduates, only ten were women, and in our entire year there were only two: myself and Hero. I had tried to get up the courage to introduce myself to her more than once that first week, only to lose my nerve and slip away before there was any chance of us being introduced. I had seen her in lectures, always at Alden's side. The two of them were cut of the same cloth: moneyed, powerful, impossibly elegant, with an intellect that cut like a whip.

"Do you know her? I'll introduce you. We grew up together, more or less. Our houses are the only human habitations for miles where we live, so it was the two of us every summer. Oh, and Eddie Gaskell, of course. The Gaskells' land is a few miles north. Eddie might be at the luncheon too, actually, if Hero can persuade him to leave his room." He stood and stretched.

"God, I'm still stiff from last night. I wonder what I did. Do say you'll come. I'd much rather keep talking about Agrippa than get drunk on Corbett's mediocre wine at two in the afternoon, although of course we could do both."

"I'd love to come," I said, before either of us could change our minds. I was finding it hard to breathe, as if the air was suddenly thin or I was very high in the sky. "Thank you."

"Don't thank me. You're doing me a favour, and probably Hero and Eddie too."

I didn't, at that point, recognise the gleam in his eye as dangerous. It was the echo of the gleam in my own, and I hadn't yet learned that mine was dangerous too.

———— ✧ ————

That was how it started, the four of us. We never meant any harm.

Follow us: